I KISSED A SCAREODACTYL

STARRING
NOA BIRNBAUM as "The Special Effects Artist"
and **LILAH SILVER** as "The Final Girl"

CAN YOU SPOT THE REFERENCES?

There are thirty-one direct and indirect references to real-world horror movies, franchises, and related subjects in *I Kissed a Girl*. Can you catch them all? Hint: Look for the "scareodactyl" hovering somewhere on the page. (Want to just sit back and enjoy the story? Check the back of the book for the answers!)

JENNET ALEXANDER

sourcebooks
casablanca

Published by Sourcebooks Casablanca, an imprint of Sourcebooks
P.O. Box 4410, Naperville, Illinois 60567-4410
(630) 961-3900
sourcebooks.com

Library of Congress Cataloging-in-Publication Data

Names: Alexander, Jennet, author.
Title: I kissed a girl / Jennet Alexander.
Description: Naperville, Illinois: Sourcebooks Casablanca, [2021] |
Identifiers: LCCN 2021001966 (print) | LCCN 2021001967 (ebook) |
Subjects:
Classification: LCC PS3601.L353815 I15 2021 (print) | LCC PS3601.L353815
(ebook) | DDC 813/.6--dc23
LC record available at https://lccn.loc.gov/2021001966
LC ebook record available at https://lccn.loc.gov/2021001967

Printed and bound in Canada.
MBP 10 9 8 7 6 5 4 3 2 1

To all my Jewish girls out there, yashar koach.
I see you, bubbelehs, and you're beautiful.

CHAPTER ONE

DEAR PROFESSOR SMITH–

Were you supposed to use "dear" when talking to a teacher? Noa Birnbaum backspaced and tried again.

Dr. Smith, thank you for your advice during our meeting. I'm going to take the job offer that I told you about—

Maybe that was too abrupt.

Yo, Phil—

Definitely not. Noa deleted the draft entirely and slumped down on the floor next to the low coffee table. Screw it. Dr. Smith would realize she'd dropped out when her name disappeared off the class list.

"Noa! *Help!*"

Noa startled at the sudden cry and shoved herself to her feet. She raced for the living room door, vaulting the pile of shoes at the end of the battered couch. Skidding into the turn on the rug that covered the peeling, fake tiles in the apartment's tiny hall, she swung into the even tinier bathroom. She half expected to find the curling iron on fire or the sink clogged and overflowing again, but nothing was bleeding, smoking, or trickling over her feet. This time.

Noa paused in the door, heart rate returning to normal after its brief jaunt into potential-emergency land. The tension that had been building in her all morning vanished along with the almost-panic, a downshift into the familiar chaos of normal life. "You rang?"

Chrissy looked away from the mirror she'd been staring into and held out a pencil with a beseeching look. "Eyeliner emergency. I *cannot* get them even. I've tried four times, I hate humanity, and I'm ready to scrub everything clean and pretend that I've never heard of cosmetics in my life."

"You could get away with that, you know. No one cares if a production assistant has wings that could kill a man at ten paces." Chrissy could get away with a lot, honestly. Tall and slim, her short brown hair buzzed in an undercut, Noa's roommate wore her confidence as a badge of honor. Except for right now, when it looked like the makeup was winning.

"*I* care." Her lower lip jutted out in a pout, and she held out the pencil.

"Yeah, yeah. Hand it over." Noa swept her arm across the top of the sink cabinet, shoving aside the jumbled litter of hair goops, toothpastes, combs—the disaster that was two girls sharing an apartment that was way too small for their combined amount of stuff. Too short to look Chrissy in the eye with her feet on the ground, Noa boosted herself up to sit in the spot that she'd cleared, butt perched on the cold ceramic ridge of the sink edge. "Hold still or I'll poke you."

The left eye wasn't a total loss, but the right needed work. Chrissy rested her pointy elbows on Noa's knees, totally at ease in her space.

There was a certain comfort level that came from living with someone in tight quarters for ages, even without having dated. Or maybe that helped. There was none of the tension that came with living with an ex or a prospective maybe. Chrissy's gaggle of girlfriends and extras didn't start drama with Noa, and Noa's current total lack of a dating life meant no stress coming from her side either. Mixed blessings.

A practiced flick of her wrist fixed the eyeliner in seconds: crisis averted. "There are templates for this sort of thing, you know. Or you could use tape," Noa advised, capping the pencil and tossing it toward Chrissy's fraying makeup bag.

Chrissy leaned over her shoulder to blink at herself in the mirror. Noa shoved her aside and dropped back to the floor, giving her a clear view. "Why pay for a gimmick when I live with a pro?" Chrissy asked, grinning as she started packing up the stuff she'd scattered across the bathroom.

"Because one day, I'm going to ditch your needy butt, and then where will you be?" Noa teased, the easy back-and-forth a welcome distraction from the tension starting to twist up in her gut again.

"One more question before you go." Chrissy held up a pair of breast forms, dangling them over her chest. "Big or small boobs today?"

Noa gave her outfit a critical once-over. "Small. That shirt hangs better with small ones. And now you are one hundred percent taking advantage of my giving and generous nature."

Chrissy snorted, dropping the forms back in her bag and zipping it closed. She ran her fingers through her hair to tousle it just so. "I am not. I provide equal returns for my rampant abuse of your skills."

"In what sense?"

"Half the rent, for one. Not to mention job leads, the pleasure of my company, and valuable life counseling."

"The 'do what I say, not what I did' curriculum?"

"You got it," Chrissy replied cheerfully. "I am a veritable font of wisdom."

"You're a font of *something*, that's for sure."

Chrissy's laughter followed Noa out the door. The sun had crept a little farther up in the sky while they'd been talking, warm light through the window softening the edges of the world. Noa's kit was still spread out next to her laptop on the low coffee table they'd rescued from the dumpster the week after moving in, the bright colors of eyeshadow palettes and tints for liquid latex eye-catching against the chipped brown particleboard. Noa glanced at her phone. 6:47 a.m. Less than an hour before they had to be on set. She ran through her checklist for the seventh time, packing everything back into her toolbox and kit bag as she went. Stipple sponge, sweat gel—surely they'd have their own face forms. Right? Maybe she should pack hers to be on the safe side...

"You're stressing out again," Chrissy pointed out, crossing the living room to grab her own black pack, filled and optimized thanks to her couple of weeks already on the job.

"But how do I know what they need? Denise said 'bring your kit' when I asked, but that could literally mean anything. What if

I blow it?" That was the thought that had been gnawing at her for days now. Dropping out of a theater degree partway through the spring semester to take an *actual movie gig* had made sense at the time. It wasn't as though union cards got handed out to techs on graduation, and the 180 days of professional, paid set experience the application required were not exactly easy to come by.

If Noa ever wanted a chance at the big movies, to work with the del Toros and Carpenters of the world, she had to start somewhere. She didn't even mind that said "somewhere" was a low-budget schlock-fest like *Scareodactyl*, as long as she didn't wash out on day one.

"You have a kit—bring it. If it's not what you need today, you'll have a chance to get different brushes or whatever tomorrow." Chrissy reached out and stretched one of Noa's brown curls before letting it spring back into place. "Relax, all right? Denise saw your portfolio, she loves your stuff, you've got the job already. Plus," she added, shoving her feet into her running shoes, "they need people so badly that you could show up drunk and doing the hula and they'd just hand you tomorrow's call sheet."

Noa made a face and threw her kit bag over her shoulder, mentally steeling herself for whatever was waiting at the other end of their drive. "I'm not sure that's actually reassuring."

———

Half an hour later, they were out of the worst of the rapidly building early-morning traffic and on the highway toward the sound stage outside Santa Clarita. Noa relaxed in her seat and drummed her fingertips on the wheel, her eye caught every couple of seconds by the moving colors of Chrissy's phone screen as she flicked through her email.

"Anything exciting?" Noa asked in response to a faint groan from the passenger seat.

"Not unless you consider eight immediate and directly contradictory schedule changes to be exciting. I'm going to have to find a way to lock Gilbert out of his calendar apps between midnight and six a.m., or I will not be responsible for what happens to his body."

"What an asshole," Noa snarked cheerfully, "putting in overtime on his job."

"Making life difficult for everyone who actually has to make his requests happen? Pretty much."

She sounded about ready to go off on a rant that Noa wasn't nearly caffeinated enough to sit through. Deflection was key. "So other than Dan Gilbert and his obsession with production timetables, what else am I going to run into today? I saw the story synopsis, and Denise gave me a basic rundown when we had that coffee interview, but that's about it."

Chrissy shrugged, a thinking frown creasing her forehead. "Not much, really. We've got a few days in the can already, but mostly, like, establishing shots and setups they didn't need the cast for. The actors have been rehearsing elsewhere, but they'll be on set today, assuming any of them read their call sheets. Tanner Blake's playing the big hero, at least until he gets eaten by the dinosaur."

The name didn't ring an immediate bell for Noa, even though it probably should. "Tanner who?"

"Blake. Square jaw, good-looking, the usual 'next Shemar

Moore' hot soap-opera type. He was in that commercial. The beer one that comes on during Dancing with the Whoosits."

That didn't help much either. "The burping-the-alphabet beer commercial, or the 'suspiciously homosocial cabin in the woods weekend' one?"

"The second one. He smashes the empty can on his forehead. He's going to make a sweet romantic lead, with those big puppy-dog eyes…" She trailed off, the teasing grin widening on her face.

"Gotcha." Noa didn't need to ask who the leading lady was going to be; she'd been avoiding the subject ever since Chrissy'd gotten the PA job in the first place. *Lilah Silver.* Noa's cheeks began to flush hot across the top, a betrayal Chrissy would never miss.

"I am going to have so much fun watching you get stupid over *Li-lah.*" Chrissy singsonged the name with a sly grin, her sideways glance at Noa knowing.

Noa ignored her, suddenly and intently focused on the car in front of them and not the little shiver of excitement that rippled through her. *Dork.* Professionals in the biz did *not* fangirl over actors, not even the gorgeous ones with perfect boobs. And it wasn't like Noa had the poster from *Killer Carousel* as her phone background. Anymore. "What did you say the key costumer's name was again?"

Chrissy kept talking, not acknowledging Noa's attempt to change the subject. "Lilah Silver's a great stage name, honestly." She tapped at her phone and the colors flashed again. "What does IMDb say…ooh. Did you know that she was nominated for an Indie Horror Award last year? 'Goriest death' for the pool umbrella skewer in *Radioactive Hurricane II: Second Wind.* Now there's an honor to call home about."

There was only so long Noa could stare stoically out the front window when Chrissy was winding her up on purpose. Noa made a face. "Don't mock. Her credits are all the greatest sort of cheese so far, but she's awesome, all right? She makes even the dumbest lines sound good. If she could get a part like...I dunno, Edith in *Crimson Peak*...she'd knock it out of the park. She's got the range."

Noa could feel Chrissy's eyes boring into her now, and she clamped her mouth shut, cheeks flushing warm. "But I am *not* going to get stupid. I know better than to autograph-chase backstage." She was green, but she wasn't green enough to risk getting booted out for being unprofessional. She'd be out of the job so fast...and then she'd be a college dropout *and* unemployable. Not going to happen.

"Mm-hmm."

"She's probably a total snob anyway. She was a pageant queen, and that's, like, mean-girl central. I'm going to hate her on sight." Chrissy wasn't buying it, Noa could feel it, and she reached for her last-ditch attempt at rationality. "Besides, I'm coming in to assist with special effects. I'll end up gluing latex claw marks onto stunt grunts and probably never even breathe the same air as the leads."

Chrissy started typing an email, her shrug a sign that she was letting the teasing go for now. "It's not that big a production," she did offer before grinning and shutting up.

"Not that big" was still ten times the size of the student films and friends' webseries that Noa had worked on in the past. She had every reason to be a little bit freaked out, a little bit worried about her ability to pull this off, and a whole lot questioning her life choices. The early morning texts from her mother reminding her that it still wasn't too late to rescind her withdrawal and go back to class weren't helping.

On the other hand, the flush of excitement, the potential, the sheer *possibility* that was unrolling in front of her was more than enough to stop Noa from pulling a U-turn and heading back to the relative security of the known.

The parking lot at the sound stage complex was half-filled with cars and vans, some looking a lot more official than others. Noa slid the old Geo Metro in beside a nondescript serial-killer white van and got out to start unpacking. Chrissy unfolded her long legs from the cramped front seat and did the same, grabbing her knapsack from the back. The bags seemed to have gotten heavier on the way over—that or everything had settled. Noa hauled them out of her trunk, ignoring the garbage bag of fast-food wrappers and the huge emergency kit that had been jammed in the rest of the space. That had been a gift from her father when she'd first bought the car, a plastic crate filled with enough emergency gear to supply a search and rescue team—everything from touch-up paint and WD-40 to emergency flares and a solar blanket.

She slammed the trunk lid on the Box of Displaced Anxiety and grabbed her gear. Chrissy looped a companionable arm around her shoulders, rumpled Noa's short curls, and gave her a reassuring hug. Noa leaned into it, taking the wordless support. "You'll be great, okay? I've got to go do the office coffee run, but I'll see you later. Makeup's right through that loading bay and hang a right past the prop shop."

"I got it," Noa promised.

Chrissy pressed a reassuring kiss to her temple, then let go and stepped aside, the teasing grin back on her face. "Have a good first day, honey," she said solemnly. "Remember that if the boys pull your pigtails, you're justified in curb stomping them."

The laugh bubbled up out of nowhere, the last of Noa's tension dissolving. She grinned right back. "Thanks, Mom."

Noa set off toward the main doors. She took the short walk as a chance to deliberately let go of the uncertainty that had been dogging her since her alarm had gone off that morning. Time to find out if the biggest risk of her life was going to pay off.

Brooke: You're stalling

Lilah: Am not. I'm thinking about it.

"Watch your back!"

Lilah jumped out of the way of the teamsters pushing the big black equipment box down the hall and shoved her phone in her pocket. Brooke and her blind date suggestions could wait. Or vanish. She'd be okay with the texts getting mysteriously deleted. Only she'd still have to answer her housemate's question once she got home.

Assuming she *went* home…

But no. Sleeping on set was a bad way to avoid Brooke, and she *meant* well, even if it came out in relentless attempts to improve other people's lives—using Brooke's definition of *improve*.

Lilah ducked out the metal fire doors and let them clang shut behind her, the gravel of the parking lot crunching quietly under her feet. The sun was up, better than when she'd arrived in the dark and crossed to the sound stages, shivering in her cute-but-useless jacket. Not for the first time, she wished she'd brought a sweatshirt. Something big and comfortable that she could hide inside until the sun came up. It wasn't exactly a glamour-girl look, but maybe it wouldn't matter as long as security and wardrobe were the only ones who saw her.

Hair was already done with her, the tidy french braid she needed for the day's scenes pinned, tucked, and sprayed into place. Makeup was next, once Denise was finished with Tanner and his artfully perfect stubble, then wardrobe, to get poured into the crop-top-and-skinny-jeans combination that was apparently what any self-respecting paleontology grad student wore in the lab.

It's fine. It's a job. And we all know that I wasn't hired for my brains. Not this time.

But every successful audition was a new networking opportunity. At least that was what Mom always reminded her when Lilah dared to complain.

Lilah's phone buzzed at her again. She glanced at it reluctantly, leaning against the rough concrete wall. It was cool against her shoulders through the chic teal faux suede, not yet warmed up by the rising sun.

Brooke: He's got a nice smile (not caps either!) and he knows the doorman at the Mondrian poolside bar. Totally worth coffee.

Lilah: Why don't you date him then?

She felt guilty the second after she hit send, following it up with a rapid-fire **LOL** and a string of emojis.

> **Brooke:** b/c the last girl he dated was my pilates instructor, and that would be weird.

Lilah didn't have a good response for that one. Or really *any* response other than a slow, somewhat confused headshake. Maybe it was an LA thing. Not that small friend group problems and weird ex network situations were unheard of in Charlevoix, but you had to expect that when your entire town had a population of less than three thousand. It should be a lot easier to avoid people in a city of four million. Maybe it was harder if, like Brooke, you knew half of them.

> **Lilah:** I've got to turn off my phone and go to work.
> **Brooke:** Don't make me bring this to the group chat. You need a life!

She heard the engine before she spotted the car pulling in and parking in the crew lot. The little blue car looked like it had been through a minor war, stickers adding blocks of color to the dented and dinged back bumper. Two women got out and started unloading, a couple of large bags and a big toolbox emerging, clown-like, from the trunk of the tiny two-seater. It was a lot of stuff to carry, and Lilah was about to kick off the wall and go offer to lend a hand. Before she could, though, the shorter of the two—petite, with a riot of short, dark curls that had been streaked with vibrant color—got her bag over her shoulder and her kit in hand. And the taller one with the undercut—*oh*.

Was leaning in. She put her arms around the shorter girl, tipped her head in and said something that Lilah was much too far away to hear. An embrace and a kiss followed, a moment too tender for coworkers. Girlfriends, they had to be. Wasn't a plaid shirt, heavy boots, and short hair practically the stereotypical lesbian uniform? All Kristen Stewart sexy grunge? There'd been one girl in Lilah's high school who'd dressed that way, and she'd moved to Portland before graduation had even officially happened.

Lilah'd been way too nervous to talk to Sam back then. She wasn't about to go looking her up on Facebook to ask about it now.

Tall One said something that made Dyed Hair laugh, and Lilah turned away before she officially became a creeper. A soft, wistful pang hit her as she pulled open the heavy steel door and slipped back inside. Maybe if she'd found the guts to approach Sam in high school, it would be easier to talk to somebody about it now. It would be so nice to have a girl look at her the way Tall One and Dyed Hair had been looking at each other, like they shared a life-affirming secret. Instead of the way guys usually looked at her, like she was something tasty to consume. It was probably a stupid fantasy, but she couldn't help imagining that it would be different with women. Softer. Easier. More cuddling with cups of hot chocolate, fewer raunchy dick pics.

Someday. When she was brave enough.

The new security guard was doing his rounds as she went inside, and he nodded to her as she passed. "Miss Silver." He was younger than the guard on the evening shift and had a leaner build, brown hair pulled back in a neat ponytail at the nape of his neck. He had a nice smile, like she was welcome and not an interruption to his day.

Lilah wasn't too distracted to remember her manners, and she smiled back, dredging her memory for the name he'd given her when she'd signed in. "Wayne," she replied, feeling triumphant in that at least when surprise flashed in his eyes and his smile grew wider. "Good morning again."

She didn't trip over any more crew members as she jogged down the hall, the muffled sounds of voices and clanging metal a faint and telling echo. The buzz of life grew louder the farther along she went, the early-morning quiet now entirely gone. Light spilled out into the hall from the open door to the makeup room. Some of the noise was coming from there, the tinny sound of music through cheap speakers and the easy chatter of people getting ready. They sounded happy to be together, and for a second, she hesitated. Didn't want to walk in.

Every cast and crew bonded. It happened in different ways depending on the people involved, but when you were stuck together for so many hours a day, in such weird and intimate situations, how could you not? It had started for her weeks ago with the cast meet and greet and her costume fittings, table reads and rehearsals, the rapid-fire introductions to the people who were going to be her entire social circle for the next three months.

So why did she still have that little day-one clench in her chest?

She had every right to be here. After car commercials where all she did was pose in bikinis, to Background Hot Girl bit parts in forgettable low-budget schlock, she, Lillian Silver, from a dinky resort town in the middle of nowhere, was finally a lead in a Hollywood movie. Screw everyone who'd assumed she'd peaked at Miss Teen Michigan. She'd knock this one out of the park, and then on to bigger and better things.

Right? Right.

Lilah took a deep breath and tried to feel it go all the way down to her feet. She'd had her moments of introspection and self-consciousness, but now she had to let it all go. *No one likes a sulky-pants, honey. Always show your best self.*

Another settling breath. In through the nose, out through the mouth. She belonged here. She'd earned her spot. Time to go be *on.*

Lilah headed in, following the light.

Makeup wasn't superbusy, and it looked like Tanner had already been sent on his way. That was a bit disappointing. He was funny and smart and had a knack for making Lilah feel at ease. A couple of the other actors were sitting in the chairs in front of the mirrors that lined three of the walls. Ishani was with hair, getting something complicated done with her neat black braids, but Peter looked up from his coffee and crossword and gave her a warm smile, then waved her toward the empty chair next to his.

She didn't have a good excuse not to join him, and he'd been charming during rehearsals, so she sat down, settling one knee over the other. "Morning, Professor," she joked, flashing him a bright smile.

"Don't do that when we're not in character. You'll make me feel old," he scolded her, his eyes twinkling. He *was* older, though, at least old enough to have been cast as the teacher in charge of the research team. His silver-gray hair was neatly trimmed now instead of the jaunty ponytail he'd sported at their first meeting, a pair of reading glasses—probably props—on the dressing table next to his coffee.

"I wouldn't want that." Lilah laughed, because it felt like the kind of response he was expecting. His chuckle proved she was right, and the last little tangle of anxiety faded away from her insides.

"To make it up to me, what's a nine-letter word for 'perfect example'?" he asked, his newspaper folded on his knee. "Second letter is an *r*."

Was it a test? Did he think she was a bimbo...or maybe he was just trying to make a connection. Lilah frowned and thought for a second. "Archetype?"

"Excellent." Peter filled in the boxes and set his crossword aside. "Feeling ready for today? It's nice that they're starting us off easy. When I shot *Blood Moon Rising*, we did my death scene first, and I sprained my ankle falling into an open grave. Talk about bad omens, right?"

"Or a sign that you shouldn't be trying to do your own stunts?" He was safe to tease, she decided, mostly based on the way his eyes crinkled at the corners when he smiled.

Peter huffed a soft laugh again, his eyes not leaving her. "Or that! But I think we'll be safe on this one, at least for the first few days. There isn't much that can go wrong with the lab scenes. At least not until they start the effects shots."

Grateful that she seemed to have read him right, Lilah relaxed—and groaned. "I know, believe me. It's the one thing I'm not looking forward to this time. I always end up covered in stage blood. It goes all crusty between takes, and you need to scrub forever to get it off." *Oh God.* Lilah clamped her mouth shut, realizing the trap she'd set for herself and then walked straight into. She hadn't intended to give him any kind of excuse for mental images of her undressed, but the gleam in his eye suggested that things might be about to get awkward.

"You know what works well for that?" Peter asked all innocently, and Lilah braced for it—the suggestion to have someone wash her back or a salacious joke about baby oil. "Lava soap. It's great stuff," he said instead, and the wave of relief that flooded her was combined with a whole lot of embarrassment for being so suspicious.

A new voice caught Lilah's attention before she could respond. "And now we're back at makeup, where we started. We're a small shop, so a lot of what would normally be done by a special effects house is split between us and props." Denise sounded like she was giving a tour as she came back into the room. The key makeup artist was older, maybe somewhere in her forties or fifties, her short-cropped, spiky hair bleached almost white. She dressed in crew blacks like almost everyone else, but her versions were high-fashion tailored things with extra zippers and funky-shaped patch pockets rather than old tour shirts and cargos.

And right behind her was Dyed Hair, looking around attentively. She was... *Oh no.*

She was really cute up close.

Lilah'd only seen her from a distance, across the parking lot when she'd been trying hard not to stare, but this was different. Now she was about to be introduced and didn't have an excuse to look away. Would she know what Lilah'd been thinking? Would she be able to tell by shaking hands that Lilah's thoughts had been less than innocent?

The vibrant purple, blue, and green streaks spiraling through the woman's dark curls were the first thing that anyone would notice, but her eyes were even prettier—blue, but not pale blue like Lilah's. Dark blue, like the indigo of her boy-cut jeans, set against skin that was more tanned than pale. The kind of olive-golden that should smell like sunshine. Dyed Hair was little, not quite what Brooke would call pocket-sized, but probably an inch or two shorter than Lilah. Firm muscles flexed in her shoulders and arms when she adjusted the kit bag she was carrying, and Lilah's mouth went dry. She had an aura about her, an almost tangible toughness that suggested that, small size or not, she could easily take care of herself.

It was stupid, it really was, but Lilah found herself wishing desperately that she'd worn that little bracelet today. The one with the pink, purple, and blue chain links, the one that had felt so transgressive when she'd impulsively bought it off the rainbow-draped table at the festival. It had looked so subtle on the rack but felt so *loud* when she'd put it on, like a screaming loudspeaker had popped into being above her head. *Bisexual—we got a bisexual here! BIIIIIIIISEXUAL in the house!*

So now the little bracelet lived in her jewelry box, tossed into a drawer with the class ring from high school that had her name misspelled. But if she'd worn it today…maybe Dyed Hair would have noticed. Maybe she would have seen it and known, somehow, that Lilah was Like Her.

It wasn't about dating. She obviously already had a girlfriend, and Lilah definitely wasn't the kind of person who would make a play like *that*. It was more of a silent, hopeful *see me*. A quiet wish into the universe for a connection to a community that simply didn't exist in Lilah's hometown. Or in LA, as far as Lilah had been able to find. At least not women looking for *new* friends in any way that she'd been able to break into.

"Lilah," Denise greeted her cheerfully, and Lilah stood to return the casual hug and the two cheek air-kisses that Denise offered as a matter of habit. "This is Noa Birnbaum, one of my flunkies. Noa, Lilah Silver. She's our Final Girl, so we'll get to slap some *fabulous* wounds on her later. Get to know one another."

Denise turned to chat with Peter after that pronouncement, and he swiveled his chair to engage with her, leaving Lilah alone and scrambling to find something instantly amazing and memorable to say. Something witty and charming that would cement her in Noa's mind as cool yet approachable, charming but spontaneous. Someone she would want to be friends with, folding her into the community that Lilah'd only managed to hover around from the outside.

It was a tall order, and she wasn't that good at improv.

"Hi, Noa," she said instead, hiding behind a pageant-fake smile as her throat closed down on the humiliating vulnerability of her thoughts. She was the star this time, she belonged here, and if she needed to fake confidence to get through, she would. "Nice to meet you."

CHAPTER TWO

NOA HAD BEEN ABLE TO keep her overexcited dorking out mostly in check through the sign in and paperwork. The security guy with the ponytail gave her an ID card with her name on it—her own ID card to swipe herself into the *sound stage*, thank you very much!—and she tucked it reverently into the pocket on the back of her phone. It had been harder to keep her cool through the ten-minute tour of the studio complex, trailing along behind Denise and her blowsy effusiveness and trying her best *not* to look like a wide-eyed newbie.

The place was huge, at least compared to the one-room base camps she'd been used to from friends' films, a whole labyrinth of halls connecting a bunch of different sound stages. Some were being used for other shoots, but at least three were filled with sets that had been constructed specifically for them—a university lab, the inside of some kind of air traffic control tower, and the major one: a rustic, woodsy cabin up on a hydraulic lift that could be shaken up and down by remote control.

Denise had sailed her through the rooms with a brief

hand-waved explanation of each, winding between pockets of people deep in conversation or walking around with diagrams and scripts or dictating intensely into headsets. Chrissy'd been one of those, able to spare Noa a wave and a wink before she was bolting off in the other direction.

"Where the hell is Denny? I need another bulb for one of the fill lights—"

"Get the science guy to check the set dressing for the lab."

"We have a science guy?"

"—start shooting in the next half hour if we want to stay on schedule."

It was all the right kind of belligerent chaos, and up until the moment they walked through the door of makeup's very own designated room—not the back half of someone's cousin's kitchen—Noa was feeling pretty good about things.

Then there she was. Lilah Silver in the flesh.

There was no shortage of really cute girls getting small parts in horror movies. That was one thing about Noa's favorite genre; it had a whole lot of room for the seemingly never-ending packs of new actors trying to make names for themselves. But Lilah Silver was different. There was something magnetic about her, beyond her long, wavy strawberry-blond hair and huge blue eyes. Even when she only had a couple of lines or a handful of minutes of screen time, Noa's gaze was drawn to her, held by her, in every frame.

It was even more potent in person, even in her own clothes and no makeup done. She still sat like she was interviewing on *E!*, legs crossed at the knee and perfectly poised. Her smile was surface only and fake, not reaching her eyes. The jeans and cropped suede jacket she had on had to have cost more than Noa's weekly salary, easy, and she wore them like a supermodel. Like she'd never been sweaty a day in her life.

She really was unfairly, perfectly pretty, and Noa had the sudden intrusive urge to mess her up, like that first compulsive, destructive splash of paint onto a pristine canvas.

They'd interrupted something when they'd come in, Lilah sitting close to an older guy at the dressing tables, deep in what looked like flirty conversation. Between that and the fancy manicure, Noa's internal filing system shuffled Lilah's card off into *yup, straight* before Noa could consciously register the result.

Noa caught up to her own brain a half second after the introductions were made, tuning in to Denise's wrap-up.

"She's our Final Girl, so we'll get to slap some *fabulous* wounds on her later."

And now she was standing nose-to-chin with Lilah, Lilah who had hugged Noa's boss hello and was now *speaking to her.* She couldn't just smile and nod, and she really should make some kind of conversation about the work they were going to do together. Maybe not mention that this film was Noa's first real chance at doing wound effects for any kind of big release, though that was a big deal for her.

Shit. She had to say something. Lilah was looking at her expectantly, all cover-girl serene, and Noa was off in la-la land. Panicking, she blurted out what was supposed to be *I'm looking forward to working with you,* but somehow in the middle of the garble of her thoughts, it came out all wrong.

"Hi!" Noa said with forced cheer, the panic in her voice bordering on the manic. "I'm looking forward to hurting you."

Which was the moment she discovered that the record-screech sound effect was an actual derail noise that could physically ring in her ears. Noa froze, panic mode engaged.

"I'm sorry?" Lilah frowned, her brow creasing.

"With the...makeup?" Noa tried to explain, her face going hot as blood rushed into her cheeks. "And the blood. The fake blood. For the effects. Kill me. Please. It will be an act of mercy."

Lilah didn't laugh at Noa directly, but she definitely looked like she was amused at Noa's expense in a faintly superior way. "It's fine. I think I get it." Somehow Noa doubted that. Picture-perfect and composed, Lilah didn't look like she'd ever been flustered a day in her life.

A quick glance showed Denise and Peter deep in another flirty conversation and no one else in the room paying any attention to Noa's slip of the tongue. She sighed, dropping her hands and tucking them into her pockets to keep herself from fidgeting. "It figures. My first ten minutes on set, and I've already managed to threaten to murder one of the leads."

"If it's any consolation, I've heard worse?" Lilah offered. She was looking Noa over carefully, like she didn't want Noa to see, probably making a mental list of every scuff on Noa's shoes and frayed edge on her cuffs. Noa knew she wasn't *pretty*, not the way women like Lilah were beautiful, but the idea of pageant queen Lilah cataloging her every fault got her hackles up before she could talk herself down.

"Somehow I doubt that," Noa fired back, and she added a

smile to make it fit in with what had almost felt like witty banter, but it probably didn't work the way she meant it.

She was saved from having to backtrack when Denise pulled herself away from what was apparently a magnetically compelling conversation with the other actor and rejoined them at Lilah's mirror. "Are we done, ladies? I have to get to Lilah's face before wardrobe sends out bounty hunters."

"We're done," Lilah replied, all sunshine and light again. "And I'm all yours. It was nice meeting you, Noa," she added, only the smile was gone and she was distant, a professional wall sliding down and closing her off.

Snob? Noa wished that wasn't the word that had come to mind, but there they were.

Never meet your heroes.

"Then let's get to work." Denise tied her dresser's apron on around her waist, handfuls of makeup brushes sticking up out of the dozen slender pockets. "Noa, get me that tray of foundations. We have magic to make."

Lilah's second coffee of the day had kicked in, her makeup was done, and she was feeling much more settled in her own skin as she walked onto the laboratory set where they'd be spending the next couple of weeks. Wayne gave her a happy thumbs-up when she passed by the security station, his enthusiastic show of approval bolstering her mood even more.

The stage contained most of a research lab, parts of it hinged to be swung away to let the cameras in. The whole thing was white and chrome; all the better to contrast with the rustic decor once they moved to the cabin in the woods. White floors, gray countertops, chrome fixtures—at least their clothes had some color in them, and there were safety posters on the walls that stopped the whole thing from looking like some Stanley Kubrick space monstrosity.

The cast was assembling, and Lilah popped herself up to sit on the counter next to Tanner. He wasn't a close friend, but they'd worked together before. When she'd first arrived in Hollywood, her big amazing First! Movie! Role! had been as "Girl Run Over by Clown Car." Tanner'd been "Jerk at Carnival," and they'd bonded over bad craft services sandwiches and coffee. It may not have been much to build a friendship on, but it was nice to have a familiar face around. "Ready for this?" He greeted her with a broad grin that reached his warm brown eyes.

"I hope so." Lilah shrugged easily in reply, looking over the room. "I've done killer clowns, hurricanes, and possessed escalators, but dinosaurs are a first."

The tech crowd was still messing with lights and moving props into place, while Ed, their director, was waving his arms around in the middle of a conversation with someone. Dan Gilbert, the producer who'd so loved Lilah at her audition, sat in a folding chair and watched the actors with a calculating stare. His eyes fell on her for a moment, and she looked away, uncomfortable at the thought of pulling his attention.

Ishani caught Lilah's eye and seemed to take it as an invitation, wandering over to join them. Wardrobe had put her into an outfit similar to Lilah's but with a button-up blouse and glasses to go with the skin-snug jeans—movie shorthand for the nerd girl, only this time, the "Bookish Girl with No Boyfriend" wasn't going to survive.

"It'll be fun," Tanner said in a tone that didn't invite argument, and it was nice to see that his absolutely relentless optimism didn't seem to have faded at all. "I'm going to tell my folks to come see this one, and they can watch my throat get ripped out by big pointy teeth." He mimed toothy jaws with one of his hands and both Ishani and Lilah laughed.

"That's one way to make sure they don't ask for a set visit." Ishani leaned against the counter, her arms folded in front of her. Lilah caught herself scanning the room rather than paying close attention to the conversation. Noa was there, half-shadowed and way in the back with the other assistants and a couple of the department heads. She wasn't looking at Lilah; her head was down and she was fussing with a camera. A second later and she looked up, like she'd realized someone was watching, and Lilah quickly looked away.

"Are you kidding?" Tanner was laughing. "My uncle lives for this stuff. He was the bad babysitter who got me hooked on horror movies, and I'm not even the first to die in this one. If he had the chance—"

A couple of sharp claps cut him off and caught everyone's attention, Ed walking out into the middle of the set with his clipboard and script underneath his arm. "Thank you! Thank you, everyone." The bright lights gleamed off the bald spot on top of his head, and Lilah stifled a grin.

"This is where I give you the big inspirational first-day-on-set speech, but no one's got time for that," Ed declared cheerily. Next to Lilah, Tanner snorted a laugh. "We all know why we're here, so let's get cracking. We'll start with the blocking we rehearsed for scene three, bottom of page twelve, and see how far we get before we feel like killing ourselves. Tallyho."

"Oh, this is going to be a fun day," Ishani muttered under her breath, but Lilah couldn't find it in her to be annoyed. She risked one last look over to the far side of the set, and this time she had the chance to watch Noa without being caught. Longing was a good emotion to hold on to; she cataloged how it felt and packed the moment away for later.

———

Noa had spent time on sets before, but it was both a blessing and a downer to realize that the slow pace wasn't merely the same on big pictures, but actively compounded. Granted they weren't waiting for someone to finish stapling the hem of their own costume, but the number of times the director made them redo shots, tweaked his setups, had all the department heads clustered around the monitors in deep consultation…four pages in a day was starting to look like a pipe dream. *It'll pick up once everyone's familiar with Ed's flow*, Denise had promised, but in the meantime, Noa sat, watched, and waited.

The scene wrapped to Ed's satisfaction at last, and the crew sprang into a flurry of action. Noa grabbed the camera that Denise had pushed into her hands and headed for the actors as they came off the side. Makeup and effects continuity photos were her problem now, and she elbowed her way in alongside the intern taking the official stills. The only trouble was the damned camera didn't seem to have a time and date stamp setting in the hundreds of submenus, and Noa sure as hell didn't have the time to go get her phone and look up the manual. "Come on, you stupid thing. You have to have a date setting *somewhere*."

The camera was lifted out of her hands, and Noa snapped her head up. The lead guy—Tanner Blake, she reminded herself, the young dark-skinned bro-dude, not the older white-haired actor Lilah'd been chatting with in makeup—had the camera in his hands and was zipping through the menus like he knew exactly what he was doing. "Hey!"

He only grinned and handed it back to her, the time and date set and showing on the bottom corner of the screen. "Better?"

Noa closed her eyes for a second against the embarrassment, caught out being incompetent. "Better," she admitted grudgingly. "Thank you."

"No problem," Tanner replied. "You've got this," he added quietly with another flash of a bright grin, this one feeling a little conspiratorial, before he was pulled away. She had the unsettling feeling that he actually meant it, unlike the cool brush-off she'd had from Lilah. At least some of the cast were genuine.

An hour later, the crew still working out the kinks in the next setup, Noa found herself perched on a chair in front of Lilah and staring right into those iconic blue eyes. A couple of wisps of red-gold hair had escaped from Lilah's braid, and Noa resisted the temptation to jump the gun on Phoebe's job and tuck them back into place. Those perfect hands of hers rested on her knees, her fingers long and slim, nails painted a pale, virginal pink.

"The hurry-up-and-wait around here is a lot heavier on the

'wait' than previous films I've worked on. What do people do to pass the time?" Noa tried to start a conversation, leaning back to get a better look at the touch-up work on Lilah's eyeshadow. Talking about something—anything—was a whole lot better than working in stony silence, dwelling on ways to impress her, or starting to babble about Lilah's career.

"A few different things." Lilah shrugged one shoulder, her head steady like the pro that she was. "The last project I was on, the stunt performers had an ongoing euchre tournament in between trying to paintball each other off motorcycles in the back lot. Peter does crosswords. He'll probably ask you for words. During rehearsals, Mikal started teaching Ishani how to crochet." She gestured with her chin, and Noa followed her nod across the set. The tall blond actor who'd been on set with Lilah was chatting animatedly with one of the others, a beautiful dark-skinned woman about their same age who'd been given glasses and frumpy clothes in a vain attempt to make her look dowdy. Lengths of yarn fell from their busy hands to vanish into a bag propped underneath Mikal's chair.

"Crafts aren't your thing?" Noa asked, mostly to keep the conversation going. Mikal hadn't seemed like the crochet type either, big and buff as he was, but actors were a different breed. "What do you do for fun around here?" If it were anyone else, that might have been a come-on, but Noa was too busy trying not to stick her foot in it again to be thinking about the surprising sweetness of Lilah's smile up close or the way the faint trail of freckles crossed the bridge of her nose underneath her smooth foundation.

Lilah glanced at Mikal and Ishani again, and her nose wrinkled adorably. "I'm not really a crafty person," she confessed. "I read, mostly, or text with friends."

"Oh yeah?" Noa perked up at that, trailing the brush across Lilah's lid to correct a smudge. "What's on your reader these days?"

Weirdly, Lilah's cheeks pinked up. Was she stashing a pile of erotic fanfic bookmarks or something? Noa's curiosity spiked the more uncomfortable Lilah looked. "Women's fiction," she said after a beat too long. "You know, Bridget Jones. Sophie Kinsella. Romances. That sort of thing."

"Seriously?" Noa wasn't sure why she was so surprised, but the words escaped with a laugh before she could stop them. "I pictured you as more of an intellectual." Ohhh, wipeout. That had been a major mistake. The recoil from Lilah was as subtle as it was instantaneous, and when she recovered, any hint of that natural smile was gone. "I mean—"

"I know what you mean," Lilah replied, and her voice was decidedly cool. "I spend most of my workdays being scared, maimed, killed, or watching other people die horribly. If I want to read something with a guaranteed happy ending, I think I've earned that."

"Totally." Noa backpedaled, her own cheeks hot. Lilah was back to detached distance, and there wasn't going to be any quick way for Noa to dig her foot out of her mouth. *Way to impress, Birnbaum.* "Absolutely you have, and when you put it that way, it makes perfect sense." She distracted herself with checking her reference photos and trying to frame the next piece of conversation in her head. She'd change the subject completely to make a snappy comment about the lab setup, then ask Lilah about her favorite moment in the script.

Only by the time Noa had the words in the right order, Lilah had her phone out and was tapping away, oblivious to Noa and her internal struggle.

Lilah Silver's obviously much more interesting social life, 1; Noa Birnbaum's big mouth, 0.

Noa: I don't think she likes me.

Chrissy: What did you do??

Noa: Nothing! It's just a vibe.

Noa: I might have insulted her taste in books a little.

Chrissy: No vibing the talent.

Chrissy: Smooth move, Casanova.

Noa: In my defense, I'm pretty sure she reads trashy romance.

Chrissy: Snobby much? That's not the defense that you think it is.

Noa: I'm hearing that loud and clear.

Noa: Do you still love me even when I'm being a butthead?

Chrissy: Buy me dinner and I'll consider it.

The shooting day wrapped on time, wonder of wonders, and Lilah made her way home in good spirits. The porch lights were on and the sky getting dark by the time she got back, the curtains already drawn across the front windows of the small shared house. She pushed a pair of scuffed work boots aside with the side of her foot and swung the door open. A blast of music hit her along with a wave of cooking smells—garlic, ginger, onions? Kayleigh had been on an Asian-fusion kick lately. Lilah set her bag down in the hall and padded along to the kitchen, sticking her head inside for a moment to say hi.

"If it's meant to *be* it'll *be*—" Kayleigh broke off her singing and waved her spatula at Lilah. "House dinner tonight, ten minutes!" She'd commandeered the shared kitchen, blond hair tied back in a long ponytail. She didn't look much like Miss Salt Lake City right now in her scruffy jeans, a dish towel shoved in the rear pocket. Pans sizzled on all the burners, rice cooker bubbling on the counter, the oven fan going, and the sink stacked high. Her laptop was perched on one of the stools, a recipe site competing for screen space with the music video in the corner, steam turning the kitchen window opaque.

Lilah's stomach grumbled, but it was in a battle with the wave of exhaustion that was about to hit her, and she wavered. "How did you know when I'd be home? And I'm beat," she confessed. "I was planning to grab a piece of toast and crash." Her stomach growled again, turning her into a liar.

Kayleigh raised a pointed eyebrow over her glasses at the sound but didn't call Lilah out on the lie. "Brooke checked your call sheet, and we added an hour. Come sit! There are, like, sixteen different vitamins in this. If you're tired, carbs are the enemy. You need some superfoods."

It smelled incredible, and Lilah's original resistance faded and died with barely a whimper. "Fine, you win," she conceded. "Where's everyone else?"

"Brooke's on the phone with Alistair, and Nadia's on her way home. She texted, like, two hours ago and said that we needed to be proud of her because she didn't murder her boss today, so I think it's going to be one of those evenings."

"Hence the feast?"

"You got it. If we don't look out for one another in this crazy world, who will?" Kayleigh asked rhetorically. Something in one of the pans started to smoke, and she hauled it off the burner with a yelp.

Lilah cranked the window open while Kayleigh flapped the dish towel over the faint plume of scorch smoke and frantically scraped the sauce-covered tofu bits into a large bowl. Once the crisis was averted, Lilah grabbed her bag again. "I love you. Don't ever change. I'm going to go wash the half can of hairspray out of my 'do and meet you back down here."

"I want set stories!" Kayleigh yelled after her as Lilah headed to the back bedroom she'd claimed for her own. The heavy, homemade pink-and-gold curtain was pulled across the living room, closing off the dining room that they'd converted into a fourth bedroom for Brooke, the faint sound of laughter coming from behind it.

"I don't have any yet!" Lilah called back.

"Then I want Tanner Blake's phone number, and I'll make some stories *for* you!"

"Don't bother." Brooke's voice filtered through the canvas-backed sari divider. "I heard he's gay."

Kayleigh sighed. "Oh well. Never mind. Who else have you got?"

Lilah did a quick mental run-through of the guys on set: Mikal had a long-term girlfriend, Peter was too old, same for the director and producer. The thought of Mr. Gilbert hitting on Kayleigh with that calculating stare of his was enough to make her shudder, and she moved on quickly. "There's a new security guy at the studio," she offered, and Kayleigh appeared in the kitchen door. "You like men with muscles and ponytails, right?"

"I could be convinced. Tell me more over dinner." She flapped the dish towel at Lilah, and Lilah took that as her cue to exit, stage left.

Once she'd closed the door to her tiny room, she flopped down on her bed, kicking her bare feet up to rest against the wall. She flipped through her phone quickly, grabbing a couple of the set photos that didn't show anything spoiler-y and uploading them to Instagram. *Back on set with the best team ever*, she added in the caption, along with a couple of hearts and heart-eyed emojis. Hashtag scareodactyl, tag Tanner, Mikal, and Ishani, and did Peter have any social media at all?

Her phone blooped happily at her. First like in less than a second after she'd uploaded. The account name was vaguely familiar; @tommyjarvis must have commented on something on her feed before.

Instagram was her favorite site, but Nancy had insisted that Lilah keep up on a couple of others as well—and her agent's word was basically law when it came to this sort of thing. So Lilah obediently opened up the next one, sent another pic and a similar sort of message.

And within a half second, @tommyjarvis had sent a thumbs-up there as well.

Huh. Lilah frowned at her phone. On the other hand, *she* had four different social media accounts open at the moment, so why was it weird that someone else was online and checking their alerts at the same time? She should be grateful for uberfans who followed her all over the place. Engagement was key, as Nancy liked to say.

Lilah hesitated with her thumb on the button, ready to post another update...but she put the phone down, something funny prickling at the back of her neck. Whatever. She was tired and imagining things, getting all creeped out by coincidental timing. She needed to go shower, wash the day out of her hair, and then go stuff her face with dumplings.

One more thing, though, most important of them all. Lilah pulled herself up to sitting and did a quick mirror check, even though it wasn't necessary. Not with him. He was the only one ever in her life who didn't care if her hair was messy or her lipstick was the wrong shade.

The program bleeped at her a couple of times, and then he was there, the camera on the phone she'd gotten him for his birthday aimed most of the way down her grandfather's ear. She heard a muffled complaint and then the camera refocused so she was looking at him, his big warm smile meant for her and her alone.

"Hi, Zaidie," Lilah chirped happily. "You're looking dapper." He was too, his white hair—once pale blond, now thin most places and gone in others—slicked back and a bow tie with a white shirt collar under his chin.

"I went to a show tonight. Senior discount, but they didn't check my ID." He chuckled, his eyelid dropping in a broad wink. "Went with the usual group: Stan, Percy, and the biddies."

"Don't let any of them trap you into a one-on-one date, Zaidie," Lilah teased him, her heart light. "You know how crafty widows can get."

"Don't you worry, my love. There's only room for two girls in my heart other than your Bubbie, may her memory be for a blessing, and that's your mother and you. Now." He settled back and she could see bits and pieces of his living room around him—the floral upholstered wing chair and matching couch, the wallpaper borders that had been on the walls since before Lilah was born, and the edge of the end table where his candy dish lived, with the seemingly endless supply of mints and butterscotch sweets. "Today was your first day filming, wasn't it? Tell me all about how it went."

By the time her grandfather'd had to sign off for the night in his time zone, @tommyjarvis had completely flown out of Lilah's mind. And by the time she fell into bed, stomach and heart full, the only memories of the day that mattered were the looks she'd stolen at Noa when no one else had been watching.

CHAPTER THREE

A FEW DAYS INTO PRODUCTION and Noa's general state of panic was beginning to settle. There was a rhythm to the job, long lulls interspersed with moments of frantic almost-chaos, then back into the downtime to build up energy for the next one.

Working across two departments gave her the chance to chat up the props guys and study the injury effects that would be coming later, her fingers itching to get sunk into the foam and latex, the painting and airbrushing that would take basic prosthetics to a whole new level of art. It was a weird art, maybe, and one her parents definitely didn't understand—the reminder especially rankling this morning, thanks to yet another early-morning phone call with her mother on the way to set. The traffic was stop-and-go, giving her no easy excuse to drop the call, and she watched the bumper of the car in front of her to avoid having to look at Chrissy's eye rolls.

"So you work thirty days on a movie set and then you get to be in the union? I don't see why you had to drop out of school for one month of work. You could do that in the summer, even with weekends off."

"That's not how it works, Mom. Union people always get called first. Productions only hire people who aren't on the roster when everyone else is already working. The only reason I have this job is because there was literally no one with a card available. That's not going to come around again anytime soon."

"Especially not in the summer with weekends off," Chrissy muttered. "What does she think you are, a bank manager?"

"Fine, so this is a once-in-a-lifetime job." The hands-free speaker crackled, and a cat meowed somewhere in the background. Noa could practically see her mother pacing around the living room, phone on speaker and set on the table so she could talk with her hands. "Thirty days on this terror-bird thing and then you're in the union, so you can go back to school."

"No. Thirty days' work and then, if I pass a review and get a strong recommendation from my department head, I can apply to be an off-roster hire for the union."

"Dropping out and you're not even in the union after that?"

"I'll be a trainee, which at least gets me insurance and the right to work. I need sixty days a year for three years to qualify for full membership. One-eighty total."

"Three years, and only *then* you'll be in the union. It sounds like a scam to me."

"It's not a scam, it's how things work, and—" Noa's volume rose as she tried to talk over her mother's incoming rant. Chrissy winced, and Noa dialed down the volume, but all that did was give her mother a window to talk over her again.

"This is a fool's errand. How can you possibly expect to

support yourself without a degree? And you won't even have the security of something to fall back on if this movie mishegas doesn't work out."

"Goodbye, Mom."

"You're condemning yourself to a life of genteel poverty, Noa, if not outright destitution, and I have no idea what I'm going to do with you!"

"Oh, look." With an apologetic look at Chrissy, Noa half shouted into the phone to get over her mother's raised voice. "I'm at work. I'll call you later. Good*bye*, Mom." And hand trembling slightly, she pushed the button to end the call.

Her phone rang again, and she sent her mother to voicemail.

"I'm going to pay for that later," Noa said mournfully. She pulled into a parking spot and got out of the car, looping her kit bag over her shoulder.

Chrissy made a sympathetic face. "Block her number for a while until she calms down," she suggested. "It's what I have to do when my nana starts in on my 'calamitous life choices' and sends me articles on detransitioning. It's like whapping a puppy on the nose with a newspaper when it messes. Sooner or later, they'll learn not to shit on your shoes."

"I do that and someone will be knocking on our door at two in the morning for a wellness check."

"Ah, parents." Chrissy rolled her eyes as they parted ways at the studio door. "It's nice that they care, but do they have to show it quite so vehemently?"

Noa snorted a laugh and dashed for the makeup room at top speed, skidding to a stop when she got there. She opened it and slipped in as quietly as possible, in the maybe-vain hope that she wouldn't get spotted coming in late.

The vibe was different that morning, a funny tension thrumming through the air that Noa couldn't quite put her finger on. Denise was busy doing Peter's final touch-ups, her shirt that morning a brilliant fire-engine red rather than her usual dark colors. Huh. Lilah wasn't around yet, and the call sheet said she wasn't due for another hour, but Ishani was there rummaging around in her bag.

Noa got onto her setups, laying out the various shades of foundation and highlighters Denise would need for Ishani, vaguely aware of a murmured conversation going on behind her. Not quite whispers, not quite loud enough for her to listen in, and all of it making her vaguely nervous about nothing in particular.

Only now Peter was leaving the makeup room, a spring in his step, and Denise was staring her down. Noa's rough morning was on the way to looking a lot worse. "Noa! Over here, please." Crap. She wasn't *that* late, was she? In an industry where "on time" meant "fifteen minutes early"…yeah, she probably was. Was she about to be fired? *Condemned to a life of genteel poverty.* Her mother's voice echoed in her head, and Noa bit her lip to stop herself from blurting out an apology or begging to be kept on the job. At least not until Denise had finished reading her the riot act.

Only she didn't. Denise waited until Noa reached her, then she pulled them into a quieter corner, away from the talent in the makeup chairs. "I am absolutely swamped," Denise began, gesturing with perfectly manicured hands, her mood positively exuberant. Was she high? "I'm being pulled in simply too many directions, and if I don't reorganize the workloads, this whole thing is going to become a dumpster fire. I'm reassigning you."

So that...didn't sound *as* bad as it could be, but Noa's heart remained lodged in her throat regardless. "Reassigned to what?"

Denise made a little sigh that sounded like relief, like she'd somehow expected a different response. "You'll be the main MUA for Tanner and Lilah from here in. You'll be responsible for them from beginning to end of day—faces, touch-ups, the works. It'll be great experience for you," she announced.

Noa stopped breathing. Main makeup artist for *Lilah*? And Tanner, but Tanner was a doll, and everything there would be fine. She didn't have a raging crush on Tanner, for one. And she didn't have the incredibly unfortunate habit of sticking her foot in her mouth every time she talked to him. The two differences were definitely related.

When Noa saw Lilah, she got stupid. Even when Noa carefully planned out nice things to say, they sounded rude when they came out of her mouth, which made Lilah dislike her more, so Noa's self-consciousness got worse and she said something even dumber the next time. It was a cycle of stupid that could only end with Noa getting slapped. Or fired.

Noa's stomach clenched. She couldn't explain any of that to Denise, not as a reason to avoid the swap. There was no way to say "Lilah would probably rather have anyone else in the building doing her face" and have it sound any less terrible than it was. And while working with the leads was usually the key makeup's place, Denise had the right to set up the assignments however she damn well pleased. There was no escape clause there.

Maybe there was still a way out. "What about when we start doing all the prosthetics work? I'm good at bruises, and I can work miracles with scar wax, but Lilah's injuries are all small pieces. Peter is going to be getting gutted, and Mikal's arm was coming off—if I'm on Tanner and Lilah only, I won't be able to help out with those." Did she sound like she was whining? She didn't want to sound like she was whining. She needed to stay on Denise's good side if she ever wanted to work in LA again.

"I'll be working with most of the major pieces, and you'll be focusing on the leads. I'll tag you in when I need an extra pair of hands. It'll work better this way," Denise soothed. "Rather than trying to handle painting up six people at once and running the chance of missing something, you'll be able to stay focused on your talent. And once the men are finished with their shooting schedule, you'll be able to devote yourself entirely to Lilah. We want her to look good after all. She's the face of this picture."

"Sure, but—" But Lilah was everything that Noa wasn't: poised, confident, *competent*. And working together that closely, without Denise as a buffer, she was going to have a front-row seat to the disaster that was Noa. Live and in Technicolor.

On the other hand, working with Lilah meant that Noa would have the same VIP access to her. And maybe, if she could get over herself, she could find a way to bridge that gap between them. It was a chance to redeem herself and, in the process, maybe learn a little more about what made Lilah Silver tick.

She'd hesitated too long and lost any chance to make a case.

"I'm so glad you agree." Denise patted Noa on the shoulder

and breezed past her, stopping to chat with Ishani and a couple of the extras waiting for their turns in the chairs.

Noa let out a puff of air, her nerves jangling louder than before. Not fired, that was a major plus. Reassigned to what was technically a prestigious position too. But she hadn't exactly made a great first impression on Lilah. Or a good second one for that matter. How was she going to cope, now that she was going to be face-to-face—and face-to-stomach, and face-to-boobs—with her for the next five weeks?

––––––––––––

The doors for the prop shop were cracked open, bright light spilling into the hallway. Lilah paused on her way over to the set and snuck a peek inside. A fan buzzed loudly somewhere, and the smell of spray paint hung thick enough in the air to make her eyes water. One of Mr. Williams's assistants was working under the fume hood at the far end, only a black-clad silhouette and the backward brim of a baseball cap visible from where she stood. She could identify some of the props laid out on the paint-splattered drop cloth—the nest of big dinosaur eggs, for instance, now mottled green and blue instead of the plain clay sculpts she'd seen on her first tour. They lay next to a handful of artfully broken eggshells, a harpoon gun, and a big crate labeled SOME ASSEMBLY REQUIRED out of which jutted a pair of blue-gray arms—severed below the elbows—and a few loose coils of red-splattered intestine. Standard stuff, except for the nest.

She'd taken a few steps into the room before she heard the voices around the corner. Colin Williams was easy to pick out; the props master had the gravelly voice of a lifelong smoker paired with a football coach's booming projection. The other voice was less familiar, as was the rumpled man it was attached to.

"You do realize that pterodactyls aren't actually a species." The balding, bearded complainer stomped out of Colin's office, an aura of frustration seemingly baked into his pores. "And *Pterodactylus antiquus* was about the size of a sparrow. How can a reptile the size of a sparrow lay eggs the size of my head?"

The assistant at the far end of the room emerged from the fume hood, wiping paint off his hands, and watched the spat with vague disinterest.

Colin followed the bearded man out, shrugging his broad shoulders. "Look, man. If you can convince them to rename the flick *Scare-anodon*, I'm all for it. But until then, I build to the specs they give me. Mornin', Lilah."

"Morning, Mr. Williams." Lilah waggled her fingers at him, flashing the other man a hesitant smile.

"Lilah, Dr. Crosby. He's our 'scientific advisor.' Crosby, Lilah Silver, our leading lady on this picture." Colin didn't actually put finger quotes around the words *scientific advisor* but he might as well have, his eyes flashing with contained amusement and his hands resting easily in the pockets of his paint-dotted coveralls.

"Miss Silver," Dr. Crosby greeted her, lighting up at the introduction. His irritation faded and he turned toward her, shutting Colin out of the conversation entirely. He stared at her intensely, as though focusing hard enough to see through her skull. "I'm very familiar with your body of work. Though someone really needed to consult on your death scene in the hurricane movie.

Unless you personally have had a rib pair removed, there were one too few splintered costae visible on each side. And your breathing pattern wasn't labored enough for a truly fatal pneumothorax."

"Um, thank you," Lilah replied, forcing herself not to look away. Was he even blinking? And she tried not to think too deeply about how hard he must have been staring at her fake chest piece in *Second Wind* to notice those details. "I'll keep that in mind? For next time?"

"Please do." He gathered himself up, tugged at the hem of his short-sleeved button-up shirt to smooth it into place, and gave her a brief nod before exiting through the same door. She watched him go, cocking her head. The door closed behind him.

"What was *that* about?" Lilah breathed out, tension draining from her.

"Sounds like you've got a fan," Colin snorted. "A scientific advisor's a waste of time for a movie like this if you ask me, but someone on the money side seemed to think it was important. What can I do for you?" He changed the subject, smile bright against his dark skin.

"Nothing much, just being nosy," she confessed, distracting herself from the icky feeling in the pit of her stomach by crouching down to poke at the biggest of the eggs. "When do we get to play with these?"

"Tomorrow, last time I checked the schedule. They're still wet," he cautioned her, and she dropped her hand. "We don't need that hatching one until Saturday."

Lilah shuddered internally. Tubes in props tended not to bode too well for her, physically speaking. A four-second shot of bleeding out on-screen equaled at least a day of being coated in corn syrup and food coloring and hours washing it off every night. "It's going to be goopy, isn't it?" she asked ruefully, rising to her feet.

Colin had reinstalled himself at his workbench amid piles of electronic parts she couldn't begin to name, though the tape labels and baggies suggested an organizational system at work. "Oh yeah," he replied with gleeful relish. "We're going to have a real good time with the slime. We're leaning more toward a borax mix than the K-Y for this one, but we'll see what happens when we do a couple of screen tests. PJ over there is going to be working the dino feet when we get to the slash-and-spray scenes," he added, nodding to the guy by the fume hood, now lighting a blowtorch and sliding a welding mask down over his eyes.

"I hate you for this, so you know," Lilah quipped, flashing him a brilliant grin to show that she didn't mean it.

Colin didn't take offense, grinning back at her. "Ah, the glamour of show biz. Wait until we get to the actual maimings. Then it's going to get *really* messy."

The clock over his shoulder caught her eye as the numbers changed—crap! Lilah backed away from the drying props and headed for the door. "And on that note, I need to get down to makeup before *they* find and maim me for being late. Have a good one!"

"You too," he called back as the door closed behind her.

Ishani was in the hall when Lilah darted out of props, getting a once-over from wardrobe. The dresser, a tall, no-nonsense woman with silver streaking through the dark brown of her hair, stared at Ishani with a concerned frown. "Why are your boobs there? Your boobs were definitely not there during fittings."

"I couldn't find my film bra on my rack. You guys must have lost it," Ishani sniffed critically. "I'm wearing my own."

"And that explains why they're an inch too high for that shirt. Come back to wardrobe, and we'll find it. The bra, I mean. Your rack's already there."

"Hah. Very funny."

Lilah slipped around them and skidded into makeup only a minute past her call time, her heart pounding hard enough to beat its way out of her chest. Noa was the first person she saw, which didn't help the pulse problem. Noa had another set of streaks in her hair today, bright fuchsia joining the fading purple and blue, and Lilah was acutely aware that she was staring. She tucked her own boring, one-color hair behind her ears, self-conscious, and took the chance while Noa was looking away to drop into the swivel chair in front of her mirror.

Operation Make Friends had been DOA since day one. Lilah hadn't been sure how to react to Noa's jokes at first, and Noa's laughing judgment of her taste still made her slightly queasy. She'd switched to something a little different on her reader after that, something telling, maybe even revealing, but if Noa had noticed that Lilah'd been reading lesbian fiction, she still hadn't said a thing. There just wasn't a connection happening, and Lilah had to reluctantly assume that it was at least partly to do with her. Sure, Noa was pleasant and professional enough when they had a few minutes here and there, but most of that time was spent with Noa's attention focused elsewhere.

Which was stupid, considering that Noa was staring into her eyes more often than not or dragging the lip brush gently across

Lilah's mouth, but looking at her makeup wasn't looking at *her*. It was a stare that stopped a millimeter in front of her, and Lilah wasn't sure she'd ever be able to explain the difference if she tried.

Only Lilah knew now that Noa smelled like a mix of coffee and rosemary shampoo, and she was kidding herself if she imagined that Noa was anywhere nearly as aware of *Lilah*.

Noa was approaching Lilah's chair, and something was definitely off. She wasn't smiling, and she usually smiled. That was okay; Lilah was pretty good at cheering people up. Kayleigh was better, with that whole Utah-sunshine thing she had going on, but Lilah tried one of her smiles on for size anyway. "Morning!"

"So they say," Noa cracked back, her joke sounding forced. She plunked her kit down on the dressing table and started unpacking product onto the folded white towel laid in front of the mirror.

Lilah stole the chance to watch Noa move, her eyes drawn and held by Noa's sure and steady hands. Short nails, of course, and unpolished, with a plain silver ring on her thumb; her fingers moved with the kind of confidence Lilah only pretended to have. The slim-cut black T-shirt that skimmed over her compact curves today was for a band called *Tenebre*—at least Lilah thought it was a band—that Lilah'd never heard of. A handful of crystal posts glimmered in odd spots in Noa's ears, and a silver chain she always had around her neck was the only other jewelry she wore. The chain was tucked in like always, the little gleaming line tracing down Noa's neck and under the collar of her shirt.

And she had a girlfriend already, which was why Lilah had to pull her eyes right back up, thank you, and not entertain those kinds of thoughts again.

Lilah's phone buzzed, and she struggled to get it out of her jeans pocket, the glitter-filled rose-gold case suddenly looking tawdry next to Noa's black-and-gray monochrome cool. It was a *good* thing that she'd never actually put on her bracelet or tried to come out to Noa. Noa probably had all the friends she needed without adding a pining wannabe to her list.

> **Brooke:** Austin wants to know if he can have your phone number. Cool/not cool?

Any other day, at any other *moment*, even, Lilah would be rolling her eyes at Brooke's matchmaking. On the other hand, going out with someone, even some guy off Brooke's endless list of random meets and hangers-on, would be a good way to keep her mind off Noa and her unavailability.

> **Lilah:** Sure, why not? As long as he knows that I've got really long days right now. I'm not ditching set to grab coffee with some farmers-market man bun, no matter how cute.
> **Brooke:** He's a *microbrewery* man bun, and you'll like him.

There. Lilah was perfectly capable of managing her own social life, thank you very much.

Apparently totally oblivious to the drama playing itself out inside Lilah's head, Noa finished Denise's setup and brushed her fingertips off on the thighs of her dark gray jeans. They left a sparkly trail of loose highlighter across Noa's hip, which she ignored. And she didn't leave. "So I don't know if Denise filled you in," Noa began, and the glance she shot at Lilah was...what? Annoyed? Stressed? Nervous? What could Noa have to be nervous about?

"Filled me in?" Lilah set her phone facedown on the counter and swiveled to meet Noa's frown. "I don't think so."

Noa let out a puff of air. "She's switched some things up. I'm going to be your artist from now on. You and Tanner, so, like, mostly you."

"Oh." *Oh.* That was why Noa was in a mood. She was probably happier doing her other job. It sucked that someone had that reaction to being told to work closely with her, but Lilah was selfish enough to be secretly thrilled on her own behalf. "I promise I won't be high-maintenance," she offered, a kind of olive branch for whatever offense she'd accidentally caused. She should really be the one to be annoyed with Noa, considering some of the comments she'd made. But there was no reason to hold a grudge and every reason to try and build a better relationship with the person who was going to know her so intimately by the end of the next five weeks. Maybe this was a good moment to try and start fresh.

"What?" Noa frowned back at her, then her expression cleared and her eyes went wide. "No! It's not—I don't think that. Honestly. It's not you. I keep digging that hole for myself." She laughed ruefully, and Lilah narrowed her eyes, some undertone there that she wasn't able to identify. Noa swigged from her coffee cup and let out a slow breath. "I was looking forward to getting to focus on special effects. Painting stunties up in gallons of ooze and silicone. It would be great for my portfolio."

The tidbit about the effects was information Lilah hadn't known about her, and she seized the tidbit gladly. "Is that what you're on crew for?" she asked, leaning her elbow on the dressing table and her chin on her hand.

Noa grabbed her primer and concealer and perched on the edge of the table, sliding effortlessly into Lilah's personal space. "Well, no, not technically. I'm here for everything that Denise and Colin need a warm body for, including coffee runs and taking out the recycling. But what I really want to do is effects makeup. Latex and prosthetics, blood and guts, that kind of thing. The bloodier and more guts filled, the better. I want to design big effects one day." She nudged Lilah to get her to sit up, and Lilah did as she was told. Noa's touch on her skin set her heart racing faster than it should, and Lilah closed her eyes so that Noa wouldn't catch on.

"Tell you what," Lilah offered. "Between Tanner and I, I bet we can talk Ed into setting up some extra gore shots." The faint pressure on her lower eyelids went away, and Lilah opened her eyes again. Noa was still leaning in close, capping the concealer, and Lilah kept going. "The final escape scene is all done in the river, and I'm sure I could do that without at least one of my legs," she finished, not letting the corners of her lips twitch upward.

A beat passed with Noa staring at her, and then Noa was laughing, with a smile that lit up her whole face. Lilah would say a whole lot of dumb things on the off chance that one of them would make Noa laugh like that again. "You'd sacrifice a leg for my career?" she teased back.

"Oh, sure," Lilah replied, still deadpan, then she let the joke go and actually felt herself start to relax. Noa smiling at her was so much better than awkward silence, and she'd only had to sacrifice a tiny bit of dignity to get it. She decided to chance it and carried on the joke. "What are friends for? As long as you're okay with it being my left one. My right is my better side."

"You and Ariana Grande," Noa snorted, reaching for another bottle.

Lilah did let herself laugh that time and settled in for the twenty minutes it would take for Noa to turn Lilah into someone presentable enough for human company. "I'm choosing to take that as a compliment."

Noa relaxed was a hundred times better than Noa stressed, and the twenty minutes flew by so much faster this time. They weren't friends yet, no matter what Lilah'd said, but maybe "slightly less awkward" would be enough.

Girlfriend, she also reminded herself sternly. *Noa's got a girlfriend. You have to let this dumb crush go.* Somehow, it was already far too late.

The next few days, Noa was on her absolute best behavior. No accidental insults, no commentary on Lilah's hobbies, and absolutely no attempts to flirt or sound clever. Lilah had called her a "friend," and there was no way Noa was going to screw it up again.

Oddly, the one time Lilah did set her phone down with the screen faceup and turned on, Noa was fairly certain that the book she was partway through was something by Radclyffe Hall. Hardly chick lit, but Chrissy'd told her off for comments like that more than once, and this time, Noa was smart enough not to say anything at all.

Now, Noa leaned in again, filling in one of Lilah's brows with a pencil. Perched on the edge of the table, Lilah sitting below her in a lower chair, Noa didn't notice her necklace dislodging itself from between her breasts until she felt the gentle tug on the chain and the brush of fingers against her collarbone.

Stifling a little yelp, Noa sat back, worried that she'd invaded Lilah's space more than she should have—only it was the little six-pointed star on the delicate silver chain that Lilah balanced on her fingertips.

"Sorry," Lilah apologized, casting her eyes up to meet Noa's gaze through her dark-tinted lashes. "You're Jewish? I guessed, when we were introduced, but so many people around here use stage names that I wasn't sure if it was okay to ask."

A faint and familiar chill prickled the back of Noa's neck, and she forced it back. There was no reason at all to be worried about what Lilah might think. There was no danger here. Noa couldn't possibly be the first Jewish person she knew—not in a city like LA, not in an industry like theirs. Unless that was why Lilah had been cool and standoffish, and it wasn't about Noa's stupid runaway mouth at all...

All those half-formed thoughts ricocheted through her head in the instant between Lilah's question and when Noa had to answer, and when she nodded, it was a little more guarded than before. "Yeah. 'Noa' is a girl's name in Hebrew." Okay, that was fine. No recoil, only a growing smile that Noa wasn't sure how to parse. It did give her the chance to go on the attack before Lilah could do or say anything awful. "So's yours, for the record. It means—"

Lilah nodded. "*Night.* I know. I used my Hebrew name for my stage name. It was easier to pick something that was already kind of familiar."

Which led to Noa's next major derail of the day. Would she ever find some kind of solid ground to plant herself on around this girl? "You're Jewish? It doesn't say that on your IMD—" She snapped her mouth shut before she could finish the sentence.

"If you say 'funny, you don't look it,' I may just kick you in the teeth," Lilah joked, her body very still and a hint of a familiar sort of wariness threading itself through her voice now that Noa knew enough to listen for it.

"Not a chance," Noa promised. "For some strange reason, no one ever tells *me* that," she added with a flash of a grin and a wink. "Polish red?"

Lilah nodded. "And Russian blond." She was thawing all around the edges now, her wariness gone and replaced with an almost-shy smile. Noa's heart dipped down into her stomach and twirled around her chest, leaving her dizzy.

"Do you keep?"

Lilah's cheeks flushed and she glanced away. "Sort of? Not Shabbat or anything. There weren't any synagogues in the town where I grew up. There's one in Petosky, but that's, like, half an hour away, and we didn't really go except for big events. My family does Passover, somewhat," Lilah offered up with an uncomfortable little laugh. "My dad really likes matzah as a snack, so he buys it year-round. Except for that week."

"Only a little backward." There wouldn't be any judgment coming from her—there were at *least* five hundred of the 613 commandments that Noa ignored on a regular basis. (Maybe more, depending on how you interpreted the one about gossip.)

Lilah ducked her head and laughed again. "Only a little! But it works for him." The self-conscious gesture broke through the shell of perfection, but the glow of her aura never dimmed. She was very human, suddenly approachable, and when she met Noa's eyes again, Noa felt a pull start somewhere in her midsection. *Ah, crap.*

"Lilah!"

Lilah turned at the sound of her name and the moment—if it had been a moment at all—was gone. "Here!"

"We're ready for you. Time for last looks, wardrobe, and makeup, and then we're on to scene fourteen."

"Back to the salt mines," Lilah joked, rising to her feet. She made a little pirouette and fluttered her eyelashes at Noa, completely unaware of the effect she was having on Noa's blood pressure. "Do I have your approval?"

Noa swallowed hard and found her voice. "Yes, yes you do. Your makeup, I mean." She scrambled to pull up the continuity photo as an excuse to take her eyes off Lilah and regroup. "Looks good," she said briskly and gave her a thumbs-up.

Lilah sketched off a salute, paused to let the wardrobe assistant tweak her shirt hem and the hairdresser replace a bobby pin, then headed for her next mark.

Noa let out a long, slow breath and tried to force her adrenaline to stand down. Her skin still tingled where Lilah's fingers had brushed against her, and she swore she could smell the sweet remnants of Lilah's shampoo. Stupid Denise and her stupid reassignments. Noa would have been safe if she'd been able to keep a little bit of distance between them, but now? A few more days like this one and she was going to spontaneously combust. She'd disintegrate like Daffy Duck in a crisis, and all they'd find of her by the end of week three would be a little pile of rubble, topped with a silver star.

Contrary to her panicked catastrophizing, Noa discovered that she was looking forward to mornings with Lilah in the chair more and more over the next few days. It got easier to ignore the adorable way her nose scrunched up when she laughed or that little frowny thing she did with her lips when she was thinking (shut up, it totally did) and replace it with admiration for her sly humor and her thoughtful way of speaking, so different from Noa's tendency to blurt out ninety percent of what crossed her mind. Tanner was more of an easy in-and-out, preferring to spend any extra prep time in his dressing room with the door closed. That meant the half hour Noa had with Lilah in the chair, often just the two of them in the room, was quickly becoming her favorite time of day.

Once she opened up, Lilah had an aura about her that made it easy to talk to her, this *thing* she did where you felt like she really, honestly cared about everything you had to say. It was a good trick for an actor to have, Noa decided in one of her more cynical moments of self-doubt. Part of that on-screen charm. It would be nice to believe that it was more, some sign that they were on their way to bonding, but their conversations never went that deep. They exchanged set gossip, stories about people Lilah had worked with before, and Noa kept her up-to-date on the prank war that props was having with wardrobe. The closest they got to anything personal was silly ice-breaker games, and even then, they stuck to safe subjects only.

"Coffee or tea?" Lilah asked, eyes closed as Noa feathered a light brush across her lids. How many times had Noa watched the scene in *Bonsai Blowout* when she'd fluttered those eyes open and practically begged the camera for that close-up?

"Pure distilled caffeine, straight into my veins," Noa joked. "IV infusion if necessary. Ryan Reynolds or—" Who were celebrities that straight girls thought were hot? "Shawn Mendes?" she supplied the first name that popped into memory from the gossip pages.

Lilah pulled a face so rapidly that Noa almost stabbed her in the eye with the brush. "Ew! Celibacy."

"Cheater."

"Am not. Holidays: Purim or Passover?"

"Neither. If you can bring in a third option, I can too," Noa added, waiting until Lilah stopped sticking out her tongue to start edging her lips with pale pink. "Shavuot. I throw my allegiance in with any holiday that includes dairy. Hurts so good," she sang quietly, a thrill running through her against her own wishes when Lilah laughed aloud. Noa was flirting, even if Lilah didn't realize it. Because she wouldn't—because she was straight.

And Noa would be a creep for hitting on talent, especially when the job involved things like gluing latex prosthetics to her bare chest and stomach. You needed a certain comfort level when it came to working with other people's bodies. They had to be able to trust you, trust that you were going to be a complete professional and keep your hands where they were supposed to be at all times, not thinking of them as anything but a coworker. "Okay, now keep your face still or I won't finish on time. Disneyland or glamping?"

"Glamping?" Lilah protested, her smile sparkling. "I have actually gone real camping before, thank you very much. Not, like, a *lot*," she amended after a beat. "And it's not my favorite thing at all. But I did the summer-camp thing."

Noa changed brushes and dusted off her hands on the thighs of her jeans. Now that was an image she could see. Lilah—no, she'd have been going by Lillian then—running down forest trails in the summer sun, long legs tanned and knees scraped, her red-gold hair flowing behind her in the breeze. "No kidding," she said with a grin. "Ramah or B'nai B'rith?"

"Tamarack, up in Michigan, for a couple of summers," Lilah replied with a grin of her own, still not opening her eyes. There was a vibe though, a hum of contentment that hadn't been there minutes ago, a moment of shared something or other that felt safe and exciting at the same time. "Definitely not Ramah—my Hebrew's awful. Did you go there?"

"Sprout Lake. It's a YJ camp. All the way through to counselor," Noa answered with a rueful laugh. "There's nothing like being a teenager in charge of a cabin of twelve-year-olds to make you child-free forever."

Lilah scoffed and Noa sat back, checking her symmetry with a critical eye. "I loved camp, and despite your cynical veneer," Lilah teased with a pointed look, "I bet you did too."

"So why'd you stop going?" It seemed like a logical question.

"Pageants started taking up a lot more time," Lilah replied so matter-of-factly that Noa barely had a chance to register it. "It's too bad, really. It would have been nice to do both."

Nice? Being shoved into evening gowns and hair teased to within an inch of the ceiling when she was still young enough to be falling out of canoes and making string bracelets? No more scraped knees from relay races. It would have been...what? Posture classes and baton twirling? Noa bit her tongue before something snide popped out, but a part of her was suddenly sad for the kid Lilah'd only barely had the chance to be. "I guess," she said as a way of continuing the conversation, doubt obvious in her voice. "So you really were a beauty queen?"

"And now I'm monster bait," Lilah replied dryly. "Go figure." She glanced at herself in the mirror. "Are we done?"

Noa'd said something wrong again, and she couldn't figure out what. The mood change had been swift, that moment of easy connection vanishing as quickly as it had been born. "You're good to go," she answered anyway, despite how easy it would be to say no, to make her linger longer. There was always tomorrow.

Noa perked up when Lilah slouched in the next morning in a janky old hoodie rather than her usual chic getup, her hands tucked deep inside the front pocket. Noa'd been on set for half an hour already, waiting for that flash of golden red out of the corner of her eye. *My Lilah's here.*

Not *her* Lilah—she'd never be that—but the little things that Noa kept locked away in her own head couldn't hurt anyone.

Lilah flopped into her chair with a dramatic sigh and a little sidelong glance at Noa that told her the drama was entirely for her benefit. She gladly slid into their little bubble of space to perch on the edge of the dressing table, her legs between Lilah's knees, barely brushing the inside seam of Lilah's tight jeans. Noa grabbed the concealer to have something to do with her hands other than flail and played along. "Something wrong?"

"Blind dates are officially the worst," Lilah announced with a sigh, and Noa had to instantly step on the totally unreasonable wave of jealousy before it could make her do something stupid.

"Speaking from recent experience?" Noa asked, trying to be as casual as possible. She leaned in and carefully dotted concealer over the darker circles under Lilah's eyes. A date that had led to a late night would explain those. And maybe even the big hoodie she was wearing. Did it belong to some guy? Had Lilah taken someone home, kissed him, touched him...?

She can do whatever she wants. Stop it.

"Ugh," Lilah groaned, sliding down in her chair. "This guy Austin, right?" She wiggled back up, and Noa had to bite her tongue to keep her focus on the shades and highlights of Lilah's almost-perfect skin. She was a canvas, Noa was the artist, and she needed to stop obsessing.

"Austin sounds like a douche name," Noa sniped, not entirely able to help herself.

Lilah giggled, covering her mouth in guilty horror. "One hundred percent, sadly. Brooke—that's my housemate. One of them anyway. She likes to play matchmaker, and she's convinced he'll be good for me. Or at least my career." Her eyes fluttered closed as Noa blended the cream into her skin.

"Did she have a point?"

"I have no idea how he's going to help me with my career when he spent the entire night talking about himself," Lilah replied archly. "He has this obsession with CrossFit."

The relief that surged through Noa was entirely unjustified, but whatever. "Oh no. One of *those*?"

"Oh yes. I now know more than *anyone* needs to know about lifting numbers and thruster intervals." Lilah rolled her eyes.

"Thruster what now?" Noa couldn't help herself, smile growing as Lilah mirrored it. "That sounds almost dirty."

"It would have been a lot more interesting if it had been," Lilah tossed back at her. If Noa wanted to really delude herself, she could imagine that there was something heated and a little flirty in Lilah's smile, a look that vanished again a moment later.

Noa turned away for a second to grab another blender and wrench her brain back on track. "Are you going to see thruster boy again? Give him a second chance to impress? Maybe he was blinded by the idea of dating a movie star and is kicking himself now for being so awkward," Noa offered generously.

"Not a chance," Lilah replied, and Noa's mean little inside voice cheered loudly. "I think I'm going to be busy from now on. Cleaning my grout with a toothbrush if necessary."

"Smart move. Guys aren't worth putting up with that kind of crap." Girls, on the other hand…Noa could apparently put up with a whole lot of nothing in order to be near the girl she liked.

"Tell me about it." Lilah paused, took a breath like she was going to keep talking. But her eyes flickered up and over Noa's shoulder at the other people in the room, and whatever she'd been about to say never got said.

CHAPTER FOUR

THE NEXT DAY, THINGS GOT a lot more interesting. They'd wrapped all the basic "argue about science and examine the monster" scenes in the lab set, and while that stage got redressed for the post-explosion scenes, filming was moving to the cabin set one sound stage over. More importantly, they'd hit a whole series of scenes where the surviving leads were bruised and bloodied up. A whole lot of blood, according to Colin, and Noa was already rubbing her hands together in anticipation. She'd even worn her vintage *Hellraiser* T-shirt special for the occasion.

It wasn't just about getting to do something that would be useful for the effects section of her portfolio, *finally*. Lilah's injuries would take a good hour to apply while Peter and Tanner were already on set, and they were going to be doing it in Lilah's dressing room rather than in hair and makeup, which meant that Noa and Lilah would have a nice long time to sit and talk. And talking would make it a lot easier to focus on her art and not on the fact that Lilah was going to have to be mostly stripped down for the duration.

Noa hummed to herself as she set up her supplies along the vanity in the small dressing room. The space was sparse, not much in it but an armchair, a coffee table, and the table with a mirror, a gym bag tossed in one corner, and a photo collage taped to the wall. Most were of Lilah and people who must be friends or family—a cluster of girls about their age all in Halloween costumes, an older couple blowing kisses at the camera, a picture of Lilah in a fancy ball gown and sash getting a sparkly tiara put on her head—prom queen? No. The sash read *Miss Teen Michigan*, one of her pageant wins. Noa still didn't get it. Maybe her parents had forced her into entering. *And maybe it's Maybelline.* Noa might not understand the appeal, but from the beaming smile she wore in the photo, Lilah definitely had.

In a gesture of rebellion that only she'd ever notice or understand, Noa hung continuity photos and the pictures from the preproduction makeup tests all over the walls around Lilah's mirror, the close-up and full-body shots of the fake, bloody wounds visually drowning out the torrent of pink and glitter. That was when she spotted it, in the bottom corner of the collage. Her hand froze over the piece of sticky tape. Lilah, her arms around two girls, in the middle of a packed street with a huge rainbow flag visible behind them. Noa knew that corner, the stores along it, the route that Pride had taken last year.

It was entirely possible—plausible, even—that Lilah and her buddies had only gone downtown for the party. None of them were wearing Pride gear other than the cheap plastic leis that had been thrown from a couple of the floats. Lots of straight people did that, allies or otherwise, or went to support friends.

But what if...?

"Is today the day you're hurting me?" Lilah asked, the door to her dressing room closing with a click.

Noa slammed the taped photo of Lilah's scratched shoulder onto the wall, covering up the Pride picture, and tried to turn around as casually as possible despite the way her mind was whirling. Lilah didn't seem to notice, flashing Noa that same sparkly grin she'd seen in the pageant photo—beautiful but not (Noa belatedly realized) entirely authentic.

"Judgment day," Noa intoned solemnly, her heart racing a hundred miles an hour. "If I do my job properly this morning, you're going to look like you went through at least one circle of hell before getting to set."

"Fabulous." Lilah offered Noa a quick flash of a smile before stripping off her shirt. She was wearing a snug tank top underneath with a little pair of shorts, and while Lilah didn't seem to care, Noa looked away before she could fall into the trap of staring. Maybe Lilah was bi or even gay, and the blind dates with guys were a smoke screen. Maybe Noa hadn't been imagining the interested glances after all. Maybe, once the shoot was done... It was a lot of maybes. She wrenched herself back to the here and now and Lilah settling in the makeup chair. "Get comfortable," Noa advised her, reaching for the silicone. "This is going to take a while."

Sitting in the chair while Noa painted oozing wounds all over her arms wasn't nearly as much fun as Lilah had briefly imagined.

Sure, they were cheek-by-jowl again, Noa's hands brushing against her skin in ways that sent tingles all over everywhere. But holding her arm up *just like that, now hold as still as you can* for ages and watching her skin get fake flayed, silicone and latex piling up in ridges, got really tedious, really fast.

The text and selfie from Nadia didn't help during the short break while Noa washed her brushes and mixed more raspberry-jam-colored goo to smear on Lilah's cheek. Lilah opened the picture without thinking twice, Nadia's dressing-room selfie in a gorgeous ball gown and uberglam hair and jewelry popping up, bright gold gleaming against her dark brown skin.

> **Nadia:** Check me out! I love this gig.
>
> **Brooke:** Looking goooooooood
>
> **Kayleigh:** Holy heck, you look amazing!
>
> **Brooke:** Holy *heck*? Your Utah is showing.

Lilah glanced up and saw herself in the mirror, her hair artfully disheveled, dirt on the tank top that Karen had handed her, and ragged claw marks built up over her bare skin. Not exactly red-carpet material there. Lilah sighed, sent a thumbs-up emoji, and stuffed the phone away.

Noa came back with another silicone scar ready to stick to Lilah's body and paused with a question in her eyes. "Everything okay? If the appliances are itchy, we can find a way to fix that."

Lilah must have been showing her feelings too much, and she fought to get them back under lock and key. "It's fine, promise." She smiled up at Noa, but Noa didn't seem convinced. Lilah turned her phone over and showed Nadia's photo, the comparisons running through her head all over again. "One of my housemates got an extra gig. It's a one-day job, but she got to be all glammed up—evening gown, jewels, the whole bit. You know? And I'm spending the week covered in chum." She grimaced ruefully. "A little envy, that's all."

"Aww." Noa sat on the high stool beside her, wiping her skin with the cleaner and laying the fake scar down across Lilah's thigh. Bite marks this time, artfully arranged. "But at least you're a lead and employed for weeks instead of days. This isn't exactly glam, but it's got its own benefits."

"You wouldn't rather be doing something else?" Lilah asked, studying Noa's face as she carefully laid the wet cloth over the paper backing, then slowly peeled it free. One scar, temporary-tattoo style. A curl fell across her cheek, and Lilah forced herself to keep her hands still and not reach out to tuck it back behind Noa's ear.

She was treading into dangerous territory now, knowing what she did about Noa's love for B movies and Lilah's ambivalence for her own genre. It would be too easy to slip up, make Noa feel as small and dismissed as Lilah had when Noa had laughed at her reading list. On the other hand, Noa had no problem expressing *her* honest and unfiltered opinions. How could she get offended if Lilah did the same?

"Oh, sure," Noa responded with a grin, and Lilah relaxed. She hadn't offended after all. "A horror flick with triple the budget and free rein over the design. A chance to really scare the pants off people. But, you know, union card first. Baby steps." Noa glanced up at her, absently swiping away the wayward fuchsia curl. "If you don't like horror, why do you keep doing it?"

Lilah sighed. "The paycheck and insurance? It's not much, but it's better than not working or flirting for tips waiting tables. And credits are credits. Maybe someone will see me and love me for a meatier role."

"I dunno about that." Noa snickered and carefully glued down the flappy edges of the prosthetic, nude-colored bite marks now plastered to Lilah's leg along with the half-dozen deep cuts on her arms that were already painted red and bloody. "This role's looking pretty meaty right now."

Lilah laughed, couldn't help herself. "You're not as funny as you think you are," she replied, the giggles turning her words into a total lie. She sobered after a second and frowned, trying to get into Noa's head even a little. The aloof bald man on Noa's T-shirt stared her down like he knew all her secrets. "Do you really love movies like *Hellraiser*, or do you wear those shirts because it's what people expect from effects artists? And if not, why do you like horror so much?"

"Some people just need killin'," Noa said in a deadpan. Then she shrugged and started to blend makeup along the edges of the scar piece to make them match Lilah's skin. "I like the work, for one. Like this guy." She gestured at the horrifying figure printed on her T-shirt. "Pinhead's one of the greats. They made the movie with all practical effects, right at the end of the stop-motion-and-slime era of horror, and unlike old CGI, it still looks amazing. It's art, and it's hard to do it well."

She was on a roll, her eyes lighting up as she spoke, and Lilah felt herself drawn in by the sheer force of her enthusiasm. Noa's eyes flashed, her smile growing, her passion for her subject so obvious and so engrossing that Lilah would have given almost anything to sit there and listen to her talk about it for hours. "Horror effects are as much fun as doing wicked contours and glitter lashes, and horror does something important. Like, the world is a mess, we all know it. When we talk about it, it's all big corporations this and heat death of the glaciers that. It's all so big and uncontrollable and terrifying.

"At the same time, being grown-up adults means we're not allowed to throw temper tantrums when we're freaking out. We end up bottling up so many things, shoving it all down because we have to 'be mature,' and that somehow means that it's not cool to have emotions. Especially guys. Gotta be all stoic and shit.

"Horror gives you a chance to let it out. To be scared and feel your feelings. You're scared but you're safe, so it's okay to scream and cry and let that whole tension-release thing work on you. And then it's, like…okay. Student loans and making rent are terrifying, but they're not nearly as bad as a six-headed shark." Noa ran out of steam around the same time as she finished blending the foundation, reaching for a paint palette covered in arterial reds and viscous, unwell yellows.

Lilah thought she understood. "Except you can punch a shark. Or shoot it. You can't punch your landlord. I mean, you *can*, but you'll end up charged with assault."

"Unless your landlord is a six-headed shark," Noa supplied unhelpfully, the light of mischief in her eyes.

Lilah couldn't help laughing. "Then you've got other problems."

The sensation of the paintbrush was muted through the layer of silicone as Noa began the careful process of making the scar look like real torn flesh. It *was* an art, Lilah supposed, if a disgusting one.

"Remember," Noa said thoughtfully after a few minutes had passed in a warm, comfortable silence. "You're the survivor this time. The final girl is the tough one who makes it through as proof that the rest of us can find ways to survive life. You're hope."

"That's a heavy interpretation for a part that boils down to 'guns and boobs.'" Lilah sounded more disgruntled than she should. Letting dissatisfaction show was the fastest route to getting reprimanded or fired or hated. She felt her cheeks start to go warm with embarrassment and fought that feeling too.

"So make it something more." Noa shrugged, like it was that simple.

"In a movie about a dinosaur?" Lilah asked, eyebrow going up despite herself. "I don't know about that."

Noa sat back, and their eyes met. "A great actor can elevate anything," she replied, and Lilah's breath caught. Noa wasn't teasing her this time but looking at her with admiration and...and *light*, and something so honest and soft that she couldn't put a name to it at all. It only lasted for a moment, but Lilah's heart shuddered at the intensity of that single perfect look. *She means me?*

Her mouth had gone dry, and Lilah swallowed to find her voice again. "It's going to take more than great acting to turn this mess into the next *Jurassic Park*."

"Even the second *Jurassic Park* wasn't the next *Jurassic Park*." Noa grinned, then grabbed the setting spray, and the moment of connection slipped away. It was just the two of them again, going through their regular routine, in a prosaic dressing room in a generic studio lot.

"Respect the dinosaur," Noa joked, shielding Lilah's eyes before she spritzed. "Don't diss the dinosaur."

A knock sounded on the dressing room door and Lilah startled, but it was only Wayne. The security guard stuck his head in the room, looked the two of them over, and gave Lilah a winning smile. "They're ready for Miss Silver on set," he reported.

"Thank you, Wayne," she replied out of habit, and he disappeared, his usual slightly off-key whistle starting up again as his footsteps moved away down the hall.

Noa looked up from her careful paint work and leaned in like a conspirator, glancing at the door in an exaggerated move. "See? The dinosaur has spies everywhere," she whispered.

Their laughter rang out again, and the rest of the painting process went far too quickly for Lilah's liking. Much too soon, Noa brushed the black and bloodied sponge over her skin in a few strategic areas to make light scrapes and made her stand and turn for new photos. "Okay, you're done. Get Denise to take a look at you, and then I'll see you for touch-ups on set."

"You bet," Lilah replied and resisted the urge to immediately start picking at one of the pieces to have an excuse to have Noa close to her again.

Noa: Remind me again why I'm not allowed to fall for her.
For real.

Chrissy: You work closely together, so a breakup would be super-awk. And Denise wouldn't be keen on your fraternizing with the talent, even though she'd be a massive hypocrite if she called you on it.

Noa: What's up with that?

Chrissy: Rumor has it she and Peter are banging. I'll see if I can get a better scoop from the guys at craft services. They see everything.

Noa: ooh intrigue

Noa: but seriously. I'm dying. I can't stop thinking about her.

Noa: I need an intervention.

Chrissy: okay okay. Text me all the things you *don't* like. I'll use them as reminders for your moments of weakness.

Noa: Ugh. I can't think of enough negatives to outweigh the way I feel.

Chrissy: I thought you wanted my help?

Noa: Fine.

Noa: She doesn't actually like horror movies that much

Chrissy: strike one.

Noa: Her taste in books is the worst kind of junk.

Chrissy: Is that an actual strike two or you being a snob?

Chrissy: She who reads Clive Barker does not get to throw genre stones.

Noa: Whatever, Barker's awesome.

Noa: She's attention-seeking. There's this huff and sigh she does when she wants me to ask what's wrong so she can vent.

Chrissy: That's def annoying. Be an adult and say things out loud.

Noa: She doesn't say what she means. She has this fake all-teeth smile that she uses when she's insincere and it drives me insane.

Noa: She's a pageant queen and she takes all that shallow tiara stuff seriously.

Chrissy: Your second-wave issues are showing again. Embrace the million varied facets of womankind.

Noa: I know, I know...okay. Fine. It's not my thing. We don't have enough in common.

Noa: Better?

Chrissy: Getting there. Lilah's cute but not for you, in other words.

Noa: Right. Different priorities.

Noa: And even assuming she is queer and was even remotely interested, the last thing I need to do right now is date one of the cast.

Chrissy: Repeat it until you mean it. Some drama you can see coming a mile away.

Chrissy: Break's over, gotta go. See you on set in five!

"You can't go out there! You'll die!"

"If I don't, *everyone* will die!" Lilah pulled against Tanner's hands, but he had her tight around the upper arms, thumbs digging into her biceps, a trickle of blood marring his cheek from the rough slash Noa had painted there earlier this morning. The camera pivoted behind him, tracking her reaction, and she tried to block it out of her awareness.

"I'll go and bring back help," she pleaded, cupping his face. Her thumb landed in the smear of red jelly, and she must have grimaced, because now Tanner was grinning at her. He could get away with it, the jerk-face, because the only part of him in the shot right now was the back of his head. "Promise me you won't do anything stupid."

Was that the line? No one had yelled cut, so she'd gotten it close enough. Tanner took his cue, hauling Lilah forward until their lips met. Even through her closed lips, he tasted like the gross Vaseline-and-fake-blood mix that Noa had used to make the blood drip not drippy.

"Cut!" Ed's voice called in the background, and Tanner let her go. "Where's Felice? Lilah's got too much shadow on her face. Move that fill light." She fell back a step, out of Tanner's personal space, and he flexed his hands.

"Check those sight lines again!"

"Zoom in tighter on Lilah." That was Dan Gilbert bossing the cameramen around, and Ed glared at him. "I want her mouth framed just like that."

"Was that too tight? I feel like I grabbed you too tight there," Tanner apologized, calling Lilah's attention back to him while the light moved around them. A reflection glinted off glasses in the crowd, and she realized that Dr. Crosby was there, watching them. Watching *her* specifically?

"It was fine," she promised and looked around for something to wipe her hand. "But I think I messed up your makeup. You've got a thumbprint on your face." She glanced over to the stool by the wall where Noa was usually perched, but this time, she was across the room talking quietly to her girlfriend. The pair of them were absorbed in their conversation and didn't notice Lilah at all.

At least Denise was there to do touch-ups, stepping in as Noa pulled herself away and came running across the set. Denise waved her away, and they reset, Lilah pointedly ignoring everything else around her.

Take two and Lilah sneezed—"In my *mouth*, Lilah. You sneezed in my *mouth*."

"I am so sorry. I think I'm allergic to something on set." She rubbed her itchy nose with the back of her hand, trying desperately not to smear any of the effects makeup as she did.

"You better not have cooties."

Take three went better, until Lilah stumbled and stepped on Mikal's hand, one of the loose body parts strewn artfully across the cabin floor. "Sorry, Mike!"

"I don't think it counts as my hand if it's not actually attached to my body," Mikal called from the sidelines, where he sat with a coffee and his script, his left arm encased to the shoulder in a bright green sleeve. "Abuse it as you like."

"I appreciate it."

Takes four through seven apparently weren't good enough for Ed's liking, even though Lilah had managed to repress the sneezes that kept wanting to come every time Tanner got close. By the eighth time Lilah and Tanner kissed, her lips were starting to feel seriously chapped. "As much as I like you," Tanner murmured in her ear, "if Ed doesn't get his act together and decide what he wants, this scene is going to haunt my nightmares."

"There's a horror movie title for us," Lilah snorted, equally as quietly, while Ed argued with someone in video village. "*Hell Kiss,* now streaming."

"*The Deadly Smooch.*"

"*Smoochageddon Two—Now with Tongue.*"

"You'd better not."

"No fear on that account." Lilah shook her head. "You're sweet, Tanner, but I'm not into you that way."

"Oh, really now." Tanner pretended to look offended, but it only lasted for a second. "I wonder who you *are* into in that case…" He trailed off, arching a speculative eyebrow. "Because you bounce around here way too cheerfully not to be into *someone.* I know you're not one of the women falling for Peter's smooth talking."

"No! No one," Lilah insisted, and with that, her cheeks ran warm. She couldn't blush now, or they'd have to do *another* stupid take after her face had gone back to normal. "I don't have a thing for anyone here."

"I dunno about that," Tanner teased her, a lilt in his voice, but he cut off as the crew came back over to where Lilah and Tanner had been left standing on their marks.

"Get a bounce card in here for some fill on Lilah's close-up," Ed instructed, and a crew member came over with a piece of white cardboard to angle in her eyes. "Last try, people. Time is money, and we have a lot of pages to get through."

"Here we go again." Tanner got his toe on his mark, and Lilah watched him disappear and the character slide across his face. It was always like that. She assumed other people saw it in her, the moment where you stepped back a tiny bit and put someone else in front of your eyes.

Lilah shook off *Lilah* and put on her character's face instead. *Make it something more.*

"Take nine. Marker!"

"And action!" Ed called.

Lilah's eyes went wide with panic and fear and a tiny thread of hope that somehow, someway, they would all be saved.

"You can't go out there! You'll die!"

"If I don't, *everyone* will die!"

"Have you seen the wing puppet? Those are *bat* wings. Pterodactyl wings are entirely different. The wings should be attached to the ankles, and the skin should be attached to the tail."

"That's the kind of thing you needed to bring up during preproduction."

"I *did* bring it up during preproduction. Ed told me I was worrying over nothing and they'd fix it in post."

"You're in luck, because we don't go into post until after filming. That's why it's called *post*production."

"Don't you condescend to me, young man. I have three postsecondary degrees!"

"I'm sorry to hear it."

Noa rolled her eyes as the unit production manager and the scientific consultant brushed past her, Crosby's complaining getting more strident the more he was brushed off. It was late, and she'd just lived through the excruciating hell that had been watching the maybe-straight girl she was crushing on kissing someone else. They'd looked cute together too, that was the worst part, Tanner leaning in and murmuring in Lilah's ear, making her laugh, then kissing her again—

Ugh.

It hadn't been real, so at least there was that tiny consolation.

Noa ducked into Lilah's dressing room to clean up the last of the scars and solvent-soaked cotton swabs from post-filming makeup removal. It was empty, naturally. Lilah'd booked it out of there with a smile and a wave once Noa'd finished peeling off all the prosthetics. Empty except for her bag, sitting on the chair in the far corner. It was the one she carried in with her every morning and probably had stuff in it that she needed.

Considering her options for a hot second, Noa grabbed her phone. The last few days' worth of call sheets were still in her email, and the cast list—voilà—had contact information. It was absolutely within her purview to use that information for this specific reason. Managing the talent was part of her job. Right? Right.

Noa: Noa here. You left your bag in your dressing room—
do you need it?

There was a long pause, long enough that Noa wondered if she'd gotten the number wrong. Or maybe Lilah was driving and had her phone off. She seemed like the kind of person who'd be responsible enough to do something like that. Or she could be in bed already—

Noa's phone blooped in the nick of time.

> **Lilah:** Omg, that's where it is! Thank you! And yes, I absolutely need it. Has everyone left already? Will the doors be unlocked if I come back and get it?

Noa took a second to save her contact just in case.

> **Noa:** No, it's pretty much emptied out. A few of the production staff are here, but I don't know for how long.
> **Noa:** I can bring it to you as long as you don't live over in Long Beach or something stupid.
> **Lilah:** Could you??? That's so sweet, thank you! :D And no...I'm in Sun Valley. It's not that far... Unless you're not going that way!!

That was a whole lot of punctuation all at once. Caught between a grin and a wince, Noa took advantage of the fact that she was alone in the dressing room and laughed to herself. She could practically hear Lilah's wide-eyed enthusiasm pouring through the text.

> **Noa:** No worries. It's basically on my way.

Not exactly, but what was a little white lie? It would be good for her, Noa decided firmly. She'd go over, see Lilah's place, probably see some guy there, and be able to put her stupid crush to bed. Bad choice of words, but whatever. She knew what she meant. A little dose of hard reality was exactly what Noa needed to force herself to move on.

Lilah: I owe you one!!
Noa: No worries.

Noa finished her cleanup in a record amount of time, grabbed Lilah's bag, and headed for the door. She dodged Tanner as he was leaving, getting a nod from him as he talked to someone on his phone, and slipped out past a pile of boxes accumulating outside the props room. EGGS, the side of the top box read. 65,000,000 YEARS FRESH.

Lilah lived in Sun Valley? Not the nicest town, but at least it was close. And if she got this over with fast enough, maybe she'd finish the errand before she had time to regret the impulse to be helpful.

CHAPTER FIVE

NOA PULLED INTO THE DRIVEWAY of the run-down house in the middle of an industrial area, the path lit by the yellow puddles of the streetlights. She hiked Lilah's bag over her shoulder and headed up the stairs. Light spilled from behind the curtained windows, and as she got closer, she could hear the faint backbeat of music. The porch was wide, a couple of garbage cans and a recycling bin on one side and an old pair of work boots, man-sized, sitting next to the welcome mat. Whose were those?

Noa pushed the doorbell before she could talk herself into or out of her confusion and waited. The door opened a minute later, but it wasn't Lilah on the other side or the housemate whose photo Noa had seen on Lilah's phone. This woman was tall, probably taller than Lilah, and white, with dark brown hair knotted into a messy bun on top of her head. She had a perfect figure, a Wonder Woman kind of vibe going, and she looked Noa over with interest. "Yeah?"

"I'm Noa." She patted the bag hanging from her shoulder. "I work with Lilah? She forgot her bag back at the studio, and I came by to drop it off."

"Brooke, hi," the woman at the door introduced herself. "Lilah's in her room. Come on in, and I'll get her."

Noa wasn't sure what she'd expected, either from Lilah's incidental mentions of her house-share situation or from the way the house looked on the outside, but the cotton-candy-colored girly hellscape she entered wasn't it. The walls were cream, not pink, really, but they gave the *impression* of pink. A string of delicate white fairy lights ran along the crown molding of the hallway ceiling, and more photo collages hung along the walls, each of them centered around one of those "live, laugh, love" kind of captions that Noa and Chrissy liked to mock every time they ventured into the wilderness of the craft supply stores.

A bunch of doors opened off the hallway, one into a kitchen, where the gorgeous Black woman from Lilah's photo was reading at the table. A blond was washing dishes, her back to Noa, but her hair was too light and too short to be Lilah's. The doorway on the other side led into what looked like a living room, one side partly cut off from the front hall by a thick pink-and-gold sari hanging from curtain rails. A couch and TV sat in there as well, the couch covered in little pillows and a fluffy purple chenille throw.

"Lilah!" Brooke bellowed cheerfully down the hall. "Noa's here for you! Grab a seat," she offered in a normal speaking voice and waved at the cushion-pit masquerading as a couch, not missing a beat. "She'll be out eventually."

"I can leave it if she's busy—"

"Nah. Chill here. She's, like, on the phone or something," Brooke left the room with a dismissive wave, abandoning Noa to her own devices.

Noa took a seat on the couch, on the edge at first. Was all that pink contagious? If there was free-floating glitter involved, she'd be leaving trails of fairy dust behind herself for days. It did look awfully soft though, and Noa's muscles ached from a full day on her feet on the studio's concrete floors. Slowly succumbing to temptation, Noa slouched into the shockingly plush and cozy embrace of the pillow pile. The chenille throw blanket tickled her cheeks, and she desperately resisted the urge to pull the whole thing over her head and curl up in a blanket cocoon. If Lilah didn't come out to talk to her soon, it might not be a battle she could win.

"Noa?" Oh, thank God. Lilah appeared in the doorway before Noa could turn into a fuzz-seeking missile. She'd changed into pale-blue-and-purple plaid pajama pants and a T-shirt from a bro-country band's most recent tour...because of course she had. Out of context, her red-gold hair down around her shoulders, her face scrubbed clean, she looked half a decade younger than she did when in full kit for filming.

And despite the fact that it was Noa who saw her makeup free and with bedhead first thing every morning, Noa who put Lilah's face on her, it was also Noa's heart that skipped tracks at the sight. A new facet, that was all it was, like seeing a bird of paradise in its native habitat for the first time.

"Hey!" Noa bolted up out of the couch—at least that had been her intent, and her muscles had tried. But the couch was wide and deep, and she'd slipped between the loose pillows. Not even momentum could get her upright without a lot more effort than she was willing to put in. "I brought your bag, but now I'm stuck."

"The soul-sucker claims another victim." Lilah laughed

knowingly and plopped herself down next to Noa instead of helping. "We rescued the couch from Nadia's old landlord when she moved in. It's deeper and shorter than it's supposed to be, or something like that. The proportions are wrong and it eats people."

"Consider me officially eaten," Noa pretended to grumble, a pillow with a sequined unicorn on it sliding slowly into her lap from under her arm. "I met Brooke at the door, and I think I saw Nadia in the kitchen. How many housemates do you have?"

"There's four of us living here. I think Kayleigh's in there too." Lilah nodded toward the door. "It's her night for dishes anyway. I like having roommates. I'm an only child, and it's a really nice change to have a lot of people around to talk to." She shifted in her seat, and something in her expression shifted too, a change maybe only Noa would notice, as accustomed as she was now to the way Lilah's face worked. "You live with Chrissy, right? One of the PAs? I've seen you drive in together," Lilah added, sounding almost cagey, as though noticing someone's habits was something to feel guilty about.

A block lodged itself in Noa's chest, and the wariness kicked in. No one was going to shit-talk Chrissy on *her* watch. Her life was a no-transphobes-allowed zone. But outwardly, giving Lilah the benefit of the doubt for a moment, she nodded. "Yup. It's just the two of us in a crummy apartment in a nongentrified corner of Silver Lake. But I'm more of a misanthrope than you are. I only want my nearest and dearest in my face more than a couple of hours out of every twenty-four."

"That's not misanthropic," Lilah objected, and she tucked her hair behind her ears. Noa's eyes followed the graceful movement, the crinkle of the smile when it hit her eyes for real, the way that cloud of bronze settled down around her shoulders again when her elegant hands fell back to her lap. "That's knowing what you want."

Yeah, sure. Only when Noa did know what she wanted, it was the thing she really wasn't supposed to have. "I have gossip on Tanner," she said, changing the subject, steering it clumsily around to something vaguely adjacent to what she really wanted to ask.

"Oh!" Lilah's eyes lit up, and she leaned in closer like Noa was about to deliver a secret, her elbow resting on the back of the couch. "Spill it!"

"I think he's started seeing someone. I overheard him on the phone when he was leaving set today. He was inviting them over to meet, and I quote, 'my new boy.'" She made the air quotes with her fingers and was rewarded with Lilah's delighted laugh.

"Okay, that's stupidly cute. Good for him!" Her joy didn't feel faked, and she didn't show any shock at the idea of Tanner dating a guy.

Noa broke her eyes away from studying Lilah's every microexpression for clues, hints, anything. *Why were you at Pride? Would you, could you ever—? Come on. I'm giving you an opening here.*

Lilah didn't take it. Probably didn't even notice there had been a cue in the first place.

"I'll give you some gossip back," Lilah carried on breezily. "You know Dan Gilbert, the producer? Of course you do—sorry. Anyway, he and Ed had a massive throwdown during blocking this afternoon. I think you were at lunch? And Mr. Gilbert threatened to fire Ed and pull funding if he doesn't get the schedule back on track."

Noa's stomach fell, like the drop at the top of a roller coaster. Lilah said it so casually, like Noa wasn't seeing her entire career flushing down the toilet right there and then.

"You mean cancel production?" Noa forced the words out, her voice squeaking in a way that would have left her horribly embarrassed if she weren't in the middle of a major internal crisis. "Just like that? Can he *do* that?"

Lilah blinked in surprise. "He can, but he won't," she said, trying to ease Noa's fears. "I've seen this a bunch of times. It's all hot air and testosterone poisoning. They'll bluster and fight, Mr. Gilbert will make up a bunch of completely unreasonable shooting schedules which Ed will ignore, and everything will work itself out in the end. They'll probably buy some stupid stock footage of bats to replace some of the creature effects shots or cheap out on the CGI."

Or ditch some of the last-minute crew hires.

"I appreciate your ability to remain calm in the face of imminent disaster," Noa said, still trying to get her brain back on track. She'd be better off assuming Lilah was right and it was nothing but chest-thumping, something to talk to Chrissy about when she got home.

"It's a talent. You should have seen the scramble when I ran out of double-sided tape right before the swimsuit section for Miss Charlevoix." Something buzzed before Noa could react, and Lilah fished her phone out of her pocket with a frown. "Sorry—I'm waiting for tomorrow's call sheet, so I need to check this real quick."

The break in the conversation gave Noa a second to regroup, though Lilah had started to frown. "Everything okay?"

"Oh yeah," Lilah replied, but her brow was still furrowed. She scrolled through something on her screen, then turned the phone off and tucked it away. "Fan mail. Professions of eternal devotion," she joked, but she didn't look flattered. "It's weird though. Somehow he got it to my personal email, not the public one. I keep all that stuff separate, so...it's fine. My agent probably forwarded it or something." She trailed off, an air of disquiet settling over her.

Noa nodded. "Or it's from one of your friends, thinking they're funny." Lilah gave her a small smile but didn't shake off the change in her mood. "Does that happen often?" she asked. Noa'd been so concerned about not looking like one of Lilah's creepy followers that she hadn't actively stopped to consider how many real ones the starlet probably had.

"What, love letters? I guess." Lilah shrugged, looking uncomfortable. "I don't see many if they are coming in. But there've been a few."

"And none of them worth dating," Noa teased, trying to find that lighthearted connection again. They'd been on the same wavelength for a few minutes, laughing and talking, and she wanted it back so badly.

Lilah shook her head, a glimmer of a smile coming back. "No. Really not. A lot of people think they know me from seeing me on screen or at conventions, like they don't realize I'm playing pretend."

That hit a little too close to home, and Noa winced. "I...yeah. That's my cue to fess up, isn't it? I've seen your entire filmography," she confessed, biting her lower lip. The sting kept her from rambling or trying to cover up the embarrassment with distractions. "But I don't think I came in with too many weird expectations."

"That's different." Lilah dismissed her with a little wave. "You're in the industry; you're supposed to have seen lots of movies."

Noa nodded and kept her mouth firmly shut about the posters. And phone lock screen.

"You've heard about my blind date disasters—I haven't gone out with anyone worth dating in ages." Lilah sighed. Then she hesitated, her fingers curling up in the fuzzy purple blanket. Her lips parted like she was on the verge of saying something, but no sound came out. She took a shaky breath instead.

And Noa waited.

Her pulse started racing for no accountable reason, but she waited.

"Guys *or* girls," Lilah added at the end. She ducked her head and looked up at Noa through red-gold lashes that Noa painted dark every morning as a frame for her sparkling blue eyes.

Now Lilah was waiting, practically vibrating from the tension that filled her body. Her confession settled into Noa's chest and expanded there, a campfire-glow of certainty that burned away the doubt, overanalysis, and nerves with two simple words: *or girls.*

"Want my admittedly biased advice?" Noa replied, her mouth dry. "Stick to girls. Guys are definitely not worth the effort it takes to civilize one. I have brothers. I know."

"I'll keep that in mind." The naked relief on Lilah's face made

Noa's gut lurch for a second. Had Lilah expected *Noa* to react badly to her coming out? Maybe she didn't know that Noa was gay, or maybe she thought Noa was one of those lesbians who had a thing against bi women, or...

Or maybe she was freaking out because coming out to someone new was nerve-racking at the best of times, and Noa needed to give her a little more credit.

The tension ebbed from the room, the metaphorical bubble popping. It was the two of them, in a powder-pink living room decorated with fairy lights and sequined pillows, and life was about as easy as it was ever going to get.

"You're not out officially, I'm guessing," Noa said. She'd know, she would absolutely have known, if it had been announced anywhere in Lilah's publicity materials or interviews, but just in case...

"I have a feeling that one or two of my friends might just be waiting for me to bring it up, but I haven't called a house meeting or sent out press releases, if that's what you mean. I guess it's more of an open secret?" Lilah hedged, pulling her knees up to her chest and wrapping her arms around her legs. "If I were dating someone, it would be different. It's not that I mind people knowing if they're cool about it. It just feels weird to make it into a big deal when nothing's happened yet."

The floodgates seemed to have burst open, and she kept talking, the visible relief and the words bubbling out of her all at the same time. "I moved to LA from this tiny resort town in Northern Michigan, right? And there's no community there. Not that kind. There was one other girl in my high school who was gay, and she bailed the day we graduated. We weren't even friends. Then when I got *here*, there was just so *much*, and I didn't know where to start. I went to Pride once and looked up some places online, but I would feel like such an idiot walking into a club alone, not knowing anyone or anything."

"It would probably be weird to hit her up on social media now." Noa was still riding the high of *maybe, maybe*, and she tried desperately to throttle it back. Lilah wasn't flirting for crying out loud! She was reaching out, opening up, because she thought of Noa as a friend. A safe space. Safe spaces didn't hit on you.

But that cover-girl veneer cracked a little more, and a rueful smile crinkled up the corners of Lilah's eyes. "I keep thinking that people will take one look at me and assume I'm a straight girl playing tourist." And thank God she didn't have dimples, because Noa would probably have had a heart attack right there on the couch.

"Tell you what," Noa blurted out, a way to redirect the conversation and not make an idiot out of herself. "You want to meet queer people? I'll introduce you to some people."

Yeah, great move. Introduce her around at ladies' night and watch everyone swarm. Lilah was beyond beautiful and wasn't already someone's ex's ex-girlfriend. She'd fill her calendar with coffee dates and open mics, and by the time filming was over and Noa was free to ask her out, Lilah would be moving out of the Barbie Dream House and in with Chrissy's ex with the five cats.

While Noa was catastrophizing, Lilah had perked up considerably. "You mean, go out?" she asked, a little hesitant. "With you?"

"As friends, of course," Noa added quickly. Maybe Lilah would be concerned about the optics. "I promise I'm not going to start hitting on you because you came out to me. I'm not like that."

"I never thought you were," Lilah reassured her, but she still looked worried.

"We've got Saturday off; we should go out. I'll show you around the gayborhood," Noa offered.

"You don't want to babysit me on your one day off," Lilah demurred, but Noa was on a mission now. And she'd show Lilah a good time, dammit—the *good* bars, the twenty-four-hour bookstore, and that one coffeehouse that didn't reek of clove cigarettes and pretension.

"It'll be fun," she said firmly. "Are we on?"

It took her a couple of seconds to decide, and Noa got to watch the way her brow unfurrowed, the clearing of the dark shadows in her eyes, the way her smile broke like sunshine across her face. *I am so screwed.*

"Yeah," Lilah agreed. "We're on."

"Ooh, we got some courtin' in the parlor!" A laugh came from the hallway, and Noa's head jerked up, her cheeks flaming hot. Somehow she and Lilah had drifted closer together on the couch, their knees almost touching, Noa's fingertips barely grazing the cuff of Lilah's shirt sleeve.

The bubbly blond had stopped halfway past the door and was looking in on them, her poofy, peasant-style blouse not doing much to conceal her curves. "Leave some room for the Holy Ghost, ladies."

"Kayleigh, ugh!" Lilah whipped one of the decorative throw

pillows at her housemate, her aim surprisingly good considering that her weapon of choice was edged in lace. Kayleigh disappeared from the doorway, her giggles echoing with her retreating footsteps.

Lilah's cheeks were flushed pink when she dropped into the couch again. "I am so, so sorry. My housemates think they're *so funny*." She raised her voice, not quite yelling down the hall.

"And on that note, mine will probably think I've died if I don't get home soon." Noa struggled out of the pillows and pushed herself to her feet. The moment was over, whatever it had been, and she needed to grab the chance to get out of there before the couch—and temptation—could sap her will to go.

Lilah rose with her, much more gracefully than Noa had managed, and walked her to the front door. Nadia, the fourth housemate, was pulling on her shoes, and she shook Noa's hand congenially when Lilah made quick introductions. A narrow scarf wound around her angelic cloud of black curls, and she moved with a dancer's easy grace. She was as beautiful in person as her photo had suggested, and really, what were the odds of all four of them being spectacular? Spending any kind of time in this house would do a serious number on Noa's self-image.

The boots were still on the porch, though from what Noa had seen of Lilah's housemates, none of them were going to be fitting into those. Had there been someone else in the house all along? "If it's all girls living here, what's with the massive work boots?" Noa asked, aware that she was grasping at straws to delay the moment when she'd have to leave but doing it anyway. What was the point of dignity, really?

Nadia was the one who answered, slinging her purse across her body. "Houses that look like a big guy lives in them are less likely to get targeted by serial killers," she answered, quite serious.

Lilah hid a small grin. "Nadia's got a thing about true crime stories."

"There've been studies!" Nadia objected, double-checking her phone before she zipped it away.

"Isn't that feeding into ideas that women need a man around to protect them?" Noa asked, trying to envision exactly how that kind of study would be conducted. Sample populations? Placebo serial killers?

Nadia shrugged off her question. "Maybe, yeah, sure. Patriarchy bad. But how many serial killers are woke enough to care?"

"Fair, actually."

"If I'm not home by three, either I've been arrested for killing my boss or my body's been dumped in the bay. Either way, phone my mom," Nadia instructed Lilah, jogging down the stairs and heading for the driveway.

"Have a good shift," Lilah called back, like that exchange was something she was completely used to.

The bannister was cool under Noa's hand, the evening getting dark, and even as the night wrapped itself around them, she found it hard to let go. "I'll see you tomorrow," she said, lingering on the stoop.

"Bright and early," Lilah confirmed, and with the porch light behind her, turning her hair into a halo of fire, Noa couldn't tell what expression might be on her face.

"Good night," she tried and this time found that her feet would move.

Lilah was still on her porch, watching, until Noa got to the street, into her car, and drove away.

There were extra shoes in the hallway when Noa got home. The recognition came a second after, then Noa headed for the living room anyway. If Chrissy wanted privacy, she had the bigger bedroom. There were no butts in the air, thankfully, only Chrissy sitting on the floor with her laptop and a sea of papers around her. A girl sprawled out on the couch behind her, one hand toying with Chrissy's hair and the other scrolling through Twitter. "I'm home," Noa announced to the room at large. "Hey, Amber."

Amber looked up from her phone and waved backward over the arm of the couch. Her pixie-cut hair was spiked and tinted blue today, coordinating with the blue socks visible under her rolled-up jean cuffs. She pulled her legs under her and made some room when Noa dragged herself over, smiling sympathetically. "Rough day?"

Noa only groaned. It hadn't been the day so much as what the day meant—or hadn't meant, or couldn't mean—and there weren't words to express the cluster of feelings trying to overwhelm her. She waved one hand in a gesture that she hoped would communicate her precise level of existential exhaustion.

Looking up from her call sheets, Chrissy fixed Noa with an eagle-eyed stare. "You ditched me and I had to get a ride home from Mikal. You owe me an explanation. He learned to drive in Moscow, and it's terrifying."

Noa had a split second to decide how much to spill in front of Amber, but whatever. She was good people. Nothing would get out if Noa asked her to keep it to herself. "I dropped off her bag," she said, compromising with herself. It was like playing the pronoun game with awful great-aunts, but at least she'd made a token stab at protecting Lilah's privacy.

"And?"

"She's bi. And I'm taking her down to the Eastside on Saturday to show her some of the hot spots."

Now Chrissy was all ears, perking up visibly. "Hot damn. So you've got a chance. Spill it."

Amber extracted herself from between them, ruffling Chrissy's hair one last time. "And that sounds like my cue to go order dinner. You eating with us, Noa?"

"Sure, what the hell. I've got some cash for once."

A couple of minutes to argue about menus and whether or not gluten-free veggie lasagna was an abomination, and Chrissy's primary girlfriend disappeared to the kitchen with her phone in hand.

Chrissy turned so she could flatten her arms on the couch and sink her chin down on them in a pose of patient expectation. "*So?*"

"It's like a sorority house over there," Noa said, still faintly shell-shocked.

"Ooh, tell me all the lurid details."

"Not a sleazy sorority house. It's more like...the unholy afterbirth of a craft store mating with a prom dress. It's pink. So, so very pink. And purple. There's glitter." Their apartment was very different: horror movie posters framed on the walls and the chipped coffee table currently buried under Chrissy's paperwork. "She listens to country music."

Chrissy made a face at her. "*I* listen to country music."

Noa waved off the criticism. "You listen to it in a Dixie-Chicks-stan Jolene-sounds-really-hot flannel dyke way. I'm pretty sure she listens to it unironically."

"Maybe it's a 'kissing girls in bikinis in the back of my pickup truck' kind of way. Don't get yourself down because you're crushing on someone whose career hinges on her aesthetic obedience to a blindingly heteronormative industry."

Leave it to Chrissy to cut right to the heart of the issue so succinctly. "I'm not sure if that's reassuring or not," Noa groaned. She sank down on the couch until she was lying on it full length, her toes stretching to touch the pillow at the other end.

Amber's voice rose and fell in the background, words indistinguishable through the wall.

"She smells really good." Noa sighed after a moment of reflection. "All vanilla or maple syrupy. She wears those flavored lip balms—I saw one on her dressing table the other day. Cotton candy flavor. *Of course.*"

Chrissy patted her foot sympathetically. "You have to face facts, No-no. Despite your sad yet predictable prejudice against all that is pink and frilly, you have a thing for femmes."

There was no logical way Noa could argue that one. Not after waxing rhapsodic over cotton-candy lip gloss. The ceiling held no answers either. It was what it was—she liked Lilah a lot, and her girliness was all part of the package. "At least I can be sure it's wife goals, not life goals," she said to the ceiling, resigned.

"That's the spirit. So now that you've asked her out, when are you going to make your move?"

"No! I can't!" Noa sat bolt upright, the couch springs protesting the sudden movement. She made a slicing gesture through the air and ended by stabbing her finger at Chrissy. "I didn't ask her out either. We're hanging out. Grabbing drinks. As friends. Coworkers. That's all."

"Weenie," Chrissy scoffed.

"I have my hands all over her every day, and she already has crazy fanboys sending her love letters on the regular. It would be super creepy and weird to start hitting on her."

"Maybe she'll make the first move and solve your guilt complex."

"It's called being a decent person, not a guilt complex. Not to mention she's the star, and I'm just one more backstage grunt." Noa sighed, forcing herself to let go of that evening's happy little fantasy and face the facts. "Even though she's queer, there's no way in hell *Lilah Silver* would ever be interested in me as anything more than a friend."

———————

Staring into her mirror, Lilah twisted her hair into a coil and turned it under itself, tucking it up around her neck. It wasn't anywhere near what she'd actually look like with short hair, hair like Noa's, but it was closer. She could photoshop one of her new headshots—that would give her a better idea. She could get an undercut, or curl it like Noa's and put in streaks...except that she'd have to change it to something else the moment she got a new gig, and right now, every director and designer liked her red hair to be long. Letting her hair go, Lilah pursed her lips at herself and folded up the sleeves of her shirt instead. She didn't own any plaid, but Kayleigh did and had handed over the flannel without asking too many questions. The rolled-up sleeves helped, even with her nightwear visible underneath. Add jeans and boots and she might even look like she belonged. Or would she? Would looking the part actually be enough to find her way?

Lilah stripped off the plaid shirt and tossed it over her chair to give back later. Opening her laptop, she flipped through some movies. Usually her recommended list was all rom-coms and feel-good things, but Noa had been so convincing—she scrolled down to the Horror tab and flipped through the options there. *Zombiesaurus Rex*? Too much like her workday. *The Exorcism of Audrey Rose*? Hard pass on the priests-and-Satan genre. *The Ring*. Okay, that sounded benign enough, and there was even a subtitled Japanese version. That practically made it high culture, at least according to her father, for whom foreign films were innately superior to anything made at home. She pulled her purple blanket around herself and settled in but couldn't concentrate on the slow-moving opening scene.

Noa had been right there, in her house, and sitting and talking to her had felt so right. Lilah'd been terrified of being honest, so unsure how Noa would react. But Noa had smiled and reached out with an olive branch of her own, and everything, absolutely everything, was going to be okay.

She was lucky to have a friend like Noa.

Someone knocked on her open door, followed by the bed bouncing under a person's weight. Lilah paused the movie and looked up as Brooke flopped down next to her. Her long dark hair pulled up in a messy bun, the cut-out neckline of her oversized sweatshirt falling down around her shoulders, Brooke was already scrolling through her contact list. Lilah braced for the inevitable. But why should she put up with it in silence? Telling Noa had gone well, and even Kayleigh's unfortunately-on-the-nose teasing hadn't even really bothered her. Maybe it was a sign that Lilah should be brave again.

"So Austin was a dud." Brooke popped her gum along with her eye roll. "You're from Michigan—how do you feel about camping? There's this guy I met at the café who runs adventure hiking tours, and his arms are *ridiculous*."

"I— Wait." Lilah blinked, confused. "What has being from Michigan got to do with anything?"

Brooke shrugged. "Isn't it, like, mostly forest up there? Forests and big lakes and shit like that."

"My hometown's biggest attractions are a golf resort and a fake castle with the state's largest model train display," Lilah replied dryly. "I'm not really a camping person."

"You went to a summer camp, didn't you? I saw you in the T-shirt."

"Summer camp wasn't *camping*," Lilah objected with a laugh tinged by happy nostalgia. "It had cabins with beds and flush toilets. And Saturday-night socials where they brought in DJs and shot confetti cannons. That's a very different sort of vibe."

"Fair. Still, *arms*. And there's something to be said for weekends alone for you-time while he's out bouldering. I can introduce you."

It would be a distraction from her growing and still-hopeless crush, but that really wouldn't be fair to camping guy, who presumably would not be into being used that way. "Brooke, you know I love you," Lilah started, setting her laptop aside and hugging her knees to her chest. "But please stop trying to find me a man."

That got Brooke's head out of her phone, but thank *goodness* she only looked surprised, not offended. "What's going on, honey? You know I'm just having fun. My nanna was a total matchmaker and it's, like, in the blood."

"I know, and I appreciate you looking out for me. It's that—" Lilah's mouth went dry. Telling Noa was one thing, but she lived with Brooke. What would happen if Brooke thought she had been predatory somehow? Or called a house meeting and told Nadia and Kayleigh and *they* had a problem living with her after this?

Maybe it would be easier to keep going along the way they had been. Why rock the boat? Why take the risk?

Except she wanted to be more like Noa, and Noa said things outright, even when she wasn't absolutely sure how someone would react.

"I've kind of got a crush on someone," Lilah confessed, and Brooke lit up.

"Tell me! Is he single? Is he cute? What kind of car does he drive? You can tell so much about a guy from how well he takes care of his wheels."

Lilah fought through the fear. She could do this. Brooke was supposed to be one of her best friends. If she couldn't trust Brooke, then what hope did she have? What good would cutting her hair do if she couldn't live her truth in her own house?

"It's not a he. She's a she."

There was a moment, a hesitation, where Lilah could imagine seeing Brooke reboot—system misfire, reset. But she didn't say anything awful. Instead, she nodded along like Lilah had told her they were out of paper towels. "Get on with your best self. Is *she* cute and single?"

Relief again, for the second time in as many hours, and Lilah wondered if it was possible to get addicted to that feeling. "Yes and no, in that order. She's way out of my league, and she lives with her girlfriend. I don't chase taken people."

"There's taken and then there's *taken*, but if you're mostly invested in avoiding messy, I can see your point," Brooke said, and it was so *her* and unawkward that Lilah felt the last of her current set of worries fade away. "Distraction, then. We should go out, see who we can pull for the short term."

It was the smart move but not one she wanted to make. Lilah shook her head, even in the face of Brooke's confidence. "Maybe. We'll see."

It made her a terrible person to hang on to the tiny, silent hope that Noa would break up with Chrissy. Not *for* Lilah, because that would be an awful thing to hope for. But maybe they were fundamentally incompatible somehow, and they'd have a civilized, mature parting of ways that didn't hurt anyone very much, and then Noa might think about Lilah as more than one of her coworkers.

Later, after Brooke vanished to her room, Lilah flung herself onto her back, hugged her pillow close to her chest, and stared up at the ceiling. Who was she kidding? Noa was sophisticated, experienced, and obviously happy and secure with a girlfriend who adored her. The last thing she needed was an insecure mess like Lilah dragging her down.

Lilah forced herself to sit up, grab her computer again, and restart the film. She needed to let the entire ridiculous idea go. Noa Birnbaum was way out of her league.

CHAPTER SIX

LILAH HEADED ONTO SET THE next morning with her usual wave and a smile for Wayne at the front desk. After her horrific mistake with *that movie*, sleep had been pretty much impossible, so she'd had time to think as she sat in bed with the lights on. She'd chosen to focus on all the good things that were coming her way rather than the hopeless despair of falling for someone entirely unattainable. Noa wanted to spend time with her, that was the main thing, and she was being wonderfully kind in the process. This was what Lilah had originally wanted after all: a chance to find some corner of the community where she might fit.

All that in mind, Lilah was humming to herself and envisioning all kinds of things about what an afternoon on the town might look like. She'd get to meet Chrissy properly, since Noa would probably be bringing her girlfriend along. Maybe Lilah should bring Brooke. It wouldn't be a double date, but it would feel less like being a third wheel if there were four of them.

Tanner was coming out of Lilah's dressing room as she tried to go in.

"Hi?" Lilah laughed, caught off-guard but still managing to hold on to her manners. "Forget which room is yours?"

He looked at the ground, at anywhere but her, before finally meeting her eyes. "No," he said awkwardly. "Mr. Gilbert asked me to drop off today's sides for you, but I grabbed mine instead and didn't realize until I...was...already here. I think his PA must have yours."

Something was absolutely up. He was downright twitchy, but Lilah couldn't figure out how to mention it without seeming rude. "Thanks? But don't worry about it. I printed a copy at home."

"Oh good, then I won't worry about it. Later!" Tanner edged around her and broke into an easy jog down the hall. He vanished into his dressing room before she thought to call out and stop him.

What the heck had *that* been about? Lilah watched him go, confusion coloring everything. *Dan Gilbert* had sent Tanner to her dressing room? And definitely not to drop off her script sides for the day, because Chrissy sent them out by email. Like she did every day.

What had the producer wanted from her dressing room that he couldn't have asked her for himself? He was an imposing figure, cold and rude to the crew when he wasn't spitting fire and invective, and sometimes when he looked at her, a chill set in along her spine for no good reason.

Uncertain and hating herself for being suspicious, Lilah let herself in and took a good look around her dressing room. Everything looked like it was where she'd left it, and wardrobe had already been in to drop off her clothes for the day: shorts, shirt, undergarments, shoes, no problem. Lilah folded her arms and stared around her, but nothing seemed out of place. Maybe Tanner had been telling the truth. But then why all the sneaking?

"Lilah? You're needed in hair!" The dresser rapped on Lilah's door, and she half jumped out of her skin at the sudden interruption. There wasn't time to start dressing now, but she could change in the hair room if Phoebe turned out to be running late. Grabbing her costume off the rolling rack and the ditty bag with its compartments full of unmentionables and accessories from the hook on the back of the door, Lilah left her dressing room and her questions about Tanner behind.

Phoebe was rubbing handfuls of gel into Mikal's hair when Lilah ducked into the room shared by hair and makeup.

The on-set hairdresser was one of those people who looked like they should be jolly and grandmotherly, with her dark brown apple-round cheeks, and the white coiling through the springing corkscrews of her black natural curls, but she had a sarcastic streak a mile wide, and everyone came to her for the best set gossip. Ishani was sitting in one of the free chairs, braids already coiled and clipped up, sunglasses perched on top of her head.

"Has anyone else noticed Tanner being weird today?" Lilah said by way of greeting. She dropped to the floor to start pulling on parts of her costume.

"Today or always?" Mikal cracked, turning to look at her. He yelped when Phoebe smacked him and made him stay still.

"He's been weird," Ishani confirmed with a grimace. "Notice how he isn't even here for his hair call right now? And Tanner's usually, like, super punctual. Annoyingly so. Maybe he's got someone stashed in his dressing room."

Phoebe snorted a laugh, tidying up Mikal's sideburns with a straight razor that had appeared like magic from one of the many pockets on the black apron strapped around her waist. "He'd have to have smuggled him past security if he did. This is a closed stage."

"That wouldn't be hard. Desk guy is always on his phone," Mikal pointed out, very carefully holding his head steady as Phoebe trimmed around his jawline. "Maybe he's looking for a date. Ishani, what do you think of him?"

She considered the question but ultimately shrugged. "He's okay if you like rent-a-cops."

"I've played many. Who am I to judge? Mobster roles usually have more lines though. And I usually get to punch someone at least once before getting shot."

Lilah pulled her socks and show bra out of her ditty bag and stood to duck into the little en suite bathroom, but something stopped her. She looked at the socks in her hand, then looked at them again. White sports socks, cuffed top, totally standard, except—"These aren't my socks," she said aloud.

"Sorry, what?" Ishani asked, brow furrowed.

"These aren't mine. They're the same kind, but they're not the same. Mine were distressed around the top, and these ones are brand-new. The plastic tag end is still in one." Lilah flipped them over and back again, but nope—definitely not any of the pairs she'd been wearing for the last week.

Phoebe glanced over at the socks in Lilah's hand and didn't seem overly concerned. "Probably a laundry mix-up. Wardrobe's got a lot to keep track of."

Lilah could accept that if it hadn't been for that weirdness earlier. "Tanner was coming out of my dressing room when I got here. You don't think he swapped them?"

Phoebe raised an eyebrow and gave a short incredulous laugh. "You think he took your socks? His feet are too big to fit in anything of yours."

"Maybe he has a foot fetish," Mikal suggested, and Lilah snorted at the very thought.

"And he's feeding it by stealing my *costume socks*? Unlikely. No, something else is going on with him. I'm just not sure what."

"Foot fetish," Ishani chorused with a knowing nod, and Mikal leaned over to high-five her.

Phoebe stuck her comb in her apron pocket and dusted her hands off on the thighs of her jeans. "He wouldn't be the first. Five bucks says you can't get him to admit it by lunchtime. Mikal, you're done. Out of my chair. Lilah, honey, you're up."

Lilah settled in. By the time Phoebe had worked her magic and Lilah was seated in front of Noa for her makeup, she'd put aside her worries about Tanner and Mr. Gilbert to focus on much better, brighter things.

———

Brooke wasn't available on Saturday afternoon but Nadia was, and honestly her quieter, more even-keeled company was a lot more soothing than Brooke's usual exuberance. Lilah had spent way too long on her own hair and makeup after lunch, trying to draw that perfect line between "no, I totally woke up looking this amazing" and "I made an effort for you because you're worth it," with as much "I absolutely belong in this neighborhood" as she could possibly manage.

Only she really had no idea what kind of makeup or hair would communicate that combination, except the kind of short or partly buzzed hair that Noa's girlfriend had, or the undercuts and pixie cuts from the photos that came up when she googled "lesbian hairstyles."

Whatever. They would have to take her as she was. Except it would never be that easy, would it? "They" didn't go through the world with all eyes on them, no matter where they went. It had been like that since birth, practically. Lilah didn't remember a time when she hadn't studied herself in the mirror very carefully, practicing—did she look better with her shoulders like *this* or like *that*? How did it feel in her muscles when her stomach was sucked in exactly the right amount?

"I'm amazed you don't walk into poles when you go places."

Lilah snapped her head around to see Nadia's lips twitching. "What?"

"You're staring at yourself in the windows again."

"I wasn't staring. I was thinking."

"Mm-hmm. So what's your answer?"

Her answer to what? Lilah's face went hot. "I, um, I suck. I'm sorry. What was the question?"

Nadia grimaced at her, and Lilah's heart sank. She really was a terrible friend, all caught up in her own head instead of listening properly. "Whether I should take the Shakespeare in the Valley gig. The pay is absolute crap, and I don't even really know if I want to go back to the stage."

The bookstore where they were supposed to meet Noa and

Chrissy was a block away, but Lilah stopped herself from squinting into the distance. *Squinting causes wrinkles.*

"Work is work. Except wouldn't showtimes interfere with your shifts?"

"Barista jobs are whatever—I can find another one if I have to. But do I want to go through the whole 'two shows a day and three on Sundays' thing? I had enough of that in school."

"There'd be better networking opportunities than at the café, on the other hand."

"True."

Lilah stared through the glass windows of the bookstore and tried to decide if the faint outline of a person in the back was Chrissy. She'd recognize Noa anywhere, even without the bright rainbow of colors in her curls.

Instead of Noa, out of the corner of her eye, Lilah saw Nadia fold her arms. A frown crossed her face, and a knot started to tighten in Lilah's stomach.

"So this thing you're dragging me to that isn't a date. If it *isn't* a date, why are you being so squirrely today?"

The d-word. Lilah froze, not sure what to say. In which case, the easiest answer was to say nothing. "I don't know what you're talking about."

"You can't try and trick me into playing chaperone and then pretend you don't know what I'm talking about. Come on. We've known each other how long now?" Nadia's voice softened again, coaxing.

"It's been, what…four years since Miss Teen USA?" Lilah counted back in her head to be sure. "Around that anyway."

"So I kind of know you a little bit." She raised her finger and thumb and held them a tiny bit apart. "And...and Kayleigh told me that she saw you and this girl cuddling on the couch."

Lilah sucked in a deep breath to try and calm her nerves. In a moment of bravado, she'd told Noa that she'd be okay coming out to everyone, but now that the moment was here, she was panicking. Brooke had been so good about it, and Lilah had thought maybe...maybe it might be safe. But what if Nadia didn't feel the same way? When she spoke, nervous and shaky, her words all came out in a rush. "We weren't cuddling, it's not a date, and she has a girlfriend. And I swear I wasn't going to do anything weird when we were rooming together for the pageant."

Nadia recoiled. "What? Dummy, I never thought that. Though Kayleigh might," she said thoughtfully. "But she's got a bunch of ex-Mormon baggage to unpack. Whatever, she'll cope. Only... were you lying to Brandon when you guys dated? Because he was nice."

"No." Lilah rejected that suggestion and pulled a face at the thought. "I broke up with Brandon because he kept bragging online about sleeping with 'the beauty queen.' Like I was some hot trophy instead of a person. I like boys. At least in concept. Real-life ones are disappointing more often than not." Nadia cracked up, and Lilah sighed with another wave of relief. "I just think I could date girls too."

"Smart move. Then you can share clothes and cut your shopping budget in half."

"I mean, theoretically, you can share clothes with a boyfriend," Lilah felt obliged to point out.

"Sure," Nadia considered aloud, "but what's the likelihood you'd both wear the same size? It's a ratio thing."

Movement and something familiar about it caught Lilah's eye. The figure at the end of the street was silhouetted against the light, but—Lilah realized with a start—she knew Noa's walk, the slouch of her shoulders, the sway of her hips. She wore jeans, Lilah could tell that much from where she was standing, her hands tucked into the pockets of a dark brown motorcycle jacket. "There she is," Lilah breathed out. Nadia was watching her reaction, though, and Lilah hid it behind a pleasant wall as quickly as possible.

"That's her? How can you tell from this far away? And I thought you said she was bringing her girlfriend."

"I assumed she would."

Nadia started texting someone, barely glancing up from her phone. "So when you asked me to come downtown with you today, it was as backup buffer between you, the girl you like, and her girlfriend? I thought I was joking about the chaperone thing. Boo, you whore."

"I didn't want to be a third wheel, that's all."

"Fifth wheel."

"What?" Lilah frowned at her, not following.

Nadia flashed her a faintly condescending grin. "Every car has three wheels. You mean fifth wheel, the unnecessary extra."

"To have five wheels today," Lilah reasoned aloud, "I'd have needed to grab Brooke or Kayleigh as well."

"Is this why you're an actress? Because you suck so bad at math?"

"Says the—oh, wait." Lilah tapped her lower lip, putting as

much loving scorn into the gesture as humanly possible. "Also an actress. Amazing."

Nadia huffed a soft laugh and tucked her phone back in her purse and double-checked the zipper. "Since there's no second wheel for you to be a third wheel on, you don't need me to stick around and run defense. Shaunda's in the neighborhood, so I'm gonna go hang out at her place. Have fun on your not-a-date."

"What, no! You can't go! What if I say something stupid and you're not there to fix it for me?"

Nadia showed no mercy, shrugging sweetly. "Own it and pretend it wasn't stupid? I don't know. You'll be fine, and I'll catch up with you later. Toodles."

Lilah stared after her, aghast. "*Toodles?* Traitor."

Nadia waved backward over her shoulder and headed off down the street, her cheerful "hello!" to Noa audible as they crossed paths.

Noa turned and looked at Nadia as she walked away, but her stride didn't break for long. She lifted her hand in a wave to Lilah as she got close. And it was true, weird and possibly encouraging, that there was no Chrissy to be seen. Noa's smile always had a hint of something wry in it, like life amused and disappointed her at the same time, and Lilah caught herself scanning her face now for some kind of reassurance.

"You look—" Noa seemed to be at a loss for words for once, and Lilah's mind immediately jumped to the worst.

She looked down at her outfit, so carefully and obsessively chosen for the day. Nadia had rocked skinny jeans and a crop top, her hair wrapped in a brightly colored scarf, and she'd looked right at home. Lilah, on the other hand, had tried on and rejected almost everything in her wardrobe *and* Nadia's before settling—finally—on a flowered sundress and knee-high boots. "Too much?" Lilah asked anxiously, painfully aware that she'd done her own makeup that day as well. What if Noa didn't like her choices? "I wasn't sure if there was a dress code for any of the places we'd be going, so I took a guess."

"No!" Noa yelped and shook her head. "No, I mean, not too much at all. I was trying to find a way to say that you look *fantastic* without coming across like some kind of—" She hesitated for a split second. "*Project Runway* judge," she finished.

Lilah was almost sure that hadn't been what she'd started to say.

"I don't see you with your clothes on very often," Noa continued, then snapped her mouth shut and flushed bright red. They got a couple of pointed looks and a covered-mouth laugh from a pair of butch women walking past them. "I mean, with your own clothes instead of someone else's." Noa flailed, dragging her hand down her red face. "Can we pretend I didn't say that? If not, I may have to run away, join the circus, and never come back."

Lilah giggled, Noa's fluster making everything so much easier. "No, it's okay! I know what you mean. If I was going to be offended, it would have been the day we first met, when you offered to punish me," she added mischievously.

"Hurt you. I said I wanted to hurt you, and oh my God, I should not be allowed to speak in public. Ever." Noa groaned. "I'm not going to live either of those down, am I?"

"Not a chance," Lilah replied cheerfully. "You have too much

power over me as it is; I have to reassert my authority somehow."
She'd meant "power over my look" or "power over my career."
Every performer knew that the crew were the ones who were
really in charge. Only from the panicked look rising in Noa's eyes,
she had the feeling that words had somehow come out all wrong
for her as well.

What had Nadia said? *Own it and pretend it wasn't stupid.*
And change the subject really fast. "Come on," Lilah coaxed,
slipping her arm through Noa's like she was one of Lilah's besties
and falling into step beside her. There was a second where she
thought Noa might have flinched, but she relaxed into Lilah's
touch without pulling away. Between Lilah's extra height and the
heels on her boots, Noa only came up to her shoulder, but then
again, Noa would be used to that. Her girlfriend was tall.

"You promised me a tour," Lilah said firmly, pushing all
thoughts of Noa's personal life aside. "So let's get touring."

In other circumstances, Lilah would have been jealous. Noa moved
through the spaces so easily, chatting with people she knew everywhere, as utterly confident in the bookstore, the store full of pride
flag kitsch, and the café as Lilah was when she was on set. She
belonged in a way Lilah was only able to fake. And every time she
pulled Lilah over to introduce her to someone new or point out
some nook or cranny with a local story, hope swelled inside Lilah
that one day, maybe, she'd belong there the same way. That she'd
find a space where she could let her armor down, relax the stage
smile, and simply *be.*

It was fun to imagine the possibilities while sitting in the corner booth of a café under a rainbow streamer, the blue, pink, and purple chain-link bracelet resting cool around Lilah's wrist. She'd put it on with a mix of fear and longing—fear that someone might see it and longing that the right people would see and understand. But everyone in here would be the "right people," purely by the nature of the space.

Her guard slowly slipping, Lilah leaned her elbows on the table and watched Noa as she talked, her hands gesturing in the dim light. They'd been at the table for ages, the sconces turning down around them as evening arrived and the later dinner crowd started to filter in.

"It's more about knowing where to begin," Lilah tried to explain as the conversation turned back to her original confession. "I even tried to get involved in a book club at one point. But it seems like everyone in this city already knows one another and doesn't have room for more friends. Or there's a password you need to get anyone to talk to you. A secret haircut?" she joked feebly. "Whatever it is women are looking for, I don't think I have it."

"I doubt that," Noa scoffed, but kindly. Her curls bounced when she shook her head, and when she leaned her arms on the table again, the side of her pinkie finger brushed against Lilah's arm. She didn't seem to notice, leaving it there. "I mean. Look at you," she said, gesturing in Lilah's general direction. "You're a movie star. A beauty queen, even! You have what people want."

Beauty queen. It was meant to be a compliment, but it curdled in Lilah's chest nevertheless. *Hot trophy*. "That's not what I meant." But what was the point in arguing? She let it go, tried to explain it a different way. "I met one girl at Pride and we danced," she offered, and Noa tried to gesture as though to say *see?* "But as soon as she found out I also dated guys, she couldn't get out of there fast enough. I guess being half-gay isn't enough."

Noa pulled a face. "Okay, no, that's awful. You're not half-gay. That's not how it works. That's not how any of it works."

"You say that now," Lilah replied skeptically. "But it's easy for you. You have a community here, and you've got a girlfriend, so you don't have to worry about meeting someone."

The pause that followed was a lot more telling than any conversation had been to that point. "I don't have a girlfriend," Noa said cautiously, and the world slowed down. Lilah had not been wrong about Noa's sexuality, she was absolutely clear on that, so it wasn't the "girlfriend" part that was throwing her off.

Unless… Oh shit. Unless Lilah'd been wrong about Chrissy's pronouns, despite her best effort at getting them right? That would be just like her to mess up something that important.

"Boyfriend?" Lilah guessed hesitantly, and the face Noa made settled that question. "I'm sorry, I'm not sure what I'm missing. I thought you and Chrissy were living together." Lilah tried to explain herself, and somehow, someway, she got the impression that she was only digging herself in deeper.

But then, oh, then, the field changed. Noa's face got totally unreadable, but in a happy sort of way, like the clouds breaking at the end of the day to reveal the red-pink sunset. "*Chrissy?* No. No, really. No. She's not my girlfriend. She's my roommate."

Roommate.

Lilah had obviously misinterpreted a whole *lot* of things. "But you guys are close," she prompted, in case it was a "friends with benefits but we don't call it 'girlfriends'" thing.

"Yeah," Noa acknowledged.

"And she's cute…" Lilah was one hundred percent fishing now.

"Very," Noa agreed readily. "But we're not a thing and never have been. She's involved in a polycule that's, like, six women deep right now. Six women and a nonbinary lesbian named Max who eats all my expensive yogurts even though they're supposedly lactose intolerant," she added with a disgruntlement so real that there was no way any of that was made up.

When Lilah got home, she was going to have to sit very still and review every conversation she and Noa had ever had and then decide if she would be able to show her face in public again. In the moment, however, she let the current flow and pull her under with it. "Oh," she said, and that was wholly inadequate, so she said "oh" again. "Okay. That's good to know before I said anything to embarrass anyone but me."

"It's fine," Noa reassured her, because Noa was amazing that way. "Even if you had said something to her, she'd just think it was funny and tease me, not you."

The low lamplight gilded her dark curls, light playing over the rich mahogany and streaks of bright color layered into the twisting spirals. Lilah was momentarily overcome with the urge to tangle her finger in one, tug it down, and see how long Noa's hair really was, then bury her hand in the rest of it and hold Noa still. For a moment, just long enough to know what her lips would taste like.

She might be allowed to do that now. Noa was single. Only

nothing Noa had done had ever suggested that she liked Lilah as anything but a very new, very tentative friend.

"For your sake, then, I'll make sure not to give her any material for target practice," Lilah replied, the moment passing.

"I appreciate that." Noa laughed, then lapsed into silence. Maybe the moment hadn't passed after all. Something…*something* ran in a little shiver up Lilah's spine. Noa's gaze flickered down to the drink in her hands, her long dark lashes casting a faint shadow. Strong-featured, that's what Zaidie would call her, not at all the sort of delicate-boned look that pageant judges and casting directors liked. Lilah liked it fine. More than fine. The way Noa's jaw set when she was sure about something, the prominent line of her nose, her full lips with their wry tilt that always seemed on the verge of bursting into a smile.

"So," Noa started.

"So," Lilah replied with a half laugh. "Nu, what's new with you? I tried watching a decent horror movie, by the way. Be proud of me, and also, I hate you."

"Oh yeah?"

"Yeah." Lilah mock scowled at Noa, even though the sheer terror of trying to sleep after the credits rolled would be lodged in her long-term memory forever. "It was some Japanese movie called *Ringu*. I've never been so scared in my *life*. I couldn't sleep at all, and I was tempted to phone you at three a.m. to yell at you, but I didn't want to wake up my housemates."

Noa started laughing, her expression a mix of recognition, sympathy, and amusement. "You don't start small, do you? That's only one of the most terrifying movies ever filmed."

"Next time, I'll have to get you to pick instead," Lilah declared, fluttering her eyelashes to make it ridiculous teasing instead of real flirting, just in case.

That got her one of those bright and brilliant smiles, and it settled warm inside her chest. "You're on. For now, did you want to keep moving?" Noa asked. "There's a bar not far from here that has great ladies' night drinks."

"Look, she's alive!"

Noa's head snapped around, and Lilah looked up at the sound of the new voice. A couple of girls their age were heading for the table, coffee cups in hand, every inch of them looking as in-place as Lilah still felt out of it. The one who'd spoken had hair buzzed short enough that Lilah couldn't guess at the color, except "maybe brown," and a ring through her lip, jeans cuffed up over well-scuffed combat boots, and a T-shirt that showed off her muscled arms. Her friend was round, all curves on curves poured into a pair of denim overalls, with black hair styled like Bettie Page and a sweet dimple in her chin.

Lilah had to take a second to remind herself that it was okay to notice that sort of thing here. It was okay to think other girls were cute, *attractive* even, without having to tamp it down or worry about getting yelled at.

"Noa! Where the hell have you been?" Buzz Cut teased, an easy camaraderie in her voice. "First you ditch halfway through term, and then it's nothing but social media silence. Sanders was taking bets that you'd actually gone into witness protection."

"Given the hours we're working some days, I might as well have," Noa replied, that almost smile blossoming into a real one again, this time aimed at the other two. "Between being wiped out when I get home and the NDAs I had to sign, there's not a lot to say." She shrugged. "How's everything going?"

"Not bad," Buzz Cut replied, her eyes dropping to Lilah's hands—first the bracelet, then her carefully manicured nails—for a long and apparently meaningful look. "I hate you for getting to skip out on the Language of Design presentations. Professor Singh almost had kittens because our slideshow didn't use the school's official template."

Lilah glanced back and forth between them, but Noa didn't seem to be in any rush to introduce her. Was she ignoring Lilah on purpose? She'd said the other day that she would introduce Lilah around, but maybe she'd changed her mind. Did she think Lilah would say the wrong thing without a script in her hand? To hell with that.

"You were in the same program?" Lilah asked, then turned on the charm, extending her hand and sparkling as hard as she could. "Hi, I'm Lilah. I'm working with Noa right now."

"Claudia," Overalls replied with an easy grin, taking Lilah's hand in hers. "This is Jordyn. She was in school with Noa, but I'm a hanger-on. Maybe we can pump you for information about Noa's supersecret project if she won't spill the beans." Lilah might not have been super familiar with the Los Angeles lesbian scene, but flirting she understood. Claudia was adorable, especially her dimple, and she was smiling right back at Lilah as though Lilah was someone important.

Lilah was a total sucker for that, go figure.

"Knock it off," Noa muttered, apropos of nothing that Lilah

could see, and shot a glare at Claudia that either the other girl didn't notice or chose to ignore.

Fine. If Noa wouldn't smooth the way, Lilah would have to take up the banner and be sociable enough for both of them. "No pumping necessary," Lilah replied, tossing her hair back over her shoulder.

"Shame," Claudia purred, her eyes alight, and was Lilah really doing this? Flirting with a cute girl in a lesbian coffeehouse like she was allowed to be so bold?

"How are your parents dealing with the whole dropping-out thing?" Jordyn asked Noa.

"Not well. They're convinced I'm wasting my time." And that was new information. Lilah's attention was torn between Claudia's dimple and eavesdropping.

"What *can* you tell me?" Claudia asked, pulling Lilah's attention back.

"Follow me on Instagram if you want all the sordid details," Lilah replied, and the absolute thrill of it all ran through her, even as she was vaguely aware of Noa's glower intensifying beside her.

Jordyn laughed, grabbing the back of the chair next to Noa like she was planning on joining them. "Sordid? Fantastic. Sounds like a porn shoot."

"And I think that's enough of that," Noa said, even as Claudia was scribbling down Lilah's handle on the back of her own coffee cup. "Did you guys want the table? We were about to head out."

"We don't have to go," Lilah objected, but Noa was already standing and reaching for her jacket. Did Lilah feel like taking the risk of alienating Noa in favor of staying with the two she'd just met? She could; no one would stop her. But Noa getting mad at her would be the utter worst.

She stood, following Noa's lead with a rueful smile of apology to Noa's friends. A couple of exchanged "see you laters" and Noa was leading her out the door, stopping for a second on the sidewalk outside to breathe in the evening air.

What was that about? Lilah wanted to ask, and *are you embarrassed to be seen with me?* and all kinds of other questions that would put a damper on the night. She settled for, "I take it they're not your besties?" and left it at that.

Noa had the good grace to look sheepish at least. "They're—No? Yes? They're fine," she settled on, shrugging before she started to walk. Lilah fell in step beside her. "Jordyn's tenacious, and I really didn't feel like sitting there for an interrogation."

It felt like an excuse, but Lilah let it go. What good could come from pestering Noa for a better answer? Movement caught her eye, and she glanced over her shoulder, catching the sideview of a vaguely familiar profile in the Saturday-night crowd before whoever it was vanished from sight. Had that been a glint off a pair of glasses or a camera flash? Or was she just overtired and overreacting to an absolutely normal evening crowd?

"So," she tried again, putting aside the faint wary discomfort for examination at some later date. "Where are we heading next?"

CHAPTER SEVEN

NEXT, NOA DECIDED, WAS A bar. She desperately needed a drink. She'd had no problem at all showing Lilah around, but when Claudia had started eyeballing her like she'd wanted to throw Lilah down on the table right then and there, Noa'd seen red. It wasn't fair, and it wasn't right, or particularly mature. Lilah didn't *belong* to anyone. But watching her flirt had started to turn Noa into a grumpy toddler.

She wasn't proud of being a little possessive. It was one of the major reasons she'd never been able to get into the whole polyamory scene. But it was worse in this case because she didn't have any right or reason to be jealous, and that only made her grumpier.

It got easier once she'd bought the first round of drinks and they were laughing over goofy electric-blue cocktails with skewers of fruit big enough to use as weapons. The evening had turned to night in the meantime, and they'd grabbed a table on the large patio, under a string of lights that twinkled like stars above them. There were no real stars to see, not in the middle of the city, but this was good enough.

"When did you know?" Lilah asked, the natural extension of their current conversation, then added, "You know—*know*."

Noa pursed her lips and sat back, thinking. *Right about now*, her brain submitted as a possible option, Lilah's glossy pink lips pursing around her straw, the light dancing in her huge blue eyes. "Hebrew school," Noa admitted with a grin. "In bar mitzvah class, everyone had to learn to put on tefillin, right? And there was this girl, Rachel—"

Lilah snorted. "It was going to be that or Naomi, wasn't it? I think we had four in one cabin at camp my last year."

"Shush or I won't tell you what happened."

"Shushing. Rachel was cute?" Lilah prompted, a flash of something in her expression that looked almost like—but definitely couldn't be—jealousy.

"Very," Noa replied unwisely. "And the teacher's pet, so she got called up to demo. We're sitting there in that stuffy old class-room, and she's wrapping the leather strap down her arm. Around the box, down her bicep, then seven around the forearm, all that black leather against her skin. And she swam, right? That was her thing. So she had more muscle than most of us did at twelve, and I couldn't stop staring. You know that meme, 'this better not awaken anything in me'?" Noa laughed ruefully. "Oops."

"You like tough girls in leather straps," Lilah teased, resting her elbows on the table as she leaned forward into Noa's space. Her hair cascaded over her shoulder and brushed against Noa's arm, spun gold in the dim light. Noa wound a piece of it around her finger, silk soft, knowing it would smell like vanilla and roses— she let go the moment she realized what she was doing.

Noa grinned, making a joke of the moment. "Hell yeah. I like a girl who can handle herself."

"Good to know," Lilah murmured, more thoughtful than a dumb wisecrack really called for. The waitress chose that point to come back around, and Noa got distracted before she could ask why.

One drink turned to three, and Noa regretted not laying down a better base for the onslaught of booze. Dinner had been some tofu-based salad thing that had felt good and healthy at the time but was absolute shit at soaking up cocktails. The tapas plate came with chili poppers, and Noa reveled in the bright crunch-and-burn of spice that tried to pop her tired neurons back into place. "What are those?" Lilah asked, reaching for one, and Noa didn't stop her quickly enough. "Are they good? Judging by the look on your face, they must be."

"Only if you like hot peppers." The look on Lilah's face about a nanosecond after she bit into the popper was a masterclass in double takes and recoils. "Which I'm guessing aren't really your thing."

"Not so much," Lilah gasped, fanning her lips with her fan. "Ow! That stings!" She grabbed for her glass and finished the last couple of gulps of her Long Island iced tea.

"That's not going to work." Noa broke a mozzarella stick into pieces, the heat of the freshly fried breading stinging her fingers, and held it out to Lilah. "Dairy kills the burn."

Lilah leaned in, holding her hair out of the way, and took the fried cheese from Noa's fingers with her teeth. Her lips brushed Noa's fingertips, a new kind of burn rocketing its way through

Noa, the sting on her own tongue entirely forgotten. "Oh my God," Lilah sighed after taking a second to chew and swallow, running her tongue around the inside of her cheeks. "What *was* that?"

"Supposedly jalapeño poppers, but this place likes to use serranos, and they skimp on the cheese," Noa replied apologetically. She fought an internal war between being chagrined and kind of amused, because honestly, they hadn't been *that* hot—*white-girl hot*, she mentally amended. "Are you okay?"

Lilah hiccupped, then slapped her hand over her mouth while her cheeks went pink. "I'm okay," she tried, then hiccupped again. "Spicy things give me the hic—"

Noa pushed her own glass, melted ice and all, across the table. Lilah had eaten from her fingers moments ago, so she shouldn't be shy about the idea of Lilah using her glass, putting her lips where Noa's lips had just been.

"—ups," Lilah finished her sentence, now blushing for real. "I'm a bit of a wimp."

"Not much call for spicy foods in Northern Michigan?" Noa teased, her heart still racing and the fairy lights draped around the patio twinkling in hazy reflections of each other.

Lilah blew a raspberry at her. "It's more of a steak-sandwich and whitefish kind of area."

"Sounds scrumptious."

"Give me a break, all right?" Lilah objected with a laugh. "I traveled! I tasted things! I was all over the state for pageants, and—why are you giggling?"

She rested her elbows on the table and leaned in, the smile

sparkling in her eyes. *That* was her real smile, right there, not the bullshit pageant/actress smile she put on when they were surrounded by other people. Noa tried to convince herself that her momentary wave of dizziness was from the booze. It wasn't. It was everything about Lilah's laugh that was making Noa feel vibrant and alive. Every fanboy on the internet could imagine they knew Lilah, but only Noa was getting to see this part of her—the silly, giddy girl with the face of an angel.

Noa waved her off, trying to get control of the laugh that was bubbling up from inside. "I was absolutely not thinking about you tasting other pageant girls," she swore solemnly.

Lilah stayed pink, her smile broadening. "Liar." Then she dropped her gaze, looking down into her empty glass with a half-formed frown curling out her bottom lip. "It wasn't like that, so forget whatever sorority/harem fantasy you're picturing. Pageants are like any short-run stage production, boring technical rehearsals and all."

"And a big shiny crown and trophy at the end," Noa pointed out. How many did she have by now? Did she have a trophy room or a shelf full of sparkly tiaras? "But fine, I concede that you have obviously seen some of the world. You weren't a sheltered princess. Not that there's anything wrong with that." Her world was getting a little fuzzy around the edges, but that was okay. Sometimes she was allowed to let go, wasn't she? Have a little fun, as long as she called a car share to get her home at the end of the night?

"I was a bit sheltered," Lilah replied, more lost in thought than she should have been. They were out! They were having fun! It wasn't the time for brooding. "Whenever we did go anywhere—at least until I moved here, anyway—I was traveling with my parents. Maybe it was more like a baby bird in the nest. Or...being cocooned." She waved it off, sitting up and getting perkier. "I'm being silly now."

It was true, Noa decided, and Lilah should say it. "You were totally cocooned, wrapped up all safe and warm. And now that you've moved out on your own, you've hatched!" she said, delighted with herself. "You're a butterfly."

"I'm a what?" Lilah laughed, caught off-guard.

"A butterfly," Noa repeated firmly. It fit her, and it would even when Noa was completely sober again. The image was perfect. If she half closed her eyes, she could see the swirls of color around Lilah, the fluttering of delicate wings, the surprising strength and intelligence it took to migrate across the continent and thrive. "Not half moth, half bumblebee or whatever. A beautiful bisexual butterfly, all yourself."

"You're buzzed, aren't you?"

"And you're not? Affirmations are supposed to be good for the soul. Say it with me," Noa coaxed, just to see Lilah's eyes light up with that smile one more time. "I am a beautiful bisexual butterfly."

Lilah hesitated at first, looking around. No one was paying any attention to them, off in their own little cocoon of a corner. "I am a beautiful bisexual butterfly," she repeated obediently, a smile teasing the corners of her eyes.

"Do you believe that?" Noa asked, setting her chin in her hand. "Because you should. Right down inside your gut. There's nothing at all wrong with you, and any woman in here would kill to have you on her speed dial."

"You're nuts," Lilah said fondly, with so *much* fondness in her voice that Noa made believe for a second that it was real. That this was a date they were on and Lilah would be coming home with her at the end of it, to Noa's tiny shared apartment and twin bed. Even that would be better with Lilah there, waking up and rolling over to find her tucked in at Noa's side, then curling around her and pulling the blankets up over their heads again to block out the encroaching day. Maybe she'd even buy Lilah a purple chenille one and a string of fairy lights, to make her feel so at home that she'd never want to leave.

Nice fantasy. Too bad about real life, which was a back table on a bar patio on a Saturday night, the floor sticky with something dubious, and the thumping bass line from the club next door reverberating through the soles of her boots.

Still, there were cocktails here, and cocktails in bed could get messy. Speaking of which—

"We should get more drinks," Noa declared.

A funny look crossed Lilah's face. She snagged the last mozzarella stick, saying, "Why don't we get you some fresh air?" She glanced over her shoulder with a thoughtful expression that dimmed her light for a moment.

"What's up?"

"Nothing," Lilah deflected. She stood, holding out her hand to Noa. "Come on. You need to walk some of this off, or you're really going to regret it tomorrow."

"I'm not drunk. I'm just tired. Our hours suck. I think I turn into a pumpkin at midnight," Noa complained, but she took Lilah's hand anyway. It wasn't the first time Noa'd held Lilah's hand, but it was the first time she let herself slide her fingers between Lilah's and squeeze, like they were friends.

Like they were more.

"Come on then, Cinderella." Lilah didn't let go, tugging Noa gently toward the door. "It's time to leave the ball."

———————

That feeling that had been prickling the back of Lilah's neck persisted even after they left the bar. It had started after that second drink, a faint notion that someone was watching them. Watching *her*. Maybe someone who recognized her from a movie, an autograph seeker, but that hindbrain awareness set in and wouldn't let her relax. Getting Noa out of the bar had been partly about that—getting out of there before something happened—but it had given her an excuse to hold Noa's hand as well. And Noa hadn't pulled away.

Except Noa was shit-faced, or at least part of the way there, so that didn't mean a whole lot. She wasn't stumbling or weaving, thankfully, didn't look sick, and after a few minutes outside, she seemed to be a lot more present than she had been back in the club. Problem one, solved.

Problem two? Lilah looked around again and shot a quick glance over her shoulder, but no one struck her as being out of place. No shadows lurking in alleyways, waiting to jump. Maybe *she* was the one who was too tired for reality.

The road transitioned rapidly from restaurants and little shops to something residential, large houses sprawling out on either side of them behind lawns and gardens splashed with color. They paused on a fancy concrete bridge with spires like old churches at either end, a garden full of ivy and flowers planted in the little ravine below. Lilah rested her arms on the guardrail and looked over the side while Noa boosted herself up nimbly to sit on the rail beside her. She'd perked up since leaving the bar, color back in her cheeks. She braced her arms and held herself steady next to Lilah, and they lingered there for a minute in easy silence.

The warning crawl over Lilah's nerve endings was gone, and she felt her shoulders unknot. "How're you doing?" she asked, keeping her voice soft so as not to shatter the easy peace.

"Much better," Noa promised. "I hope I didn't offend you when I suggested another round—if it seemed pushy or something. If you're not usually a drinker?"

Lilah shook her head. "It's not that. There's, like, a billion calories in one of those." She made the easy excuse instead of explaining the way her skin had been crawling like eyes were on her, some vague spider-sense tingling a warning she couldn't define. "If my weight changes too much during filming, wardrobe will murder me for real."

"I...never really thought about that," Noa confessed. "The films I've been on before were like one-week shoots—bang out all the scenes, bam-bam-bam, then right into editing. No one had to keep their look for longer than a few days. That's got to suck, having to watch what you eat all the time."

"It comes with the territory. I knew what I was getting into. It's still worth it," Lilah added, trying hard not to go on the defensive.

"Oh sure," Noa teased, resting her chin on her shoulder and grinning at Lilah from her perch. "Having guys like Ed telling you that you're breathing wrong and can't eat what you want, then add idiots like me poking you in the eye with lash curlers four or five times a day. Worth it."

"Says the girl who'd happily spend her working life up to her elbows in vats of fake blood," Lilah shot back happily. "I don't get how you can love that side of moviemaking so much. At least I get my face on-screen for my troubles."

Noa snickered. "Could be worse. I could have to kiss Tanner."

Lilah laughed. "Compared to some, he's an absolute delight. His breath smells great, he knows his angles, and he never, ever tries to slip me tongue. Some films I've been on, the cast really didn't get along, and that was rough. Pretending to like someone enough to make out with them on-camera right after having a fight backstage is *real* acting," she added with a little shudder.

"What's it actually like to kiss on-camera?" Noa blurted the question out like she hadn't meant to verbalize it at all.

Lilah couldn't help it—her eyes dropped to rest on Noa's perfectly painted lips. She caught her own lower lip between her teeth to stop herself from blurting out something equally as impulsive. It didn't exactly work. "Not nearly as much fun as kissing in real life," Lilah said, holding Noa's gaze. Her stomach flip-flopped. Would Noa take the invitation? Would she even notice it for what it was? Lilah wasn't used to being the forward one. Guys were usually a lot happier if she let them think they were in charge. Maybe it would be better if Noa didn't notice. Then they could go on being friends and Lilah wouldn't have to face what she'd just tried to do.

But oh, it would be nice to kiss Noa. To rest her hands on Noa's hips and feel the sleek warmth of her skin, to taste her—would she be all spicy still, like the hot peppers she was eating, or would her mouth be sweet?

"I believe that," Noa replied, all lighthearted and noncommittal, either not noticing or being very careful not to indicate it if she had. "Most people don't have a camera guy, a lighting designer, and a boom operator within spitting distance when they're kissing in real life either. Unless you're in a very specific industry," she added as an afterthought.

Lilah sighed inside and resigned herself to failure. She'd tried an obvious hint and Noa hadn't gone for it. Now she had to let it go and be normal for once. "But then it's not real life, by definition. If everything's blocked and scripted for you already."

"Scripts are nice," Noa said wistfully. "Wouldn't things be so much simpler if life had a script? Then we wouldn't have to stress out all the time about saying the wrong thing at the wrong time to the wrong person. Someone else would have done all the thinking for you already."

"Sure, as long as you get an author you like. Given the scripts I've read, I'm not so sure I'd trust most of them with reality." Lilah wrinkled her nose at the idea.

A breeze kicked up and tugged at her hair, and she scooped it back behind her ears. What was going on in Noa's head when she looked at Lilah? There was something intense behind her stare now, and the sounds of the rest of the world dropped back a step, quieter and somehow removed. Like a bubble was forming around them, only them, the universe receding to give them privacy.

"You are so beautiful," Noa sighed, her eyes not leaving Lilah's.

And that hurt in a way Lilah didn't have words for. Because of course she was; that was practically her reason for existing. Noa's job was to make her even prettier, so maybe that was all she saw. Like Brandon, Austin, Lilah's parents, or a dozen different fan sites. A beautiful girl. A trophy. A mannequin to be trotted out and given scripts with all her lines predetermined, and—

And the alcohol was obviously getting to Lilah as well, because Noa didn't mean it that way, and she needed to get over herself. "Beautiful" was the reason she kept getting work after all. It was stupid to think otherwise. "I know," she said, not able to get herself as far along the road to "thank you" as she should.

"No, really," Noa insisted, her knuckles tight on the guardrail where she sat. "I've always thought so."

"Can we not?" Lilah interrupted, despite her own better instincts, then instantly felt guilty for it. "I'm sorry. I—Thank you. But can we talk about anything else?"

Noa frowned, her mouth setting in a flat line. "Does it bug you that I said that?"

"Yes, but not the way you think." Noa was upset, and it was Lilah's fault, and all she wanted to do was turn back time a minute and a half so that she could stop herself from getting defensive and ruining the end of what had been an incredible evening. Lilah's hand tightened on the rail next to Noa's. It wouldn't take much to slide over half an inch, rest the side of her pinky finger against Noa's and connect the circuit. One move, one touch, and she could barely bring herself to breathe at the thought.

"I'm more than that, you know," Lilah managed to say around the growing lump in her throat.

"Oh my God. Yes, you are. You are absolutely and completely more than that. You're smart and you're so *nice*. You have this thing you do where you make people feel important just by looking at them. And you're *funny*, not like you're doing stand-up or anything, but this sniper kind of funny where you're quiet for a while and then *zing!* And no one sees it coming, and that's funny as hell—" Flustered and panicking, Noa looked...vulnerable. For the first time since that first apology, she looked totally vulnerable. Only Lilah hadn't known her well enough to read it back then.

Something clicked over inside Lilah, a feeling that had been building all afternoon, a new and utterly sacrilegious notion that Noa wasn't someone to idolize after all. Not the gatekeeper or the wise guide or a model to emulate, but a girl, like Lilah, capable of making the same kinds of foot-in-mouth mistakes Lilah was forever kicking herself for.

Now, all of a sudden, she was endearing and sweet—and Lilah had the odd thought that *Noa* might be worried about impressing *her*. It made no sense, but there it was. "You're babbling," she pointed out fondly, the red flush across the tops of Noa's cheekbones definitely more embarrassment than alcohol.

Noa's usually wicked mouth was all turned down, her expression teetering between freaking out and crestfallen. Lilah leaned in, running on the desperate impulse to make Noa feel better, get rid of that stricken look on her face. She leaned in and pressed her lips to Noa's, soft, tentative, almost chaste. Blame it on the night, on the cocktails, on the answers she imagined Noa might hold for questions she could barely articulate.

Lilah kissed her, and after a moment's hesitation that sent a jolt of panic right through Lilah's system, Noa kissed her back.

Her lips parted beneath Lilah's, a burst of bright spice still on her tongue. The warmth of it infused Lilah straight down to her bones. Noa's fingers clutched at Lilah's sleeve, twisting up in the fabric, another point of contact to keep her grounded. Lilah's head spun anyway, and she broke the kiss, pulling back and trying desperately to read Noa's face *now*.

Noa looked as dazed as Lilah felt, and she brushed her fingertips against her lips. "What was that for?" she asked, laughing a little. Was it nerves? Or had Lilah overstepped, taken Noa's compliments for more than what she meant in the moment?

"It stopped you from freaking out." Lilah offered the excuse to cover up the ripples of terror and longing that were clashing into each other inside her chest, the *I want* echoing through her in the wake of the kiss.

Noa didn't seem to buy it. Weirdly, Lilah almost felt relieved. "Is that all?" Noa asked.

"Only if that's what you want." Was that a cop-out? It was totally a cop-out, putting the choice for *what happens now* back onto Noa, a volleyball serve of emotional responsibility, a hot-potato metaphor that she was currently beating to death rather than facing what she'd just done.

The breeze tugged at Lilah's skirt and the ends of her hair, a reminder that the world still existed around them. Car horns sounded in the distance, music somewhere else, but the only thing that mattered was Noa's reply.

"What about what *you* want?" She wasn't going to let Lilah off the hook. Nuts to that.

And Lilah didn't have a good answer. Ideally, she could say *Yes, I want this. Go out with me.* Only the what-ifs kept bouncing around in her head, and *What would people say?* echoed louder than anything else. Except this was her life, not anyone else's. She had the chance to reach out and take everything that she'd wanted—right up until the moment it was being offered to her.

"Maybe?" Lilah said softly, and that was the wrong thing. "That is, I don't want to make your life complicated, and I'm probably not the kind of person you usually go out with, other than tonight. I know this was a favor, not a real date." Why was Noa looking at her that way?

"Could it be?"

"Could it be what?" Lilah furrowed her brow. *Don't do that, honey. It leaves wrinkles*—her inner voice sounded exactly like her mother, and she forced the muscles to relax. "A date? I wouldn't say no, but not if it's because you feel sorry for me for being so dumb at this."

"No!" Noa yelped, then recovered. "No, I promise you, there's no pity here. This is about to be the highlight of my adult life."

Then Noa was the one who leaned over—leaned over and kissed her again. It wasn't sweet or chaste or innocent this time, not in the least. Noa kissed her, and the heat went beyond the serrano peppers—not a stage kiss with closed lips but a messy, sliding moment of communion. Something raw and empty inside

Lilah healed over, a loneliness she'd noted before but never truly understood. The nagging, critical voices in the back of her mind fell silent, drowned out by the wave of unblemished joy that crashed over her. Lilah tangled her fingers in Noa's silk-soft curls and held on, sinking forever into the feel of her, the taste of her. A missing piece slotted neatly into place, and she was left breathless at the enormity of it all.

It ended too soon, the air cool against Lilah's wet lips when they parted. Somewhere in the distance, the world kept on moving, traffic made noises, and music was playing, but nothing mattered more than committing to memory every last detail of this perfect moment.

I kissed her. She kissed me. And it was incredible.

"So," Noa began unsteadily, her fingertips brushing her lips in something like shock. "What does this mean?" She wobbled on her guardrail perch, and Lilah grabbed for her, stopped her from sliding off backward to fall to the flower-filled ravine below.

It means run away with me. Lilah slid her arm partway around Noa's waist to stop her from falling. She tucked herself in tight, Noa's arm pressed against her front. The closeness started that telltale rush building deep inside, a tingling, swooping sensation halfway between flying and drowning that left her tongue thick and her head swimming. *Take me home with you tonight*, she wanted to blurt out. *Bring me in from the cold. Show me everything I still need to learn.*

Lilah wasn't bold enough yet to ask for anything even remotely close.

"Talk about it tomorrow?" Lilah suggested, and she let go of

Noa's arm. She should do some research, learn something about what Noa might be expecting, before she flung herself at her. Noa might laugh at her fumbling, make fun of her inexperience, and that would be the utter worst. Her own cowardice embarrassed her at the same time as she retreated into the safety of excuses. "We're both tipsy and exhausted, and I know for sure I'm not going to make the right words like this."

"Tomorrow." Noa sounded disappointed even as she got her feet under her, but she didn't push. Still, she grabbed for Lilah's hand and gave it a tentative squeeze. "But we're good, yeah?"

Lilah nodded, relief not nearly enough to counteract the mess inside. She needed space and time and a long soak in a hot bath to sort out exactly...anything. "We're good."

It would be too late for that kind of soak by the time she got home, after the quiet walk back to the main street and bundling Noa into her Lyft. Lilah watched the car drive away, still sorting through her thoughts. The world was already precarious, and now it was tilting on its axis, threatening to tip her off into the unknown.

Did she dare jump?

Claudia: Where've you been hiding her?

Noa: I haven't been "hiding her"—she's a coworker

Claudia: Just a coworker? Cause she's cute as all hell and if you're not going to hit that...

Noa: NO.

Claudia: mmhm.

Noa: shut up.

Claudia: I'm just saying.

Noa: yeah, and if I said "go ahead" you'd do that thing you always do

Claudia: which is what, precisely?

Noa: you know exactly what I mean. You give a girl that 1000-volt smile and within an hour she's looking up U-Haul rentals.

Claudia: nah. Two hours at least. We stop at the humane society to pick out a new cat first.

Noa: It's all about the pussy with you.

Claudia: Tooshay. Bring her to ladies' night at Mollyz next week or I'm texting her those photos of you wearing the beer-chugger hard hat.

Noa: can't. we're on location.

Claudia: the week after, then!

Noa: you realize blackmail is a federal crime, right?

Claudia: so turn me in.

Claudia: I'll see you at the bar!

Noa tossed her phone onto her bed, and it bounced once before settling to rest safely on the plain green duvet. She spun around in her desk chair, watching the room turn lazily around her. The clock blinked at her: 3:20 a.m.

"What am I doing with my life?" Noa asked the four walls. The vivid red-splotched poster of William Marshall didn't answer her. Neither did Kate O'Mara and Ingrid Pitt, who pouted at her silently from their poster, 1960s frosted lips parting around mouthfuls of plastic fangs.

"She kissed *me*. And she was super into it when I kissed her. That means something, even if she did start backpedaling, like, immediately. But if I sleep on this," Noa reasoned aloud, "then Claudia will swoop in and ask Lilah out before I can. Lilah might prefer that, mind you. Claudia's a lot of fun. More fun than me." Claudia was great, that was the worst part. Noa couldn't even feel mad about Lilah hooking up with her, except for the pure jealousy part of the whole thing. *My Lilah.*

"She won't be my *anything* if I don't do something."

William, Kate, and Ingrid seemed to agree.

"Only if I ask her out for real and she says no, then we're right back to the first problem, in that we have to work together and it could be creepy and weird." Except tonight, oh, tonight... There was every chance that Lilah would actually say yes, wasn't there? That she hadn't been messing around? Lilah had kissed her. And then kissed her back. But after that, she'd backed away and put off talking about it. She could be having a good old gay panic. Or maybe the kiss had sucked and she was trying to come up with a polite rejection before moving on to someone who could do a better job. Unlikely given how incredible that kiss had been, but then, she was an actress. Maybe she was really good at faking that too.

Middle ground, then. Something plausibly deniable if Lilah didn't want to acknowledge it but that showed Lilah exactly how much she already meant to Noa. Noa threw out a hand and grabbed the edge of her desk, stopping the lazy spin of her chair. Most of her desk was littered with work-related debris and other tchotchkes, but somewhere in one of the drawers, she had the supplies she needed. A few minutes and a trip to the bathroom later, she had her inks, watercolors, and cardstock all set up. She had to be on set in less than six hours, but some things were more important than sleep. The sketch and then the black ink lines took careful shape under her fingers, a different medium than her usual, but the muscle memory came flooding back as she brushed the colors onto the sweeping curves.

Done, Noa set the picture on her desk to look at it with a critical eye. The morpho butterfly swooped across the cream-colored card stock, outlined in black, its wings shaded in a watercolor haze: pink, purple, blue. She'd let that dry while she grabbed a couple of hours of shut-eye, then slip it onto Lilah's dressing table tomorrow. A little gift and a reminder of what they'd come so very close to sharing.

CHAPTER EIGHT

WAYNE GAVE NOA THE STINK eye when she barreled through the studio doors at top speed the next morning, and she resented every second it took to stop and swipe in. Lilah's call wasn't technically for another hour, but she was also one of those crazy morning people and tended to be in early. This was something Noa needed to do before that happened.

She'd expected the place to be quieter this time of day, but today the halls were more chaotic than normal. A big stack of boxes had gone up outside the door to the props shop, and PJ was adding another one to the pile as Noa passed by. The label on the newest black crate read *GUTS—DO NOT SPILL*.

"Morning." She tossed off a quick wave to PJ and paused in her stride. Chrissy'd assured her that the fight between the producer and director had blown over hours after it'd begun, but there was still the off chance of another crisis. "Packing for strike, or packing for location?" she asked as casually as she could muster.

"Location," PJ grunted, levering another box onto a nearby dolly. "We're going up to base camp this afternoon to make sure all the hydraulics work before you all get there tomorrow. Hooray us."

"How bad could it be?" Noa asked without as much sympathy as she could probably have mustered.

"I can't find my goddamned work gloves, the coffee maker in the crew room is leaking, and if the truck supervisor doesn't pull her thumb out of her ass and start actually sending guys in the right order, it's gonna get a whole lot worse," PJ grumbled darkly. "Watch out for Ed this morning. We're behind schedule again, and all the department heads are on a rampage."

Noa's hopeful mood deflated, and she nodded along. "Thanks for the heads-up. Any idea what they're going to do?"

"Colin was saying they're gonna start cutting corners on costs, which means I need to quit chatting and get these on the goddamned trucks before some dipshit in production decides that they don't need practical effects at all," he said pointedly, scowling at her from under the brim of his ball cap.

"Point. Have fun with that." Noa headed away, PJ cursing a stuck wheel on the dolly as she left him behind her in the hall. Her gut started churning more with every step, worries from last week raging back. Chrissy'd assured her that Lilah's gossip had been just that, that the scheduling and budget drama would all blow over quickly, but obviously not so much. Heart thumping and worries cascading through her head, Noa ran through the numbers. She needed her thirty days of work this year to stay on track for her recommendation, and so far, she'd been on the production for what? Fifteen? Losing this gig now was not an option.

The dressing room was empty, and Noa slipped inside and

flipped on the light as the door swung quietly shut behind her. She swept a space clear on the top of Lilah's cluttered dressing table, pushing aside a jumble of personal cosmetics, a hairbrush, crumpled script sides, and a gift bag. Taking a minute to make sure it was framed nicely, she propped the butterfly watercolor card against the mirror where Lilah would see it as soon as she sat down. Then second-guessed herself, picked up the card, stamped down her irritation, and put it back. It was a gesture of her affection, something Lilah could choose to follow up on or not without adding pressure to a life already filled with people placing claims on her attention.

Noa forced herself to leave, the card sitting half propped against the mirror and the bag. And now to get on with her day, like she hadn't left a little piece of herself waiting to be brought in from the cold.

Despite the mild hangover and the way her coffee was sloshing around uncomfortably in her stomach, Lilah was walking on cloud nine on her way into the studio. She'd kissed Noa, and Noa had kissed her back. Kissed her! Even leaving things on an awkward note couldn't dim her excitement. She'd lain awake most of the night reliving the moment. Brushing her teeth, getting rid of the last traces of Noa on her lips, had felt like some kind of betrayal.

That was probably weird. But good-weird, like she was on the verge of something tremendous. All that time thinking in the dark had brought her a new clarity. She'd been scared as hell last night, worried about a dozen possible awful futures, but why should she be? This wasn't the 1950s, her parents were good people, and she was an adult. She wasn't going to be sent to reform school or some weird Christian pray-away-the-gay program. The absolute worst that was likely to happen was a few raunchy gossip blog comments, and her mother sucking her teeth about the possibility that she might not get grandkids. Lilah wasn't sure she wanted kids anyway, even if she did end up dating a man, so disappointing her parents on that score might be inevitable.

The more she thought it over, the more it seemed like all the obstacles had been swept aside at exactly the right time. They were moving to location tomorrow. And in the mountains and the woods, away from the chaos of the city, who knew what wonderful things might happen?

Last night, Noa had kissed her.

Humming to herself, Lilah swept into her dressing room and tossed her things on the chair. Then stopped. Someone had been in before her. A beautiful card sat propped up against a gift bag that definitely hadn't been there when she'd left for the day on Friday, and she picked the card up eagerly. The watercolor butterfly had been painted in the same colors as her bracelet—pride colors, *bi* colors—and it didn't take any thought at all to realize who must have left it. Lilah pinned it to her wall, grabbing a thumbtack from another picture without a second thought.

She tore into the bag, squealing a little when she saw what was inside. A teddy bear, a sweet little teddy bear with fluffy fur, shiny glass eyes, and a satin bow around its neck. Lilah hugged it impulsively, only a little dismayed when it was pokier and not as cuddly as she'd anticipated. Didn't matter, the thought was the important thing, and it would look supercute on her dressing table. She balled up the old script pages and tossed them toward the trash can, ignoring the ones that bounced off the rim onto the floor. The teddy bear got pride of place against her mirror, right under the butterfly card, where she could see them both every time she came in the room and know that she was admired.

Admired for her looks. Noa had called her beautiful before she'd kissed her. That was the first thing she'd said. Funny, smart, kind—she'd only said those after Lilah had prompted her for more. But if Noa wanted her to be beautiful, if it meant more days together like yesterday, Lilah could do that. Brandon hadn't been worth the nonsense, but Noa would be. She could feel it.

Her phone buzzed and she glanced at the screen, her mood deflating all at once when she saw the scrambled, anonymized email address on the top of the preview. This would be the fourth email from @tommyjarvis in as many days. Blocking his email address had given her a few days of freedom, but it apparently couldn't stop him from making new ones.

Despite her better judgment, Lilah swiped it open.

You looked beautiful last night.

A chill ran up and back down her spine again. Okay, now *that* was super creepy, far more so than the "I loved all your movies, show us your tits next time" fanboy stuff that she was sadly more used to. Was that the reason she'd felt like someone was staring? Because someone had been? But why? She lived in LA for crying out loud! There were plenty of other more well-known actresses to track down and harass. Why did he have to pick on her?

That was nothing more than the plot of its own bad movie, a creep messing with her for funsies, and she wasn't going to let some...some *weirdo* with too much time on his hands throw her off-balance. Not when things were finally starting to really go her way. Lilah tossed her phone on her dressing table and left it there. She needed to focus now, not get distracted by electronic pranksters.

"I have to go be someone else for a while," she told the teddy bear. He needed a name if she was going to talk to him, but nothing came to mind immediately. "Don't you worry—I'll think of something."

The light from the hallway seemed to catch the bear's eye as she closed the door, a flash in the lens making it look like the bear was winking.

They were surrounded by people that morning, no way to ask Noa privately what had inspired the gift, but Lilah couldn't hide her giddy joy when she found herself settling down in the makeup chair.

"Noa, pass me the setting spray!"

"So I said to him, Murray, I know we have kind of a theme going here, but there is no way in hell I'm reading for *Hamstergeddon*. Did you *hear* what Alejandro did with *Attack of the Fifty-Foot Squid* last year? The lawyers had a field day."

"Has anyone seen my dressers' apron? It's the second time it's gone missing."

"'Great expectations,' seven letters."

"High bar?"

"Cover your eyes and nose. I'm going to spritz now."

"Are you hungover at all?" Noa asked Lilah with an air of uncertain cheer. "You don't look it, and I hate you."

"Cucumber slices on my eyelids this morning and a whole lot of coffee," Lilah admitted, her eyes not leaving Noa's face. Noa was a lot greener around the gills than Lilah felt, but then, she'd had more to drink with a lot less body to contain it. "How are *you* doing? You were pretty giggly by the end there." Denise looked at her sharply over Noa's shoulder, and Lilah shut her mouth. Was she doing something wrong? She wasn't gossiping about anyone else and not talking nearly as loudly as Phoebe and Ishani.

Noa didn't seem to notice, carefully smoothing the primer under Lilah's eyes. Lilah stole the chance and leaned into her touch, savoring the smooth brush of Noa's gentle fingertips.

"I'm fine," Noa promised, her voice pitched low. "Did you get a chance to go to your dressing room this morning?" she asked ever so casually, and was Lilah imagining it, or was Noa looking nervous? Despite Lilah's big epiphany the night before, that was definitely the wrong way around. *You have too much power over me*, Lilah had giddily proclaimed, and now in the light of day, it felt true again.

Lilah nodded, her teeth catching her lower lip to prevent herself from breaking out into a wide smile and throwing off Noa's rhythm. "Did you paint that?" she asked breathlessly, dropping her voice lower when Denise glared at them again. "When did you find the *time?*" The card, the *shopping*—unless Noa had already gotten the bear and had been waiting for the right time to give it to her? She didn't know which answer she liked better.

Noa lit up, her smile reaching her eyes. "It's amazing what you can accomplish at three in the morning when you're really motivated."

"The butterfly..."

"That's you. It's how I see you anyway."

"I want—"

She never got the chance to say what it was she wanted or to find out what her own next words would have been because Denise swooped over and started pointing out the blending spots Noa had missed. Lilah fell quiet, closed her eyes, and let them work.

Lilah: You know tech stuff; how do I filter emails so I don't have to see them?

Brooke: you mean block the sender?

Lilah: no, like stick them somewhere so I still have them, but they don't show up in my inbox.

Lilah: Someone's sending me weird stuff and it's freaking me out

Brooke: weird stuff? Like nudes?

Lilah: That's not weird, that's gross. More like the marriage proposal kind of stuff, but it's starting to get creepy. I'm not so sure I should delete them, but I don't want to read them.

Brooke: gotcha. I'll send you a link that shows how to make filter folders. If it doesn't work, bug me when you get home.

Lilah: you're the! Best!

Brooke: you know it, bb!

Their pages that day mostly involved Tanner getting ripped to shreds by PJ from props, who was wearing massive dinosaur feet on his arms. Noa was particularly proud of the fake skin over the blood tracks and the color blending that made it vanish into the throat sleeve Tanner wore. That had taken ages while he practically vibrated in the chair with the adrenaline left over from rehearsals. Arterial spray was even more fun, both in the rigging and the deploying. Colin let her play with the plunger during setup, viscous red stage blood shooting out of the small ends of the rubber tubes, mimicking human arteries and veins. Some days, she really, really loved her job.

The actuators that powered the shaking floor for the raised cabin set were in full sway. Built on a platform six feet off the ground, the three-walled replica of the cabin in the woods was jolting around like it was being tossed in an earthquake or landslide. "Back it off about five percent and run it again" came the order, and the cabin creaked to a shuddering halt before restarting.

Down on the sound stage floor, PJ waved the huge scaly feet around, opening and closing the claws a few times. A faint squeak and pop of metal came from one of the mechanisms. Colin unbuckled the harness and handed him a bottle of WD-40 that PJ made disappear somewhere deep inside.

"There's not enough blood in these takes," Ed complained through his megaphone, a whine settling into the edge of his voice. The cabin shuddered to a halt, back in starting position. "This isn't a goddamn Hallmark chick flick here. We need gushers!"

Colin let Noa stand next to him and watch as he put the final touches on the setup. Tanner gave them a thumbs-up as Colin backed away, playing out the clear rubber tubing as he went.

"Less ooze," Ed ordered from his chair, "more spray! I want people ducking away in the theater seats!"

"Less ooze, more spray," Colin repeated solemnly. He winked at Noa, and she grinned back at him in reply. The secondary hose running from the pump in his hand to the second water-cooler-sized bottle of blood under the props table made her take a step back.

"Ooh, Tanner's about to get it." Lilah's gleeful murmur came from directly behind Noa, and she struggled to keep her focus on the job. Lilah's pickups and reaction shots had been cleared first, and she wasn't even really supposed to be hanging around the set, but Noa sure as hell wasn't about to complain. Lilah leaned in right behind Noa, a little too close to pretend that it was an accident. The heat of her spread all up and down Noa's back, a bone-deep awareness of her closeness, the tickle of the end of her ponytail on the side of Noa's ear. Noa caught a faint whiff of cotton candy and vanilla on the air, and her racing nerves picked up another notch.

"You may want to step—" Noa tried to warn her but didn't get a chance to finish.

"Last looks, and quiet on the set! We're rolling for this one, so everybody shut the hell up."

Oh no. Noa waved Lilah away as subtly as she could, Lilah's pastel outfit not nearly as practical right now as Noa's washable blacks.

"Action!"

PJ came in for the kill and Tanner bellowed, a broken man's dying rage. A soft rubber claw the size of a carving knife swung across Tanner's bared throat.

"Cue the blood!"

Colin depressed the plunger. Blood bubbled out of the slash in the throat sleeve and Tanner bit down on the capsule in his mouth, sending foaming red cascading down his chin.

The pneumatic pump kicked in a half second later. Lilah hadn't moved.

Hissing like they'd cracked open the gates to hell, the five-gallon bottle emptied in under ten seconds, blood shooting in a fan arc halfway across the set.

The wave crested, arcing over the side of the set and splattering down in a fervid mist over the watching cast and crew below. Ed got it full in the face. The spray splattered across Noa's chest and stomach and Colin's jeans, and PJ, standing next to Tanner, was soaked from head to toe. When Noa turned, Lilah was spluttering, wiping stage blood from her mouth and nose with the back of her hand and managing to smear it more.

There was a beat of silence, broken only by the hiss of the pump.

Ed bolted up from his chair and roared, pumping his fists into the air as stage blood dripped off the end of his nose. "Colin, you utter arsehole! Now *that's* what I'm talking about! Cut, print, tell me for the love of all that's good and holy that we got that shot. We'll do one more for safety if we have to."

A faint whoop sounded from Tanner, collapsed in a heap on the wooden floor of the set. A black-clad crew member climbed up the ladder to the cabin to help PJ slide his arms out of the claw puppets, and Noa tried desperately to remember if she had any wet wipes in the bottom of her kit.

Behind her, Crosby was griping to Colin again. "The human body only holds about a gallon and a half of blood, you know. That kind of pressure buildup would have triggered a massive embolism in that young man long before something could have cut his throat." He gestured to Lilah next to him, her shirt splattered with the back spray. "If I were to cut Miss Silver's lovely little throat here, you'd see blood burbling down her chest, not a geyser across the room! A knife would be a better choice as well," he mused aloud, eyes fixed unsettlingly on Lilah's neck. "A claw's just not as efficient."

Lilah edged away from him, alarm registering on her face.

Colin shook his head as he started to flush and reset his tubing. "Embrace it, Doc. This just ain't that kind of movie."

The science consultant sank his head into his hands in despair, and when he lifted his face again a moment later, his glasses were smeared with stage blood. "I wonder if it's too late to demand to be left out of the credits?" he asked the air, then took off his dirty glasses, tried to rub them clean—leaving red streaks on his shirt— and wandered off blearily in the general direction of the hall.

Props and wardrobe were seeing to Tanner's reset, which gave Noa a couple of minutes to find somewhere to wash herself off. Or better yet… She deliberately bumped her arm against Lilah's as she passed her and cocked her head toward the door. "Let me give you a hand cleaning that goop off," Noa offered, a statement that got no raised eyebrows from anyone in earshot. Awesome.

Lilah joined her as they passed into the hall. "I'm told lava soap is my best option," Lilah replied, grinning at whatever private joke that stemmed from.

"I don't think we've got any of that in makeup, but I can probably find some bar soap that'll do the same thing."

"A thousand bucks a minute!" Dan Gilbert stormed down the hall, Noa and Lilah jumping aside and clearing the way so they didn't get trampled. "That's what this bullshit is costing me, and he's wasting everybody's goddamned time with practical effects and shot setups like he's a goddamned auteur! He thinks he's Kubrick, but he couldn't find the Stanley Hotel up his own ass with two hands and a light meter!" He raged into the headset shoved in his ear, his phone in his hand. Chrissy scrambled behind him, clipboard and binder shoved under her arm, and made an apologetic face at the two women as she hurried past.

Noa winced, and Chrissy made an exaggerated shrug before she had to grab the door to the sound stage and haul it open. They vanished through it, the door slamming shut behind her.

"I'm going to venture a guess that Ed and Mr. Gilbert haven't made peace," Lilah suggested into the quiet that followed the slamming door.

"Wait until he sees what we did to the set." A muffled howl of rage came from behind the door, and Noa bolted before they could get caught up in whatever happened next. Lilah grabbed her hand and they ran, half giggling, down the hall and around the corner, to collapse in a heap outside the dressing room doors.

When she could catch her breath, laughter subsiding, Noa tipped her head back against the concrete wall and caught Lilah's eye. Her cheeks were flushed under the smeared red syrup, the sparkle alive in her eyes. Her chest rose and fell with her rapid breaths as Noa's pulse picked up speed.

"Is it always like this?" Noa asked, wrenching her eyes back up to Lilah's face, a desperate grasp for something—anything—to take her mind off the moment. Off the way Lilah was pressed against her side, her shoulder and thigh tucked in neatly beside Noa's; off the way she smelled, all sugar and sunshine, despite being locked in the same concrete bunker as Noa for the last three weeks of sixteen-plus-hour days.

"What?" Lilah asked in all innocence. "Studio films?"

Studio films or what? Noa burned with the question: What else would Lilah think she was talking about? Crushing on someone? Wanting to touch, so badly, and having to keep every impulse under careful control?

Even after the not-date, the kiss, the way Lilah had beamed at her this very morning, Noa was still caught in the terror. If she opened her big mouth, if she had made the wrong assumptions after all, she could disrupt this tight-wire act and fall, screaming, to be impaled on the shards of her own presumption.

Wow, she was in a mood today, the sleep deprivation and hangover having her *thinking* in purple prose. Gross. She took the easy way out. "What else?" Noa drawled, the sarcasm a shield against the dangerous truth.

"In that case, no. Not always." Lilah took her question seriously, though her eyes were still bright and focused on Noa, like she saw through every pretention and careful layer of armor that Noa could fling between them. "Sometimes the producers and directors actually *don't* get along."

Noa snorted a laugh. "Then I hope to God I never end up on one of those, if this is what friendly looks like."

Lilah hadn't moved and Noa didn't either. No one was around, and even Dan Gilbert's shouting had died down to inaudible.

"Friendly looks like a lot of things, I think," Lilah started slowly, and Noa knew—she *knew*—that the subject had completely changed. Not suddenly, either, even though it might have sounded it to others. She'd been having this same argument with herself for three weeks already. Almost half the shooting schedule, done. They were on location as of tomorrow, and then once they got back, the countdown to wrap really started.

And then what? She'd never asked Lilah what her next gig would be or if she was flying somewhere far away. And what if she was going on location to…who knew? South America or Tunisia? Somewhere where her new castmates would be her next family and Noa would be a distant memory. She should. She should really pay attention to where she actually was, because Lilah was still talking, and Noa crashed back into her own body a half beat behind.

"Like us, for instance," Lilah was saying, still hesitant, like she was choosing her words very carefully. "Are we friends?"

"Of course we're friends!" Noa jumped in to reassure her, because how had she somehow managed to make Lilah think they were anything less?

"Friends, or *friends*? Because friends don't usually kiss the way we kissed last night." Lilah left it there, the words hanging in the silence.

The world went very still.

She didn't sound mad.

More like...hopeful?

Was that really possible?

It wasn't *im*possible. Lilah had kissed her first.

"That's true," Noa replied quietly. "I mean, sometimes they do, if people are friends with benefits, which is a thing that happens sometimes. Not with us, that is, I don't—I wouldn't be *upset* if that was the kind of arrangement you were looking for, but—" She blinked at Lilah. "I'm supposed to shut up right now before I make a huge mess of a good moment, aren't I?"

"Wouldn't hurt," Lilah offered with a smile so sparkling that Noa didn't care about the teasing. They were almost nose-to-nose now, Lilah drifting in toward her with unmistakable intent.

Lilah Silver is about to kiss me while we're sober.

"And I've been kind of hoping for something a little different than friends with benefits."

Lilah freaking Silver just asked me out?

Noa could die right then and be assured that her life had been worthwhile. *Teshuvah, tefillah, tzedakah—I must have been a very good girl last year to have been given this.*

"I could be down for that," Noa agreed as calmly and serenely as she could muster, her heart thumping so loud that there was no way Lilah could be that close and not hear it. "I—"

"Noa?" Footsteps echoed in the hall behind them, and the crystal-glass moment shattered. Lilah scrambled to her feet, Noa a beat behind her, so that in the next moment when Denise rounded the corner, they were standing by the door to Lilah's dressing room rather than practically in each other's laps on the floor beside it. Noa's boss rolled in like a thundercloud, loose black sleeves cracking in the air with the swinging of her arms. "There you are! What do you think you're doing? You're needed back on set!"

"Wardrobe was working with Tanner," Noa reasoned aloud, trying desperately to drag her brain back off the spin cycle Lilah had thrown it into. "So I figured rather than stand around and waste time, I'd help Lilah—"

"Lilah's off the clock until her afternoon call, but you're not. Come on. I need you!" The key makeup was freaking out in a major way, and Noa could practically *see* her head on the chopping block. Which meant she was going to do whatever Denise told her to do, at least until she had a recommendation letter in her hands. She sent a look of silent apology to Lilah, hoping that she'd understand.

Lilah had a fakey-fake pageant grin on her face. Not a full-on solar-flare type of smile, but the patient "yes, yes, get on with it" media smile that Noa was starting to be able to recognize. "It's no problem," she replied, and Noa fought the urge to grab her hand and run again. "I'll jump in the shower and get out what I can on my own," she added with a faint laugh in her voice and a look directed at Noa that she hoped Denise neither noticed nor understood.

Lilah vanished into her dressing room, and the tension built up in Noa's shoulders. Alone with Denise now, what was she going to say? Denise started walking, and Noa wrenched herself away from Lilah's door to follow.

"You two have been getting awfully close," Denise observed, her heels clacking on the floor. Noa had to take a step and a half for every one of Denise's long, angry strides, and she found herself scrambling to keep up. Did department heads learn that trick from experience, or was it a class Denise and Dan Gilbert had taken on *how to keep your minions from feeling confident in their jobs?*

"Lilah's great," Noa replied, trying—and probably failing—to keep the grin from showing on her face. "We've really hit it off." That was a good thing, right? A keep-your-job thing if the talent liked you.

Or maybe it wasn't. Denise paused halfway through her next step. She looked Noa dead in the eyes this time. Her gaze was sharp and penetrating, and weirdly, her eyes seemed red around the edges. Probably not enough for most people to notice, but Noa knew a few things about covering up post-cry eyes. Denise didn't look sad now though. Right now, she just looked pissed. "One thing to stick in your head and keep there," she said, her words and voice sharp. "Anyone who works for *me* has to keep things purely professional. I don't care what other departments do, but if I hear word one about any fraternization with the cast—flirting with Tanner, for instance, or *Peter*—you're out. The talent is the talent, and they don't get involved with crew."

"Yeah." Noa had the presence of mind to clamp down on her scoff of laughter at that suggestion. And then the moment of decision. Come out, or don't come out? Sets were notorious for the speed at which gossip moved. Say something to Denise right now, and everyone, including the grips, would know Noa's life story by lunchtime. She was out, but she preferred the details to be on her own terms. Hard pass. She went the more subtle route. "That won't be a problem."

"Make sure it isn't. Because if I catch any rumors about you hooking up with the actors, I'll kick your ass back to UCLA so fast you'll be spitting shoe leather for a month." And she left Noa standing in the hall, her head awhirl.

Shit.

She couldn't say yes to Lilah now. Not until filming was over. And if Denise caught wind that they'd been on a date already or that Noa had left love tokens, her career would be over before she'd even be able to prove to her parents that dropping out had been worth it. She had to sit down with Chrissy and chew over this little bit of information later. Once she was done freaking out.

Noa: I can't do any more bar nights until we've wrapped.

Lilah: What?

Noa: Denise gave me major shit over getting too friendly with the talent. She said she'd fire me if she caught me flirting.

Lilah: Oh no! Are you serious?? Why does she even care?

Noa: Dunno. It sucks, but at least it's only for a few weeks.

Noa: But after filming's over? Maybe we could…

Lilah: Yeah. We can wait. If it means keeping your job!

Lilah: It's too bad though. I had fun. 😣

Lilah: I guess I'll see you on set

Lilah: night

CHAPTER NINE

THERE HADN'T BEEN ANY TIME to talk to Lilah properly between the long shooting day and packing for the drive to location the following morning. A couple of texts before Noa's phone battery died hadn't been nearly enough to explain everything that Denise had both said and not said, but Lilah seemed to understand. There hadn't even been a chance to offer to drive Lilah up to the shooting location so they could make plans in the car, what with Noa packed into the crew van and hauled up the mountain like so much cargo herself.

The crew van shuddered to a halt in the gravel parking lot of the base camp on the side of a wooded hill, pulling in beside a half dozen other cube vans that would be piled high with gear. Trucking had moved half a sound stage's worth of equipment sometime in the night, and tents and trailers and port-a-potties had popped up like mushrooms all over the field. A path led behind a copse of trees and wound its way off into the distance, a cabin sitting halfway up the slope. Cameras and lighting gear had already been set up, reflective walls blocking off Noa's view of the film crew at work.

Already halfway across the parking lot, Denise stopped and waited for Noa to catch up, one imperious hand on her hip as she watched Noa struggle with the heavy bags. The sun was only barely up, and Noa cracked her mouth open in a yawn she couldn't control, turning her face into her shoulder, her hands full.

"Trailer three is crew break room," Denise told her, and it almost sounded kind. "Ditch your crap in hair and makeup, and get yourself a coffee before you touch anything important."

"Oh, thank God," Noa uttered, clamping her lips tightly together even as the pointed comment made its escape.

There was a pause. Then a small smile cracked Denise's tightly pressed lips, the first one Noa'd seen her wear in a while. She took the heaviest of the bags from Noa's shoulder and slung it over her own. Was that...compassion? It was something anyway, and Noa wasn't nearly caffeinated enough to deal with it. Thankfully, it didn't last long.

"Don't take an hour," Denise warned her as she headed off. "Today's the start of the sausage factory. We've got a dozen marines to slaughter, so don't forget the condoms. Colin's got the blood for the squibs in the props truck, and the buttons for the head-shot gags are with my kit. Bring everything over to makeup once you have your coffee, and we'll start the assembly line."

"You got it," Noa confirmed, running through the list in her head—*boxes of condoms and the blood to fill them, buttons and fishing line, the rubber head.* She started off toward the trailer, taking a shortcut through a patch of uncut grass. Something slithered past her feet, long and beige with brown spots. *Rattlesnake!*

Noa shrieked and jumped back to the gravel, the snake vanishing into the grass.

"Watch out for snakes," Denise called over a second too late. "This place is lousy with gopher snakes. Stay out of the grass, and they won't bother you."

"This day keeps getting better and better," Noa grumbled low enough that Denise couldn't hear her. Catching herself, she took the long way around, on the gravel, and dropped her bag inside the door with a cheerful wave at Phoebe and her hair dryer. On location, dream job. Up at four in the morning to get here on time, the fields were full of snakes, and her boss was using Noa as an emotional punching bag, but it was a small price to pay overall.

"I love my job," Noa reminded herself, trailer three firmly in her sights.

She wasn't the first one in there. Noa did a double take at the red-haired figure eating a fancy grain salad out of Tupperware, but it wasn't Lilah noshing on couscous and pine nuts. It turned out to be her stunt double, a woman named Sadie in a red wig and an identical version of Lilah's costume, who was far too chipper about the mistaken identity to cope with so early in the morning.

One embarrassment over with, Noa stopped in the kitchenette, looking around for the coffeepot. PJ had beat her to it, the last few drops falling to splash into his oversized Troma travel mug. "Oops," he said, deadpan. "Did you want some of that?"

"Asshole," Noa replied automatically, and he flashed her a toothy grin. He dumped the grounds into a plastic box sitting next to the stained, old sink and started making a new pot before she could say anything else, so at least someone had taught him how to be a decent person.

The break trailer was definitely not in the kind of league the star trailers had to be. Those were probably swank, with soft couches and wide-screen TVs. This was more of a camper gone to seed, with a handful of distressed chairs, a minibar fridge with dented corners whirring in the corner, a toaster oven, and an ancient microwave that was probably leaking enough radiation to turn all their future children into versions of Swamp Thing. Still, the coffee was free, even if the wood paneling inside the trailer made her feel like she was on a sitcom set abandoned since the 1960s.

The fridge was full already, crammed with energy drinks and bottles of dubious-looking condiments. "Don't touch the thermos," Sadie advised with a grin from the other end of the trailer. "One of the gaffers is breastfeeding."

"So?" Noa asked, not making the connection.

"So she doesn't have her kid *with* her on set," PJ said pointedly. "Unless you want to fluid bond with her by accident—"

Oh. "Noted." Noa closed the door hurriedly, then blinked at PJ. Where the hell did a kid who looked like the second coming of Marky Mark learn a term like "fluid bonding"? The door swung open before she could ask, and they were joined by a gaggle of other crew. The little trailer filled quickly, laughter rising, and Noa boosted herself up onto a clean section of the peeling Formica countertop to wait for the new pot of coffee to finish brewing.

Noa: On set now, where are you?
Chrissy: w/DG, doing paperwork. Kill me.

Noa: We're living the dream, aren't we?

Noa: coffee's on, I'll bring you some?

Chrissy: thx but no thx. If I have any more caffeine right now, you'll have to peel me off the ceiling.

Chrissy: Your girl's over at the cabin in rehearsal, btw.

If only. If Noa was brave enough to take the chance, to run the risk of Denise finding out. Wasn't Lilah worth it? Wouldn't it be absolutely, completely worth it to kiss her again? Her lips had been candy sweet, and she'd leaned in to Noa's hand, all warm and soft and willing.

Lilah *was* worth it. But if Noa could hang on a few more weeks, she wouldn't have to choose. And what was a few weeks in the grand scheme of things? Once shooting wrapped, she would ask Lilah out properly, take her to dinner, moonlit walk on the beach, botanical gardens? Something romantic like that.

It would be worth the wait.

Noa: She's not my girl yet. Not unless I want to get fired.

Chrissy: Right, b/c you play by the rules now. Want me to go back to reminding you why you shouldn't date her? I have a handy list.

Noa: Please no.

Chrissy: Trying to be supportive here

Noa: you suck at supportive.

She didn't wait to see what rejoinder Chrissy would fire back. One was definitely coming—having the last word was kind of her thing. That gleeful sparring had started at their first meeting and had been one of the first signs that she and Chrissy were destined to be fast friends. Sometimes, though, she wished Chrissy'd put a sock in it.

"Ow!" Phoebe yanked her fingers back from the toaster oven, then grabbed a threadbare dish towel to pull the door open and grab for her bagel. "It gets hot, so watch out."

"Livin' the life," Noa replied dryly, and Phoebe laughed.

"At least we *have* a trailer, honey. I've been on a project where all the crew got was a tent in a field."

"You have?" PJ asked with interest.

"Sure, but only once, and only until I found out that all we were getting was a tent in a field," Phoebe answered with a grin. "This woman deserves better."

The coffeepot finished perking, and Noa grabbed for it before anyone else could slide in there first. The rich, warm smell soaked into every pore as she filled her mug, and she took a second to appreciate PJ's brewing skills. Maybe she'd misjudged the guy. It wouldn't be the first time. "Thanks." Noa lifted her cup in his direction and hopped off the counter. He gave a taciturn nod in return, but she liked to imagine it had been a little bit friendlier than before.

More cars and vans had arrived in the time she'd been cooling her heels inside, and Noa exited the break trailer into a milling crowd. A PA jogged toward the trees with a box full of annoyed gopher snakes while Sadie had joined a group of guys in copies of the cast's costumes. One of Ed's PAs passed in the other direction, talking rapidly into her headset. "I'm bringing a bunch of extras your way for background. Is wardrobe ready?"

Shaking off her fears about Denise's mood, the producer's temper tantrums, and the embargo on hanging out with Lilah, Noa sucked in a deep lungful of the cool morning air. The collective excitement—and a hefty dose of caffeine—rippling through her, she struck out toward the makeup trailer.

———

Rehearsals over, the cast was in hurry-up-and-wait mode, a part of the day that Lilah guarded jealously. She needed her quiet time to go over lines and get mentally ready. And watching the crew clear the snakes out of the cabin set once had been more than enough.

Her trailer had a star on the door. She'd taken a photo, then stopped with a ripple of fear before uploading it to Instagram. The inside was small and cozy, her fuzzy purple throw blanket tucked over her feet enough to make the place feel like home. The teddy bear from Noa sat on her dressing table, the first thing she'd set up when she unpacked. She scrolled through her email on her phone, stopping every so often to reread the most recent one from her agent and let the excitement run like a shiver over her skin.

Somewhere around the ninth or tenth time through, reading the message wouldn't have the same effect anymore. She wanted to savor it.

> They loved your audition, want you in for a screen test for chemistry.
> Ready to make an offer.
> We got this one in the bag, kid.
>
> —Nancy

And even if it had to be another horror flick, at least this one wasn't cheesy. No improbably resurrected dinosaurs, no implacable zombie men with machetes, no sharks in tornadoes. Just a creepy house, a new marriage already falling apart, and some really good, juicy scenes that she could *act* in.

She'd have to move to Paris for three months, but that wasn't terrible, and she'd have a chance to practice her French. The production covered housing, so she wouldn't need to look for an apartment or find someone to sublet her part of the house share. It was all very neat and tidy, except for one specific person she'd be leaving behind. Noa was on a tight leash while they were filming, and now Lilah was considering leaving the country soon after. What would happen to her promises then? Maybe it would be better to ask Noa to wait a little longer again, until Lilah got back from her next location. Or they could try doing something long distance, but was that even worth it when they'd barely even begun? It would be so selfish to ask Noa to wait for her when, if Lila's career took off the way she wanted it to, she'd be jetting all around the world all the time.

Noa would find someone else in town more likely, and Lilah would be pining away in France all alone. Maybe that was why so many actors hooked up with other actors. It was just easier when you knew that there was an end date already stamped on something. Or Lilah was being a scaredy-cat and was using travel as an excuse. If she wanted to be with Noa—and she did, she was so sure that she did—why would she be scared?

Her brain was a whirling mess with no escape hatch in sight. There was one thing guaranteed to make her feel better and get her settled back in her own skin. Lilah swiped her email closed, her thumb finding the speed-dial button without need for conscious thought.

"Hello?"

"Hi, Zaidie? It's me."

"Lillian, bubbeleh! How's my little flower?"

He didn't want to hear her be sad or confused. It would make him feel good to hear that she was doing well, so that was what she had to be. Lilah summoned up her chipper voice and focused on her agent's email instead of worrying about a future that might not ever happen. "Great!" she bubbled with as much enthusiasm as she could. "I got some wonderful news today. Do you remember when I auditioned for *Night of Anubis*? I got the callback! They want me in for some screen tests with the male lead so they can see if we'll work well together, and Nancy's absolutely sure that I'll get signed."

"That's fantastic!" His warm voice soothed her down to the core, insides starting to match her outside smile for the first time that day. "This is the European production, yes?"

"American production, but filming is in France. I'd be gone three months, but I promise I won't forget to call, even with the time difference. I'll hopefully be back before the High Holidays."

"What an opportunity, eh? I'm so proud of you, following your dreams like this. You should take an extra week or two and visit the old country when you're over there. See exactly what your great-grandparents were running away from as fast as their legs could carry them." He chuckled.

Lilah giggled, settling back into her chair and pulling her fuzzy blanket around her. "That's not exactly a rousing recommendation, you know."

"It never hurts to know your roots." He paused. "Well, sometimes it does, come to think of it. Sometimes roots hurt a great deal. But it's always better to know things than not know them. And there's your pithy grandfather quote for the day," he added with a laugh. "You can write it up in sparkly ink and that pretty handwriting of yours and put it on the instant-gram."

Lilah burst out laughing. "It's *Insta*."

"You think I don't know?" He teased her right back. "My favorite grandchild can't tell anymore whether I'm teasing."

"I'm your only grandchild," she felt obliged to point out.

"I could choose not to have a favorite at all, you know. Maybe I'll rewrite my will and leave everything to Herschel. He's an excellent cat."

Lilah couldn't stop giggling, tears stinging the corners of her eyes. "Sounds like a plan. Maybe we should let Herschel pick out your nursing home as well."

"A kosher kitchen and a bevy of pretty widows, and I'll be happy anywhere."

"That's more information than I needed, you know—" Lilah cut off at the sound of a knock on her trailer door. "Hang on a sec?"

"I need to get going. You caught me on the way out the door to bowling. Call again tomorrow!"

"I will. I love you."

"Love you too, bubbeleh. Be good."

Lilah tossed her phone on the couch and moved to answer the

door, her fuzzy blanket wrapped around her shoulders like a cape. She half expected to see one of the PAs on the other side of the door when she opened it, or maybe Ed to go over some notes from rehearsal. She didn't expect Noa to be there, bouncing on her toes and casting nervous glances over her shoulder.

"Okay?" Lilah asked, not sure what to say.

"Can I come in?" Noa prompted, still bouncing. Lilah stepped back, and Noa took advantage of the motion, sliding into Lilah's trailer under Lilah's outstretched arm. "I'm on break supposedly, and I wanted to see you. I feel like I haven't seen you in days, though that's ridiculous. It's like the moment Denise tells me I'm not allowed to do something, it's the only thing I can think about."

Lilah let go of the door, and it swung closed on its own. She drew the edges of the blanket around herself, her caterpillar cocoon. "Are you okay?" she asked cautiously. "Your texts were a little dramatic." A little disheartening, a little devastating? That was overkill, but it would have been nice if Noa had been a little more reassuring. "Are you vibrating?"

"PJ in props makes really good coffee," Noa confessed, setting down her empty mug on the table. "Did you know he could do that? I've had, like, three cups already. Do you think anyone saw me come in here?"

Lilah wanted to laugh or maybe yell at her, because Lilah was the rule-following one, the careful one, not Noa. She was supposed to be the flip-the-bird, impulsive one who swept Lilah off her feet despite Denise's stupid new dictates. "You're my makeup artist, Noa. Even if anyone saw you in here, why would they care? It's not like we're doing anything wrong. We're only talking." She wanted more, was pretty sure Noa did too, unless she was about to use Denise's tantrum or Lilah's travel as a reason to call everything off for good. Lilah had to sit on that news, at least until she could figure out how to get to that place they'd been yesterday, when Noa had looked at her like she was wonderful.

Noa groaned. She didn't move farther into the room, though she glanced briefly at the couch behind Lilah. Lilah wanted her to push through and flop down on it like she belonged there. She wanted Noa to belong there. "Denise is a total shitshow today. She's watching me like a hawk, and this is unauthorized free-time fraternization."

"Why is she so mad?" Lilah glanced out the window reflexively, but the only movement she saw out there was a couple of the teamsters heading back to the trucks. "I was kind of hoping you'd tell me more about what happened."

At least Noa had the good grace to look sheepish. "Yeah, sorry—my phone died, and I crashed hard. I'm pretty sure Denise had something going with Peter that maybe didn't end so well. I'm her prime punching bag right now."

"What can she even do? Complain to Ed that you're doing your job too well?" Lilah shrugged the idea off, but Noa didn't seem to relax.

"Fire me or not write that recommendation letter, and that's my career down the drain. I need this job." Noa's cheeks went pink across the tops like she was embarrassed by the admission, like she thought Lilah didn't have to hustle to get auditions. "My dad keeps sending me emails about how it's not too late to go back to school and catch up on my classes, and if I blow this shot, my

mother's going to make going home for the holidays a living hell."
There was so much there that Lilah recognized and so much she
wanted to ask about, pull on the threads a little and see what new
parts of Noa's life would unravel for her to see.

She opened her mouth, though, and none of that came out.
Instead, it was tepid, careful, testing the edges of what was and
wasn't allowed. "I mean, it's not like we actually did anything
wrong by going out as friends. People do that all the time." Friends
didn't kiss the way they'd kissed, but if Noa wasn't going to bring
it up, she wouldn't either.

Noa winced, her fingertips drumming out a complicated
rhythm against her thigh. Nerves or coffee? Was there a difference
right now? "Right. As friends."

She didn't move, and Lilah didn't either, a few inches apart in the
aisle of her little trailer. Memories rocketed through Lilah's mind,
her lips tingling with the remembered feel of Noa's mouth on hers,
the bright burn of being the center of Noa's attention. Her pulse
raced, and her cheeks got hot. Any minute now, Noa would notice
that something was wrong, that Lilah couldn't find her words, that
without a script in front of her, she was useless. She would—

Would look up at Lilah with stars in her own eyes, the flush
not fading from her face.

If this were a scene, there would be a camera pushing in over
Lilah's shoulder right about now, milking the breathless tension.
Later, a composer would thump a bass line to imitate her heart,
swell the violins. Only it wasn't a scene, and the only sounds were
the rise and fall of distant voices and the click-hum of the trailer's
tiny fridge.

Lilah caught her lip between her teeth, pushed her breath past the sudden lump in her throat. Noa needed to be the one to say something, to tell her what to do.

Direct me, because I don't know how this part of the story goes.

Another knock sounded at the door, and Lilah just about jumped out of her skin. Somehow, she and Noa had drifted closer together, close enough for Noa's curls to brush against Lilah's jaw when she whipped around to stare at the door, panic in her eyes.

"Shit!" Noa hissed. "What if it's Denise? I'm supposed to be on coffee break!"

"You don't need any more coffee," Lilah advised, but all the while, her mind was racing at top speed. If Denise really was as pissed off as Noa suggested, she might actually fire her. And then this would be the last time Noa would see her, because she sure as hell wouldn't want to be spending time with the girl who got her *fired*.

"Hide me!" Noa pleaded.

"In here!" Lilah grabbed Noa's upper arm and pushed her toward the trailer's small bathroom. Noa tripped over the edge of the carpet and half stumbled in, slamming the door behind herself.

A muffled curse came from behind the door, and Lilah shushed her, rushing the handful of steps to the door. A deep breath—*act casual*—and she pulled it open, the words already on her lips. *I haven't seen Noa all day.*

Only it wasn't Denise this time either. Tanner blinked at her from the top step, his confusion probably looking a whole lot like hers.

"Tanner? What do you want?" Lilah asked, keenly aware of the click of the bathroom lock. Normally, she'd just welcome him in, but Noa didn't want to be seen with her outside of work duties, whether Lilah considered it overkill or not.

Movement drew Lilah's eyes down, and she stopped worrying about Noa's paranoia. Tanner had a massive shopping tote over his shoulder, and the bag was wiggling. A sneeze built, and she pressed her finger against her upper lip to try and kill it.

"Let me in?" Tanner pleaded, looking over his shoulder at the lot. Lilah stepped aside this time and wordlessly invited him inside. Noa was still hiding, but her coffee was sitting right there—should she try and get rid of it? She could probably move it to the sink if she acted really casual. Would Tanner either notice or care that Lilah was suddenly the kind of person to own a *Bride of Chucky* travel mug?

The bag jumped and squirmed, bumping against her thigh. Then it barked. Recoiling, Lilah covered her little gasp of surprise and what was starting to become understanding. "You have something alive in there."

A thump came from the bathroom.

"You have something alive back there?" Tanner replied with an equally suspicious look.

"No!" Lilah objected, her mind racing. Would Noa be mad if *Tanner* caught them? He could be trusted, except for that one weirdness with her dressing room. He certainly wasn't going to tattle to Denise. She pointed at the bag. "Promise me that isn't snakes."

Something bumped behind the bathroom door again and water turned on, then abruptly turned off.

Tanner shifted from foot to foot, trying to see around her. "Promise me that's not Peter!"

"Peter? No! No one's here but us—" Lilah said at the same time as the bag barked again.

The door flew open, and Noa emerged, drying her hands on Lilah's pink hand towel and leaning against the doorframe in a way Lilah suspected was meant to be casual and unaffected. It didn't exactly work. "Oh, hey," Noa said, acting totally surprised.

"And Noa," Lilah sighed.

Tanner didn't bat an eye at Noa's sudden appearance, though he did smile knowingly in a way that didn't do much to soothe Lilah's frazzled nerves.

The bag barked, wriggled its way out of Tanner's arms, and dropped to the floor as he scrambled to try and regain his hold. "Hey, wait, stop!"

"Oh, *sweetie*!" The fluffy head that shook its way out of the tote bag was covered with soft white-and-black curls. Huge brown eyes looked up at Lilah from halfway under the mop, and the puppy staggered out of the bag on feet easily twice as large as they should be.

She couldn't resist. Lilah scooped him up in her arms and buried her face in the warm fur of his side. The puppy wriggled around until a wet tongue slorped across her forehead, sending her giggling.

And sneezing. Once, twice, three times—the puppy struggled in her arms at the sudden burst of noise, and Tanner grabbed him back from her before he could fall.

"That's why I've been sneezing!" Lilah accused as she let off another rapid-fire burst into the crook of her elbow. "Dog hair!"

"If you're allergic, why'd you try and neck with him?" Tanner pointed out, and she stuck out her tongue.

"I didn't know that's what it was until just now! I've never had a dog."

The puppy wriggled and struggled until Tanner put him down on the floor, where he started very carefully sniffing everyone's shoes. "What kind is he?" Noa asked, carefully picking up her feet and shuffling closer to Lilah and Tanner while the puppy growled at her boot lace.

"A big one. Look at those feet!" Lilah cooed.

"He's a teddy bear schnoodle," Tanner replied proudly.

Noa's expression was all skepticism. "A what now?"

"A teddy bear schnoodle," Tanner replied, scooping him up again and holding him protectively. "He's a poodle-schnauzer mix. Meet Rasputin." He waved Rasputin's paw at Noa solemnly. "Say hi to Noa, Rasputin."

Lilah stifled a giggle, and Noa rolled her eyes. "Could you *be* more of a stereotype?"

Tanner was unabashed. "I could, yes. But I refuse to be shamed for loving this sweet little face. Look at his nose, Noa. Boop the nose." He held Rasputin out at arm's length and, grudgingly, Noa tapped the puppy's nose. He promptly licked her finger, then made a dive for the floor again.

"You're ridiculous," Noa informed him, and a little part of Lilah rebelled. How could Noa not turn into a gooey puddle over the sweetest little ball of fluff to ever...get into her bag?

Tanner yelped and dove across the trailer. "No, don't eat that!"

In the less than five seconds they'd been ignoring him, the

puppy had found one of Lilah's socks and was happily growling at Tanner over their sudden game of tug-of-war.

"Let go!"

"He's only playing."

"With my sock!"

Tanner managed to wrest Rasputin's new plaything free and held it up to Lilah with a look of deep chagrin. "I'm so sorry. He has a thing for fabric."

"That's where my costume socks went," Lilah realized out loud and somewhat belatedly. "And why you were in my dressing room. You replaced them?" Not Dan Gilbert's doing after all, and she felt an old knot in her spine untangle and release.

He nodded, his dark cheeks flushing, and Noa cackled. "That's why things keep disappearing? Phoebe's apron? PJ's work gloves? Ishani's bra? Because kibbles 'n' bits here has an oral fixation?" Noa grinned wide and flopped onto the couch, the way Lilah'd been wishing she would.

"He keeps getting out of my dressing room," Tanner replied, shoulders slumping in the picture of misery. "Ed said it was fine to have him on set as long as I kept him out of the way, but he's faster than he looks! He got into Peter's stuff in our trailer this morning and ate his lucky boxers. Did you know Peter hates dogs? Cruella de Vil has nothing on that guy."

Lilah hadn't known that, and now she took the chance to sit on the small couch next to Noa while they talked. She slipped in, oh so casually, Noa's arm resting across the back of the couch where she'd first draped it. She didn't move, even when Lilah leaned back far enough for her shoulders to rest against Noa's side. She was warm and solid, lean muscle and rolled-up black shirtsleeves, and her breath caught a tiny bit when Lilah settled in. Lilah heard it, felt it against her ribs where there were only a few millimeters of space between them. Tanner straddled the back of her desk chair and folded his arms across the back, not calling attention to the way the women were sitting.

"Peter had lucky boxer shorts?" Noa asked, and her fingertips played lightly along the shoulder seam of Lilah's shirt.

"Emphasis on *had*," Tanner grumbled. "He wears them on every movie. He said the one time he didn't, he hurt himself falling into an open grave, like that was the underwear's fault? And now he's kicked Rasputin out of the trailer, even though he was only being a puppy. The guy can't be reasoned with."

Deprived of the sock, Rasputin looked around, then hopped up on the couch in a tumble of fur and paws. He flopped over on top of both their laps before Lilah could pull away. She could already feel her eyes starting to tingle, but then there was *puppy belly* in her lap, and really, what was a girl to do? She scritched him, already regretting the choice.

"So I need somewhere for him to stay," Tanner finished, and the pleading eyes he gave both of them were bigger and more devastating than anything Rasputin could manage. "He's too little to stay by himself all day, and if Peter sees him in our trailer again, he's going to lose it."

"He can't stay here," Lilah objected, shaking her head. "I'm going to—*wachoo!*—swell up or stop breathing."

"I'll pay for a week's worth of antihistamines," Tanner promised, one hand over his heart. "And Kleenex."

"He's going to pee on stuff," Noa pointed out.

"I've got pee pads. He's already trained to use those if he can't hold it."

Rasputin wuffled and nosed Lilah's hand to make her keep scratching, and she knew she was sunk. Besides, Tanner was a friend, and if she said no when he really needed help, then what kind of person would he think she was?

"If the antihistamines don't work, you need to find a different solution," Lilah compromised aloud.

"Promise," Tanner replied. "And I'll come to take him out whenever I'm not shooting a scene, so it won't be like you'll have him all the time. You're a lifesaver, Li."

"You owe her, big-time," Noa said, looking over Rasputin and Tanner with a jaundiced eye. "You're lucky she's too nice to say no to you."

Lilah sneezed.

CHAPTER TEN

COFFEE BREAK HADN'T BEEN LONG enough. Noa'd had to run from Lilah's trailer, leaving her alone with Tanner's ridiculous ball of fur, to make it to the hillside where Troy was shooting with the second unit. The gaggle of stunt performers were hanging out in various stages of fake dismemberment, and Noa kept half an eye on the assistant director as he set up a shot.

"Roll it down toward Sam, and try to land it against the rock with his face pointing up," Troy instructed. One of the PAs took the direction, nodding very seriously and in deep thought as he dropped to one knee, a rubber head in his hands. Noa applied a line of blood syrup along the fake scar on the cheek of the costumed stuntman in the chair in front of her and referenced the photo of said rubber head clipped neatly to her clipboard. *Don—decapitated* read the caption underneath.

"Ready to die messily?" she asked. Behind him, the PA rolled the head gently down the slope. It tumbled along the grass, hit a divot, and bounced into the air, landing at Troy's feet.

"Just another day at the office," Don cracked, flashing a quick grin. "Is this your first time with a condemned man?"

"Take two." His head double bounced down the hill and landed facedown in a mud puddle a foot away from the mark.

"Heck no," Noa snorted, deflecting what might be an attempt at flirting. "I serve guys like you up to the dark lords of movie-making on a regular basis. You should see what's going to get pulled out of Peter's rib cage later this week."

"Take three."

"Hang on. Dead Don's got mud up his nose. I gotta pick it."

"Get your finger right up there, kid," Don yelled over his shoulder, his call followed by a volley of good-natured insults back and forth.

"Once we get this shot, we'll put Don up on the hill." Troy gave instructions while Sam rolled the head down the hill a few more times, crossing his fingers with each attempt. "The wing comes down this way, and the claws go across his neck like so. To get the head to roll that way, we want to frame the shot from here." He gestured, his fingers up to make the box of an imagined view screen.

"And we're done," Noa proclaimed, stepping back to cast a critical eye over Don's wound FX. "Out of my chair."

"Ma'am, yes, ma'am," he replied cheerfully, pushing himself out of a soft-backed folding chair. "Dead man walking!"

Noa peeled a wet wipe out of the package and cleaned off her hands, scanning the tree line in case Lilah suddenly decided she wanted to come hang out with second unit instead of kicking her heels in her trailer, but who was she kidding? Noa couldn't compete with new-puppy cuteness. A flash of red hair caught her attention, though it was Sadie, not Lilah, who collapsed happily in

Noa's makeshift station. It was disconcerting, looking at a woman who was dressed and styled to *be* Lilah from a ten-foot distance but who definitely, absolutely wasn't.

"I thought you were principal talent only," Sadie greeted her with a grin, the muscles under her white tank top more defined than Lilah's and her smile less guarded. "What got you demoted to hanging out with the cannon fodder?"

"Denise keeps changing her mind. And since Lilah and Tanner are off duty right now while first unit films Mikal on the cabin roof, *voilà*." Noa gestured at herself. "You guys get me." She frowned at Sadie. "I didn't think you were in this scene?"

"Background action," Sadie replied. "I'm rolling down the hill after Don's shots. Guess they don't want Lilah to worry about scraping her knees."

Noa nodded and flipped through her photo gallery to try and find Sadie's setup for the scene she'd described. "That doesn't sound all that exciting. I thought you guys got into stunt work for the thrill."

"I get swept down river rapids on Wednesday, if that's any consolation," Sadie offered, her grin not fading even as Noa uncorked the blood bottle. "Hey, a bunch of us girls are getting together for drinks later tonight. You should come."

Noa hesitated for a beat, but it didn't feel like Sadie was flirting. "Denise has got a bug up her butt right now about fraternizing with the cast," she apologized.

Sadie snorted. "I'm not cast. I'm fresh meat for the grinder. But suit yourself." She shrugged. "My number's on the call sheet if you change your mind."

"Got it!" Sam cheered in the background. Noa looked up to see him punch his fists in the air as he performed a victory dance on the crest of the hill. Dead Don rested on the mark, staring in frozen and bloody horror up at the clear blue sky.

"Awesome," Troy called up to him. "Now do it while the camera's rolling."

"*Goddammit.*"

Noa slumped back to the motel room and collapsed on the weirdly orange-and-taupe blanket draped over her bed. The motel hallway had smelled suspiciously of bleach, the carpet an undefinable shade of mushroom, but at least rooming with Chrissy was familiar territory. It wasn't a fancy trailer like the lead actors got, set up along the wooded edge of the location's parking lot. But with the mess of electronics and clothes already all over the place, it felt a little bit like home.

"Dan didn't mention anything about letting Tanner bring a dog to location," Chrissy said from the second bed, where she was sprawled out to her full almost six feet of height. "What a pain in the ass! Who gets a puppy when they're going to be filming for a month and a half? Are you both committed to Tanner's babysitting gig now?"

Noa was torn between annoyed and grateful at the reminder. Tanner had interrupted them right when Noa had been about to cave in to her baser instincts and Lilah's gentle persuasion, to instigate something that she was one hundred percent bound to regret. Going over to Lilah's trailer in the first place had probably been a mistake, Denise's warning preying incessantly on every anxiety Noa's brain could produce.

You're going to screw this up.

What "this" was remained unclear—the job, her relationship with Lilah, her relationship with her parents, her chance at a good future, all of the above?

Her brain skittered sideways from trying to parse it all out. She wouldn't be able to anyway—not at one in the morning, when she'd been working sixteen hours straight.

"Not me," Noa replied, rummaging through her backpack to find her battered toiletry bag. Worn-out at all the seams and frayed in the corners, the canvas pouch had been with her on every trip since her first summer of camp. She could afford to replace it now, probably should, but what kind of message would *that* send about loyalty? "Lilah's got him with her back at her trailer now."

"That's kind of sweet, but puppies are a lot of work." Chrissy folded herself up to sitting and dangled her bare feet off the edge of her bed. "I wouldn't want to be the one getting up to let the dog out every two hours. Maybe that's why Tanner dumped him on her."

Noa headed into the motel's small bathroom and dropped her bag on the tiny shelf next to the sink. Chrissy's stuff was already spread everywhere in here as well, taking over most of the counter space. "It wasn't a dump; it was more of a beg. But it's entirely plausible."

"Now that you know she responds well to begging, how long before you get her to tie you up?" Chrissy called out after her, laughing as she teased.

Noa grabbed the first thing to hand—one of Chrissy's breast forms—wheeled around, and chucked it at her head. It hit with surprising accuracy, considering she hadn't stopped to aim. Chrissy yelped, still laughing, and ducked out of the way when the second one followed the same arc through the air.

"You left your boobs in the bathroom," Noa announced sweetly and slammed the door.

She turned on the water and stepped under the half-hearted spray. The water ran down over her body, first hot, then cold when someone down the hall turned on a tap, then flushing warm again a moment later. Noa stood there and let the water run over her, puddling at her feet and around the slow-moving drain.

This morning, she'd had a plan. One that even made sense. Keep away from the temptation of Lilah except for when necessary, explain the problem to her and get her buy-in, then when filming was over, seal the deal. Only none of it had worked out the way she'd wanted it to. Standing there on Lilah's step, faced with reality, it had all vanished from her head in a heartbeat. The moment Lilah was nearby, every carefully constructed plan in Noa's head had popped and vanished, and she couldn't remember what they'd been to begin with. Being in her presence, the light in her hair, the way she moved through the world, skimming over every surface like a dancer, like she was being careful not to leave a mark—it was intoxicating. So was the sound of her voice, warm and soft, honey mixed into tea that soothed every ache and pain in the world, the way her entire *being* lit up with delight when she was happy. The way she'd lit up around the dog.

The way she hadn't lit up around Noa today. Except when

Noa'd tried to back off and give her space, Lilah'd followed her. Not only followed but sat down close enough to practically be in Noa's lap. Her fingertips still remembered the soft, much-washed cotton of Lilah's T-shirt, the sleek feel of the purple throw that Noa recognized from Lilah's house. What did Lilah want? A short-term experiment, a long-term relationship? An on-set fling? So much of who she was was still a kind of mystery, one Noa was sure she wasn't even close to unlocking.

Maybe Noa was overthinking things. It sure as hell wouldn't be the first time. Lilah was sweet and flirty and kind and funny, but that was also what she was paid to be. Her entire childhood had been spent training her to be appealing to other people. And what was that line from Sondheim?

"She was raised to be charming, not sincere."

Noa only realized she'd said that aloud when her own voice echoed off the tile. How long could she cope with this limbo, being so close to Lilah without being allowed to touch, to kiss her the way Noa wanted to? Three weeks had felt doable this morning, but now she was second-guessing everything. It didn't help any that Lilah probably thought Noa was running hot and cold. Like the water in this goddamned motel shower.

Lilah probably wasn't worrying about any of this. Lilah was probably stretched out in her personal star trailer, with her fuzzy blankets and a puppy lolling at her feet, reading her fan mail. It was a good image. A deserved rest. And Noa wanted to be a part of it so badly that it burned.

In the dark of the night, the only light in the trailer coming from the distant set, Lilah wished Noa were there.

There was nothing specifically wrong. Only that it was the witching hour, the countryside was the kind of quiet she wasn't used to anymore, and her mind kept playing tricks on her as she tried desperately to fall asleep.

At first, she'd blamed the coffee, or the adrenaline of having spent a huge chunk of the day running and screaming, or the newness of the trailer. She always had a hard time falling asleep on the first night in a new place. Breathing exercises and relaxation tricks usually worked, but not this time. Rasputin seemed to be picking up on her nerves as well, lifting his head from her feet to stare intently out the window at the black night beyond.

Was that a footstep? There'd been a sound for sure, one that had made Rasputin's ears prick up. Lilah sat very still, knees drawn up to her chest, and listened. Someone whistled in the distance, or maybe it was just the wind. *This is what I get for watching horror movies.* She should text Noa and yell at her for even making that suggestion. But even if she called Noa, bunking down with the rest of the crew at the motel twenty minutes away, what could Noa possibly do?

Her fingers itched to call someone, anyone. Wake up Tanner in his trailer and make him come over, or call home—only it would be 5:00 a.m. in Michigan now, not quite daytime enough to justify waking up her father.

Another faint sound that could have been a person outside or could have been an animal. A raccoon, maybe, scavenging the lunch and dinner garbage from the day. Raccoons weren't scary.

There wouldn't be any bears in these woods. It was a whole different kind of wilderness, a controlled, film-friendly staged hinterland where the worst danger she could face was one of those snakes that Ed had promised her were harmless or an autograph seeker with no respect for basic boundaries. And they were what security was for.

Lilah hauled herself up and wrapped her throw around her like a cape. A superhero cape this time, giving her the powers she needed to protect herself. A cape and a weapon—her travel hair dryer lay where she'd left it on the table that afternoon, and she grabbed it as well. In the dark, maybe it would look enough like a gun that she could fool the prowler long enough to figure out her next move. She'd learned self-defense moves for *Second Wind*, after all. She didn't need anyone to save her—she was the Final Girl.

Which implies everyone else on set is dead already, so maybe I need a better pep talk.

The scuffling sounds had stopped, and so had the whistle. The night was silent. A car raced by somewhere in the distance, engine revving.

Lilah laid her hand on the door handle. She flipped the lock.

She opened the door.

No one was there.

Flinging it wide, hair dryer clutched in her hand, she stepped to the threshold and looked around. Tanner and Peter's trailer sat about fifty feet down the path, hair and makeup beyond that. Stacks of equipment and boxes covered with tarps made black silhouettes against the night sky. And that was all.

Lilah let out a long, shaky breath, her shoulders sagging in relief. She glanced quickly along the sides of her trailer in case she could spot a raccoon or skunk doing its thing, but there was no sign of wildlife either. None except for the puppy, who jammed his head between her ankles and sniffed at the air. He let out a high-pitched bark into the darkness.

A flashlight lit up and swung her way. An indistinct shape formed out of the darkness, picked out only by the cone of light.

Lilah muffled a shriek, hand slapping over her mouth to try to deaden the sound. She aimed the hair dryer at the shape. The flashlight beam swung up to blind her, and she heard a yelp that mirrored her own. The shape ducked away from the hair dryer, the light playing over her again a second later. "Miss Silver?"

The voice was familiar. "Wayne?" *Oh, thank goodness.*

"Don't shoot," the security guard requested, a laugh in his voice. "I thought I heard something, but I didn't expect to be held at hair-dryer point. Everything all right, Miss Silver?" The light still shone in her eyes, and Lilah tried to shield them with a hand. He lowered the beam after a moment, and Lilah blinked to clear the purple spots from her vision.

"Yes, yes thank you. Everything's fine." She lifted her hair dryer and kept her head high, grinning as though she was sharing a joke rather than being totally embarrassed at being caught waving it around like an idiot, by *security* of all people. "I'm armed and ready for anything."

Wayne nodded at her companionably, almost confidentially. He wasn't in his uniform, she noticed absently, but a gray collared shirt over a T-shirt. He had a bucket under his arm that rustled in a familiar way. Snake patrol. He must have been doing a final sweep after shift change or heard her and Rasputin on his way to dump the bucket. "I can see that. Armed and dangerous. Is there anything I can help you with? Some serving and protecting in your hour of need?"

He was kind, and she felt even more foolish for her moment of suspicion. Rasputin tried to push his way out into the night air, and she struggled to keep him inside, behind the door. "No, thank you! Everything's good," she added in a strangled tone, the puppy getting more insistent behind her.

The security guard craned his neck like he was trying to see inside, lingering on her bottom step.

"Good night," Lilah said firmly.

"Good night, Miss Silver." He didn't take the hint until she closed the door, and even then, it took a half a minute before she heard his footsteps moving away.

Rasputin whined, and she knelt down to smoosh his curly face and sweet-talk him, despite the warning tingle in her eyes. "Don't you worry, sweet baby," Lilah cooed. "Wayne's not going to turn you over to mean old Peter. Even if I did threaten to blow-dry him to death."

Knowing security was on duty made her feel a little better, honestly. Still, she double-checked the locks and made sure the deadbolt slid home. She drew the curtains tight over the windows, even though it would block out the morning sun. Waking up with the growing light was a lot easier than doing it with the insistent beep of the alarm, but she'd forego that tomorrow in return for knowing that no one was going to be looking in.

Flopping down on the small couch-turned-bed, Lilah popped

open her email. She hoped for an email from Noa, something to soothe her nerves and reassure her that they were still on the same page. Sending one herself felt dangerous, like she'd be asking for more than Noa might be prepared to give. If you had to beg for someone's attention, then it didn't mean anything once you got it.

There weren't any emails from Noa, explanatory or otherwise. There was a very sweet card from her parents on a hearts-and-flowers background, congratulating her on the callback for *Night of Anubis*, and she dashed off a quick thank you. Then, on second thought, she scheduled it to send in about three hours. Otherwise, Mom would look at the time stamp and be all up in Lilah's texts about why she was awake in the middle of the night.

That folder she'd set up for fan mail, following Brooke's instructions, had three unread messages.

Unwisely, she looked.

Are you blocking me? That's very rude to do to your biggest fan. I thought you looked great on set today, by the way. Your knife work is really improving.

Cold chills and nausea settled into her stomach worse than last time.

Lilah shoved her phone into her bag and curled up in bed. Rasputin wuffled his way over, sniffing every inch of the floor between them, and pushed his cold nose against her arm. Curling up around him, she considered grabbing the teddy bear from Noa as an extra comfort. But it would only serve as a reminder now that Noa wasn't here. And if she was, would she be any help, or would she tease Lilah for being a silly girlie-girl waiting for someone else to save her? She liked tough girls after all.

Could you be any more of a stereotype? Noa'd been teasing Tanner, but the question echoed with a deeper resonance.

Ten minutes ago, Lilah'd felt like a superhero. Now she just felt tired.

"You'll protect me, won't you?" she asked Rasputin. He licked her nose and didn't judge.

CHAPTER ELEVEN

NOA'D INTENDED TO PLAY EVERYTHING totally cool the next morning. It didn't last long.

Lilah was curled up in the makeup chair in a baggy gray hoodie, the sleeves pulled down over her hands as she cradled a cup of coffee between them. Faint purple smudges marked bags under her eyes, her strawberry-gold waves pulled back in a hasty, unbrushed ponytail.

"Rough night with the new man?" Noa asked as a joke, but the wan smile she got in return was hardly worth the effort.

"I don't sleep well the first night in a new place. I'll be fine once I've had my coffee," Lilah explained, but there had to be more to it than that. Her attention jumped to over Noa's shoulder when the door swung open, and Noa could have sworn that Lilah'd flinched at the sound. Noa's protective instincts swelled up inside her. Lilah was everything gentle, kind, and soft; she couldn't say no to anyone to save her life. Noa'd seen that firsthand yesterday. Which meant if she was in trouble, Noa needed to be there to save her from herself.

"Seriously," Noa said quietly, perching on the counter next to Lilah's chair. She grabbed a concealer stick and leaned in, pretending to be looking at Lilah's skin while she spoke. "You're all upset—something's wrong."

Lilah shook her head, leaning away, expression blossoming into one of her big pageant smiles, all teeth and no sparkle. "I'm fine, honest! The running and screaming wears on you after a couple of days, and it's all the 'escape the burning cabin' exteriors today and tomorrow. I'm not looking forward to this part, even with Sadie doing the worst of the stunts."

"Liar. That's a fake smile," Noa pointed out. Denise wasn't in the trailer, and no one was watching, so she laid a hand protectively on Lilah's arm.

"Know me that well, do you?" Lilah murmured, turning her head in toward Noa, some loose tendrils of hair sweeping across her face.

"I like to think I'm learning. Don't pretend around me anymore, please? I like the real you. The more I learn about her, the better I like her." Was it a pipe dream? How could you really know what went on in someone else's mind? But Lilah had her tells, and Noa resonated along with them.

Lilah met her eyes for the first time that morning, the dark circles a sign of how stressed out she had to be. "Not a lot of people want that, you know," she said, trying to tease, the lightness in her voice falling flat. "Pretending is the thing I'm best at."

Oh, there it was, an undercurrent of sadness that Noa hadn't really noticed before, so preoccupied with her hair, her eyes, her laugh—she would do better, for Lilah's sake and for her own.

She'd *be* better. "Pretending's your job, but it's not everything you are."

Noa stroked the pad of her thumb along the inside of Lilah's wrist and felt a tiny shiver go through her at the touch. She felt Lilah's stress down through every fiber of her being and ached to be the one who could soothe it. "Be real with me, please. No more false faces or stage smiles? I can see when they don't reach your eyes. Let me help."

Lilah hesitated, her teeth pressing white into her lower lip as she searched Noa's expression for something. Evidently satisfied, she nodded slowly. "Deal. But you have to promise not to laugh at me when I do."

"I promise." Noa nodded emphatically, curling her fingers around Lilah's hand to give her something grounded, someone to lean on.

"It's nothing. At least, I'm sure it's nothing. I—"

The trailer door opened again, and Lilah and Noa jumped apart, put professional distance between them again as Denise swept in like a storm cloud.

"After," Noa promised and caught Lilah's eye to try and impress on her how much she meant it, even as she reached for her kit.

"Burns today, Noa," Denise shrilled. "Don't forget to consult the design pack!"

"On it," Noa called back, the interruption rankling even though she knew she shouldn't let it. All these shouldn'ts and shoulds were starting to grate in new, awful ways, chafing against what she really wanted to do, which was pull Lilah into her arms and rub her back until all that tension bled away.

Lilah set her mug aside and stripped off her sweatshirt, her arms bare in the tank top she wore underneath. Noa fought the flush, the ache, the sudden rush of *I want* that surged up inside. Wrong place, wrong time, wrong mood, wrong everything!

Noa caught Lilah's eye the moment Denise turned away. Lilah's shirt didn't cover her shoulder where one of the wound prosthetics was going to go, a claw slash two inches long and a good inch wide. Right now, her skin was clean and bare, a dusting of pale brown freckles scattered haphazardly across the curve. Noa reached for a liquid eyeliner from her kit and leaned in close.

Uncapping the eyeliner, she stroked the tiny brush across Lilah's skin, leaving a fine black line behind. Lilah shuddered, or maybe it was a shiver, her thigh pressing tight against Noa's knee.

"What are you doing?" Lilah murmured, the faintest low rumble meant for Noa's ears alone.

"A reminder, to have with you all day," Noa murmured back, lips so close to Lilah's ear that she barely needed to make a sound. Lilah's hair swept against Noa's cheek, her body so warm and tight against Noa's that even the smallest breath made her feel like she was about to shatter apart.

Denise would be back around to them any moment now. Noa willed her hand not to tremble as she finished the big curve, then the little one, a flick of the brush—another shiver running across Lilah's skin—and a kiss of the finest hair against a freckle for the curled end of the butterfly's wing.

"It'll all be okay," she vowed, not knowing exactly how but knowing that if Lilah needed it, Noa would make it happen. "You're a butterfly, Final Girl, and everything's gonna work out okay."

"Promise?" Lilah asked equally quietly.

"Promise."

Lilah craned her neck to look at her reflection, a real smile replacing the fake, glassed-over look in her eyes. "I believe you."

"Time is money, people!" someone shouted from the trailer door, and Noa jumped away. The moment broke, crystal shards of almosts and maybes spinning free and turning to mist in the air. Within minutes, she had the butterfly doodle covered up with the wound makeup, and the rest of Lilah's glue and paint followed as quickly as Noa's hands could move.

Denise hovering and pointing out corrections meant they couldn't talk anymore, not until they were released and Noa was walking Lilah across the field to the cabin. "I'm sorry I suck at texting," Noa tried, and that worked.

Lilah nodded, smiled, and Noa was apparently forgiven. "It's fine," Lilah said. "We'll talk later? Right now, I've got to go panic for a few hours."

Noa nodded, holding on to that thin thread of hope, one getting thicker by the moment. "Later definitely. Now go show them how a scream queen gets things done."

She held out her fist to Lilah, who obligingly bumped it with her closed knuckles, then jogged off toward the camera crew. Noa followed at a more sedate pace, trying desperately to keep her mind where it needed to be—on the job.

The morning was a lot of the same take from different angles, Lilah and Sadie taking turns going in and out of a window onto a mattress lying out of frame while Ed got a million and one reaction shots. Noa was on call for touch-ups and photographs and a lot of waiting and watching. Dan Gilbert hovered, watching the video screens over Ed's shoulder and complaining incessantly about the schedule.

The tension on the set was a new and unpleasant thing as well. Peter stuck by Lilah's side and was snide and dismissive to Tanner, especially after his pant hem caught a spark. Three crew guys dogpiled him with fire extinguishers to get it out. The end of his tirade "...wouldn't have happened if I still had my lucky boxers!" carried on the wind.

During the break that followed for resetting, it took three of the grips and the set dresser to remove a particularly persistent gopher snake from the inside tubing of Ed's folding chair.

Denise was wherever Peter *wasn't*, which generally meant right under Noa's nose or looming behind Ed in video village with her arms folded, looking like some demented gargoyle. She started in Noa's direction when break was called, but Ed intercepted Denise long enough for Noa to make her getaway. She bolted for the crew trailer and the promise of the coffeepot before she could get hauled up by the scruff of her neck for some other imagined infraction.

The trailer was buzzing, snippets of conversations rising and falling around her as Noa made her way through the crowded space.

"At least four safety violations on the fire bars alone..."

"Who's going to call the fire marshal on Dan? You?"

"...working a Fraturday call; the night shoot's going to four a.m. I haven't seen my kids awake in three weeks."

"And no one checked to make sure the trucking supervisor had a valid driver's license?"

One of the casting assistants pushed past, an earpiece and dangling cord the only sign that she wasn't running lines or talking to the air. "What do you *mean* she's six months pregnant? Can we maybe...I don't know. There's no time to recast, so rework the shot. Make her carry a plant. I'm sure there are plants in forest ranger offices, they're *forest* rangers for crying out loud! Give her a potted fern and move on!"

The coffeepot was down to the dregs, and PJ wasn't there to refill it, worse luck. Noa dropped her phone and keys on the toaster oven, the only clear space, and started searching the cabinets for the filters.

A few minutes later, the coffee was perking away happily, the blissful smell of hot caffeine sinking into every one of Noa's brain cells. Caffeine and...something.

Something acrid, that smelled an awful lot like burning.

Noa whipped around, sniffing the air. The coffeepot was clear, the microwave was off, the toaster oven was glowing red, a tray of pizza bagels bubbling inside and her phone sizzling happily on top.

Yelping, Noa lunged and grabbed her phone, the case burning hot against her fingers and the cards shoved in the pocket drooping toward her fingers as they squished into the melting plastic. What to do, what—inspiration struck, and she wrenched open the freezer door, shoving her phone and the melting cards inside before slamming it shut again.

"Ow," Noa hissed, shaking her stinging fingers.

"My pizza bagels!" one of the grips complained and wrinkled her nose at the smell.

"Forget your bagels, you set fire to my phone!"

"It's not on fire, and I didn't see it there. Why would you put your phone down on an oven?"

"Ovens are only supposed to get hot on the *inside*," Noa huffed, feeling entirely within her rights to be annoyed. She left the freezer door closed until she absolutely couldn't stand the not knowing a second longer. Her phone looked okay, at least at first examination, but the cards shoved into the pocket on the back—her driver's license and her set ID—had gone all wobbly and rippled, like the world's ugliest Shrinky Dinks.

"Oh *shit*," Noa sighed, mostly to herself, as she tried to flatten the set swipe card out with her fingers. No dice. The now-cool surface was still kind of rectangle shaped, but the new wavy edges weren't budging. Maybe if she ironed them...

Or that could end up melting the cards to her table. Noa shoved the cards back into the phone pocket, the edges of that starting to curl up as well. Great. Denise was up her nose, Lilah was seriously on edge, and now Noa was going to look completely irresponsible whenever she had to show her ID for anything.

Eight hours left on the day's schedule. Surely they could make it without something else going wrong.

———————————

"Truck's on fire."

PJ, not a man of many words in the best of circumstances, was downright monosyllabic when he came charging into the makeup trailer seven and a half hours later. He raced for the sink and the buckets next to it, turning on all the taps at once.

Noa looked up from the silicone patch she was peeling off Lilah's thigh, her hands stilling in shock. "I'm sorry, what?"

Already halfway across the room, mostly full bucket in hand and the water left running, PJ only repeated, "Truck's on fire!" and vanished out the open door.

"Like, *fire* fire?" Noa asked, pushing to her feet and trailing along in his wake. The panic and the yelling in the parking lot proved he wasn't messing with them; small flames jumped out of the back of the truck where the fire bar, hosing, and gas tanks had been packed away. A couple of the stunties in fire-retardant gear, Sadie among them, were hauling ass in and out of the truck, rescuing props and equipment. Dr. Crosby was in the middle of everything, flailing and generally getting in the way, while PJ ran back and forth with his water buckets. Behind her, she heard Lilah on the phone. "Hello, 911?"

She couldn't just stand and watch. Noa vaulted down the trailer steps and ran for her car. The tub of junk from her father was still in the trunk. She grabbed the first thing that looked like it might be useful and bolted in the direction of the shouting.

"Smother it!" Someone yelled the general request at no one in particular.

"Wardrobe's coming with wet towels."

"What started it?"

"How the hell should I know?"

PJ flung his buckets over the base of the flames and they died in a billow of steam, smoke, and charred bits of paper. Noa coughed at and choked on the rancid air, waving it away from her face. A steady stream of hissing steam continued to pour from the pile of wet debris. She went to pull the pin from her extinguisher, only to find that she'd grabbed the tiny 8" one meant to do things like douse sparks from a blown fuse.

Still! Noa pulled the pin and hit the trigger, half expecting the canister to kick in her hand. A tiny lick of flame popped up underneath a wet coil of rope, and she zapped it with the fizzle-y stream of powder until it vanished in a pathetically quiet hiss. So there.

Noa stood silently with PJ in the middle of the sodden mess of the smoke-filled truck and surveyed the damage with a grimace.

"Whoa," she said.

Sirens blared in the distance, fire department on their way.

PJ nodded and tugged the brim of his cap down over his brow. He sighed heavily, shoving his hands in his pockets. "We're all gonna get fired."

The smell of smoke lingered in the cool night air long after the flames had died and the fire engines had pulled away. Lilah sat on the steps of her trailer, Rasputin's head on her knee like he knew she needed him, her fingers buried in his thick, curly fur. Crew members walked between the piles of wet and partly charred parts recovered from the back of the truck, voices rising and falling on the breeze.

The fire shouldn't have happened. What could possibly make the back of a truck suddenly go up in flames when no one was in it? Maybe it was a warning. There'd been another message waiting for her when she'd called the fire department, one that she desperately wanted to forget.

You'll warm up to me, like it or not.

Had *he* done it to get her attention? Would Lilah's trailer be the next thing to go up in flames?

Lilah hugged Rasputin tighter, and the puppy whined softly until she let him go. It was his wriggle and wet tongue against her elbow that settled Lilah's mind. It wasn't just Lilah in danger. If her "biggest fan" was crazy enough to set fire to the effects truck, what might he do to a helpless baby animal that got in his way?

She pushed herself to her feet and chewed her bottom lip, trying to make up her mind. Peter was standing at the edge of the circle of light being cast over the mess by the big set lamps, watching the cleanup process with faint interest. Lilah shut Rasputin in her trailer and headed toward him, pulling her purple blanket tight around her shoulders to ward off the night.

Final girls are supposed to be tough and save ourselves. I don't want to be that anymore.

Peter looked up as she approached, the furrowed brow smoothing out into something kinder when he caught sight of her. Did she really look that awful? "Hey there, kiddo." He greeted her genially, a far cry from the sourpuss he'd been on set all day.

"Hey, Professor." She forced a smile, but even she couldn't keep up the act for very long and felt it faltering much too soon. He didn't even grumble at her for teasing him with the nickname, so she must look like hell warmed over. Lilah cringed inwardly at the thought and pulled the blanket closer around herself. "Watching the mess?"

"What else?" Peter snorted, nodding at the chaos surrounding the unloaded truck. "We're surrounded by incompetents."

And that sounded more like the Peter she knew. "I think," Lilah began to say, then faltered under the weight of the shame. "I think this was my fault," she confessed, the words coming out in a whisper.

He cocked his head at her, and the frown settled back in on his thick gray eyebrows. "Come again? You don't strike me as the secret-smoker type."

"I don't smoke," Lilah answered before she understood what he was implying.

"So not your cigarette butt, then."

"No! Cigarette?"

"I'm assuming." He shrugged. "Half the cast and crew light up when given half a chance. One carelessly tossed butt later and half of California's down to ashes again."

"I don't mean like that," Lilah answered, her gut churning over the words she had to force out. "I mean I think someone might have set the fire. On purpose. Because of me."

"Don't be ridiculous," he scoffed, but his laugh stopped when he looked at her, *really* looked at her, and his face twisted in a funny way. "You're serious."

Lilah nodded miserably. "There's this guy who's been sending all kinds of messages and commenting on my pictures on social media, and it got weird. So I started blocking him. And then this happened."

"Oh, kiddo. You must be freaking out. Come here," he offered, all solicitous and kind, the way he'd been that first week of filming. Peter slung his arm around her shoulders, and she gave in to the urge to rest her head on his, all warm and safe and protected. At least for a moment. Noa had promised not to laugh at her, but Noa wasn't there, and Lilah had run out of the energy she needed to pretend to be tough.

She pulled away after a moment, super conscious suddenly that they were in full view of everyone—and possibly someone she couldn't even see. "Anyway, I'm definitely freaking out now, and I don't know what to do about it," she confessed. "I can't go to the police, not without any kind of proof. You must have dealt with creepy fans before."

"Autograph hunters, sure, but it's not the same, and I think we both know why," Peter said, and his pointed reminder did nothing to help her mood. "This is above my pay grade. Come with me, and we'll go find Dan. If there's someone creeping on his set, he'll make the call."

Lilah sucked in breath. "And do what? He wouldn't shut down production." Not over her, not and make everyone else lose out on so much! Noa wouldn't have a job, and she needed at least another couple of weeks. Lilah could have kept her mouth shut. Only, what would have happened if PJ or Colin had been in that truck? Her head swam, and she blinked away the tears that threatened.

"Over some nutcase star chaser? Not likely," Peter scoffed. "More likely he'll bring in a bunch of extra security guys. Even a tightwad like Dan Gilbert can be shaken down for a little extra cash if our leading lady's safety is on the line. You'll see, honey," he reassured her, resting his hand familiarly on the small of her back as he steered her toward the trailer that doubled as the production office. "Everything's going to be fine."

Fine meant something a little different to Peter than it apparently did to Lilah, but in the end, she couldn't complain about the arrangements. Maybe it was Peter's solid presence behind her, and maybe it was the look on her face, but the producer actually took her seriously when she described what had been going on. And the fire, though Dan frowned and shook his head when she suggested that her stal—*admirer* had been responsible. "The fire bars weren't cooled down enough when they were loaded in," he said, dismissing her fears. "Someone packed the blackout curtains on top of them, and the heat buildup ignited the moose. The timing is shitty, but it wasn't deliberate. Just stupid."

He said it with such confidence that Lilah couldn't help but believe him, the guilt replaced by sheepishness for raising a problem where one hadn't been. Not for anyone but her at least. "That does make me feel better," she admitted, and Dan nodded reassuringly.

"And the other issue," Peter pressed, and Lilah shifted in the hard office chair.

"Maybe I shouldn't have said anything," she said, second-guessing herself out loud. "It's like you said, there's lots of set security, and I didn't actually *see* anyone."

Dan sat on the edge of his desk, arms folded, and his face

read full of concern—so much so that an ungrateful part of her wondered if it was fake. "I want you to feel like you can come to me about anything, Lilah. You're important to this movie—to all of us," he added, not quite as an afterthought. "Let me handle it. I only need one thing from you."

"What's that?"

His eyes narrowed at her, and that unsettled, unsafe feeling surged up again. "Let me handle *all* of it. The studio and the investors are already on edge about the financing, and you know how panicked people get over schedule changes. If rumors start spreading about the set being unsafe or our star being targeted, well…you know what gossip is like in this industry. The story would grow—"

"And you don't want any bad publicity," Peter added dryly from over Lilah's shoulder.

"Do you?" Dan asked him, whip fast in his reply. "Remember what happened to the *Twilight Zone*? Or *Poltergeist*? The last thing we need is to have idiots declaring that there's a curse on the movie. Then there'll be lookie-loos all over the place and no way to tell the threat from the fanboy bloggers. Then how will we be able to keep Lilah safe?"

Despite the way he kept using her name, Lilah didn't exactly feel like the focus of his concern. And she wouldn't even be able to talk to Noa about anything that had happened? "You don't want me to mention it to anyone? Not even security?"

"You wouldn't want to be the reason filming gets shut down, would you?"

"No!" Lilah answered quickly, shaking her head. "Absolutely not. So many people have already put so much work into this."

"Exactly. Trust me, I'll take care of everything," Dan said, trying to soothe her, his hand resting lightly, chastely, on her knee for a brief moment. A smile that was probably supposed to look reassuring turned up the corners of his mouth. Her skin crawled at the touch, and it took all her willpower to move away subtly instead of kicking him. "All you have to do is focus on your job. Keep your mouth shut, and everything will be all right."

It made sense, sort of. And when it came down to it, did she really have a choice? Lilah nodded hesitantly. And when she and Peter left Dan's office, the only answer he gave to her questioning look was a shrug.

The long and short of it was that a new rule came down, blamed on insurance after the fire. No one was to spend the night on set, at least not until it was confirmed as an accident. But rather than drive everyone back to LA at one in the morning, Lilah found herself deposited at the crew's motel with her overnight bag, another warning not to spread unfounded rumors, and very little else.

"Are they going to have enough rooms for all of us?" Ishani asked, coming up behind Lilah with her backpack slung over her shoulder. They'd been left for the last round in the hastily arranged carpools, given time to pack their essentials from their trailers. Lilah hadn't been sorry to leave location behind in the dark.

"We're doubling and tripling up for tonight" came the answer from one of the harried PAs, a checklist in hand and a blaring phone on his hip. "Chrissy made up a roster, and we'll figure out different billets in the morning. Please, guys—don't bitch to me about this one. None of this was my call."

"I don't care what Gilbert's assistant decided, I'm *not* staying in a room with Tanner and that garbage disposal that he calls a dog," Peter huffed.

"Unwad your jock." Tanner scowled at him, shifting Rasputin protectively under his arm, and the puppy barked.

Peter scowled back. "I would, but he *ate it*."

"Tanner's with Mikal and PJ in twenty-one; you're in with Ed in twelve. Ishani, the motel's putting a cot in with Phoebe and Karen for you. Room fourteen."

Ishani nodded. "Hair and wardrobe, sweet. I'll be ready before any of y'all tomorrow."

"And me?" Lilah asked, heart thumping loudly for no reason she could immediately name. "Where am I sleeping tonight?"

The PA flipped the page and scanned down the list as what felt like a million awkward seconds ticked loudly by. Or maybe that was Lilah's breathing, the weight of the evening and...and *everything* beating down on her at once.

"Room eight," he replied, and the lump in her throat didn't subside. "Noa and Chrissy. You know them, right? One's Mr. Gilbert's PA and the other is—"

"Makeup assistant," Lilah breathed out, part of her resigned and mortified, the other screaming incoherently inside. "We're friends. It's cool."

"Awesome. The time is now..." He looked at his watch, a black line against his wrist in the lobby lights. "One a.m. Breakfast is at six, everyone on set for quarter to seven. Get sleep."

"Oh, for Pete's sake—"

"Not my call, man."

"Five hours? That's not enough sleep."

"It'll be four if you don't get a move on."

"If I can't get a decent shower before bed, I'm quitting this turkey operation. They can edit Kevin Costner over my face for all I care."

Lilah left the complaining behind and headed down the hall, the smell of cleaning supplies making the air hard to breathe. It wasn't going to be anything fun, she scolded herself. Noa's roommate was there, and Noa was running so scared of Denise, it would be amazing if Lilah even got a word out of her all night. Which was going to be barely enough time to sleep a little and then shower.

Oh God. Noa in the shower. Sharing a bathroom, seeing her with her hair all mussed up first thing in the morning—the thought was almost enough to make Lilah miss her step, catching herself before she could do more than a little shuffle stumble that would have cost her poise scores once upon a time.

She wasn't being watched now. She was going down the hallway to knock on a door and have a safe, warm space to sleep with trustworthy people nearby. People who knew her and with whom she could be...well, no. Not herself, but a tougher, brighter, *better* version of herself. With Claudia's flirty sensuality and Jordyn's self-confidence, Noa's sharp humor, Chrissy's presence when she entered a room... See? She knew *four whole lesbians* now, and she could pull enough inspiration from each of them to make a newer, better version of herself.

One who didn't run scared because of some dumb internet comments.

Some comments, emails, and potentially a prowler outside her trailer, but Peter was probably right. They'd add more set security, and in the end, everything would be fine.

Having talked herself back into a better state of mind, despite the exhaustion and worry clawing at her temples, Lilah drew to a stop in front of the door to room eight. She lifted her hand to knock, pausing only at the sound of thumping inside.

She hesitated, then leaned in to listen and try and make out the muffled voices.

"Can't believe you!"

A laugh, then indistinctly: *"Please, like you don't want—"* followed by what sounded like...a closet door?

"That's not the point! I'm...to talk to—" The door opened, and Lilah jumped away, hand still in the air and face flushing hot. "—front desk," Noa finished lamely, her arm halfway into a hoodie half-on over a *Ginger Snaps* T-shirt that was obviously part of her sleepwear, considering the small plaid boxer shorts that were all she was wearing underneath. "Uh," Noa said eloquently. "Hi."

Noa's fluster gave Lilah the chance to recover, at least a little bit. Her eyes kept going down to Noa's legs, the most skin she'd ever seen on Noa, the muscles defined in her calves, and the boxers that ended at midthigh. "You forgot your pants," Lilah said, the first words that came to mind. "Is this a bad time?"

"I was, um. Going for ice. Figured the ice machine wouldn't mind." Noa's lie wasn't convincing, but Lilah decided that she didn't want to care.

"It won't." Transfixed by the closeness, the bare inch of space between them, Lilah was frozen in time. Noa's chin tilted up, and their gazes locked, a thrum of energy pulsing between them that was almost tangible in the air. The tip of Noa's tongue touched her lower lip, a nervous gesture that drew all Lilah's focus, imagining in a single moment of exhausted vulnerability—*what if*. Those first two kisses had been so sweet.

The guys were behind her coming down from the lobby now, and Lilah really didn't want to be explaining Noa's lack of pants to the mob, so she took a step to the left to go around as Noa stepped to her right, blocking Lilah off again.

"Sorry, I—" Noa stuttered as Lilah said "oops," and then went to her left just as *Lilah* went right—

"Let her in already!" Chrissy's cheerful voice came from around the corner, and muttering under her breath, Noa backed inside. Lilah grabbed the door before it closed on her foot and followed.

It didn't look like she had been expected, even though Chrissy had been the one to make the new rooming list. Clothes, makeup, and paperwork were scattered over every flat surface and draped over the nonflat ones, a bundle of cords and chargers already a massive spaghetti tangle from the single outlet in the wall. Chrissy had taken over one of the two queen-size beds, her long legs supporting her laptop, a tablet, binder, and portable printer all taking up half the bed beside her. The other one had to be Noa's, the covers flung back but otherwise empty.

There was no couch.

"Thanks for letting me crash here with you." Lilah directed that at Chrissy. Noa followed Lilah inside, tossing her hoodie toward the nearest chair. It slid off into a heap on the floor. "How long until the front desk gets a cot in here?"

"Oh, they ran out," Chrissy replied, still smiling like the cat that ate the canary. Noa made a muffled sound of agony behind her, but by the time Lilah turned, Noa had vanished into the bathroom and closed the door. "You'll have to share the bed with Noa. I hope you don't mind."

CHAPTER TWELVE

LILAH'S AND CHRISSY'S MUFFLED VOICES rose and fell outside the bathroom door, but Noa hadn't heard a scream of anguish that would suggest Lilah had objected to the setup. What were they talking about out there? About the situation? About Noa? Chrissy was supposed to be Noa's best friend, only this was…this was… this was a mess, and Chrissy was doing what she did best, which was meddle with the best of intentions. Would it have killed her to call dibs on a cot?

Noa stared at herself bleakly in the motel bathroom mirror, the crack that ran across one corner jarring her reflection into two distinct sections. "Come on," she coaxed herself, one side of her mouth quirking up in the mirror to laugh at the other. "You're being stupid. And tired. You'll go to bed and pass out in seconds— nothing awkward about it."

But oh, the soft heat of Lilah's skin under her hands, the way she'd shivered under Noa's touch, and the intensity in her eyes when she'd stared at Noa only moments ago—and now they were supposed to share a bed?

"Actors do this kind of shit all the time," she told her reflection firmly. "Sex scenes even. Behave and pretend this is normal."

Normal meant acting like professional adults who didn't have a thing for each other, and the wreck in the bathroom definitely wasn't that. Noa took control over the one aspect of life she could control and swept the scattered toiletries and cosmetics into the drawer beside the sink. Once the counter was clear, the towel hung up, she started to breathe a little easier.

"Everything okay in there?" The knock on the bathroom door was followed by Lilah's quiet concern, and Noa drew in a deep breath.

"Oh yeah," she replied breezily, opening the door and striding out as confidently as she could muster. "I'm cleaning up so you have somewhere to put your stuff. Bathroom's all yours now."

Lilah looked like she was about to say something more, but all she did was frown and head into the bathroom, door closing behind her.

Chrissy grinned.

"You are such an asshole," Noa said quietly, and only once the water had turned on in the room behind her. "*Such* an asshole."

"You love me," Chrissy replied, all smug.

"I hate you."

"Bullshit. Cuddle your girl tonight and stop stressing out."

Noa bit her tongue, *hard*. "She's not 'my girl,'" she hissed at Chrissy, flopping down onto the bed that she was going to have to share with Lilah in only a few short minutes. "Not yet anyway," she mumbled under her breath. "Maybe not ever."

"Denise can go piss up a rope," Chrissy retorted, cutting to the heart of the matter.

"You only say that because she can't fire you. Besides, that's not the only issue. We're probably not long-term compatible," Noa said, justifying her fear out loud, though in her heart of hearts, she knew it for what it was: total bullshit. Lilah was already opening Noa's eyes to new ways of looking at the world, and she was having a hard time imagining what this gig would have been like without her.

Chrissy snorted, closing her laptop and putting it aside. "You keep on telling yourself that."

She went about her evening routine, the makeup the last thing to come off before bed, while Noa tried to become one with the sheets. She folded her hands behind her head and stared at the ceiling, trying not to listen to the sound of the shower turning off and imagine what Lilah would be doing right now. She'd squeeze the water from her long hair, the trickles running down over her forearm and dripping to the floor—was her towel on her now or not?

It was a particularly personal form of mental torture that Noa was too weak to avoid inflicting on herself, especially since she could map out ninety percent of Lilah's body in her mind's eye with perfect ease, every curve, divot, and sweet round swell.

"ARGH." Noa flipped over and shoved her head under her pillow as the door opened and footsteps padded across the room.

"Is...she okay?" Lilah asked again, muffled by the pillow.

"Oh yeah" came Chrissy's cavalier response, because Noa's best friend was a traitor. "She's a little stressed. Ignore it."

The bed dipped on the opposite side, and Noa dared a peek

out from under the safety of the pillow. Was she...? No, to both Noa's deep disappointment and sweeping relief, Lilah was wearing pajamas, pink ones, with big red lips on the side of the butt that Noa could see from her sideways vantage point. Tacky pajamas, then, but better than a towel or some little lingerie...thing.

Noa sat up, desperate to shake the images out of her head and replace them with something more innocent, friendly, and professional. "Every project has a moment where you've just got to scream into a pillow, am I right?" Noa improvised, hoping that didn't sound as dumb as it seemed.

Lilah finished tying her hair into a loose braid and nodded, maybe a little less convinced than she might be. "Tonight definitely qualifies for that. You should have heard Peter out there. He was ready to walk off the project if he had to have Rasputin in his room."

"Never trust a man who doesn't like dogs." Chrissy finished at the mirror and tossed the cotton makeup pad at the garbage can. "Nothin' but net. You ladies ready to hit the hay? Because I'm wiped."

"Yes," Lilah replied immediately, still sitting on the edge of the bed and not looking at Noa. She was not-looking so carefully that it had to mean something, didn't it? Was it the same thing that had been stressing her out that morning? Or the fire that had apparently annoyed the producer enough to move all of the cast back to the motel? Noa hated not knowing, but Chrissy hadn't had any more details about the evening's events than Noa did, and almost two in the morning when everyone was exhausted and on edge was not the time to ask. "The sooner today is over and tomorrow happens, the better."

"I hate to tell you, but tomorrow's already happening all around us. Not it for turning off the lights," Noa replied, trying to keep things light. She made a show of settling in on her side of the bed, waaaaaay over on her side of the bed, and closing her eyes.

The mattress dipped after a moment, and on her other side, Noa heard Chrissy get up with a sigh and a groan and pad across the room to flip the light switch.

"Good night," Lilah said softly beside her.

"Night," Chrissy replied, halfway through a yawn. "Sleep tight, you two."

"Night," Noa muttered, folding her arms across her stomach and lying stiffly underneath the cheap cotton-blend sheet. The darkness should have made it easier to tune out, but it made things so much worse. Lilah turned over and Noa felt it. She breathed in and Noa heard it, the air filling her own lungs in the same rhythm without her consciously deciding to synchronize. Every nerve ending of her left side resonated with the knowledge of Lilah's presence, her warmth seeping into Noa's pores from inches away.

What was the point of this dance, this push and pull Noa had been living for the last few days? When they were apart, she could come up with a dozen different very good reasons for waiting, for putting her hopeless pining on hold until it was safe to ask Lilah out for real. Then when she was nearby, like now, and her body yearned for Lilah's touch, it was as though she'd never made a list at all. None of the problems felt like problems, melting away in the sunshine of Lilah's smile.

Until the next time Noa had to face real life and the confusion came raging back.

Noa'd thrown away everything else in her life for this job. And now she was seriously considering throwing the *job* away for a chance at a girl? Stupid beyond words. But no one had ever looked at her the way Lilah looked at her, like she was someone amazing, like her opinions mattered. And there was so much about Lilah that Noa still didn't know, so much left to unfold and discover, peeling the layers of her public personas off her one careful, tender inch at a time.

Frustration bubbling up inside, Noa turned over and faced Chrissy's bed instead, her back to Lilah and the aching loneliness of being this close—and no closer. Maybe if she didn't look, she could forget long enough to sleep. Seconds ticked by into minutes, Chrissy's soft breathing turning to gentle snores. Lilah still radiated tension, and Noa slowly let herself fall onto her back again, returning to Lilah's space. Lilah lay on her side, knees curled up to her chest, facing away from Noa and looking so very vulnerable that Noa's heart gave up its spikes and exploded into softness all over again.

"Can't sleep?" Noa murmured into the darkness. Chrissy's even snores didn't change.

Movement beside her, and the slightly darker lump shifted under the covers. Lilah turned to face her, and as Noa's eyes adjusted, she could make out the pale contours of her face in the night.

Lilah drew in a shaky breath. "Not really," she confessed, just as softly. "Too tired to sleep, if that makes any sense at all. My brain keeps buzzing."

Noa knew that particular feeling all too well. "It totally makes sense. Talk to me for a while? I bet I can be boring enough to knock you right out."

"Pfft, hardly. I like talking to you." Lilah's murmur already sounded steadier, a win that Noa would gladly take credit for. Only now she'd gotten herself stuck, because the kinds of things she desperately wanted to know weren't the kinds of topics designed to be calming or sleep inducing. Asking about this morning or the fire on set would be the exact opposite of relaxing and would have to wait for a better time. Conversations about family had the potential to go horribly wrong, and considering they spent so much time together on set, she knew basically everything about how work was going.

"Okay...so," Noa started, taking the easy way out. "No-stress small talk. You know my favorite movies, but you've never told me yours."

Lilah huffed a soft laugh—at least Noa thought it was a laugh. The night folded around them, dark and soothing, even the sounds of traffic outside distant now and the zip-zooms of engines further apart. "If I say *Confessions of a Shopaholic*, you're going to make fun of me."

"Am not!...maybe a little. Is that really your favorite movie of all time?" Noa tried to keep the incredulity out of her voice, but it was a hard go. On the other hand, that kind of fluffy stuff fit in perfectly with what she'd seen of Lilah's house. *And that attitude would be why Chrissy yells at you. Stop it.*

"No," Lilah replied, and Noa frowned at the shadow shape in the bed with her. "But it is a comfort watch. A fuzzy slippers and hot chocolate kind of sick-day film. I like movies like that."

Noa propped her head in her hand, other hand brushing accidentally against Lilah's where it rested against the sheets. Noa left it there, fingertips tingling where their skin had swept across each other's for a hot second. "It sounds pretty nice when you put it that way. Your actual favorite, then," she coaxed. *Show me who you really are underneath.*

"It's old."

"I won't judge. Most of my faves are, like, twice my age."

"You totally will."

"Cross my heart," Noa objected, catching herself as her voice began to rise. Chrissy's snore interrupted for a moment, and she muttered something, the bed creaking as she rolled over. A minute passed and Chrissy's breathing settled down into a regular rhythm again. Lilah shifted, and in the shadows, Noa realized she was propping her own head up, a mirror image of Noa's pose. When she spoke, it was quiet enough that Noa had to lean in closer to hear. "It's called *Getting Married in Buffalo Jump.*"

Noa'd never heard of it. "Getting what with the who?"

Lilah's shoulders sagged, and Noa's chest contracted with a pang of instant regret. "See? I knew I shouldn't have said anything."

"I'm sorry. Shutting up now," Noa promised. "I'm listening."

"It's a romance, okay? And it's from, like, thirty years ago, and it's the usual tropey thing where a girl goes back to a small country hometown from the big city and there's the guy from high school who teaches her how to love again and whatever.

"But it was the first time I saw a romance where they were equals. Where it wasn't some broken-down girl being swept off her feet by Prince Charming, but two people, both kind of messed up, who find something in each other worth holding on to. And I like that idea. I like it a lot." Lilah sounded so wistful, something lonely ringing in her voice. What had some dumbass boy put her through that the idea of equals was such a pipe dream? Noa had the rising urge to go find and fight him. She might be little, but she was mighty.

"I don't think you're messed up" was all she had to offer there in the dark. That and her hand, fumbling until she found Lilah's and curled protectively around it. "It sounds like fun. We should watch it together sometime. Get one of those ten-gallon cans of popcorn and make a movie night out of it."

"I'd like that." Lilah's fingers tightened, curling in return until their hands were laced together in the no-man's-land of the sheets between their bodies, unspoken and unacknowledged. "And I kind of am. Messed up. I think everyone is, one way or another. But it's about finding someone whose mess matches yours, you know? Where your issues make each other better, not worse."

"That's pretty wise."

Lilah laughed, a soft sound like water. "Thank you. I stole it from Kayleigh."

"Good old down-home wisdom?" Noa teased, her heart fluttering with the speed of hummingbird wings—no, not a hummingbird. A butterfly.

"Don't let the 'aw-shucks' routine fool you. She's from a big city."

"I dunno. I don't think I can envision her hobnobbing it with the Real Housewives of New York."

"Don't people ever surprise you?" Lilah asked, her pulse thrumming against Noa's wrist. "Or do you have us all pegged from day one?"

Noa swallowed hard. "You surprise me all the time," she offered. "It's a good thing. I like what I'm learning."

Lilah's hand squeezed hers, and she knew she'd answered the right way. There was something about the darkness that made it easier to speak her mind, to worry less about what Lilah might be thinking. She still couldn't let it all go though. Some part of her was still on guard, choosing her words carefully in case she shattered this perfect, precious moment.

"Surprise me now," Lilah asked—ordered, really, all imperious, but with a smile in her voice that meant Noa didn't have to take her seriously. "Tell me something about you. How did you get into all this in the first place? It's not a direct line from blush and highlighters to gluing on latex skin diseases."

"You'd think, but you'd be wrong." Noa laughed, then fell quiet as Chrissy snorfled and turned in her sleep. Voice lower again, Noa lay her head down on the pillow, and she slipped her hand from Lilah's. Lilah made a small noise that sounded like disappointment until Noa dared to slip her arm around Lilah's waist. Her heart jackhammered inside, surely loud enough that Lilah could hear it. She must have, because she pressed her palm to Noa's sternum, right there above and between her breasts, where her pulse thudded in her chest. It was more intimate than anything else Lilah could have done, anywhere else she might have touched, the heat from her hand soaking in through Noa's well-worn T-shirt.

Imagine—if the stars aligned somehow, she could have this all the time. The two of them, murmuring easy conversation in the darkness before sleep, Lilah's breath sweet as mint and her body warm against Noa's. Noa's breath caught at the idea, and she tried desperately to remember what she'd been saying. Lilah'd asked her a question, and Noa was supposed to answer.

"It's all about transformations and disguises. Making something different from what was there before. Figuring out new gags, new effects, what I can do with a specific palette to make the camera see something that's never been there before—it's fun," Noa finished lamely. "Also, messing with people."

"You're so mean." Lilah laughed, but she snuggled closer under Noa's arm as though she hadn't just told her off. Noa could bury her face in Lilah's hair like this, slip her foot between Lilah's calves and hold her, safe against the world. "Like practical jokes?"

"When I was first getting into makeup as a kid, I used to make liquid latex burns and stuff all over my older brother. My parents rushed him to the ER once because they thought he'd really hurt himself, until the doctor pulled the whole wound off in a sheet." Noa snickered at the memory, both her parents' fury and the realization that *her work* had been good enough to fool *real grown-ups*. That had meant something.

Lilah shifted in the bed, settled her head next to Noa's on the pillow without dislodging Noa's arm from her hip. From here, Noa could see her eyes in the faint light from the window, and she was watching Noa with real interest. "What do you want to do with it? Years from now, I mean. Where do you want to be?"

"I want my name to be said along with the greats," Noa confessed. "To be somebody."

"Hitchcock?" Lilah guessed, missing her point. "Or more modern, like Ari Aster?"

"Tom Savini," Noa breathed out reverently. "Greg Nicotero. Rick Baker. The *legends*. They were the guys who invented whole genres out of nothing, and their monster shops were the reason horror *worked*. CGI's changed everything—there aren't nearly as many practical effects now. But makeup's something no computer guy can replace, no matter how many pixel dinosaurs they make."

The soft hum Lilah made sounded like agreement, and Noa decided to take it at face value. She wasn't laughing anyway, or telling her that her dream was something ridiculous and outdated. "Where do you want to be in five years?" Noa asked, daring to try for something equally personal. "What's your big dream? Not more horror, you said that already."

"I don't mind some horror," Lilah objected. "Just not splatter stuff. If I'm still doing this by the time I'm approaching thirty, I'll be in real trouble. Slasher flicks don't like older women. Not unless you're Jamie Lee Curtis, and there's only one of her. I want..."

She trailed off, and Noa curled her arm tighter. "Go on."

"I want to be taken seriously," Lilah whispered, and Noa's heart broke. "You know what it's like, how easy it is to be overlooked just because we fit a type, and I'm so tired of being 'pretty girl number three.' I want people to see me as a real actress, someone who can tell stories that mean something and touch people's hearts.

Not just their spleens," she added as an afterthought, and Noa almost woke Chrissy up trying not to laugh aloud.

"You are good," Noa promised her, meaning every word. "And you'll make it."

"Do you have any idea how many girls there are exactly like me in this town, all trying for the same thing?" Lilah asked softly. "There are only a few amazing parts to go around."

"Yeah, but you've got something most of them don't." And then Noa had to try and find the word for it, which wasn't as easy as it seemed.

"What's that?"

"Star power? It factor."

"I'm not so sure about that."

"Gumption?" Noa tried next. "Moxie?"

"You're making this up as you go along." Lilah huffed a soft laugh.

Noa sighed. "Is it making you feel better?"

"A little."

"Then I'm good."

"Yes, you are." Lilah's voice was fuzzy, hazed with sleep and punctuated by a yawn. "Sorry."

"Go to sleep, it's cool," Noa urged, squeezing Lilah's fingers with light pressure. "That was the point, right?" Sleep was clawing its way around the edges of her own brain no matter how she tried to fight it, exhaustion a constant companion these days. But oh, her heart was warm. Lilah had a face that she showed to the world, a sparkling, shiny persona that was as much of a fiction as any of her movie roles. Noa had seen the real girl underneath that mask, the sweet, vulnerable yearning, the doubt and the hope. She'd be a megastar one day, and all Noa wanted was to be by her side as it happened.

There may have been more murmuring as the dark swept up and claimed her, but with her hand in Lilah's, Noa sank happily into the black.

CHAPTER THIRTEEN

NOA WAS FLYING, GLIDING THROUGH a sunset sky, the rays falling on her skin and warming her through. She dove down into the pink clouds, and Lilah was there in the mist, naked as Venus rising from the seashell in that one painting in every art history book. Noa ran for her, grabbed her up in her arms, sank her lips against Lilah's. Lilah melted into her, and Noa died right there, resurrected, and died again.

"I like you so much," she whispered in Lilah's ear.

"The fish is in the bathroom," Lilah replied solemnly.

Noa blinked, the clouds beneath her resolving to something firmer, more solid and cotton-like. Sleep parted around her, the curtains of dream drawing back. The sunrise melted away, and so did the clouds. One thing that didn't was the girl in her arms, pressed up against her, lips brushing sweet against Noa's forehead. Somehow during the night, Noa's intent to stay firmly on her own side had abandoned her, and she was nose-to-chin with— and boob-to-boob, and her legs firmly tangled around—Lilah. It felt too good, which was the worst thing, Lilah's thigh wedged between hers, right up against her, where it would be so easy to move against her, sink into the desire that rushed through her like a bullet train.

Or bury her face in Lilah's hair and stay there forever, wrapped up in the warm and the acceptance that she'd found there. Lilah didn't want her to be anything other than what she was, seemed to actively like the parts of Noa that Noa herself was so uncertain of some days. She was safe in Lilah's arms. She didn't have to front.

She didn't have to move either, because Lilah *liked* her. She'd kissed her! Twice!

Noa could have this, at least here, in the early light and the stillness of the morning.

A door closed in the distance as Noa drifted in the haze. She barely registered the noise until it was followed by a loud banging.

"Noa! Rise and shine!" Denise's voice shrilled through the door.

Did she have a key? Would she come in and see Noa and Lilah snuggling? Oh God, Noa was going to get fired!

Barely a second had passed between realization and understanding, and Noa shoved herself backward and out of Lilah's arms like she'd been electrocuted. She misjudged, and her hip barely grazed the edge of the bed before she was falling, hitting the floor with a loud thump.

The shock was worse than the pain, and Noa lay there dazed for a beat. She opened her eyes to find both Lilah and Chrissy peering down at her from the pair of beds, wearing equally confused expressions.

"Noa?"

"I'm okay!" she announced, her cheeriness sounding forced even to her own ears as she jumped to her feet. "I'm up, Denise! I'll meet you outside in five!"

Her tailbone hurt from the landing, feeling like it was definitely going to turn into a bruise later. The bathroom door was only a few feet away, so she headed for that as nonchalantly as she could manage. "I...rolled over too fast. Anyway, now that everyone's up, how about we get some coffee? Gonna be a long day!"

Noa closed the bathroom door behind her and sagged against it, sliding down to sit on the floor and bury her head in her hands. Muffled, back in the room, the alarm clock started beeping noisily until someone whacked it with a shoe.

She might have made a massive fool of herself, but at least Lilah had been asleep. It was better that way, better that Noa's heartfelt confession had been in her dream instead of real. At least the origins of the kiss that had made her insides bubble and fizz had been more than a figment of her fervid imagination. They'd fallen asleep with their arms around each other; she'd woken up with Lilah curled into her, peaceful and warm—

Only this wasn't the right time. Not yet. Nor the right place. Noa picked herself up off the floor for the second time in as many minutes and turned on the shower full blast. She only needed to keep Denise off her back for a couple more weeks at most. She could do it.

So why did doing the right thing feel so wrong?

Noa's hesitation was starting to wear very thin as far as Lilah was concerned. She left the motel room while Chrissy was still putting on her face, and Noa had barricaded herself in the bathroom. She could shower in her trailer, thankfully, so there wasn't any need to wait around to see how Noa was going to try and avoid her this time.

She'd woken up in Noa's arms and lain there for a while, very still, soaking in the feeling of Noa against her, touching her, Noa's face slack with sleep and utterly soft and vulnerable in the predawn light. Lilah'd fallen asleep again like that, trusting, trusted, and safe, only to find Noa *flinging* herself away from Lilah as fast and as far as humanly possible. Who would want to stick around for more of that kind of rejection?

Disgruntled and seriously under-rested, Lilah slunk into the lobby where a line had formed by the ancient coffee machine on the corner table. Joyous barking met her as a little furry missile launched himself at her knees. Lilah dropped to a crouch and buried her face in Rasputin's curly fur, a smile blossoming on her face for the first time that morning. "Hello, baby," she crooned gently between licks from the tongue attacking her face. "Did you miss me?"

"We're not sharing custody, no matter how much sucking up you do," Tanner warned her, grinning as he approached with the leash. "Coffee?" he asked, holding out a fresh cup.

Lilah took it and held it in both hands, the heat warming her up her arms and into her bones. "Yes, thank you, and you are a god among men."

"I wouldn't go that far, but I'll accept 'minor deity of costars,'" he teased. "How'd last night go?"

"Awful," Lilah replied without thinking. "I feel like the walking dead, and my hair still smells like smoke." The rest hadn't been so bad, especially falling asleep in Noa's arms, but she wasn't tired enough to let that slip out.

"Tell me about it," Tanner commiserated. Lilah sneezed. "Mr. Gilbert's stress about the schedule would be a lot funnier if all the corner cutting wasn't putting us at actual risk. Stressed-out people make dumb mistakes."

"I'll feel a lot better once this part of the shoot is over and I'm home in my own bed," she confessed, avoiding the crawling feeling that came with hearing the producer's name.

"I hear that." Tanner glanced over his shoulder at the groups straggling into the lobby. "Time to roll; the AD is my ride. Who's taking you over to set today?"

"Same," Lilah confirmed, shouldering her bag. "Dibs on shotgun."

She didn't see Noa or Chrissy in the general hubbub, though they did pass the new props van in the parking lot. PJ was loading in boxes again, the one in his arms labeled LIMBS: MEDIUM RARE—EXTRA CRISPY. It wasn't a threat, but Lilah still caught herself in a shudder. Right now, fire was the last thing she could bring herself to find funny.

———

The shower in her trailer was a gorgeous thing, hot water easing out all the cramps in her neck and shoulders from the rough half night of uneasy sleep. Lilah tucked her bathrobe snugly around herself as she stepped out of the bathroom, barely having the chance to throw on clean underwear and a bra before a knock sounded at her door. Tanner dropping off Rasputin again? She glanced out the window, craning her neck to see who it was before rushing to throw open the lock.

The coffee, long drive, and shower had done wonders for her mood, and the residual annoyance she had over Noa's weirdness had long since faded. Of course Noa had been out of sorts at having to share a bed, and the closeness they'd stolen under the cover of darkness was something to savor and remember. Still, when she opened the door, it was hard to figure out exactly what she was supposed to say in the light of day. "Come on in." Lilah gave up on trying to figure out anything clever.

"You left without us," Noa accused, setting her makeup bag down on Lilah's small couch.

"I wanted to use my own shower, not get stuck if the motel ran out of hot water." It wasn't entirely a lie, especially since Lilah's hair was obviously wet and dripping down her back. Telling Noa she'd been annoyed by the way she'd woken up wasn't going to do either of them any favors at this point, so why bother bringing it up? "Are you here to make me pretty?"

"Who could improve on perfection?" Noa riposted, her exhausted face brightening with a smile, and Lilah melted all over again.

"Flatterer."

"I thought stars liked that kind of thing. You know, yes-men and flunkies to tell you how awesome you are," Noa teased, starting to set up her kit along Lilah's dressing table. She gave the teddy bear a funny look, then nudged it slightly out of the way to get her fake scratches ready.

"Only if it's believable, and you saw me with serious bedhead this morning," Lilah replied with a laugh, immediately breaking her own internal promise not to bring up the awkward night.

"You're beautiful even with bedhead," Noa said, reaching out for Lilah's hand, and the mood in the trailer shifted sideways before Lilah could catch her breath.

"You didn't seem to think so this morning." The snide remark was out before she could bite it back, remorse flooding over her as soon as the words were out. "I'm sorry. I didn't mean it like that."

"No, that's fair. I freaked out because Denise was there, but sleeping with you—*sleeping* sleeping, not...yeah—was one of the highlights of my life. I've been a huge idiot. I spent the whole drive over reminding myself why we have to keep it cool, and it's not working," Noa confessed.

She reached for Lilah's hand again, and this time, Lilah let her take it. Trembling inside and unsure, she let Noa's hand slide into hers. There she found stability, like when she'd curled up in Noa's arms only hours before. Unbidden, a memory of that first day jumped back into her mind. *I'm looking forward to hurting you*, Noa had said, then tried to walk it back, and Lilah had still somehow decided that Noa was a cool girl to look up to. Her first impression hadn't been wrong, Lilah decided firmly, only maybe that pedestal was a little closer down to ground level now. Low enough for Lilah to step up one day and join her there.

"The no-fraternizing rule is really bothering you?" Lilah guessed, the disappointment no doubt written all over her face.

Because that surely hadn't changed in the last couple of hours. Part of her still wanted Noa to fight for her, for Noa to decide that Lilah was worth a little bit of risk.

Noa nodded, vibrant instead of glum, and Lilah's attention was caught by the light in her eyes. "But to hell with that, and to hell with Denise," she said firmly, squeezing her hand and making Lilah's pulse leap. "I spent the whole drive over thinking about this—"

"You said that already." Lilah laughed lightly, unable to resist.

"Shush. You're not the only one allowed to have retakes. As I was saying." Noa cleared her throat, her cheeks pink beneath the olive gold of her tan. "Denise can't stop us from hanging out unless she reassigns me completely, and that's not likely to happen now. Not this far in. And once the filming's over, what can she do? If I did a good enough job, I can probably even get Ed to recommend me if I have to. But I happen to think you're kind of amazing, and I want you in my life."

"I like you too." Lilah tried that line on for size. It went over pretty well if the smile on Noa's face was any indication. "I said that back at the studio, remember? But if this means that all that back-and-forth nonsense is over, then I'll take it. I want—" She hesitated, pulling Noa a step closer instead of knowing what to say. "I want to go out with you, like on a date date. Not a friend date or even a coffee date. A for-real date with the possibility of interesting things happening afterward."

And *those* images were enough to fire up her blood, making everything inside fizzy and hot. Lilah tugged Noa forward that one last step until they were practically against each other, her bathrobe too warm and stifling in the trailer's still air.

"I think we can arrange something along those lines," Noa murmured, her eyes half-lidded as she rose up on her toes. There was nothing tentative or rushed about this kiss, no alcohol or adrenaline involved, only a solid thumping of Lilah's heart against her ribs and the silk-sweet taste of Noa's mouth on hers. This, this, *this*—this was what she'd been missing, been craving, as essential as cold water or life's blood. Noa's arms came about her neck, and Lilah pulled Noa into her embrace, tasting Noa's mouth, her tongue, suckling gently, then hard, at the sweet plumpness of Noa's lower lip. Her curls were a cloud around them both, her hips full and round under Lilah's cupped hands, and the little half gasp she gave when the kiss broke was enough to send all the air flying from Lilah's lungs.

"We can't tell anyone," Noa urged, sinking back down and her hands sliding to rest against Lilah's shoulders. "But it's only for a couple more weeks. Once principal photography is over, we'll have time to do things properly."

And there it was, the confession Lilah couldn't avoid any longer. "I might be going to France once *Scareodactyl* is done shooting," Lilah blurted out, her eyes closing to block out Noa's stricken expression. "For three months, for a movie. I still have one more screen test to do, with the guy they've already cast for the lead, but my agent thinks it's a sure thing. If she's right, then I'll be gone for a while. But then I'll be back. Or maybe you can come with me. Maybe I can ask for my own makeup artist as part of the contract. It's far away from here, and far away from—" *From @tommyjarvis,* she was about to say, but Dan's admonitions kept her mouth closed about the stalker and his screen name. "From Denise and her nuttiness."

"European adventure? You'd do that for me?" Noa asked, surprise and something like awe in her voice, like back on that first day.

"Depends if you take me dancing or not," Lilah teased and was rewarded with Noa's glittering, sharp laugh. "We can talk about it later. I just want you to know that we've got options. Things to look forward to."

"Oh, I have all kinds of things in mind now." Noa laughed, her hand slipping down Lilah's side to rest securely on her hip. Her eyes spoke a hundred promises that made Lilah want to lock the door and call in sick for the day. Stupid work ethic. "But first, you have to go run away from a dinosaur."

"Ugh. I'm about at my limit with this one," Lilah grumbled, pulling away from Noa and heading for her dressing table. The teddy bear's eyes caught the light, looking for all the world like it was winking at her, and she patted it lightly on the head as she took her seat. "Give me a flamethrower and I'll wrap the ending up nice and fast."

Noa laughed and followed close behind, like even a little distance was too much right now. Lilah could sympathize. "Settle in then, because you're all mine for the next hour. It's too bad that putting my hands all over your body means *liquid* latex."

"I don't know. I'm sure you could come up with all kinds of fun ideas for that too," Lilah said, flirting, the words coming out of her mouth before she even really registered what she was going to say. Was this how she was supposed to feel around someone, all giddy and bubbly, like she was going to float away on the sensation? It was utterly, entirely new and wonderful, and all thanks to

Noa. Lilah looked at her, took in every detail of her face the way she hadn't been able to in the dark of night. But there was her generous mouth, full, plush lips, and the strong line of her nose above them, all of which defined her face so fiercely. Her indigo-blue eyes, outlined today in purple and smoky gray, framed by dark brows that drew together in the middle in furrowed bewilderment as Lilah continued to stare. Lilah smiled and Noa relaxed, not a lot, but enough.

"Do I have something in my teeth?" Noa asked, covering her mouth with her hand as her cheeks flushed pink beneath the olive gold.

"No! No, I like looking at you," Lilah confessed, her own cheeks heating up at the admission. "You're beautiful. Is that okay?"

Noa's mouth moved, but no sound came out except for a faintly strangled cough. "Yes? I think. I mean, look who's saying it. You're pretty much the dictionary definition of gorgeous."

That was enough to poke a hole in Lilah's blissful bubble, but she ignored the vague feeling of deflation in the name of not ruining the moment. "No one ever thinks that about themselves," she deflected, somewhat uncomfortably. "Now, are you going to put your hands all over me?"

"Your wish, my command, et cetera, et cetera." Noa perched on the edge of Lilah's dressing table and reached for the eyeliner brush first, not the primer or toner or any of the first stages Lilah'd gotten used to.

"What's that for?"

"Luck." Noa made eye contact and, with two fingers, tugged

the bathrobe off Lilah's left shoulder. She only had a bra on underneath, and while Noa had seen her in less before, now everything was different. Her beating heart and Noa's faint inhale confirmed that without need for words. Noa traced the eyeliner brush gently over Lilah's shoulder, the same place as last time. The butterfly formed under her quick, clever fingers, and this time around, Lilah knew enough to watch it happen. Noa's breath fogged warm on her arm, raising goose bumps and tingles all the way down to Lilah's fingertips.

The butterfly grew on her skin, first the black outline and then the colors done with eyeliner. Lilah made Noa wait for a moment before covering it up with the latex appliance, taking a long look in the mirror so she could impress its shape and swirls into her memory. It was like and unlike her watercolor card, because it moved with her. If she were to get it as a tattoo—but no, that was one step too far. Zaidie would never forgive her for that one.

One lingering stare later, she flopped into her chair and nodded to Noa. Noa tucked her phone away and gave her that same wonderful, life-affirming smile filled with the approval that Lilah craved. "Ready?" Noa asked, two questions in one.

And Lilah smiled. "Ready."

CHAPTER FOURTEEN

THE MOTEL-ROOM SHARING ONLY LASTED one night, unfortunately for Noa. As soon as she and Lilah had gotten to a point where things might be happening, the production had actually coughed up enough money to give the actors their own rooms. Go figure. Worse yet, most of Noa's next two days were going to be devoted to Peter's evisceration instead of closed up with Lilah in her trailer, painting her lips in shades of pink.

How had she come to the point, Noa reflected as she followed Colin with the bucket of intestinal loops, where she was actively disappointed at getting to set up an effects gag? That was what she got for ignoring her own better judgment. Nudging a snake aside with her foot, she climbed the trailer stairs. *Girls*—she sighed to herself happily—*were the best kind of trouble.*

The scans and molds for Peter's fake torso had all been made months ago during preproduction, before Noa had even been interviewed to join the crew. Colin had that under his own arm as they joined Peter in the trailer that he and Tanner were sharing. Already shirtless and sitting in his chair with earbuds in, Peter looked up with a wary smile when they entered. "FYI, four in the morning is the devil's own wakeup call," he said to Colin and Noa jovially enough.

"Hit the bathroom now, my friend, because once we get started packing the blood squibs in, you won't be doing much of anything easily," Colin replied with a chuckle. "Let me know when you're comfortable, and we'll take it from there."

Noa hid a yawn behind her hand and waited for the double espresso she'd shotgunned on the way over to kick in. Big effects project now, and later on that day, she'd get to see Lilah and tell her all about it. Considering what a disaster Monday had been, she'd take it and smile.

———

It took no fewer than four hours to get the appliances and prosthetics built onto Peter's torso and neck, Noa's hands dotted with blowback from the airbrush and drips of fake blood drying sticky on her jeans. But it was done and it was a masterwork, and all she could do was hope and pray that they got everything right on the first take, or it would take another two hours to reset and try again.

Colin had sent her off to find food for all three of them, and Noa was on her way back from craft services with bags of sandwiches and a tray of coffee when her phone started buzzing in her back pocket. Lilah? It could be Lilah! Looking around for a bench, Noa set everything down and fished out her phone, not stopping to look at the number before swiping it on and holding the phone to her ear. "Hello?"

"Noa, honey! How are you? It's been days!"

Noa deflated at the sound of her father's voice on the other end. "I'm working right now, Dad, and I can't really—"

"Working? At this hour?"

"I've been on set since four. We've got a big gag filming today, and they needed me in early to set up."

"What kind of gag? I thought you were filming a horror movie, not a comedy."

"A special effects shot. That's what it's called. What's up, Dad?" Noa caved and asked the dreaded question, rubbing her eyes to get the sudden wave of tired out of them. "Is everything okay?"

"Of course everything's okay. I can't call to talk to my daughter for five minutes? The news said there was a fire on your movie set."

Noa groaned aloud. "How many Google alerts do you and Mom *have*?"

"If you'd tell us more about what was going on in your life, we wouldn't have to," he said cheerfully, no guilt whatsoever leaking into his voice.

Sighing, she leaned against a tree and let it become her spine for a while. "It was an accident. No one was hurt and the damage was really minor. Some equipment from a fire stunt didn't cool down quickly enough, that's all." That didn't come close to touching on the rush of fear Noa had felt when she'd seen the flames, but what choice did she have? The moment she let slip that things were less than perfect, her parents would shove a wedge in that crack and use all their strength to push her back to their vision of her ideal life. Lying and minimizing sucked, but it was a lot better than another round of *get a real job, and why would you want to make your mother cry?*

For a moment, she let herself indulge in the kind of wishful thinking that she usually avoided. What would it be like to have parents who understood why she wanted to do what she did? Who didn't try and force her into the mold they'd practically designed for her at birth? Doctor, lawyer, CEO—professor would have been acceptable to them too, she supposed, though the thought of that much school still filled her with an unnamable horror. *Special effects artist* had never been on the list of Things Good Jewish Girls Did.

In the meantime, however, her father was still talking about workplace safety regulations, and she supposed that was as good as saying that he cared about her.

"You're worrying too much, Dad," Noa told him when he stopped to take a breath. "I'm behind the scenes; it's not like I'm one of the stuntwomen. Lilah's in more danger than I am on a daily basis."

"Lilah—that's the actor you're working with, isn't it?"

"One of them, yeah." Noa sighed a little with relief at the subject change and at the somewhat surprising realization that at some point, he'd been listening when she'd told him about the job. She glanced at the time and fished out her earbuds as she spoke, trying to organize her phone, the coffee tray, and bags of food so that she could walk and talk at the same time. "She's the lead actress, and she's pretty amazing. I'm not working on her today though. I've got to help pull a guy's guts out."

"And you'd rather do that than go to anatomy classes for

medical school. I see how it is." Her father chuckled. "Is this Lilah the same one that had you sighing and bookmarking every movie poster on the internet last year?"

Noa couldn't have been more flabbergasted, stopping with one earbud hanging from the cord next to the microphone. "You paid attention to that? I wasn't even living at home!"

"I may not always agree with you, sweetheart, but that doesn't mean I don't listen."

She could hear the warmth and, yes, the love in his voice, and it caught her off guard. That was probably why she slipped in her resolve, the desire to be known too strong. "We're going out on a date in a couple of days," she confessed. "Once we're back from location. I really like her, Dad. I know I shouldn't be into a coworker, but she's not like anyone else I've ever met."

"Ah," he said, teasing still lacing laughter through his voice. "And the truth will out. What's she like, other than amazing?"

A couple of the set dressers headed past with armloads of boxes, and Noa realized with a start that the set was filling up with people. She was taking too much time and talking much too publicly, and both were going to get her in deep shit trouble if she wasn't careful. "She's a perfectly nice Jewish girl," Noa replied dryly, starting to jog back toward Peter's trailer. "So don't worry."

"Better a Jewish girl than a non-Jewish boy," he replied, like she knew he would. It hadn't been the way she'd hoped her parents would react when she'd first come out to them years ago, but it was a well-worn routine by now, and there was no avoiding it.

"You don't get to choose either way," she found her spine and told him. "And that stopped being funny years ago."

The line crackled, and she had the image of him shifting in his office chair as he spoke, the sight so familiar that she momentarily ached. "Who said it was supposed to be funny? In any case, I hope it works out the way you want it to."

"Thank you. And I have to go," she reminded him. "I need to get back to work."

He made a noise that sounded like an acknowledgment but didn't hang up. "Look, if you're not going back to school next year, you at least need to come home for the holidays. 'I'm too busy in September' won't be an excuse."

"We'll see. I really have to go, Dad."

"All right, I'm sorry. We'll talk about it more later. Happy Shavuot, Noa," he said.

Noa stopped dead outside the trailer door. "Shit, wait, when is that? Already?" Wasn't it still April? No, they were already in May, and Pesach had been early this year, because she'd used winter term exams as an excuse not to fly home. She'd regretted that later, Uncle David's table-pounding lectures fading in importance against the realization that she'd missed her grandmother's kugel entirely.

Her father's exasperation was faintly obvious in his reply, but he didn't call her out. This time. "It starts Sunday, but I'm not likely to talk to you again before then. Chag sameach, hmm?"

"Chag sameach," she replied more by rote than anything else, caught between the pull of two competing calendars, two sets of priorities and schedules that the modern world had ensured would never align. "Love you, Dad."

"Love you too, honey. Talk to you later."

Noa hung up and bundled everything into her pocket before pushing the trailer door open and heading in, shifting back to the world that was most immediately pressing on her here and now.

Chrissy: We might make it back to LA in time for that open mic night after all.

Noa: what? Why?

Chrissy: Gilbert's losing his shit over the extra expenses re: the van fire. Cutting location filming by a day and a half. We're going back to town Tuesday.

Noa: How the hell are we supposed to get all the pages shot by then?

Chrissy: He says, and I quote, "that's Ed's fucking problem, that's what I pay him for."

Noa: ...wow. Classy.

Chrissy: Get ready for a couple of seriously late nights.

Chrissy hadn't been kidding. The fourteen-hour days they'd been pulling already turned into eighteen and twenty, as Ed tried to get as many of the outdoor scenes in the can as possible. Scenes intended to be daytime were moved to night without any changes in the script that Noa could see, and grumbling got worse even among the more cheerful members of the cast and crew.

Lilah got off easy, since her scenes had mostly been put to bed earlier that week. She got to go back to LA and do her screen tests, while Noa gave up on going back and forth by Saturday and spent the night sleeping on folded-up jackets under the counter in the makeup trailer. To heck with the insurance company's rules; it wasn't like anyone was checking up on her. And it was all the better to be up at crack of sparrow fart to get Peter into his disembowelment gear without having to deal with a drive at the same time. Lilah really hadn't been happy when Noa texted that she was crashing on location, but California could have earthquaked itself right off into the ocean, and as tired as she was, Noa was certain she'd have slept right through it.

Sunday evening, Noa collapsed onto the couch in the miraculously empty crew trailer as the sun set outside. Ed shouted at someone in the distance, but she was on break for the next half hour. Anyone who disturbed the nap she was about to take was going to be picking teeth out of his intestinal tract.

"Noa?"

Noa sat bolt upright on the tweedy and faintly smoke-scented couch, ready to lay into whoever had woken her up. Lilah stood there with a shopping bag in her hand and sunglasses perched jauntily on the top of her head, and Noa instantly forgave her for everything. "Oh, hi! Why are you here? I didn't think you were filming tonight."

"I'm not. I didn't want to disturb you when you were napping, but I wanted to make sure you got this, instead of the vultures we call a crew." Lilah sat on the couch next to Noa and curled her legs up underneath her as she handed over the bag. "Chag sameach."

Noa glanced out the window where the sun had already set, making it well and truly the holiday. "And a gut yontif back atcha. What's this?" She was already peeking into the bag as she asked, finding a bakery box inside.

"Open it and see."

Noa was way ahead of her, wrestling the fancy cardboard box out of the bag and popping the sides. The smell hit her before she had the lid all the way open, starting her mouth watering and stomach grumbling. "Oh my God," she replied reverently at the sight. "Is this for me?" The massive slab of caramel-covered cheesecake would take her entire break to get through, but the nap was a sacrifice she was more than willing to make.

"To share, if you don't mind my cooties," Lilah joked, and indeed there were two plastic forks tucked inside along with the slab of cake. She shook a little bottle in her hand and grinned. "I even brought the Lactaid."

Noa laughed ruefully. "You really did think of everything. How did you know?"

"It was a pretty safe bet." Lilah shook a couple of the pills out of the bottle and took one herself before handing the other to Noa. "For a people so prone to lactose intolerance, there's irony in having a holiday celebrated with dairy desserts."

Halfway through sinking her fork into the point of the wedge of cake, Noa dry swallowed the pill and chuckled softly. "But what sweet pain it is. So how did your audition go?" The thought of that had lingered, the possibility of adventure tempting to the extreme.

Lilah lit up, the honest excitement in her eyes something Noa wanted to see on her all the time. "Really well! There were three of us there to read with Luca—that's the lead. I thought he was French, but it turns out he's actually Italian. He was very nice."

Lilah's eyes lingered on Noa as she took the first bite. Noa's eyes fluttered closed and she moaned inadvertently, the smooth, rich cream of the cake exploding across her senses like a first kiss, all her pleasure centers firing off at once. "Holy shit that's good." But she was changing the subject and pulled her thoughts back to Lilah and her news. "So should I be jealous? Luca and Lilah, the gossip headlines write themselves."

Lilah scoffed. "Don't be silly. There's no one else I'd rather pig out on cheesecake with. Especially caramel." She reached over Noa's arm to sink her fork into the cake. "My turn."

Were her cheeks a little flushed? She sank her fork in where Noa's had just been, lips closing around the heaping pile of cake she retrieved. Her throaty sound of appreciation sent a shiver down Noa's spine.

"Why caramel in particular?" Noa asked, her breath coming in shallower when the pink tip of Lilah's tongue darted out to retrieve a drop of caramel that lingered on the swell of her lower lip.

"Because both you and caramel can be so sweet, deliciously well rounded, but disappointing when oversalty?" Lilah's elegantly delivered roast was so unexpected and well-timed that Noa almost choked on her next bite.

"And there's the sniper in action," Noa laughed, tears coming to her eyes. "Mean but true. Nicely done." She wanted to be the one to lick the delicate smear off Lilah's lip, but she settled for taking another bite on her fork instead. Just because the trailer was empty now didn't mean it would stay that way.

"Do you think you'll get the part?" Noa put her fork to her mouth, and her lips met Lilah's by three degrees of proxy.

"I think so. I'll hear from them next week sometime. The

casting director seemed very positive and had us go through three different script sides before releasing me. Apparently I'm good at generating chemistry," Lilah added impishly, locking her eyes with Noa's.

"I could have told them that," Noa murmured, the air in the room getting warmer as they sat, Lilah's knees brushing hers, her smile lighting up the room.

Another bite, this time an offering instead of something selfish. Lilah leaned forward and took the cheesecake from the tines with her mouth. Caramel lingered on the corner of her lips, and this time, Noa didn't resist. The lamp on the table kept the light dim, the noise of the outside world fading away. Noa set the fork down and reached for Lilah, sinking her fingers into her torrent of red-gold hair. Lilah followed, her cheeks flushed pink and her lips parted, her breath as ragged as Noa's when their mouths finally met.

Kissing her was like falling, not terrifying but comforting, a soft landing in a warm ocean, or a couch covered with pillows. She tasted of caramel and promises, tangy sweet and needy, and Noa was on fire with all of it at once. Lilah snaked her arms around Noa's waist, slipped her hands into the back pockets of Noa's jeans, and pulled her close. Noa breathed her in and pressed a hundred tiny kisses to the corners of her mouth before Lilah objected, then captured her mouth for real.

She could be sure of one thing, and that was that Lilah was sure of her. Lilah kissed her with a confidence that set Noa's head spinning. She tugged Lilah's shirt from her waistband so she could feel the skin there, the strip of silk-soft temptation she'd dreamed about too often and too vividly for words.

Some indefinable time later, the door of the trailer rattled, and they sprang apart before the incoming group of techies could see anything. Noa grabbed the box of cake again while Lilah hastily tugged her shirt back into place, her cheeks red and hair mussed, her eyes and mouth both laughing.

"I should get back to set," Noa said apologetically, all her senses suffused with the scent and taste of Lilah and dessert combined.

Lilah sighed dramatically and pouted out her bottom lip in a move that did a lot of things to Noa, none of which were conducive to getting her ass back to work. "Spoilsport," she said, her voice low under the noise and laughter of the group crowded around the coffee maker at the other end of the room.

"Thank you for the cheesecake," Noa replied with a grin. "What if we saved the rest for later?"

"Later when?" Lilah asked, one golden eyebrow arched as though in challenge, like she didn't expect Noa to bite. Nuts to that.

"Later tonight, if you're willing to stick around. And…"

"And?"

"And there's a thing on Thursday night," Noa offered, nervous for reasons she couldn't put her finger on, not there with Lilah's thigh pressed tight against hers and her body resonating with Lilah's nearness. "An open-mic thing. A bunch of my friends are going."

"Noa Birnbaum, are you asking me on a date?" Lilah asked, quietly delighted.

"If I do, will you say yes?"

"After the way you kissed me, how could I say no? I can't stay tonight though," she added, much to Noa's disappointment.

"Thursday, then, after the shoot."

Lilah stood and brushed herself down, ostensibly getting rid of a couple of wayward crumbs but also making sure her clothes were all back in place. "It's a date. I'll put this in the fridge in my trailer? Otherwise, it won't survive the night," she added, turning the statement into a question.

Getting up herself and grabbing her bag again, Noa nodded. "Save it for us. It'll be worth the wait," she added with a grin.

"Counting on it," Lilah replied, and Noa felt Lilah's gaze burning into her back until the trailer door closed behind her.

Noa made her way across the dark lawn, toward the burning lights and the hubbub of the crew, a lift in her step and a hum in her throat. She was ninety percent of the way to being able to call Lilah Silver her girlfriend, and after Thursday, everything was going to fall into place. *Not bad, Birnbaum. Not bad.*

CHAPTER FIFTEEN

"THIS IS WHERE BODHI LIFTS Peter up—Peter, pretend it's the pterodactyl. Bodhi lifts him, and his weight's taken by the wire. Peter screams, tries to pull away, the wires slack, and he lands on the ground. You have to land hard, Peter; no farting around and trying to break your fall. We need the audience to really feel it."

Peter nodded, already walking bow-legged thanks to the tight safety harness under his costume. The lights around the field cut through the 3:00 a.m. darkness, casting all kinds of shadows across the fake intestines looping out of the torso build strapped to Peter's chest. It looked pretty damn good, if Noa did say so herself. Between Colin's build and her paints, Peter would fit right in at the local ER. Or morgue, considering the amount of goo they'd already layered on him. He glistened under the spot lighting, almost every inch of exposed skin smeared with red fake blood.

"Can he handle it?" Noa overheard Sadie muttering to one of the other stunt performers. Sadie was almost unrecognizable out of costume and without the long red wig that turned her into Lilah's on-screen clone. "He's an old dude. Bob should be doing this."

"It's not supposed to be a rough stunt, and Ed wants to get close-ups at the same time. Stupid schedule."

"Makeup, last looks! Get some more blood on there; it's starting to look sticky."

Noa hurried over at the AD's call and carefully layered more gore onto Peter's already-gruesome prosthetic. "We're good to go here," she announced, Denise nowhere to be seen to give the all-clear. In a move that did wonders for her confidence, Ed took her at her word and waved everyone away to start the take. Look at that. Noa was a full member of the crew now. She'd earned her stripes, her expertise was respected, and the scene was going to look incredible once it was done.

"Action!" The first piece went off the way Ed had talked it out. Bodhi lifted Peter up, the talon prosthetics on his arms clenching and clawing. Peter squirmed, the rigger on his controls dropped him, and Peter hit the ground, hard. He held it. A beat. Two.

"Cut and print!"

Peter sprang up to his feet, clutching his wrist and yelling in pain. "Son of a *bitch!*"

There was more blood now than there had been a minute ago, Peter's palm oozing in a place Noa had definitely not laced with her squirt bottle.

"Medic!"

"Told you so," Sadie snorted behind Noa.

Ignoring the commentary, Noa headed over to Peter, driven by curiosity more than any kind of ability to help. She was good at making people look like they were falling apart, not necessarily putting them back together.

"There's glass in there," the on-set EMT was explaining, shining her flashlight on a shard that had sliced across the meat of Peter's palm. "I don't think it hit anything important."

"Bull*shit* it didn't hurt anything important!" Peter objected, supporting his wrist with his uninjured hand. There was a glint in his eye—not exactly *amusement*, but some kind of resigned humor. "If you're saying that because I'm not a lead…"

The medic looked at Peter, her set lips not betraying any kind of a smile. "I mean tendons. It's going to need some stitches; I'll run him into town."

"Looking like that?" Noa blurted out, Ed, Peter, and the medic all turning to look at her. She gestured to the prosthetic, complete with painted-on fat bulging out of the fake abdominal wall.

Ed grimaced. "How long will it take to get him out?"

"Without destroying the body cast? About three hours," Noa replied, running the mental calculations. The medic shook her head, applying pressure to the gauze pad she was wrapping around Peter's injured hand.

Peter grinned through his wince of pain. "I'll tell them I've got a stomachache. See what they do." He dropped an obvious wink at the medic, and Noa rolled her eyes.

That made the stone-faced medic crack a smile. "You're a terrible person," she informed him somberly.

"I'm a terrible *bleeding* person. How far away is that hospital?"

He was griping as the medic led him away, which was probably a good sign for his overall survival. Ed, on the other hand, looked like he was halfway between murder and suicide. "Tell me, for the love of God and little fishes, that we can use that take," he was saying to his AD. Noa lingered, unnoticed behind him, to find out the answer.

Troy peered at the screen, watching the replay, then slowly nodded. "Looks good, boss."

Ed sank into his chair and sighed expansively in relief. "Oh, thank God. Peter's a tough old jerk, but that shot would be impossible to get again." He flipped through the schedule pinned to his clipboard, and Noa held her breath. Sleep? Sleep would be good. This had been the only scene left on the schedule for the night, which meant—

"Since we've lost Peter, let's use the last hour we've got. We'll pick up some of these other shots we put off yesterday. Set up for cabin exterior, page ninety-four," Ed announced, and Noa died inside.

Sleep hadn't been easily won, Noa's makeshift bed in the makeup trailer horrifically uncomfortable for the second night in a row. No one else was around to peel Peter out of his appliances when he came back with seven stitches in his hand though, and there hadn't been a whole lot of point driving the half hour to the motel only to turn around and come back to set the moment he got released. Stumbling out into the midmorning sun, rubbing her eyes and yawning, Noa decided *against* doing the math to figure out how many hours she definitely hadn't gotten.

If there was any justice in the world, then someone would have started coffee in the crew trailer. On her way over, Noa took in the sights.

The place was in strike mode, every department rushing

around to get their gear broken down, packed, and on the trucks as efficiently as humanly possible. Noa's was small and easily contained, thankfully, a privilege not afforded to the lighting and set decoration departments. Filled crates sat next to dollies waiting to be loaded. One of the riggers turned an empty box upside down and shook it, a snake sliding out and away into the grass. Even wardrobe was hustling, and Noa had to jump clear of a rolling rack that decided to make a break for it down the hill and across the parking lot, Karen in full flight after it.

Noa caught snippets of conversations as she passed, the general sentiment somewhere between worried and hopelessly resigned.

"Aren't we supposed to be white-water rafting? The river escape—"

"Off the schedule. They're going to try and do it in the tank back at the studio."

"That's going to take some work to sell."

Crosby, the perpetually frowning scientific consultant, was deep in conversation with PJ from props and Troy, the AD, by the door to the crew trailer.

"I don't see why we have to leave location," Crosby complained. "How do movies ever get made if schedules are changing like this all the time? It's not as though anyone was hurt."

"You're unhappy about being able to go home instead of crashing in a cheap motel?" Troy asked, nodding to Noa as she went by. Crosby looked as well, the intensity of his stare through his thick glasses not helped by the way he held that stare just a beat too long for comfort.

Crosby shook his head. "It's not that I prefer the admittedly subpar accommodations, but the camaraderie of the set was more pronounced on location, away from other people. The brotherhood," he expounded. "Getting to know one's colleagues on a more *intimate* level. The *bonding under fire*."

"Literally, apparently," Troy interrupted, his annoyance showing. "I'm sorry that you're not having the personal growth experience that you hoped for, but it's time to pack and get moving."

Noa let the door close behind her, cutting off Crosby's reply, if there had been one at all.

By the time she'd claimed her coffee and was leaving again, Troy and Crosby had moved on. A figure stood in the tree line, just too far away for her to make out anything more than a shadow, but for a moment, she could have sworn that whoever it was had been watching *her*. She took a step that way and the shape moved, then was gone. She stood there for a moment, waiting for it to reappear, but the only thing that happened was Denise coming around the corner and yelling at her for wasting time. Noa stayed quiet and followed her boss, trying to let that eerie feeling go.

––––––––––––

Having a couple of days off was a privilege, and Lilah slept through at least fourteen hours of her first one. She felt a little bit guilty, stealing the chance for a long, hot bath and reading her script in bed while others were working through the night, but her turn would come. Once they got back to LA she, Ishani, and their stunt doubles were going to be spending almost an entire week in the water tank pretending to be rafting, swimming, and almost drowning, and then it would be Peter's and Tanner's turns to feel smug.

At least she got to blow up a puppet at the end of it. Learning how to use a grenade launcher was definitely going to be the high point of this shoot. That, and Noa.

She'd been surprised at her own boldness a few times recently, but Noa's reaction in the trailer on Erev Shavuot had been ample proof that it was appreciated. Things were going well, too well, and that was setting off alarm bells of its own, because things like this never went well for Lilah. Not for long. They'd start dating officially—that part seemed inevitable now—and then Noa would turn out to have a secret girlfriend. Or she'd start expecting Lilah to cook for her, or brag to all her friends about bagging the beauty queen, or Lilah'd catch Noa selling Lilah's underwear on eBay...

Or maybe Lilah was simply jaded and a little damaged by previous dating disasters. Noa seemed like she'd be a good girlfriend, and Lilah still wanted desperately to find out. She needed to put her paranoia on hold.

Stretching her feet out under the crisp white sheets on her bed, Lilah scrolled aimlessly through her various social feeds. She should be running lines, but focusing was hard. She wanted to daydream about Thursday night, once Noa was back from location. About finishing what they'd started in the crew trailer. An alert pinged, and Lilah clicked absentmindedly on the pop-up that came with it. A search alert for her own name was tacky, yes, but her job practically demanded it. At least until she was rich and successful enough to hire someone to do it for her. This one was a message board posting, and Lilah felt the blood drain from her face and her chest get heavy as she read through it.

Blind Gossip Today: This red-haired scream queen is as dumb as she is pretty, and her new flick looks to be as flightless as the last. She's desperate to be seen as a serious actress and is one of three ingenues in the running for a plum role overseas, but who's going to take her seriously when she's banging her makeup artist? Wake up and smell the mascara, honey—temporary tattoos are super tacky, the rookie's using you for cred and contacts, and the casting couch only works when you're sleeping up, not down.

Thanks to the faithful reader who sent in the tip!

> **Tommyjarvis:** Lilah Silver! I'll watch anything and everything she ever does, no matter what. She'll come to her senses and dump that leech, you'll see.

> **MacheteKillSquad:** If she takes her shirt off, I'm going. Need to see those tits.

Eyes filling with horrified tears, Lilah swiped the window closed and tossed her phone to the end of the bed before she could let herself read any further. Tommy Jarvis was everywhere she turned, and she had the terrifying notion claw at her throat that he'd be there for her next job as well. No matter where she went, the creep would find her. Her heart hurt, and it was her own damn fault for reading stupid blind gossip lies.

Only they weren't lies, not all of them. Because she *was* in the running for a good new role, and she *was* with Noa, something they'd been trying to keep somewhat under wraps. And the only tattoo-like anything that she'd had done in a very long time were the butterflies that Noa painted on her shoulder.

Some of it could be coincidence or a good guess. It wasn't a huge leap to imagine that an actor was going to auditions. But her butterflies? No one had been close enough to see the one that Noa had painted in the makeup trailer, and she and Noa had been alone in her trailer for the others. Noa was the only one who knew everything in that blind item. The only one who could have put all those pieces of information together.

But why would she do it? Did she get paid for information about Lilah?

It wouldn't be the first time.

Before Brandon, there had been Carter, and Carter had seemed so nice. Right up until she caught him taking photos of her sides for *Bonsai Blowout* and uploading them to fan sites. When he'd been so protective over his phone, she'd assumed he'd been trading nudes. In some ways, that would have been easier. At least naked pictures of other girls couldn't get her fired as a security leak. She'd only barely talked her way out of that one.

Noa couldn't. She *wouldn't*.

Would she?

No, Lilah decided firmly. She had to show a little faith. The blind item had been a lucky guess, a lie that happened to hit too close to one of Lilah's insecurities, and the only thing she needed to do about it was delete the alert.

That little inkling of doubt lingered though, long after she closed her eyes in the dark. Who could possibly have made guesses that specific? If it was someone from the set, someone close enough to have seen all of what they claimed, then maybe the rest was true as well.

At least she could be sure about one thing: Noa liked Lilah for herself.

Didn't she?

———————

By Thursday night, Lilah had mostly managed to shake off the unease that had been lingering since her ill-advised wander through the wilds of online gossip. Work helped, even though they were back at the sound stage and not marooned together at the cabin in the woods. Having the afternoon off and no call until noon the next day found her parking in front of Noa's apartment building slightly earlier than they'd originally planned. She'd consciously set aside her fears and concerns about fans and leaks and stalkers. She was going to have a good time tonight.

The run-down building didn't have an elevator, and Lilah jogged up the stairs, the cake box in hand, eager to get out of the dimly lit, faintly claustrophobic space. Her heart raced faster than even the stairs would account for, her pulse thrumming in her veins in anticipation.

Taking in a deep breath, she steadied her nerves and rapped at the door. Then waited.

And waited.

And waited. Lilah frowned, putting her ear to the door. There was a faint thumping inside—had she gone to the wrong address? Only this was definitely the one Noa had given her, so—

The door was flung open, and Lilah almost stumbled in before regaining her footing. Noa stood in the doorway, a sleek tank top outlining every delicious curve, snug jeans sitting low on her hips. She blinked at Lilah a little owlishly, only one side of her eye makeup done.

Lilah smothered a giggle, the reason behind the panicked thumping suddenly becoming clear. "I'm sorry, did you need more time?"

"No, that is yes, that is—I'm running on Jewish time. I didn't think you'd be here early." Noa backed up and let her in, sublimely flustered. Her curls were pinned back, her lips red, only the lopsided liner and shadow-less eye making her look anything less than perfect. And honestly, if they weren't going out, Lilah wouldn't care about that at all.

"I had to switch over to show scheduling in theater school; on time is late and fifteen minutes early is on time," Lilah apologized, holding up the box as she stepped inside. "Can I pop this in your fridge for later?"

"Absolutely, yeah!" Noa led the way down the hall, Lilah's gaze landing and fixating on the easy, confident movement of her hips. Everything about her read *strong and fierce*, and Lilah liked to imagine that she was one of the few who knew how unsure and flustered Noa could be. It was a gift, getting to see that side of her, an intimacy she promised herself that she would never take for granted. Maybe Noa felt the same way, that she was privileged to get to know the fragile parts of Lilah. She wanted desperately to believe that she could trust Noa with more.

"Is Chrissy here?" she asked, trying to break out of the intensity of her own thoughts.

"Nah. She's over at Max's place for the night. I think it's their anniversary."

Stepping into the tiny kitchen, Lilah opened the fridge and scanned the shelves for somewhere to stash the cheesecake. Beer, leftover pizza, three jars of pickles? "Any particular shelf I should use?"

"Top shelf is Chrissy's, so either middle or bottom." Noa paused, one hand on the doorframe. "I'm running a bit behind on the makeup, obviously—gimme five minutes. Ten? Maybe ten. Wi-Fi password is on the chalkboard!" she announced when Lilah waved her off, vanishing into what Lilah supposed was the back of the apartment and her bedroom.

Lilah looked around and found the message board on the wall, covered in magnetic notepads with grocery lists and reminders of things like Noa's essay due dates—obviously not an issue now—and Chrissy's estrogen and spiro refills. And scribbled in the corner, the Wi-Fi password. But not the network name. And when Lilah called up the list on her phone, more than twenty networks with creative names scrolled by. The Batcave? Black Mountain? The Love Shack? Charming.

Noa's phone sat on the counter, and Lilah grabbed it. When she picked it up, the only thing on her mind had been checking the network ID, but the main screen opened in her hands. The phone was unlocked. Lilah hesitated, temptation gnawing at her from all directions. The stupid gossip item kept replaying in her head, impossible to unsee.

Using me for cred and contacts. Could she really be so self-serving?

Noa wouldn't ever betray her like that. She was sure of it.

Temporary tattoos are super tacky.

But Lilah had been sure—and wrong—before.

Lilah fought against her worst impulses for a good thirty seconds before the need to know became too fierce to ignore. Carter had leaked scripts, Brandon had bragged about their sex life online—what was lurking on Noa's phone? It wouldn't take long, she rationalized. One quick look and she'd prove to herself that there were no terrible betrayals waiting to be uncovered. Then she could put everything behind her.

Noa would be in the bathroom for at least another five minutes, maybe more. Lilah took a deep breath and searched for her own name.

The search results made the blood drain from her face, and she sat down in the kitchen chair with an audible thump. Okay, fine. Noa had disliked her enough to want to keep a constant reminder on hand of all the reasons Lilah was terrible. Maybe it was sarcasm not coming through properly in text, or...or some private joke that Lilah didn't understand. *List of all the things she doesn't like about me.* How very grade school. And Lilah got to see all of Noa's thoughts about her faults written there in black and white, saved in notes as though just the message thread itself wasn't enough.

CONS

» Total snob
» Doesn't like horror

» Shallow pageant princess

» Reads trashy romance

» Annoying attention-seeking habits

» Vain—always checking herself out in mirrors

PROS

» Gorgeous

» Crush on her for for-freaking-ever

» Cotton candy

And that was it. The only things Noa had thought were important enough about Lilah to put on her stupid burn-book list were comments on Lilah's looks. Nothing else meant enough to her? Nothing else mattered. Nothing Lilah had said or did, no personal quirks that Noa found appealing...and what the hell did "cotton candy" even mean?

Lilah's stomach churned, her chest throbbing and tight as though she'd been punched, tears threatening at the corners of her eyes. She'd offered to bring Noa with her to France—had that been part of Noa's plan all along? Getting into her confidence and then using her, as everyone used her? For her looks, her contacts, her...cotton candy?

No! She did not cry, she *would* not cry, and she sure as hell wasn't going to let Noa realize that she'd snooped.

Closing everything and putting it back where she found it, Lilah sat back down in the chair and waited, staring at the fridge door, until she heard noise in the hallway again.

Lilah was an actress, and despite everyone else only caring about her red hair and her tits, she knew in her heart she was a good one. She could get through the first part of the evening without letting on that she knew. After that…she had no idea.

CHAPTER SIXTEEN

SOMETHING FELT OFF WHEN NOA and Lilah left her place. Noa tried apologizing for keeping Lilah waiting, but Lilah waved it off and gave her a big smile that sent Noa's pulse skyrocketing. The clothes she'd chosen didn't help lower Noa's blood pressure at *all*. Lilah'd shown up at Noa's door with her hair down, red-gold waves tumbling down to the small of her back. Her tiny waist was on display under a pair of black denim overalls that dipped way, way too low at the open sides for Noa's sanity. Lilah wore a snug crop top underneath that left her skin bare practically from her rib cage to her hip bones, and while Noa knew every inch, somehow seeing it on display like this—available for touching but also so very *not* at the same time—was entirely different.

She was a showstopper the moment they walked into Mollyz, conversations literally fading into silence as Noa scanned for familiar faces in the crush of the almost-the-weekend partygoing crowd. Lilah paused for a beat in the lights by the bar almost like she'd planned it, found her light, and took advantage to draw everyone's eyes to her. It wasn't hard to understand. If Noa hadn't been the one walking in with her, she'd have been one of those moths swarming to Lilah's incendiary flame.

"I see Jordyn!" Noa returned to Lilah's side in time to interrupt a gorgeous bald woman asking to buy Lilah a drink. "Come on," she urged, sliding her arm possessively around Lilah's waist. "They saved us seats."

"Oh, good," Lilah replied easily and followed, pausing long enough to give an apologetic smile to her hopeful suitor. Noa bit back the comment she wanted to make about flirting, adding more swagger to her step as they walked to broadcast the news loud and clear: *This girl is here with me.*

Lilah's nerves, or whatever it was, had her back and shoulders tight under Noa's hand. She was all smiles when she was introduced around to the gang though, greeting Jordyn and Claudia like they were old friends, repeating names, shaking hands, and laughing like a politician's wife on the campaign trail. It was verging on the fake smiles and false front that Lilah'd promised she wouldn't use on Noa, and even though Noa mostly understood, it still rankled.

"You can let up a little," Noa murmured into Lilah's ear when they slid into the empty chairs around the table. It was only Noa's gang from college and a couple of extras they'd picked up along the way—Sophie, Claudia's most-recent-but-one ex, and Madelyn, who was Jordyn's brother's girlfriend's cousin...or something like that. However she'd gotten there, she was family now. "No one here is Hollywood powerful. You don't need to impress."

She got a tight smile back from Lilah for an instant, one that blossomed into a full-on pageant smile a half second later.

"I don't know what you're talking about," Lilah said, dismissing her, and an alarm sounded somewhere in the back of Noa's brain. Something was *definitely* wrong, and she had no idea what. The obvious answer was to order drinks, strong ones, and hope to God that whatever bug had bitten Lilah was something that a little relaxing could easily solve.

Seeing Lilah in this new environment was an eye-opener on more levels than one. She matched the gang round for round, and once she had a couple of shots inside her, that awful tension had drained away from her muscles. But her attitude didn't change, and the fake persona didn't go away. She laughed and chatted with Noa's friends like she'd been part of the group for ages, picking up Sophie's habit of tapping her nails on the edge of the table, the little giggle tail of Claudia's laugh. Rather than worry how she was going to help Lilah fit in, as the evening went on, *Noa* was the one who felt more and more invisible.

Some date.

The failure was probably Noa's fault. Who took a date to a group event in the first place? But Noa's friends were an important part of who she was, and Lilah had wanted to be part of the community—it had all felt like a great idea at the time. Now, watching Maddie fondle the pink, purple, and blue chain-link bracelet on Lilah's wrist, Noa was second-guessing everything.

"Piercings are absolutely hot," Claudia was saying to mixed reactions around the table. "I dated this girl with a tongue stud once, and if I hadn't been a total dyke since grade school, that thing would have been enough to turn me."

On a normal night out, Noa would have taken that as her cue

to tease Claudia about her taste in girls, but she was too slow off the draw, too distracted to play the games.

"You'd do anything with a tattoo," Maddie snorted.

"Good thing they're so popular these days," Jordyn added with a grin, flexing her bicep. The lines of poetry written around her upper arm undulated with the movement, and Claudia pretended to swoon.

"Do you have any mods?" Sophie asked Lilah, one blond eyebrow arching.

"No." Lilah shook her head. "Only the basic ear piercings. Casting directors like having options, and makeup artists get stressed out if they have to cover up too much." She laughed, shooting Noa something that looked a lot like a teasing grin. And if Noa hadn't seen her use that exact look on Tanner during filming last week, she might have bought it.

The others at the table were eating it up though, and Lilah seemed to glow under their attention even as Noa pulled away.

"But you like piercings, right?" Claudia egged her on. "I need someone on my side!"

"Oh, sure," Lilah agreed readily. "I had a girlfriend in high school who used a fake ID to get her nipples pierced. Her mom eventually found out and made her take them out, but in the meantime..." She trailed off suggestively, shooting back the rest of her drink as the table hooted and applauded.

Wait, what? Noa frowned, and Lilah ignored her.

"Hoops or bars?" Claudia asked, waggling her eyebrows and leaning her elbow on the table, as she moved closer to speak over the music's noise.

"Um. Hoops. Awesome, am I right?" Lilah improvised, only then shooting Noa a quick and uninterpretable look.

Noa shoved herself back and away from the table, pushing herself to her feet. If she didn't get out of there and cool off, she was going to say something stupid in front of everybody. What was Lilah *doing*?

"Noa?" Lilah asked, her laugh turning into a frown—and she at least had the grace to look a little guilty.

"I just need some air," Noa ground out between gritted teeth, and she strode away from the table before she could call Lilah out right there and then. Even angry, she couldn't make that kind of scene. The cool air outside hit her like a slap in the face, a sobering rush of awareness cutting through the fog of limoncello and betrayal.

Why? Why would Lilah lie about something so dumb when Noa knew the truth? Or maybe she'd lied to Noa to make herself seem what? Less experienced? How did that make any sense?

Noa wrapped her arms around her middle and paced back and forth along the concrete, trying to wrap her head around the whole scene. Lilah'd promised to be honest with her, and now Noa couldn't figure out which way was up. The night breeze was supposed to help her focus, but the only thing she was getting was more confused.

A hand landed on her arm and she whirled around, startled out of her thoughts.

Lilah backed up a couple of steps when Noa jumped, her face contorted with something Noa wished was guilt but was probably closer to annoyance. "What's going on?" Lilah asked, not contrite at all. "Why did you take off?"

"Because I couldn't sit there any longer and listen to you lie!" Noa shook her head, words bubbling out as her temper got the better of her right there on the sidewalk. "You told me you've never dated a girl before, so either you lied to them or you lied to me. And ignored me to flirt with the whole table all night, making up stories, picking up their habits, trying to be what? Some kind of fantasy version of yourself? You promised me that you'd be you," she finished, hurt drowning out her anger as she stared Lilah down.

"They're your friends. You care about what they think—and I care about what they think of me. I didn't want to tell them how inexperienced I am or how little I know." Lilah looked away, cheeks flushing pink. "I just wanted them to like me."

"That's no reason to pretend to be someone you're not." Noa raked her hand through her hair, fingers getting tangled in her curls. "Why wouldn't they like you as you are?"

"You don't." Lilah finally made eye contact and said it calmly, calm and cold.

The world got very still around Noa, the sound of the blood rushing in her ears the only thing that proved she hadn't stopped dead as well. "What are you talking about? I like you—"

For the first time ever, Noa saw anger, raw and under tight control, burning in the depths of Lilah's eyes. She moved closer, narrowing the gap between them until they were almost nose to nose. She spat out her list of Noa's sins, a liturgy of atonement meant for Noa alone. "You told Chrissy that I was a snob. That my taste in music is basic. That I read garbage books."

"Chrissy told you?" Noa blurted out, a confession in her

question before realizing, no, there was no way. "You looked at my phone? You snooped!"

Lilah tipped up her chin, defiant even in the face of the ringing accusation. "I needed to know. A lot of people have gotten close to me in order to get something from me or said horrible things behind my back. I thought you would be different. Except you aren't."

Shame and guilt washed over Noa because she had done exactly what Lilah was accusing her of, only...only outrage welled up inside, easier than apology. "That doesn't change the fact that you invaded my privacy! That was a personal conversation, and you read it entirely out of context. Eavesdroppers never hear good things about themselves, and the same goes for phone snoops!"

"Is that the fault of the eavesdropper or the people who talk shit about them?" Lilah fired back, arms wrapped around her middle like armor, a shield gone up between them. "I wouldn't know. I'm just a *shallow pageant princess*, remember?"

Noa froze completely, her brain a stuck signal skipping back and forth over the words *you snooped* and *people who talk shit about them*. "I...but you..." She sputtered, anger, shock, and mortification combining to white out any words she might have been able to find. "You had no right!" she settled on, wholly inadequate. "That list was never meant for you to see! It's not how I feel. I wanted... I was trying to—"

"Trying to make fun of me behind my back," Lilah said, filling in all the wrong words, her voice rising as she tore Noa down to her component parts. "Why? Because you were offended that doing beauty pageants made me feel good about myself? I met my best friends that way, my very best ones, and they're a hell of a lot nicer than you! And so what if I like things that you don't? You of all people should understand that there's more than one right way to be a girl."

She fired that arrow straight and true, and Noa all but staggered from the impact.

But Lilah didn't stop there. "I wanted to be like you," she said, and her voice caught for the first time. Caught, and then she recovered and carried on. "You told me I was special, and I *believed you!* I wanted you to like me for who I am *inside*, and instead the only things you liked enough to put on your stupid list were my looks? You wrote down everything you think I do wrong, and now...now I'm sorry I cared."

Noa's head spun, feeling *everything* so hard in that moment that it split between all at once and nothing at all. Her own protective instincts—always prickly, always geared toward *attack* rather than *defend*—took over before she could even fully process what was happening, and the words flew from her. In the moment, she wanted them to hurt. "Be like me? But you don't even know who you are. You care so much about fitting in and changing to be what you think other people want to see. You're even *dressed* like Jordyn tonight, and I can't believe I didn't see that before. Is there anything under there at all, or are you as fake as your smiles? Fake stories for a fake person?"

That was too far, and Noa knew it even as the words came out. *This is the moment where I destroy everything.* A single perfect tear ran down Lilah's cheek, and in that instant, Noa hated that too. She even *cried* fake.

"And what about you?" Lilah replied, the cool fury replaced

by shaking, a tremulous quaver in her voice that Noa hated and relished at the same time. "You hide from conflict, avoid hard conversations. How many times have you literally locked yourself in a bathroom to get out of talking about something this month alone? And what about *your* promises? You said dating me was worth the risk, and you're still hiding from Denise! You said you wouldn't judge me, and you're standing there looking like you've bitten into a lemon!

"How dare you tell me how I'm supposed to act or talk or dress when you're the furthest thing from comfortable in your skin? Maybe we're not supposed to have it all figured out yet, did you ever think about that? But you'd rather run away and judge from a distance and feel superior to everyone who doesn't act exactly like you." Lilah's voice caught, and she drew in a shaky, trembling breath. That was real—the devastation in her eyes was real, and it was all Noa's fault.

"My mistake was thinking that made you cool, but all it really makes you is an asshole." And with that, Lilah turned and started to walk away, receiving a totally uncalled-for smattering of applause from the bouncer at the door and some of the women waiting in line.

"I can't believe this," Noa spluttered, reeling from everything that had just been lobbed her way. How long had Lilah been sitting on all that? Long enough to have come up with the perfect words to read Noa for filth. "You're the one who broke into my phone, and *I'm* the one in trouble?" Her hands curled into fists, nails digging into her palms, but the sharp sting wasn't enough to ground her. "*I wore a matching underwear set for you!*" she shouted at Lilah's receding back.

No response, though Noa hadn't really expected one. She turned and ran, eyes filling with the burn of incoming tears, trying to put as much distance as possible between herself and the scene of the massacre before she broke down for real.

"Chrissy?" Noa burst through the apartment door into silence and darkness. Only the faint clinking of the pipes heralding that the guy upstairs was taking a shower. Right. Because Chrissy was over at Max's tonight, so that Noa could bring Lilah home.

Only it hadn't exactly worked out that way, had it? Lilah was two-faced and a liar, and Noa was perfectly justified in all the things she'd said. Totally justified. And Chrissy would agree with her! Only Chrissy wasn't home. Noa wouldn't see her until tomorrow, on set.

On set. Oh no. Noa was going to have to spend four hours alone with Lilah tomorrow, putting on fake scratches and burns and then peeling them all off again. What had been an intimate, special ritual for the two of them was going to be a disaster.

Anger was safer than guilt, and Noa let it take over. She stormed into the living room, grabbed the couch cushion, and kicked it across the room in a burst of frustration as visceral as her rage. "That stinking, lying, plastic princess *faker!*" How could Noa have gotten so sucked in by an act? And by someone who would stoop so low as to snoop through her phone! Her private messages and her personal notes and—

And if I hadn't made that list in the first place, there'd be nothing for her to be mad about.

"I should never, ever have gotten involved with her," Noa announced to the empty air in the apartment, her voice sounding scratched and broken, the world hollow. She sank down on the cushion, now toppled over in the middle of the floor, and buried her face in her hands. What did she need Lilah for anyway? She had plans of her own, and friends and goals...none of which needed a girlfriend or to have to deal with Lilah's insecurities.

Or her kindness, the way her face lit up from within when she smiled for real, the wicked sense of humor she only let fly when she felt comfortable, the sweet vulnerability she'd let Noa see in tiny glimpses.

The pain hit her from all sides, a wrenching agony at the loss of what might have been, paired with the desperate knowledge that somehow, it could all have been avoided. If she'd only been less...everything. Less judgmental. Less jealous. Less focused on her own drama at the expense of really listening to what Lilah had been trying to tell her.

Sprawling out on the floor, Noa stared at the cracks in the off-white builder's paint across the living room ceiling. The last two hours of her life kept replaying in her head, every nuance, every ugly expression on Lilah's face, every excruciating second of the fight. And Lilah's voice kept echoing in her ears, no matter how hard she tried to block it out. *All it really makes you is an asshole.*

That wasn't entirely unfair. Noa had laughed at her to her face and behind her back. She'd made fun of Lilah's decorating style, said some nasty things about her books, movies, musical tastes—and Lilah'd called her out on it. Noa'd wanted Lilah to be herself, but only when "herself" wasn't something that Noa had decided was cringy. Yeah, she was definitely the asshole for that.

But Lilah wasn't perfect either! She told people what they wanted to hear and retreated behind that plastic smile whenever she didn't want to be vulnerable. It was basically the same as hiding in the bathroom, just the person you were hiding from couldn't call you on it.

Because everyone watched the actors, and no one cared about the crew. Lilah was always on, always in the spotlight. So maybe that was how she'd learned to deal with it. But that was a coping mechanism for work, not relationships.

Noa cursed and pushed herself to her feet, pacing circles in the small living room, light and noise from the street seeming to mock her in her solitude. Being alone with her anger and her misery right now was the worst possible thing. She could call a friend, but they were all still at the club. Lilah was out, obviously, and there wasn't anyone else from work that she'd gotten close enough to to talk about life stuff. Tanner came close, but he'd been Lilah's friend first.

There was always her parents.

How about no.

Noa's phone buzzed. She grabbed it, hoping for a half second that it was Lilah.

No such drama. As if they'd heard her thoughts from a hundred miles away, it was her parents' number showing up on her screen. Time for the weekly reading of her flaws? Noa couldn't describe how little she was in the mood to deal with that. On the other hand, they were a distraction. The call was going to suck, but at least getting nagged about school and calling her grand-parents would be a different kind of misery than the agony that currently clawed at her gut.

"Hello?" Noa answered, her voice dull and lifeless.

"Noa!" Her mother's voice started off cheerful but quickly veered into concern. "What's wrong? Are you sick? You sound sick."

"I'm not sick," Noa objected, flopping down onto the floor. She propped up the cushion on its end beside her and dragged the other couch cushion down with her free hand. She needed a blanket. Lilah liked blankets. "I had a fight with...someone I liked." Her voice caught on that, and she bit her tongue to stop herself from breaking down on the phone. Like her parents needed more ammunition to poke holes in her current life.

"This was the actress you told Dad about? The one who does all the horror movies? Didn't she get an award recently?"

Noa barked a laugh. "Did you look up her IMDb entry or something? How did you know that?"

Her mother dismissed the question with an airy sigh. "Of course I did. You don't tell us enough about what's going on in your life, so what else am I supposed to do?"

"If you didn't Google stalk me, I might be more inclined to open up."

"Ahh, the classic chicken-and-egg problem."

"Hi, Dad. I didn't realize you were on the line."

"Anyway," Noa's mother continued, as though her father had never interrupted from the extension. "She's very pretty. Is she nice?"

"Yeah, she is," Noa sighed. Twisting her body, she managed to grab ahold of the hoodie that Chrissy had flung on the arm of the couch. She pulled it across the top of the cushions and curled up inside her fort. There. She lived here now.

"But so are you."

Dad picked up the conversation as soon as Mom finished talking. "What's with that pageant nonsense anyway? What kind of parent would want their children to be focused on their looks all the time? You want someone who does math olympiads. Those are pageants for the brain," he proclaimed, obviously pleased with himself. "Beauty fades, but smarts are something no one can ever take away."

"Except Alzheimer's," Noa's mother replied, water turning on and off somewhere in the background. "That can take intelligence away. And not getting enough sleep. That'll do it too."

Noa couldn't help but laugh, even as the tears had started to slip silently down her cheeks. They were trying to make her feel better, but they were wrong. Lilah *was* smart, and sweet, and so much more than her looks, and Noa...Noa was the one to blame for messing everything up. Her parents loved her, but they didn't know both sides.

"Honestly? At the start, I thought she was stuck-up. Only she's really not." Noa started babbling, the words pouring out without filter. "She's amazing. She shows up every day off-book and totally prepared for her scenes. The early wake-ups for makeup make some actors really crabby, but Lilah—she's this ray of sunshine. The whole world perks up when she's around. And she's just so *nice*. She never divas, never steps on anyone's line or in their light.

And she was pet-sitting for her costar at a moment's notice even though she's, like, stupidly allergic to his dog. She's just like that."

Noa drew in a painful breath, the thought hitting her like a blow to the solar plexus—had she ever told any of this to *Lilah*? The words kept tumbling out in a rush, everything she should have said and hadn't.

"...and she's *interesting*. We have the best conversations in the makeup chair, everything from really obscure indie cinema to music and books. She's smart and open-minded, always willing to consider other points of view. Even though I haven't been. And she's so good on camera. She's going to be a megastar one day. I've never met anyone quite like her." And now Noa would be watching it all from the sidelines.

There was a pregnant pause on the phone. Too much? That had probably been way too much. Her father coughed gently. "It sounds to me like you may be a little in love with this girl, sweetheart."

"What? No!" She rejected the idea before he was even done speaking, but it echoed incessantly in her ears.

"Are you sure? The only time I've ever heard you talk so passionately about anything was when you were trying to convince us to let you go to that Tom Savini school instead of UCLA," her mother reminded her, also being way too gentle. Oh crap. Why were they being so nice? What had they figured out that Noa hadn't? "We didn't listen and said no, and look where you ended up anyway. Maybe this time, we should be telling you to go with your gut."

"You're both ridiculous, you know that?" Noa deflected,

everything too upside down and backward for her to make sense of. Not now.

"Of course," her mother replied, all fond and soft in a way Noa had almost forgotten she could be. "But we can be ridiculous and embarrassing and love you and want the very best for our girl all at the same time. Parents are magical that way."

"Get some sleep, honey," her father said. "And tell Chrissy we said hello. Even if you can't make it home for Rosh Hashanah, remind her that she's still welcome. But she has to tell us how many girlfriends she's actually bringing so I have enough chairs this time. Last year, we had to run across the street and borrow from the Glazers."

Noa scrubbed her hand across her eyes, the button on her shirtsleeve hard against her cheek. "Will do. Love you guys," she added on impulse, then ended the call.

And now she was back to where she'd been in the first place: alone in her quiet apartment, the world outside moving along without any regard for what Noa had just thrown away.

CHAPTER SEVENTEEN

LILAH MADE IT HOME BEFORE the tears started. The moment she walked through the door, greeted by the strings of fairy lights, all her armor fell apart. Her stomach hurt, her heart hurt, and by tomorrow morning, her head was going to hurt from all the crying that was bound to happen any second now. She sagged against the wall and hugged herself tightly, trying to keep it together. The nagging reminders surfaced again, voices she'd been starting to be able to ignore. *Cover girls don't cry. Crying makes you ugly. Makes your face swell up and go all splotchy.* Music played in another room, and dragging in a shuddering breath, Lilah managed to push the urge back down for a moment. Who was around? No guests or boyfriends, please not tonight!

Rhythmic thumping came along with the music, and after a moment of hot-faced shame, Lilah recognized Kayleigh's workout routine. She turned the corner into the living room and sank down into the soul-sucker couch with relief, pulling the blanket around herself as Kayleigh bounced and high-kicked her way through the dance sequence on the television screen. One blanket wasn't enough, so Lilah pulled at the edge of a second one and wrapped that one around herself as well. Almost better.

The song ended, and Kayleigh shook her arms out, dropping the controller on the table. She turned and frowned at the bundle of Lilah sulking behind her. "What're you doing home? Didn't you have a…a thing tonight?" She shied away from the word *date*, still hard for her to say, but regret crossed her face right away, so Lilah forgave her.

"I did," Lilah said, her voice partly muffled by the chenille of her purple throw. It cracked as she spoke, and she was grateful for the shield, but there was no hiding the hot tears that slid down the sides of her nose. "And now I don't. And life stinks."

"Oh, honey." Kayleigh wrinkled her nose, as adorably as everything she did, and gave her own armpits an exaggerated sniff. "Life stinks and so do I, I'm telling you. Don't you dare cry over some dumb girl who doesn't appreciate you, or…or I'll rub my sweaty pits on you."

It was one of her weirder threats, but she advanced on Lilah like she meant it, arms up to show off the damp circles under her arms. "Ugh, gross!" Lilah objected and tried to bounce herself away, but she was mummified in the blankets and couldn't get farther than a butt cheek over. Instead of rubbing her stanky shirt all over Lilah though, Kayleigh dropped onto the couch next to her and wrapped her arms around Lilah and her blankets.

"You deserve better," she said, and that was it. None of Lilah's defenses were strong enough against *that*, and the wall of grief and rejection slammed into her with all the force of an eighteen-wheeler.

Sobbing, Lilah buried her face in Kayleigh's shoulder. "I…

really…liked…her," she got out between gasps for air, and Kayleigh squeezed her tighter. A door slammed, and footsteps announced the arrival of at least one of their other housemates, though Lilah was too busy trying not to get snot all over Kayleigh's shoulder to worry about which one.

"What happened?"

"Her date didn't go well."

Nadia sucked in air. "Not *that* kind of not well?"

"No!" Lilah shook her head, unable to get a word in edgewise as she was surrounded by three people instead of one. "Not like that. I… She said…"

Someone handed Lilah a tissue, and she blew her nose, but the hiccups started and wouldn't let go. She tried to explain, but it came out all garbled, a mess of syllables and hiccupping sobs that weren't in the right order at all.

"What did she say?"

"That Noa was trash-talking her behind her back," Brooke translated, and Lilah nodded vigorously.

"No!" Nadia exclaimed.

"That…that fudging *witch!*" Kayleigh shot off, which made Brooke giggle, which made Nadia smack her in the arm. Brooke fought back, and Lilah started cry-laughing at their antics, which sent snot all over Kayleigh's shoulder.

By the time the tussle was over, Brooke was hauling the comforter off her bed in the dining room and wrapping it around Lilah, Kayleigh was passing her more tissues, and Nadia had gone off to the kitchen to raid the freezer.

"I thought you had a yoga class," Kayleigh said to Nadia as

their housemate came back to the living room with two half-pints of ice cream and four spoons.

"Whatever, it's online and it can wait. This is house solidarity." She held out one of the spoons, waving it slowly back and forth in front of Lilah's face until she snaked a hand out of the mountain of blankets to take it.

"Shove over. Your butt's where my butt needs to be."

"Shove it yourself."

"Stop bickering or I'm pulling this couch over, and Lilah and I will eat this all ourselves."

"Thank you," Lilah said quietly when she could trust her voice again.

Brooke was the one who answered, nudging Lilah gently in the side. "Anytime, boo. That's what friends are for."

Another tissue was handed over Lilah's shoulder, she wasn't sure by whom, but the girls waited until she could breathe without hiccupping before the gentle interrogation started. There was no way to explain everything without starting further back than she wanted. If she breathed a word about the stalker, Nadia would lose her mind, so that part had to be left out completely.

So she started with the blind item and how someone had known about the audition and about Noa, the way the words had gotten under her skin until she hadn't been able to take it anymore. By the time she got to the part where she'd been standing in Noa's apartment with Noa's phone in her hand, her voice had gotten steady, and the enormity of it all was starting to break over her again, distant this time, like she was telling a horror story about someone else.

Noa hadn't been responsible for the gossip leak. Lilah'd been so distracted by what she had found that she'd forgotten what she'd gone looking for in the first place. Noa had been trustworthy and Lilah...hadn't.

"Ooh." Kayleigh winced. "Invasion of privacy. Phones are, like, sacred space."

Nadia made a face at her. "Not if you're using them for nefarious purposes. How would Lilah even know that Noa was shit-talking her if she hadn't checked?"

Lilah curled up, her chin resting on her knees and her stomach a block of ice. "I think I knew all along that she hadn't done it," she said quietly, letting the sequence of events play out in her mind one more time, in proper scene order. It didn't make any sense for Noa to betray her that way. It would make more sense if it was someone else on set. Someone who'd seen something he shouldn't have, someone who didn't like them. Like Dan Gilbert or creepy Dr. Crosby.

When you boiled it all down, what had happened? She had snooped, found old messages on Noa's phone, gotten her feelings hurt, and then...then she'd done the exact thing that she'd promised Noa she wouldn't: pretended everything was okay when it really, really wasn't. "I yelled at her for running away from hard conversations, but when I got scared and mad, I embarrassed her in front of her friends."

"And what would have happened if you hadn't looked? You'd have gone on thinking that she respected you when she doesn't. Ends justify the means," Brooke said, and now even Kayleigh looked uncertain about her original stance. "You can't be too careful."

It sounded good, a pat and certain way to let Lilah off the hook. Only Noa hadn't looked disdainful or snobby at the end. She'd looked betrayed and hurt, and it hadn't felt nearly as satisfying as Lilah'd thought it should.

"Maybe. But I don't think I like that philosophy," she confessed. "The means have to matter too. And if they do, then I really messed up." Admitting it didn't fix the problem of Noa's burn book, but maybe something that big couldn't *be* fixed.

Lilah curled up against Kayleigh while Nadia passed around the ice cream, Brooke wielding the TV remote like a weapon. "I'm putting on something light, and we don't stop streaming rom-coms until you feel better. Unless you'd rather watch *Fury Road* and imagine Noa's face on everyone who gets blown up?"

Shaking her head fervently, Lilah rejected that idea even as the pain in her heart swelled. "No, definitely not. I don't want revenge. I want to forget."

"You're a better person than I am."

Lilah waved off the compliment and dug her spoon into the ice cream that had ended up in her lap. Rocky road, awesome. It wasn't caramel cheesecake—there went the punch to her chest again and the tears burning in her eyes—but it tasted like love anyway.

———————

Lilah had already been dreading parts of the upcoming work week. Spending days on end splashing around in a water tank pretending to fall out of a boat was not her idea of a good time. But the events of Thursday night made the entire prospect of going to the studio feel like some new form of torture. "I'd prefer bamboo spikes under my nails," she confessed mournfully to Brooke over coffee the next morning. "At least I could pull them out."

"Ignore her," Brooke advised, slurping loudly enough from her mug to make Lilah cringe. "Put on your best stage smize, give her the old-fashioned cut direct, and make her feel like a total asshole for ruining the best possible thing that could have ever happened to her."

Lilah laughed but shook her head. "You're an amazing friend, you know that?"

"Damn straight I am," Brooke replied cheerfully. "And you're my boo. Anyone who messes with you goes through me. So get out there and fake it like there's an Oscar on the line."

It was an excellent pep talk, enough to get Lilah on the road to the sound stage, but any extra pep Brooke had managed to supply wore off long before Lilah got off the freeway. All her friends were angry at Noa, and so was Lilah. But Noa had said some things that Lilah…well. She wasn't sure that Noa was wrong. Not about everything.

On the other hand, if she hadn't snooped, then maybe Noa would still be smack-talking her to anyone who would listen. Maybe everyone on set knew that Noa thought she was a fluff-brained idiot and had been laughing at Lilah behind her back. Maybe—

Maybe she was exaggerating, because that didn't sound like Noa at all. If she was lucky, it was only Chrissy who actually knew what Noa really thought of her. She could probably cope with that.

Lilah pulled into the parking lot with the early light and swiped away the tears from the corners of her eyes. Noa was going to be spending the next two hours looking carefully at her face, and there was no way in hell that Lilah was going to let Noa see her cry. Not now, not *ever*. The sky looked the same as it had that first day, when she'd seen Noa unloading her car in the parking lot and thought *gee, I wish I were her*. How quickly things changed. The sky was the same, but Lilah wasn't.

Steeling herself, she slipped in through the main doors, pausing to say a quick hello to Wayne, back at the front desk. He smiled when he saw her, so at least there was one person at work who didn't think she was hopeless. And he'd been kind, checking on her when she'd freaked herself out imagining things on location. That night hadn't been her best for obvious reasons, but that was hardly Wayne's fault.

Wayne waited a moment after she said hello, watching the door like he was expecting someone else to follow her, but when no one did, he visibly relaxed. "Late night last night?" he asked, and his smile widened, though somehow, maybe, it didn't quite touch his eyes? She understood Noa's hatred of polite smiles now, the coldness behind them. Something felt off with him today. His skin had a pallor to it, and his eyes had circles under them, and for the first time, something in his steady, unblinking gaze made her want to bolt down the hall and out of his line of sight.

She was imagining things, and Lilah silently told herself off for it. *Be nice*, her mother would say. *You never know who's got connections that could lead to your next break.* It was good advice, even if it meant that Lilah had ended up with a long list of networking acquaintances and only a few real, true friends. That was just grown-up life, wasn't it?

"Not too bad," she answered breezily, trying—and failing—to hold on to her equilibrium. She could make small talk for heaven's sake! She'd only been practicing this sort of inane, impersonal conversational gambit all her life. "Went for some drinks with friends and then back home to watch movies with my house-mates." There, that sounded absolutely normal! "Any big plans yourself?"

"Oh, always," he replied, leaning forward on his folded arms and that eerie, slightly-too-wide smile never flickering. The desk creaked with his movement, and she had the sudden thought that he was probably stronger than he looked. "Not up to your usual standards, I'm sure. No red-carpet premieres or cocktail parties with the high rollers."

"Believe me, there's nothing that glamorous about my life either." Lilah forced a tinkling laugh, despite the discomfort inching up her spine. Her skin crawled, alarm bells going off for no reason she could name.

Wayne waved off her disclaimer, his eyes leaving hers only long enough to do the creep-crawl down her body and then slowly back up to her face. "Oh, no, I can't believe that. Not from an artist like you. I see red-carpet premieres in your future, Miss Silver."

"You're very kind," Lilah replied and seized the opening for her escape. "I've got to run, I'm afraid—makeup's expecting me—but I'll see you around!"

"You can bet on it." He tossed off what was probably supposed to be a jaunty salute, but Lilah couldn't bring herself to find it either charming or reassuring. "Welcome back," he called as she retreated quickly down the corridor. "And don't forget to unpack!"

Heart in her throat, Lilah braced herself before walking into her dressing room. Everything from her trailer had been moved for her after striking location, her belongings in a cardboard box on the coffee table. Even the bear from Noa had been thrown on top, feet sticking out of the box as it stared sightlessly toward the ceiling. The lights were off, and no one else was around. Lilah breathed out, her shoulders unknotting.

She might have gotten away from Wayne's intensity, but the respite was only momentary. Any minute now, Noa was going to come through that door, and Lilah was going to have to ignore her broken heart and put on the best performance of her life. Better to change into costume before Noa arrived. Lilah shucked off her clothes and tossed them onto the rack in the corner, shimmying into the shorts and tank top that wardrobe had left for her.

Watching herself in the mirror, Lilah practiced her faces. Calm! Cheerful! Did that look realistic or forced?

She's so vain, has to look at herself in every mirror she sees.

Noa's voice rang in Lilah's head, words she'd never said but had certainly implied blending with Nadia's gentle teasing and Lilah's own internal chorus of failings. Now Noa joined Lilah's mother—and acting coaches, photographers, journalists, backstage "advice"—in the chorus of critiques and little reminders: *Stand up. Don't slouch. Pull your tummy in. Pull your seat up. Don't frown. Smile. Pretend like Noa didn't stab you in the back and then rip out your still-beating heart with her bare hands.*

It was too much all at once, and Lilah's lip started trembling despite herself.

Any minute now, Noa would walk in. Any second now, Lilah was going to have to come face-to-face with the first girl she'd ever kissed, the girl she'd screamed at, and pretend like neither of those things had ever happened.

Any minute now.

A brisk knock sounded at the door, and Lilah jumped out of her skin. She clutched her heart and tried to catch her breath.

Moment of reckoning.

She pulled herself together, turning into a different person in the mirror as she watched. "Come in!" Lilah sang out. She would face whatever Noa said with every ounce of strength she had.

The door opened.

"Good morning, my dear," Denise trilled cheerfully as she sailed in, apron on and kit in hand, her kimono-style black jacket tied at the waist with a brilliant red cord the color of blood. "We're going to be waterproofing you today, so settle in."

Was this a reprieve, or...? Lilah furrowed her brow in confusion as relief flooded her brain for the second time in five minutes. "Is—is Noa not going to be doing the appliances from now on?" Had Noa said something? Had she asked to be moved to work on something else? Did Denise know about the fight, about the awful things Lilah'd said and what Noa had yelled at her in return?

"Noa's coming in a bit later today," Denise replied, seemingly unaware of the worries ricocheting around inside Lilah's skull. "Poor thing has a migraine, so I'll be starting you off. It's a good thing I'm the one who designed these makeups, hm? Don't you worry at all. You're in good hands." She set out her supplies as she spoke, adding a bottle of pure alcohol to the cosmetics and silicone pieces on the table.

"A migraine! Oh. I hope she feels better soon," Lilah replied on autopilot, settling into her chair. A migraine her *ass*. Noa was avoiding her, like she avoided everything difficult or complicated. And when Lilah had gotten herself all psyched up to deal with it too. Fine. If Noa wanted to stay away from Lilah that badly, Lilah wasn't going to go out of her way to stop her. Putting her earbuds in, Lilah settled back in her chair and closed her eyes while Denise got to work. Listening to podcasts wasn't going to be as wonderful as spending the hours giggling with Noa had been, but it was far less likely to end in makeup-wrecking tears.

Not that tears would have wrecked the makeup Lilah found herself in that day. The tank was her new home, the water thankfully heated, though that didn't stop the shivers from setting in every time she had to haul herself out between shots. The water was red with the gallons of fake blood that the crew kept dumping in, swirls and rivers of it sticking to Lilah's legs as she kicked through the goo, and the gallons of milk they'd added to make the clear water look like a silty pond gave the whole thing a faintly spoiled smell.

The production team had built up two of the sides so they looked like the riverbank, the other two left open with clear glass for shots of her kicking feet and the puppet pterodactyl. Pumping the water through the hoses gave them an approximation of rapids, and that morning, Lilah and Ishani fell out of the raft seven times, clutched desperately to each other at least eight, and had to watch the props guys inflate and deflate the raft remotely another five before Ed was happy with the shots.

She boosted herself up onto the side of the tank and gratefully accepted the towel handed to her. Ed and Troy were reviewing the footage at video village, and Lilah headed over to join them, the bank of monitors showing her attempts at drowning from four different angles. Her thighs could use some toning, Lilah decided with an inward sigh, critical eye picking out every potential flaw and ripple in her skin.

"Looking great, tiger!" Sadie draped her arm over Lilah's shoulder and rested her chin there for a beat, watching the footage. "Love what you're doing with the twisting reach. I'll try to nail that as close as I can."

Lilah glanced her way and smiled as best she could while her heart still hurt. "You're very sweet." Sadie was in costume as well, red wig pinned over her brown hair, and a rebreather hose looped over her shoulder. She wore it better though, exuding a reckless confidence that Lilah tried and failed to match. Maybe it came with being a stuntwoman instead of an actor. Her face wasn't the one on the posters, and filming didn't rise or fall with her. Did stunt performers get crazy fans? She ached to tell someone, anyone, what had been going on, but Dan was lurking within earshot, and she didn't dare. Not where he would hear her going so flagrantly against his direct orders.

"Do you ever—" Lilah began anyway, then her courage failed her. "Worry about how a scene will look? How you'll look in it?"

Sadie frowned, then shrugged. "Worry as in 'will the stunt work properly'? Sure. Worry as in 'does my butt look big in this'?

Not really. I know that I'm good at my side of things. Stick me in a stunt, show me my safety nets, and I'll hit my marks every time. The rest of it is someone else's problem. Yours this time," she said cheerfully, clapping Lilah on the shoulder. She looked at Lilah a little closer, then at the shot of Lilah's bare legs on the monitors in front of them. "If someone thinks my butt is too wobbly to be yours, then they needed to give us longer pants. Otherwise, they can suck it."

"You have a great butt," Lilah objected with a laugh. "I'm proud that casting thought mine was as good as yours."

"Aw, thank you." Sadie made a little heart out of her hands and pressed it to her chest. "I'm proud to be your butt too. We're besties now, for the record. Butt besties."

"I'll take it." Lilah smiled, some of the ache in her soul soothed, if only for the moment. "You wouldn't really tell Ed to suck it, would you?"

"Damn straight I would," Sadie snorted. "I know my own worth without my name on a marquee, and you should too," she added pointedly. The stunt coordinator called her from across the stage, and Sadie jogged off, a light slap on Lilah's apparently objectively great butt thrown into the goodbye for good measure.

Lilah watched her go and sighed. "It's not always that easy."

Linoleum was cold. And there was a spiderweb in the corner of the kitchen ceiling that Noa had never noticed before. No spider though. That was good. Or was it? If it wasn't there, maybe it was currently crawling across the floor toward her prone body, coming to investigate. "I'm too big for you to eat, Charlotte," Noa announced to the empty room. "Shove off."

Calling in sick had been a coward's move, but mental health days should be a thing even in film production. She was going to get it in spades from Denise when she did go in, but when it came to blowing up her own life, Noa was a master.

Her parents had been right. She was in love with Lilah. Beyond attraction, beyond simple desire or affection. She loved Lilah, every crinkle of her nose and ripple of her laugh, every time she warmed a room, gave of herself so openly, in every way she inspired Noa to be a better, kinder person. So she exaggerated some stories in order to fit in. Who hadn't wanted to make themselves look better every once in a while?

She was in love with Lilah Silver. And Lilah probably didn't want to be reminded that Noa existed.

Her phone rang somewhere on the floor with her, and she groped around blindly until her fingertips scrabbled against the case. "H'lo?" she answered, flipping the phone around until the speaker was by her ear instead of her chin.

Chrissy's voice sounded at the other end, echoing like she was walking down a hallway. "Are you planning to lie on the floor all day?"

"I'm not lying on the floor," Noa lied. "Why would you think that?"

"Because that's your 'I give up' pose, and today you're giving up."

The wave of despair broke over her once more, and Noa

squeezed her eyes shut against Chrissy's concern. "I hate my life," she sighed mournfully.

"Hang on. I'm going somewhere I can talk."

Noa stayed on the floor. It was quiet down there. She could think with her eyes closed and push out everything that clawed and gibbered at the edges of her mind. Only nothing could prevent the litany that repeated over and over again, an extremely short playlist on shuffle.

I screwed up. My dream is over. I hurt Lilah, and now she won't ever work with me again. I'm going to lose my only shot at breaking into the industry. Denise will fire me, and then I'll be blackballed forever. I'm going to have to go back to my parents and tell them I messed up.

Scratch that. I'd rather live under a bridge.

Was she falling asleep? It almost felt like it, the tips of her pinky and ring fingers tingling faintly and her spine pressed against the cool floor.

The darkness spoke, a still, small voice sounding inside her ear. *So what are you going to do about it?*

What *could* she do? Noa was in the middle of wrecking her own life, and there was no way to pick up all the pieces.

A door opened and closed on the other end of the line, and Chrissy's voice came back with less echo. "Are you spiraling? Because you won't have to live under a bridge."

"I wasn't going there," Noa lied again, struggling to sit up. "Though I was maybe spiraling a little. I think I've earned it, don't you? Everyone needs to marinate in self-pity occasionally." Maybe cracking jokes would get Chrissy off her back.

"Nice, real mature. In the meantime, Denise had to recruit the second assistant director's second assistant to help her do setups, no one can find the continuity photos because some of them are on your phone, and Colin's stressing out because you were supposed to be assigned to him to do gag setup for tomorrow. We can drink and anxiety-spiral tonight, but right now? Get your ass to set."

She was right; that was the worst part. Noa groaned and held her head in her free hand. At least helping Colin would keep her out of Lilah's line of sight. "Fine, yes, I'm coming. Guilt works. But if I break down crying in front of people, it's your fault."

"There's no crying in baseball. Just get here."

The minutes ticked by as Noa sat there, the linoleum cool against her legs. Finally, unable to put it off any longer, she shoved herself to her feet and padded into the bathroom. Washing her face, she paused and stared at her reflection in the small dusty mirror. The exhausted woman looking back at her wasn't a villain, but she sure as hell wasn't a hero either.

So what am I going to do about it?

Damned if I know. But I should probably start with an apology bigger than any I've ever given before. And hope to God that Lilah's willing to hear it.

By early afternoon, Lilah was ready to chuck it all and tell Nancy only to book her for period pieces. She could do a Jane Austen, all pretty white dresses and parasols and posing on manicured green lawns. That sounded delightful. She boosted herself up onto the fake riverbank, the cool air hitting her hard through the wet white

T-shirt that clung to her clammy skin. Everything had a faint green tint from the light reflecting off the green screen taking up the entire wall behind her, making her look as sickly as she felt. The tank creaked beneath her, and she rebalanced her weight. Someone handed her a robe, and Lilah took it gratefully, only realizing as she slipped it on that Noa was standing beside her instead of Karen.

"Thank you," Lilah said, flustered.

Noa stared at her for a second, mouth working like she was going to say something, but all she did was make a noncommittal sound that might have been acknowledgment. Lilah's heart clenched despite herself. Noa looked exhausted, as wrung out as Lilah felt.

Lilah ached, and her first instinct, as always, was to say something that would make it all better. Brush the hurt under the carpet and ignore the fight for the sake of peace. But then what? Pretend and keep on pretending, locking the hurt deeper and deeper away until it ate her alive? She wasn't strong enough to keep that going forever. But she could keep Noa at arm's length until filming was over, keep her from getting under Lilah's skin again. And maybe by then, seeing her wouldn't hurt so much.

"I need," Noa began, and Lilah tensed. Noa glanced back over her shoulder, and Lilah followed her gaze to where Denise was talking to Ed. "To check the edges of your appliances," Noa finished, the whole conversation so unbearably awkward. "In case the glue is lifting."

Lilah nodded stiffly. "Of course. It's your job." She stood, wrapping the robe as closely around herself as she could, while Noa poked and prodded at the seams of all the bits of latex and silicone glued to Lilah's skin. The sharp chemical astringent of the glue and latex hit her full in the face, a scent that up until now had meant safety and intimacy—now it made her stomach turn.

"Looks good," Noa proclaimed after an excruciating five minutes, during which Lilah had to stand perfectly still and think about all the ways she and Noa had disappointed each other.

Noa looked over her shoulder, and when Lilah followed her gaze, she saw Denise walking away. Noa opened her mouth, and she was going to say something—something Lilah didn't want to hear. Not now, not yet, maybe not ever. She was wet, cold, sleep deprived, hungover, sore, and miserable, smelling like Karo syrup, chlorine, and sour milk. Everything stunk, both figuratively and literally, and Lilah couldn't take another emotional blow on top of it all.

"Thanks very much," she said loudly, and across the set, Troy saw her nod.

He gestured, calling her over, and she had her escape. "Lilah, we're ready for you again!"

She turned and left without looking back, feeling worse, not better, with every step. She should be happy that Noa was out of her life and all the drama with her, and yet that last wounded look that Lilah had seen flash across Noa's face stuck with her even as she perched on the edge of the raft and got ready to lose Ishani in the rapids. What had Noa been about to say? Lilah wanted badly not to care. She wasn't quite there yet.

I got the call from Gina's assistant; they want you for *Night of Anubis*.

Luca loves you, they love you together, they're sending
me all the paperwork this afternoon.

You're going to France!

-Nancy

Lilah read the email and grabbed for her phone. She needed to call
Noa, tell her that France was on, that all her support had paid off,
that they could celebrate—

No. She didn't because Noa wouldn't be coming with her.
They were over, even if in her excitement—just for a moment—
she'd forgotten.

———————

The next few days saw Noa still dragging herself onto set looking
haunted, but Lilah didn't engage. She'd taken to wearing her
earbuds the whole time she was getting glued in. Maybe it was
petty, but it was easier this way. No more hoping for connection, just waiting for enough time to pass to turn it all into a bad
memory.

She was still in the tank most of the day, so much so that her
fingers and toes stayed wrinkled for hours afterward, and her hair
was starting to crispy fry at the ends from the amount of chlorine
pumped through the system to stop it from growing Legionnaires'
disease or something equally hideous. Saturday morning's scenes
involved a whole lot of treading water and screaming while PJ
poked her with rubber claws, and Noa was nowhere to be seen.

Karen handed Lilah her robe this time, and she cuddled into
it gratefully, jumping off the bottom of the gently swaying ladder.
"Dry off and then get changed before you catch your death of

cold," Karen reminded her, handing her a towel. Lilah nodded, taking a moment to squeeze the worst of the water out of her hair.

"I'll keep the robe until I come back from lunch, if you don't mind? That way if I drop anything on my lap, you won't come after me."

"Smart woman." Karen chuckled, warm and easy. She was the mom sort of wardrobe lady, Lilah's favorite kind. "You must be glad to be out of the tank."

"I am going to be so ready to blow that thing up," Lilah said reverently, nodding toward the full-sized dummy of the pterodactyl sitting in a folding chair near some of the background performers. Someone had tucked a leftover script side into its claws and a highlighter between its jaws. "So extremely ready."

"At least until the Karo syrup starts flying," Karen replied cheerfully, taking the hair towel back from Lilah and tossing it into her basket. "Your dry costume is in your dressing room."

A shower was going to feel so good. Once she stepped under the hot water, she'd be able to wash the stress—and the goo—off her skin and let all the bad roll right on down that drain. She could practically feel it as she hurried down the hallway, Lilah's pace picking up in anticipation of that first glorious splash.

A whistle meant Wayne was coming, and Lilah stepped aside to let him by. He passed her in the hallway, his friendly nod and smile more distracting than anything when she was so tightly caught up in her own head. He said hello, called out something else to her, but she was four steps past him before it even registered, and she didn't bother going back to fix her rudeness.

Turning the corner, her treacherous memory pelted her with images of when she and Noa had run that same path from the set to her dressing room together, covered in fake blood and giggling. The beginning.

The door to her dressing room was slightly ajar when Lilah got there, and she caught herself hesitating for a second before pushing it all the way open. "Hello?" she called out and was met with silence. She waited a beat, still nothing. Lilah rolled her eyes at herself as she headed inside. A quick glance around showed her to be completely alone, and she breathed a sigh of relief. Karen probably hadn't pulled it fully shut when she'd dropped off the clothes, that was all.

And yet. A faint whisper of fear tickled at her hindbrain, a sixth-sense niggling that something was off, even if she couldn't put her finger on it.

The bathroom door was closed. Lilah stepped toward it, leaving a trail of faintly damp footprints from her running shoes. Stepped toward it, paused, and then flung the door open to reveal...absolutely nothing except her bathroom, even the frosted shower door set open and very obviously not containing any kind of threat.

"You are such a scaredy-cat," Lilah said aloud, padding back into the room and pushing the door closed with her hip. "Even Nadia would be embarrassed for you."

The box from her trailer still sat on the end table, a sad and lonely plush foot sticking out of the top. Hit with a sudden and unwelcome pang of melancholy, Lilah reached in and pulled the teddy bear out of the box. He didn't seem to be any worse for wear after having been flung in with her extra shoes and laundry, and she brushed the shaggy brown fur away from his gray glass eyes. There was nothing wrong with keeping him, was there? There had been some good moments before everything went sideways.

She set the bear on her dressing table where he belonged, threw the lock, and showered, her paranoia still trying to trick her into being freaked out. Shadows made her jumpy, and at least once, she was sure she heard Wayne's whistle echoing in the hall long after he should have been finished with his rounds.

Something still seemed off after her shower, and the feeling nagged at her as she toweled off and dressed, looking over the room again as she reached for her clothes. Her costume change was where Karen had said it would be, her own clothes hanging over the rack where she'd tossed them that morning. Shirt, pants…bra?

No bra.

How was that possible? She'd left it right there, and wardrobe had made a big fuss on the first day about how their dressers weren't going to do personal laundry. If it had fallen in with the pile, maybe Karen had taken it without noticing?

Fear rolled back in, the feeling of something *off* raging into full-blown panic. Lilah grabbed her outfit, shook out her shirt, rolled the rack aside to see if it had fallen down the back—nothing. She stood in the middle of her dressing room, looking around, her heart thumping painfully.

Was that why the door had been cracked open? Someone had come into her dressing room? It wasn't unusual; lots of people had keys for the dressing rooms. Wardrobe, for one. Hair and makeup, various PAs and set assistants, security—but none of them had any reason to be messing with her personal possessions.

Breathe, Lilah.

There had to be a logical answer.

And she was getting in a state over nothing. The answer was right there, staring her in the face: the silly polaroid of Tanner and Rasputin tacked up with the others around her mirror. Cute he might be, but Rasputin was becoming an expensive little terror. Forcing herself to slowly exhale and calm down, Lilah rehung her clothes and shimmied into her costume for the afternoon shoot.

No clothes left out, check. Remind Karen to close her door properly, definitely. Give Tanner grief about his menace of a pet, next thing on her list.

Detouring past craft services and—for once—loading her plate up high with all the worst sorts of comfort-food carbs, Lilah spotted the rest of the main cast hanging out in a circle of armchairs in the corner of the break room. She headed over, hand raised in a tentative wave. Why did this feel so odd? Because up until this week, she'd been spending all her free time in her trailer or dressing room with Noa and not socializing with anyone else. That wouldn't be an issue anymore.

"Hail, hail, the gang's all here," she joked and lowered herself to sit next to Tanner on the couch as he scooted over to make room. Tanner had his throat sleeve on again, the foam latex appliance cut through to show tubes and fake veins, his shirt liberally splattered with blood. Mikal was back in his long green opera glove, the shoulder of his shirt above it torn and bloodied where the post-production wizards would CG in a torn shoulder joint.

The effects explained where Noa had been all morning; that much work must have called for all hands on deck. Mikal had a cigarette in his hand, blissfully ignoring the no-smoking sign above them, waving it and leaving a trail of smoke in the air behind him as he spoke.

Peter sat next to him, his stomach piece on and gory intestinal loops piled in his lap. His hand had real stitches in it thanks to his nasty fall, but he had his pen in his other hand and another page of his crossword book open on his knee. "Small scraps, fit for the birds. Nine letters."

"Tittynope." Ishani dropped into the final empty chair and stole a french fry off Lilah's plate. She was already dried off and in sweats, her head wrapped in a towel. Fake injuries still criss-crossed her arms, though the blood smears had mostly washed away. "Anyone know why I just watched Sadie cart two Segways over to the stunties' bullpen?"

Peter scribbled the letters down and nodded in satisfaction. "Brilliant. Also, I have no idea. But whatever it is, it's bound to be better than that time on the set for *TimeSiege* when the knight extras got bored enough to build their own catapult. They acciden-tally launched a pumpkin into the middle of the grotto lake. Took six hours to dry out all the equipment."

"It's going to take six hours to dry me out," Lilah complained with as much cheer as she could muster. "I'm completely waterlogged."

"Tell me about it," Ishani commiserated ruefully. "My hair's going to be a disaster after this. Not even Phoebe's deep condi-tioner routine can save it."

"On the plus side, you both will look adorable with buzz cuts," Mikal teased, and Ishani threatened him with a raised fist.

"So what brings you over here to hang out with the plebes instead of Noa?" Tanner asked Lilah, settling his chin in his hand. He was making conversation, not fishing for gossip—though, on edge, that was exactly where Lilah's mind first went.

"A girl can't hang out with her costars for lunch break once in a while?" Lilah shrugged the question off. "I was getting sick of the same four walls of my dressing room."

Tanner frowned. "You guys were really tight for a while. What's up?"

"Nothing!" Lilah protested, her voice a little too loud. Mikal and Ishani glanced over from their side conversation, and Peter looked up from his crossword. "Nothing's up," Lilah repeated more quietly this time, her cheeks warm.

Mikal raised a skeptical brow. "Lilah, you are a good actress but a terrible liar. What happened?"

She shrugged one shoulder gamely. "We had an argument, that's all. Too much time in close quarters will do that with anyone."

Mikal nodded sagely. "Ah, 'bitch eating crackers' time."

Lilah frowned at him. "'Bitch eating crackers'?"

It was Tanner who answered, and Ishani took Lilah's distraction as a chance to steal another fry. "You know, when you get so fed up with someone that everything they do annoys you. Like, 'look at that bitch over there, eating crackers that way just to annoy me.'"

"No!" Lilah objected, shaking her head firmly. "It's not like that. We disagreed about something, that's all." *I snooped where I shouldn't have, and she was meaner than she should've been.* Simple, tidy, and wholly inadequate to capture any of it. "Some friendships aren't meant to be anything more than acquaintances."

The others seemed to accept it, the conversation moving on, but Tanner leaned in close enough that she could feel his breath brushing warm against her ear. "What's a five-letter word for 'delusional'? Starts with *L*."

"Shut up," Lilah muttered, her face going hot and tears starting to prick at the corners of her eyes. She needed a subject change, and fast. "Where did you stash Rasputin during lunch?" she asked Tanner, and Peter rolled his eyes. "The little creep stole one of my bras. I want it back if you can even find it among his other trophies."

"That dog's on his way to becoming a serial killer," Ishani laughed, but Tanner looked puzzled. "Taking underwear's just the beginning. Next it'll be someone's ear in a cigar box."

"Rasputin's not on set today," Tanner replied.

The world slowed to a dead stop around Lilah, rushing blood ringing in her ears. "He's not?"

"I took him to the vet this morning. The big snip-er-roonie," he said, miming a pair of scissors near his own crotch. "The dog world will be down one potential puppy daddy. I pick him up on my way home tonight."

"So he hasn't been here since yesterday?"

"Nope. So wherever you left your bra, or with *whom*ever..."— Tanner grinned, not picking up on the rush of fear that engulfed Lilah—"it wasn't him."

"Here, have these." Lilah set her plate on the table in front of Ishani and bolted before her stupid emotions could betray her. If Rasputin didn't steal her underwear, who the hell did? One name kept ricocheting around in her head, a screen name she couldn't escape no matter how far or fast she ran.

This time, the door was exactly the way she'd left it, and so was the room beyond. No cues or clues to suggest that anyone had been in there at all, much less who that person might have been. Lilah stood there and shivered, the cold seeming to reach right into the marrow of her bones. All sense of safety was gone, her former sanctuary now just another room.

CHAPTER EIGHTEEN

LILAH WAS BADLY DISTRACTED THAT afternoon, so thank goodness they were only doing blocking for the fight tomorrow. She second-guessed the way everyone looked at her, from Sadie's hyped-up excitement to Dr. Crosby's intense stares and even Wayne's cheerful whistle. But how could she figure it out? She wasn't allowed to tell anyone about That Guy. There were people who already knew—Mr. Gilbert and Peter—but what if one of *them* was Tommy Jarvis or the blind item leaker? Either one of them could have come up with the information, and both could have gotten access to her dressing room without anybody asking questions.

By the time she was released from rehearsals, Lilah had made up her mind. The production office was buzzing with activity when she walked in, a half dozen assistants and coordinators on headsets and phone calls, others hunched over laptops. Fluorescent lights flickered overhead, and the industrial-gray carpet muffled her footsteps. Her own eight-by-ten-inch photo greeted her, one wall of the office filled with headshots of the cast all neatly labeled with their roles.

The head of security was in the producer's office when she approached and knocked cautiously on the partly open door. Good. A witness would make this easier if Mr. Gilbert tried to scare her again, or worse. And if it *was* him, then he'd know that she knew, and then…that was where her plan died a little. But this was the first step toward sticking up for herself.

"Can I interrupt for a moment?"

Mr. Gilbert waved her in, his usual look of pinched irritation softening when she obeyed. "Lilah. What can we do for you?"

"Things are going missing from my dressing room," Lilah informed him calmly. "I think someone's been in there who wasn't supposed to be." He looked surprised, so that was a good sign. But surprised that something had been stolen or that she was bold enough to call it out?

Mike had his hands folded over his stomach when she came in, his foot up on his knee, and he barely shifted his attention from Mr. Gilbert when she made her accusation. "Things go missing all the time on set," he said, trying to soothe her but doing so dismissively. "Are you sure you haven't just put something down somewhere else? You've got busy days, and it's easy to get distracted."

"I didn't get distracted. I went to set, and when I came back, my *bra* was gone."

"And the last time you had a problem, you thought someone set fire to the props truck when it was just an equipment accident," Mr. Gilbert reminded her, and Lilah's face flushed hot. "I'm sure this is another mistake. You'll find it on the floor, or it got mixed in with the costume shop laundry."

Cowed, Lilah shrank under his callous glare. *Don't make waves. Don't be "difficult." Actresses like me are a dime a dozen, and the pains in the butt don't get hired again. Be pleasant, smile, keep sweet, thank him for his time—*

No.

I know my worth.

"I am not imagining things, Mr. Gilbert, and I would appreciate you taking me seriously." She said it as firmly as she could manage, keeping any quaver out of her voice. Not because she was playing a role but because she deserved to be more than invisible. "I'm not asking for an inquisition or for you to fire anyone. I want a lock on my door. Given the circumstances, I think that's perfectly reasonable and well within the film's budget."

"There are already locks on the doors for when the rooms aren't in use, but they all use the same master key. I can't give it to you. It'd be a security risk. Makeup and wardrobe," Mike blustered, "they need access."

"Give Denise and Karen a copy of the key, or they can have the combination. Or make it a swipe card system like our entry passes," Lilah suggested, her fear thick in her throat. "But *given the circumstances*, I need some more assurance that the production has my back." She snapped her mouth shut before she said too much and irrevocably crossed that line, half convinced she already had and he'd decide she wasn't worth all this trouble.

Only he didn't. Mr. Gilbert just looked a little relieved, maybe that she hadn't asked for more? She should probably have asked for more.

"A lock can be done," the producer confirmed. "Mike, take care of that work order for us please."

"A second lock for Miss Silver's dressing room," Mike grumbled, searching his jacket pocket and pulling out a crumpled paper pad. "Should I post extra security on the room too? My new guy's got nothing better to do."

"By 'new guy,' do you mean Wayne?" she asked, and that tightness in her chest came back. Only this time, it didn't seem to have a source, and she tried to ignore it. Being overly friendly didn't make someone a bad guy. "He was very kind to me on location."

Mike snapped upright in his chair and looked at her sharply. "I'm sorry, can you say that again? He was on location?"

Alarm bells set up a chime in Lilah's ears, and she sank down in her seat. "The night before the fire. I was sleeping in my trailer, and I thought I heard someone prowling around outside. I got up to look, but the only person around was Wayne. He was doing his rounds and took me seriously even though it turned out to be nothing," Lilah admitted, still a little embarrassed by the whole thing. "I guess he didn't file a report?" The burst of confidence that had been pushing her through the whole interview flagged, leaving her uncertain and very much in a spotlight she didn't want.

"Wayne wasn't assigned to location security," Mike replied, and Lilah's self-consciousness stopped dead. All her thoughts did, and she blinked at both men in confusion.

"What do you mean?"

Mike shifted his bulk and stabbed at Mr. Gilbert's desk with an emphatic finger. "I mean, he didn't have any shifts on location.

We're studio security only. All he's supposed to do is warm the desk, make sure people sign in and out. He's a sub, a friend of one of my regular guys. He asked to work on this shoot, and we needed the extra body, so I figured what the hell."

God, it was such a cliché, but Lilah's blood and guts actively turned cold. Every smile Wayne had given her, every word he'd said when he'd been staring her down, all of it ricocheted madly through her head. She was back in the trailer, straining to hear the sound of footsteps, listening to the sound of off-key whistling coming from nowhere in particular, back in her dressing room staring around at walls that suddenly felt unfamiliar. Violated.

He asked to work on this shoot.

Mouth dry, not wanting to know the answer, Lilah asked the question anyway: "So what was he doing there?"

Mr. Gilbert scowled. "I don't know the answer to that yet, but you can be damned sure we're going to find out. And in the meantime, I want that guy off my lot. He's not union, so no one will give a shit, and I don't need the liability hassles. I don't want to see him here again."

———————————

Noa's life sucked. Forget all the phone calls and trying to explain to her entire friend group why she and Lilah had bailed on Thursday. She still had to work cheek-to-cheek with Lilah, hands all over her body, and what had been a mind-blowing thrill at the beginning of principal photography was suddenly a horror show worse than any movie in her collection.

Not because Lilah was yelling at her—that would have been

bearable. But because she *wasn't*. It was either the silent treatment with her earbuds in or a fake professional smile, no more personal than the one she gave to the guys filming the behind-the-scenes extras. It was awful, and every second Noa spent in her company was a knife-through-her-heart reminder of what an idiot she'd been. If she'd deleted that stupid list or maybe...maybe not have made it in the first place. Then even if Lilah had snooped, she wouldn't have had anything to find.

This is the lesson I'm supposed to take from this? Hide the evidence better?

That didn't feel right either, but any deeper introspection left her nauseated and exhausted, easier to blank it out and spend all her time elbow-deep in buckets of fake blood and gelatin. On the other hand, at least she wasn't that security guard.

Noa stopped in her tracks, cup of coffee warm in her hands, and watched the head of security frog-march Wayne the desk guard out the front door. She stopped a PA passing in the hallway to ask the obvious question.

"No idea. Probably stealing from one of the dressing rooms. Money or something," the PA replied with a diffident shrug. "Or selling drugs out of his car. I hear it happens all the time with those rent-a-cops."

"You'd think they'd do security checks on the actual security guys," Noa said dryly, watching the removal turn into a heated argument out in the parking lot. Wayne saw her, stared right at her through the glass doors, and suddenly, the whole thing wasn't so funny anymore. *A shape in the tree line, watching her.*

The offensive-lineman-sized head of security was on his way

back in when Wayne made a break for it, grabbing the door after the other guard passed through.

"She doesn't get it!" Wayne shouted incomprehensibly, stabbing his finger directly at Noa. "She doesn't understand yet. But she will, and so will you!" He didn't make it any farther into the building, the head of security spinning surprisingly lightly on his heel, grabbing Wayne by the arm, and escorting him right back out the way he'd come in.

What the hell? Noa shuddered, cold as the blood that drained from her face slowly started to work its way back to its proper place. Her fingers clenched on her coffee cup, and she watched until Wayne had been escorted out of sight of the main doors, waiting for her heart to settle back into rhythm.

"Understand *what*?" she asked the empty hallway and got no answer back. And who was "she"? There were a whole lot of "shes" working on this movie, but when had any of them had anything to do with the desk security guy? Did he mean Lilah? But why would he care?

Noa's phone beeped at her, warning her of the time, and she drew in an unsettled breath before moving again. Wayne's shouts lingered in her mind, the sheer *weirdness* of it all hanging over her head like the proverbial sword of Damocles. At least there was some faint comfort in the knowledge that she wasn't the only one having a terrible, horrible, no-good, very bad day.

Hurrying through the halls to the props shop, Noa skidded in the door to see Denise and Colin wrestling the full-scale pterodactyl head onto the dolly. Time to shake off the feeling of impending doom and focus on what was right in front of her. Today was explosion day.

I KISSED A GIRL 321

"Noa! Just in time," Colin greeted her cheerfully. "You and PJ get Fluffy here over to set, and I'll follow with the air mortar. Denise has the brain refills."

"You named him Fluffy? Not 'Rodan'?" Noa asked with a grin, shooting back the last half of her coffee and wincing at the burn on her tongue.

"Of course. Isn't it obvious?" PJ mocked her right back, looping his arm around the distinctly non-fluffy rubber dinosaur's neck and flicking a finger at one of the dozens of vicious-looking teeth planted firmly in the mouth. The tooth bounced back from the snap, the whole jaw section wiggling. Noa burst out laughing despite everything that was awful. How had she ever thought of him as some generic teamster lunkhead? He'd become a friend without her noticing it, and...

And that was exactly what Lilah had been saying all along. That Noa was a judge-first-decide-later person. The way she'd treated PJ was a prime example.

"Okay, I can see it now," Noa joked back, the revelation fighting with a new rush of chagrin.

"Flirt later, work now!" Colin called over as he loaded up the second dolly.

PJ turned red, and Noa had to head that off at the pass right now or she was going to be in worse trouble. "Sorry, man," she offered. "You're fun, but you're really not my type."

"Thank God for that," he snorted, but his smile let her know that it was all in good fun. Popping the brakes on the dolly, he nodded toward the door, and Noa ran to pull it open. "And we're moving."

They rolled into the sound stage in a cluster, arriving as rehearsal was still underway. Lilah was there, as was Sadie, both redheads paying close attention to the stunt coordinator's safety talk. Noa was left with far too much time to reflect as she watched the team walk through Lilah's next take.

"Hit the ground and roll to this mark, then come up holding the grenade launcher. The camera will be here, so hair flip to the right side, and deliver the line to this point—Bodhi will be holding the tennis ball for your sightline." Ed gestured and Lilah nodded, her arms folded. "Ready?"

Lilah glanced over her shoulder, and her gaze landed on Noa. For a moment, the character slipped, and Noa was looking at *Lilah*. Not her role, not the fakey-fake smile, but a wistful, sad sort of frown-smile that twisted Noa up inside and spat her out raw. Then Lilah looked back at Ed, and the moment was gone, just an actress and her director, with Noa on the sidelines.

"Hell yeah," Lilah said, her bravado sounding as natural as anything Noa had ever heard her say. "I love the parts where I get to kick some butt."

"That's my girl," Ed replied approvingly, and Noa had to bite her tongue to stop from calling him out. Lilah didn't flinch at being condescended to, walking off-camera while Ed put the grenade launcher back beside the bloody, headless dummy dressed in fatigues. "And go."

Lilah started moving, her chest heaving with ragged breaths as she took the dive and rolled back up to standing, grenade launcher in her hands. Backward, the butt end pointing at the tennis ball. She glanced down at it but didn't break character, flipping her hair dramatically back over her shoulder and staring Bodhi down as he snickered. "And *this* is for tanking my GPA, *asshole*," she cried in vengeance and mimed shooting the backward launcher like a rifle, tucked against her shoulder. Laughter rippled through the crew, and she set the launcher down, shaking her arms out as they reset for another take.

It was hard to watch and amazing all at the same time. Lilah was in her element, that glow of the spotlight matched by the glow she was exuding as she did the job she loved. Noa had to force herself to turn away, Denise gesturing for her attention.

Troy was crouching by the four-foot-long puppet head and talking to Colin and Denise when Noa rejoined the group. "So how's this work?"

"It's a sweet little build, if I do say so myself," Colin replied, popping open the fake skull with a squeeze of his hands. The inside had been painstakingly painted in purples and greens, laced with 3D-printed structures that looked both biological and alien. "Based on a KNB design. The skull's hinged so we can blow it open with the air mortar. The pressure shoots the gelatin and blood squibs out the back, and when we need to reset, we pack the skull again and push the pieces back into place. Simple yet effective."

Troy nodded approvingly. "Anything simple is a go from me. What's the splatter radius gonna be?"

Colin grinned, his eyes alight. "Son, let's just say everyone's going to need a raincoat."

"And grenade, go." Noa sat back on her heels and watched as Bodhi pulled on the end of the long wire, tugging the grenade projectile out of Fluffy's mouth and back along the monofilament line of its trajectory. The film would be reversed later and tweaks done by the computer guys to turn that into Lilah's shot flying straight down the toothy lizard's throat. "Good. We've got it."

That piece disassembled, Bodhi retreated behind the splatter line, and PJ grinned at Noa. "We're on."

Getting raincoats for the entire crew hadn't exactly been practical, but Noa ended up handing around dollar-store plastic ponchos and covers for the cameras. Tarps were laid out, and from the corner of her eye, she noticed the actors gathering to watch.

"Are we ready?" Ed called down from his chair, and Colin gave him the thumbs-up. "Go hot on the effects, please."

"Three," Noa called out, her adrenaline bumping. Everyone's attention was on her, and all she could do was hope to heaven that the gag worked. "Two, one!" PJ hit the button.

The air mortar went off inside the head with a thud like a shock wave. The skull, rigged with its hinged flaps, exploded open. Rubber pieces shot backward, followed by a shower of crap that splattered not only the cameras and their operators but also sprayed viscous fluid all the way back to the director sitting in his chair. The plexiglass shields in front of the more sensitive tech streaked purple and green, lines of gelatin and colored Karo syrup sliding down the glass in oozing puddles. Cheering erupted from the onlookers, with scattered applause.

Noa turned, hoping, even though it was probably pointless— but Lilah *was* watching, had moved up to the front of the crowd of onlookers, and was laughing with the rest. Then, when Noa's eyes met hers, Lilah raised her hands and sent a little golf clap Noa's way. She clapped *and* she gave Noa a small smile, a real one, and Noa's heart lurched sideways in her chest. The only thing she could think of to do was smile back, stick both her thumbs up, and hope.

Did it mean anything? Probably not. Lilah was gone when Noa glanced over the second time. But it was more reaction than Noa had had out of her in three days—not that she'd been counting.

"Review the footage," Ed called out while Troy was laughing too hard to comply immediately.

"We got *chunks*. That's fantastic!"

"Do one more for safety."

"Noa? Start repacking the brain. Noa?"

"Coming!" Noa shook off the distraction and tried to focus on the job. She'd been watching Lilah, who'd also been watching her. Maybe it was permission or a sign. Oh, that whisper of hope!

Lilah doesn't hate me.

It was enough.

Well, no. It wasn't *enough*. *Enough* would be forgiveness, a chance to make it up to her, to prove forever and always that Noa didn't think Lilah was dumb or shallow or any of those things she'd been so stupid as to think—or write or *say*—in the first place. Noa could change. She absolutely could be a better person, if only Lilah could be convinced to give her one more chance.

CHAPTER NINETEEN

"TELL US ABOUT YOUR CHARACTER."

"My name is Lilah Silver, and I play Clea. She's a graduate student, and she's part of a special research group studying a clutch of fossil eggs that were found in the Amazon jungle. Only everything starts to go wrong when the eggs hatch."

The light burned in Lilah's eyes, but she kept the smile pinned to her face as the PA behind the camera gestured for her to keep going. Sunday morning and instead of having brunch with her housemates, she was delivering studio talking points to a bored cameraman for DVD extras that no one in their right mind would ever watch. She was a mess wearing a Lilah face, pretending more fiercely than when she was delivering her lines in front of the green screen on the studio wall. "We spend a lot of time running away from the dinosaurs, and then we get a chance to get our own back. The action is really intense!" she chirped inanely.

Surely he had more than enough footage now to call it, but no. Here came another question, and this time, it wasn't one she'd prepared a cutesy story for.

"What about conflict on the set?" he asked, reading the question off a list on his phone. "What's it like to be working with everyone on such an intense film?"

"Conflict?" Lilah repeated as though she hadn't heard him, grabbing for any little bit of time to focus her thoughts. "No, not at all," she lied through her teeth. "Ed likes to tease me about doing my own stunts, but that's what we have Sadie for. Sadie Graf is my stunt double, and she does the things my agent won't let me do—like getting set on fire. She's great to work with. Really, everyone here has been!"

It was one of her best performances ever, only this wasn't one she could ever put on an awards reel. Lilah had been walking around with her brain floating an inch behind her eyes all weekend. Even seeing Wayne get perp-walked out of the studio yesterday hadn't done much to assuage her fears. Sure, Mike and his guys would be on the lookout to make sure he didn't get back in the studio, but what about when she went home? If Wayne was capable of sneaking onto location in order to get closer to her, then he was capable of a lot worse. Including stealing her bra, sending invasive emails, and posting awful things online.

But worse than that, what if he wasn't her stalker? What if there were two of them or more, waiting around every corner, ready to violate her sense of safety again and again? She felt like Nadia, who watched hours of crime TV and saw serial killers around every corner.

Only this time, the threat was real, and it knew her name, phone number, and cup size.

The thought broke through the dam that she'd been building

to hold in her feelings, and she felt the turmoil begin to swell up from her gut. "Are we done?" she asked brightly, every nerve brittle and her fingers closing tightly on the arms of the folding chair. "Thanks so much!"

She escaped, fleeing for her dressing room and the safety of a closed door. She swiped her card through the new lock and pushed the door open when the light obediently flashed green. Biting the bullet, she fished out her phone and fired off a text. It wasn't failure to admit to needing help.

> **Lilah:** I need puppy cuddles and no people. Can I borrow Rasputin?
>
> **Tanner:** He'll be right over.

A few minutes later, something scratched at her door. Curious, Lilah cracked it open. The puppy sat there, head cocked as though waiting for her, the plastic cone around his neck the only sign that he'd been through minor surgery. A bag was tucked into his collar, and when she bent down to take it, Rasputin dragged his wet tongue all the way up her face. "Yuck," she complained half-heartedly, and he licked her face again. "Come on in."

Cookies. Tanner had swung by craft services and liberated a couple of her favorite cookies, tucking them into the little ziplock baggie. The note inside said *eat these before he does*. Done and done.

The crocheted afghan thrown over the old chair was a poor substitute for her purple blanket, but it would do. Lilah pulled it around herself and curled up in the chair, Rasputin in her lap.

He nosed at her elbow and only settled in for a head scratch once she'd popped the cookie in her own mouth and the chance to beg for treats was gone. The butter-sweet melt on her tongue helped a little but not as much as being able to bury her hand in Rasputin's curly mop and watch his tail wag in appreciation.

She fought the urge to look at the emails again. Or see what new horrible things people were saying in that blind gossip thread. Squeezing her eyes closed, she swallowed hard and tried to stop the tears from coming. They came anyway, her breath catching as she tried to choke them back. Rasputin tried to lick them away, bumping her face with the edges of the cone, and she shushed at him to settle.

She needed to do something, anything, other than sit and mope. Cuddles were good, but maybe a friendly voice and a distraction would be better. Her finger found her speed dial before she made the conscious decision to call. When her grandfather answered, her tears started silently coursing down her face once more.

"Lillian, bubbeleh! What's new with you?"

"Only everything. Life is awful right now, Zaidie." Lilah filled him in quickly on some of the things that had happened, leaving out the fact that she'd been on a date with Noa and the reasons for the fight. Some things were still too personal, too real to put into words with her grandfather, even though he'd probably be accepting. Right now, she couldn't take one more risk.

"I admired her so much. I tried to be like her, and that didn't work; then I tried sticking up for myself in my own way, and that worked a little bit. But what if the producer decides that I'm too much trouble to work with because of this *creep*, or what if he *is* the creep and…I'm just…I'm lost," she confessed. Rasputin tried to chew the corner of her phone, so she set him down on the floor, curling up again once he was exploring the room. "Help me, Zaidie. I don't know who I'm supposed to be right now."

"The creep, that's a problem for the police. The rest of it, that's a bigger question." There was a slurp on the other end of the line, a drinking-coffee sound, so blissfully *normal* that she melted a little inside. "When my parents moved here after the war, they had to change their names in order to find work. So they did. Changed their names, bought a house in a nice suburb, tried to be exactly like everyone else. And you know what they found out?" he asked her.

"What?"

"It didn't make them any happier. Don't be in such a rush to give up the things that make you special. The world won't love you any better, and you'll have lost something precious along the way. Just be you, bubbeleh. Not someone else's idea of who you should be. You're perfect exactly as you are."

Lilah smiled against the phone, even though he couldn't see it. "That's very profound. When you were young, did you ever think about becoming a rabbi?"

"Thank goodness I didn't. I was a much better architect than I ever would have been a scholar," Zaidie replied, and she could hear the fond smile in his voice too. "But I have flashes of insight every now and again."

"I want to see—" A low growl interrupted Lilah's thought, and she squirmed around in her chair to see what was going on. Rasputin had somehow managed to stretch his neck up as high as her dressing table and had snagged the teddy bear. "Give that back, you little monster! Sorry, Zaidie, dog-sitting. Gotta go."

She jumped out of the chair, tripped over the corner of her afghan, and almost took a header into the mirror but managed to catch herself before she fell. "Rasputin! Drop it!" He had the toy's arm in his mouth and was shaking it for all he was worth, growling and snarling and backing away into the corner of the room as Lilah advanced. She grabbed one of the legs and tried to haul it out of his mouth, accidentally triggering a game of tug-of-war. "Give! What command did Tanner train you with? Drop! Leave it! No!"

That did it. Rasputin shook the teddy bear one last time, and something let go. Lilah stumbled back with the remains of Noa's gift in her hands. The fluff was everywhere, but so were… wires? The stomach area had ripped open, as had the head, and something was inside. Something hard and black and connected to a battery pack. Lilah tugged on the wire and pulled the object free. It popped out of the bear's head, trailing fluff along with it, and she got a good look for the first time.

A camera, with a tiny microphone and a little lens attached to one of the bear's hard glass eyes. The teddy bear was a nanny cam.

"Oh my God," Lilah breathed out, stumbling backward and falling hard on her butt. She sat there in shock, staring down at the device. Noa had given her a nanny cam? *Noa* had bugged her dressing room? Why? To get nudes?

That didn't make any sense at all. Noa had access to her room whenever she wanted, and if Noa had asked…at one point, Lilah might have considered posing for her. Had she given it to Lilah not realizing that it contained a hidden camera?

Only…only Noa had never mentioned the toy, had she? She'd made a big fuss about the butterfly card but never the bear. So maybe it *hadn't* been from her. But if not Noa, then…

Lilah sucked in air as the realization hit, another blow in a week full of psychological beatings that she was sure would never heal. A camera in her dressing room. *That* was how someone had found out about the butterflies and Noa and all the rest.

She needed to talk to security and to Ed. And the police! This was so much bigger than anything she could deal with alone. Grabbing the pieces of the nanny cam, Lilah shoved them into her bag and headed for the door.

It opened before she got to it. And framed in the doorway, a nightmare.

"Lilah. Lillian, if I may." Wayne stood there, backlit from the hallway, dressed all in black. He held a bag over his shoulder, and the master security key dangled in his hand, his face lit up with an eager smile. The combination of everything together made every word he spoke sound sinister. "Before you go anywhere, I have a proposition for you. And you're going to want to hear me out."

CHAPTER TWENTY

RASPUTIN BARKED AT THE INTRUDER, and Lilah backed up, her stomach tangled in queasy knots. "You were fired," she said unnecessarily, because of course he would already know that. "You were stalking me on location."

"Stalking? Never!" he objected, spreading his hands wide. "I needed to protect you, Lillian. No one else was doing a good enough job. No one else could. I know you, you see," he continued earnestly, backing her into the corner by her chair. "I know everything about you. I've been to all your appearances. You even signed an autograph for me at HorrorHound Weekend last year. I was dressed as Bongo, so I know that's why you didn't recognize me here," he assured her confidently.

That jolted her memory, the fan in full costume as the clown that had murdered her in *Killer Carousel*. Her first onscreen death, first line on her IMDb, first for a lot of things. He'd followed her around that weekend, a jolt out of the corner of her eye every time she saw the red nose lurking. She'd written that off as convention silliness at the time and forgotten about it. After all, there'd been no harm done.

Not then. Now as he waited expectantly for a reply, she wasn't so sure.

"Of course I remember," Lilah assured him, darting a quick look at the door, which had swung closed behind him. She couldn't make it without getting past him, so she tried a different tactic. "You were protecting me then too, weren't you?"

His eyes lit up, and his whole body softened. "I was. You're so right. You see? I've been beside you since the beginning. You got me fired, which is a problem." He scowled, then rearranged his features into something more closely resembling but otherwise utterly unlike a smile. "But you can make it up to me. It's going to be great. We'll have a wonderful time, Lillian. I'll treat you so well. You'll wonder what you ever saw in any of those muscle-bound morons you dated before."

The way he switched the smile on and off was eerie to the extreme, leaving her off-balance, wondering if she'd really seen the scowl after all. "I'm not sure what you mean," she stalled, edging closer to the door. That also brought her closer to him, an unfortunate side effect with his eyes trained on her every movement. Drinking her in, consuming her. Like she was a *thing* to be consumed in the first place.

"I mean us," he explained and gestured back and forth between them, still with that faux ease. "You and me. You're going to be my girlfriend. We'll be a power couple—my smarts, your beauty, it's a perfect match. I've got so many ideas for your career. You can leave it all to me."

"That's very sweet to offer," she lied, clutching the bag that rested heavy on her shoulder. Where was Rasputin? "But I've already got an agent, and I'm kind of seeing someone." Except Noa was a lost fantasy already, but Wayne didn't need to know that. Maybe the less available he thought she was, the more likely she could get out of this without setting him off.

Wayne shook his head, moving to plant himself squarely between her and the door again. "See, now I know that's a lie. You already gave Noa the heave-ho, and good for you. She doesn't deserve you."

Lilah shook her head. "How could you possibly know what's going on in my private life, Wayne? We don't talk all that much." Wrong move.

Rasputin growled from behind her legs, and Wayne's reply shattered the illusion of good cheer he was still earnestly trying to project. "Because that little toy of mine in your bag has been recording you since the day you got it. I've been keeping a close eye on you, Lilah. Because I knew that one day, you'd recognize all the work I've done for you, and you'd be grateful."

There it was, the thing she'd been terrified of.

She'd had the bear with her in her dressing room, in her trailer, and now he'd seen everything. Dressed and undressed. Kissing Noa and crying over her. Every time she'd thought she was alone, he'd been there with her.

The fight with Noa faded instantly into insignificance, and now all she wanted was Noa behind her. Noa would clock him one and never miss a beat. Her phone—she grabbed for it, finger hovering over the emergency speed dial. "But I can make it all go away by what? Dating you? Sleeping with you?" Lilah's voice cracked, the pitch rising as she got closer and closer to hysteria.

"That's never going to happen. What's your next step, blackmail photos?"

"See, that's what you don't understand, not yet. I'm not here to hurt you, Lillian. I'm *protecting* you. Like I've always protected you. Here, on location, online—though you really need to stop blocking my messages. How am I supposed to take care of you if you block me?"

Oh. The realization hit her square between the eyes as Wayne kept talking. *He's the creep.* "Tommy Jarvis?"

"So misunderstood as a character. And like him, I'm the hero you need. You just need a little push to see it." The bag moved on his shoulder, and he brightened, a look of excitement that sent daggers of fear into the pit of her stomach. "Like this. I found him on location, and it reminded me of that scene in *Snake on the Plain*, you know? Where you were stuck in the tree and Graham fought off the snakes to rescue you and carry you away. We can do that now! I'll be Graham, and you'll be you." He gestured back and forth between them with growing enthusiasm, like he was Ed or Troy setting up a shot rather than an overly possessive fanboy in her dressing room.

"And this will be the snake." He reached into the bag on his shoulder and drew out a tan-colored snake, long enough to wrap up his arm and around his shoulder, open mouth full of pointy fangs. "My cousin is an animal trainer. Did you know that? He does exotic animal work for films. He's the one who got me into movies in the first place, and now it's brought me to you. It's amazing how these things work themselves out, don't you think?"

Rasputin lunged in a flurry of barks and yelps, and Lilah grabbed him, her phone slipping from her hand and sliding under the coffee table. Shit! She couldn't grab her phone like this, and Wayne looked so *happy* to be holding the rattlesnake, babbling on about proving himself as a protector... Playing along made for a crappy backup plan, but whatever worked to get her and Rasputin out of there unbitten.

"Sure, Wayne, sure," Lilah soothed, backing away until the backs of her knees hit the edge of her chair. "But you know that was just a character I was playing. This isn't the Congo, and that's only one rattlesnake, not a nest of tree cobras. It won't be the same as when I was filming."

He paused partway through his monologue and considered that for a moment before nodding seriously. "You're right, of course. You're so right. We can greenscreen the Congo background, of course. It's amazing what they can do with computers. And the chair can stand in for the tree. And don't you worry about the number of snakes. I have just the thing." His eyes alight with excitement, he started for the door.

Lilah let out her breath. Just a little longer and he'd be gone, then she could run—

"Why don't you start rehearsing? Don't go anywhere until I get back." He dropped the snake to the floor and left, closing the door. The lock clicked. The snake landed and coiled immediately into a figure eight on the floor between her and the door. Its tail set up a steady rattle, and its closed-mouth head lunged at her when she went for it anyway, Rasputin squirming and barking in her arms.

Lilah screamed and jumped away, the snake's lunge missing her ankle by scant inches. She scrambled into the chair, Rasputin still in her arms, and sucked air into her panic-constricted lungs. From the hallway, she heard Wayne begin to whistle, the eerie tune fading away with the sound of his footsteps leaving her behind.

Her phone was out of reach, her door locked, and any minute now, Wayne was going to be back with God knew what. And if he didn't get what he wanted from her, then what? Leave her with the snake until she got bitten? Release nanny cam footage of her all over the internet?

Someone would come looking for her when she didn't show up to her next call. Noa, Phoebe, or Karen. Or Tanner would come to get Rasputin. All she had to do... Lilah put her foot down on the floor, and the snake lunged again, hissing and making a rattling sound. She yanked her foot back up, biting back the scream. Did snakes care about loud noise? If she yelled for help, would it attack?

Think, Lilah, think! She needed to get her phone. All she had with her was what was in her pockets and her bag. It didn't amount to much: the remains of the teddy bear, a change of clothes, her makeup case...nothing like a yardstick that she could use to reach her phone without getting down from the chair and getting in range of the snake.

Her frantic search did turn up a pair of workout leggings and a maxipad. If she tied a knot in the end of the leggings and wrapped the pad around that, maybe she could get it close enough that the sticky side of the pad would stick to her phone. Then, she reasoned, calming Rasputin down enough that he wouldn't start losing his mind again, she could call for help.

It wasn't exactly a dignified plan, but it was better than nothing. Reassured by a breath of hope, Lilah kept an eye on the snake, still sitting vigilant and coiled by the door, and set to work.

———————

Noa pulled into the studio parking lot and unpacked her gear, remembering to take the lunch bag with her this time. The box jostled inside the insulated pack, all part of the plan. She'd had time to think, after the chaos of yesterday, and now she was determined to set it all in motion.

Wayne wasn't at the desk this morning, which on one hand was a relief. His weird threats had set her on edge. On the other hand, no one seemed to have replaced him yet, and the security desk sat empty. Noa dug for her key card and swiped it, but the toaster-melted plastic mess refused to be read, the light staying red. She cupped her hands and looked through the glass, to no avail. No one was in the hall.

She pulled out her phone as she headed around the side of the studio, intending to text someone to let her in. Only she didn't need to bother anyone, because the door wasn't just unlocked but propped open. A small wooden block had been shoved in the door to keep it from swinging closed on itself, not super unusual, and today someone else's laziness was her salvation. Hauling the door open, Noa headed inside. It took a moment for her eyes to adjust from the bright summer sun outside to the dim lighting indoors, and by the time she blinked away the spots, the other person in the room had realized she was there.

Wayne jumped to his feet. He'd been messing around with

a large plastic box at his feet when Noa'd interrupted him, and she could swear she heard something like movement coming from inside. It was hard to tell over the noise of the compressors for the building's AC, the dull roar settled under everything in this area of the sound stages. "What are you doing here?" Noa asked. "I thought Mike gave you the boot. Everything work out okay?"

"Oh yes," he replied, his eyes bright and grin wide. "Everything's working out exactly according to plan. I won't let you get in the way, of course. Not again."

"What are you talking about? I've never said anything to you except hi and occasionally bye. You're the one who went off on me yesterday totally unprovoked." Noa racked her brain, but nothing even remotely offensive in their interactions came to mind.

"You kissed her when she's not yours," Wayne informed her seriously. "You don't know the first thing about what she needs. How to treat her right. I bet you don't even know her first screen appearance," he sneered.

Noa didn't need to ask who he was talking about. There was only one woman she'd kissed in the last six months. "Uncredited background action in *Cannibal Carnival*. Dude, what is your *problem*?" How Wayne of all people knew anything about the two of them was an entirely different question. All the alarm bells in her mind began ringing in cacophonic dissonance, unexpected goose bumps raising the hairs on the back of Noa's neck. Wayne had been a little weird, but now he looked downright manic, his movements jerky and erratic. She wanted out of this interaction as fast as possible.

His affect changed, the bright grin vanishing to be replaced with a creepy little smile. "That barely proves anything. She needs me, not you. So you're just going to have to go away."

Something was definitely moving in the box at his feet, a lot of somethings, and Noa's eyes narrowed in suspicion. "What's going on, Wayne? Why are you back on set, and what are you planning to do with Lilah?"

"It's not planning. It's already underway. I just need to get the rest of these over to her dressing room and prove to her that I'm the hero she needs. You're just crew," he added loftily, picking up the plastic box. "You wouldn't understand art."

The movement startled whatever was in there, and something scaly pressed up against the fogged-over plastic. Scaly, slithery, and long. Snakes? Noa stared, the pieces not fitting together until the moment they did. "The rest of these? As in there are snakes with Lilah already?" Frozen in disbelief for a beat, Noa's mouth worked like a goldfish as words eluded her. "What the hell is wrong with you? Put those down, you little creep!" It wasn't exactly Shakespeare, but something in her face or her tone must have been impressive enough, because Wayne started speed-walking away, balancing the box in his arms.

Noa let out a yell and gave chase, her bag thunking solidly against the small of her back.

Wayne whipped around and saw her coming, his eyes flashing wide and smile slipping. He yelped, ducked, and ran, and she overshot the corner, skidding on the recently mopped floor. Wayne stumbled over the Caution: Wet Floor sign, the box falling from his hands and tipping over on its side. He barely paused, vaulting over the sign and taking off down the hall at a dead run.

The world slipped into slow motion. Noa's jump followed his, clearing the tipping storage tub. She looked down and saw the mess of tubes inside before the tan-and-brown spot pattern fully registered.

Her foot hit solid ground. The box finished toppling over. The side hit the floor with a slam and a hiss and a series of angry rattles.

Snakes spilled out from the tub in an angry, writhing mass.

Noa didn't stop to count how many or wait for the angry death tubes to untangle themselves. Still yelling, this time a warning—"Snakes! Snakes in the hall!"—she bolted down the hall and turned the other way, heading for the dressing rooms and Lilah.

Please let her be okay. I'll start going to shul every week. I'll light candles again. I won't sneak sips of Coke on Yom Kippur no matter how bad my headache gets by afternoon. I'll do the Four Questions at the seder without complaining, even though it's stupid as hell to be in my twenties and still the youngest at the table. Please, please, please. Just let her be safe.

The shouting started as Noa skidded down the hall to Lilah's dressing room, doors slamming behind her in the complex as cast and crew responded. Lilah's door was locked, a new swipe thing on the frame, and once more, Noa's card didn't work. The light flashed red, and Noa yelled out her frustration, slamming her balled fists against the door in impotent fear.

Barking echoed from inside, a torrent of puppy-sized yips and yelps that could only mean one thing. "Rasputin?" Noa called through the door, but it was an actual human voice who answered.

"Noa?"

Relief crashed over her, a tidal wave that made her feel even more like she was drowning than the fear had done. "Lilah! Thank God! Wayne made it sound like he'd done something terrible. Come on. We have to get out of here!" The words spilled out of her in a torrent, her hands pressed flat to the door as though she could absorb herself through it and out to the other side.

"I can't! He locked me in here, and there's a rattlesnake between us and the door. It keeps hissing at me! Can you get me out?" Her voice was faint but strong, and Noa sagged against the door, not able to hold herself up for a second while she adjusted to the new task in front of her. Operation Find Lilah had turned into a rescue.

"Did it bite you?"

"No! Not yet, but I can't get down from the chair without it trying to."

She tried shaking the door handle, just in case the new lock hadn't been properly activated, but no dice. Another swipe of her melted card—because *fuck* that toaster!—proved equally useless. Something thumped inside the room, then a scrambling sound and another thump, and Noa pressed her ear against the door to try and hear better. "I can't get past the lock, but I'm going for help," Noa promised. "I'll be right back, Li. I won't leave you."

Now the question—where and how? Noa headed back down the hall to where she knew there was a room full of tools, some of which *had* to be useful for breaking locks. PJ ran into her before she got to the props shop, a bucket in his hand. "Did you know there are snakes on the loose? Some asshole let motherfu—"

"I know. I saw it happen. It was Wayne, that security guard

who got fired yesterday," Noa explained in a rush. "He locked Lilah in her dressing room, and there's a rattlesnake in there. She's freaking out, and I can't get in. Help?"

He was moving before she finished explaining, leaving her alone in the hall. Noa ran back to the door, nothing registering in her mind except getting back to Lilah.

"Lilah?" Noa called out, hands pressed against the door once more. "I'm here. PJ's gone to get tools to get you out. You'll be okay." A soft noise came from the other side that Noa assumed was acknowledgment. "I know this isn't the best time, but I also know you can hear me, and—and I'm not running away from things anymore."

Well, maybe a little. She was definitely running from Denise, because she'd missed her call time. And Wayne. And absolutely from the tub full of snakes. But not from Lilah. Not ever again.

Her phone was blowing up in her pocket, buzzing like crazy, and she pulled it out. "Hello?" she answered quickly, not looking at the caller.

"Seriously?" Lilah asked over the line, her voice coming in much more clearly than through the metal. "You're picking now to have this conversation?"

"I've been trying to figure out what to say for days now, but I really suck with words, and nothing sounded right," Noa confessed, embarrassment curling hot through her stomach. "Everything either sounded like another awful list or way too cheesy and you'd hate it. You have your phone? Why didn't you phone someone for help?"

"I only just got it back. The police are supposedly on their way, but God only knows how long *that* will take. I don't think the dispatcher believed me." There was a thump sound and barking that Noa could hear through the door and phone at the same time. Where the hell was PJ?

"Can I at least say that I'm sorry? I know that I messed up, big-time, and I hurt you," Noa began, and Lilah huffed a short, sharp laugh.

"It's what you said you were going to do. Maybe that should have been a sign."

Noa frowned. "What?"

"The first thing you said to me was that you were looking forward to hurting me. I didn't think that was supposed to be a warning." Was that a poke intended to hurt? No—she sounded almost wistful, so maybe that was a good sign.

"Yeah, well. You fluster me, and I can't think straight when I'm near you. My brain short-circuits, and I get dumb."

"Is *that* what it is?" Lilah laughed warmly, and Noa melted. "I'm not taking responsibility for you being dumb around girls. That sounds like a you problem."

"Fair," Noa sighed. "We can absolutely agree on the fact that I do stupid things. And I want to fix it. This. Us. Which I hope isn't another stupid move."

"Can this wait until I'm not being menaced by a ten-foot killer snake?" It wasn't a no. Noa held on to that thought as PJ came around the corner with an oversized drill in his hands.

"Hammer drill," PJ explained with a wide grin and a look of faint glee. "Colin never lets me near this baby."

"Glad to provide the excuse?" Noa stepped back. "PJ's here with a death-ray gun. Step away from the door."

"I'm holding a dog and standing on an armchair. He'll have to deal" came the answer from inside the room. PJ set to work drilling the handle out of the door, the overkill-sized drill bit chewing pieces out of the old door. Splinters flew and Noa moved aside, grabbing for a weapon from the janitor's cart parked a few feet away. There was a snake in that room, and while a rag mop wasn't exactly a harpoon gun, it was something to have in her hands.

PJ drilled the last screw out of the doorknob plate. The handle fell to the floor with a clank, and PJ blew imaginary smoke off the bit. Noa rushed forward and shoved the door open with the mop held out in front of her like a sword, Lilah shrieking "the snake!" as she did so. The door hit something and sent it flying, Rasputin wriggling out of Lilah's arms in a hail of barking. Lilah jumped off the armchair and dove for the dog, grabbing him by the collar as he barked his curly little head off at something in the corner of the dressing room.

Lilah hurtled out of the room into Noa's arms—no, wishful thinking. She hurtled out the door *past* Noa and into the hall, sucking in gasps of air like she'd been in a cave-in and was finally seeing the sun. PJ took Rasputin from her and checked him over as the puppy wriggled out of his arms.

"Are you okay?" Noa asked urgently. "Do you need the medic? The hospital? Antivenom?"

"I'm okay," Lilah promised, grabbing Noa's arm for a moment. Their eyes met, locked for the first time in three days, a static shock of regret and longing rocketing deep into Noa's core. There was the real Lilah, vulnerable and reaching out, her lips parting as though she were about to speak. Noa held her breath.

Lilah looked over her shoulder and gasped. "Rasputin, no!" She let go of Noa's arm and started running. Another snake slithered along the hallway, whipping its long body back and forth on the slippery surface of the linoleum. Rasputin gave chase, and the snake pushed ahead, vanishing underneath the janitor's cart. Rasputin didn't give up, sniffing and barking underneath and banging the cone against the side of the cart until the tail flickered and the snake zipped underneath the dolly full of boxes.

Rasputin chased the snake, Lilah chased Rasputin, and Noa followed them all, mop in hand and her backpack bouncing off her shoulder.

"Noa, we gotta evac!" PJ called after her, but she didn't turn around, running down the hall, ducking and weaving through the two-way traffic. PAs in headsets, crew guys with toolboxes and belts full of rolls of tape, Rasputin gaining speed with four legs rather than her clumsy two—

"Hi! Can't talk now!" she called out in response to Denise's shouted greeting, skidding around the corner as she went. She caught up with Lilah by the door to sound stage B, the cabin set and the riverbank visible through the half-open door. "Rasputin, wait!" The puppy didn't listen, charging full steam ahead into the set, barking at the snake. The snake was going to bite him, and then Rasputin would die, and Noa would have to tell Tanner that she'd let his puppy get venomed because she'd been too busy wishing she could hug Lilah to catch him in time. Lilah skidded to a halt next to her, looking around the empty stage. The cabin set was already reset and redressed for the next shooting day, no one else in sight.

"Do you see him?" Lilah gasped, winded.

"No, but I hear him! You go right, I'll go left. We'll cut him off at the water tank!"

"Got it." Lilah broke right and vaulted over a stack of lighting gear, disappearing behind the water tank that towered above them. Noa headed left and almost collided with Rasputin as he skid-bounced toward her. She scooped him up, barking and wriggling the whole time, his head shoving itself over her shoulder to yell at the snake making its escape under a pile of boxes behind her.

"Do you have him?" Lilah panted, rounding the corner past the ladder leaning up against the tank. "Here, let me take him back to Tanner. He'll obey me."

Peter stuck his head in the open doors and gestured to them both. "Get moving, ladies! There's an invasion. Animal control's been called."

Noa glanced from Lilah to Peter, then to the wriggling animal in her arms. "Here." She gave Rasputin over—not to Lilah but to Peter, who backed away and wrinkled his nose. "Please? Take him to Tanner? I need to talk to Lilah for a minute, and then we'll be right behind you," she promised, taking the chance that Lilah wouldn't object. The second of hesitation seemed to drag out for hours, the silence punctuated by sounds of shouting and equipment being dragged through the halls.

"Please?" Lilah asked Peter, and Noa sagged with relief.

"Fine. But only because I like you." He pointed at Lilah, then took Rasputin from Noa, holding the puppy away from his body at arm's length. He left, arms stiff in front of him and Rasputin joyfully wriggling to get his tongue in range of Peter's nose.

Then they were alone. The building was in chaos, but the sound stage was silent. Lilah looked around, and her shoulders sagged in what might have been relief but also may have been grief or exhaustion or something else entirely. Noa obviously wasn't as good at reading her as she'd once imagined.

Coming around to be face-to-face gave Noa a second to get herself together and remember the speech she'd been rehearsing. Only when Lilah made eye contact and Noa saw the bags under her eyes and the red rims that she'd covered up with three different layers of primer and foundation, the guilt and regret made her catch her breath and stumble all over again.

"I," Noa started and then swallowed hard. "Focusing on 'I' is how I got into this mess in the first place. Let me try again?"

The door slammed open, and Troy stomped in, talking on a headset and gesturing around him as he yelled at someone on the other end. "Animal control is going to need access to all of the sound stages—get some guys in here to move the boxes out." Great.

Crosby trailed along behind him, arguing about something unrelated while Troy ignored everything except the walkie and his headset. "...disrespectful and completely unprofessional. Adjusting to my new trifocals has been distressing to the extreme without people complaining that I'm staring too much! It's ableist, that's what it is, and I don't have to put up with it..."

Any second now, Troy was going to see them. Knowing Noa's luck, he'd be taking his role as safety officer super seriously and would evacuate the two of them as well, even though there weren't any snakes in sight.

"Come on," Lilah muttered under her breath, watching Troy as well. She stepped in close behind Noa, the pair of them hidden for a moment behind a lighting screen. "Scram."

Barking echoed down the hallway, and in that same heartbeat, a snake—maybe the same one from before, maybe not—slithered into the room through the door that Troy had left open. Rasputin followed it at top speed, tongue lolling out like this was the greatest game of chase ever, his leash flapping in the air behind him. He was followed by a panicking Tanner, his arms waving wildly.

Rasputin ricocheted off a stepladder that began to wobble from the impact on his way toward the two men arguing by the water tank. Before Tanner could reach him, Rasputin ran under a table and chased the snake toward Dr. Crosby and Troy.

Crosby let out a sudden shriek and flung himself away from his one-sided conversation. He hit the water tank with his shoulder, and it creaked alarmingly, a faint snapping and popping echoing through the sound stage. "Snake!" Crosby howled, his face turning as red as his hair. "Rattlesnake!"

"Oh shit," Lilah said softly and grabbed Noa's arm, dragging her away from the tank. Noa dropped her mop and followed, putting distance between them and the men.

Rasputin barked loud enough for the noise to echo off the high ceiling, and Tanner grabbed him before he could get away again. Troy grabbed Noa's abandoned mop, and Crosby backed away again, stumbling in his haste. "That is the last straw, the absolute last straw! I *quit*!"

"That's a gopher snake. Chill *out* for once!" Troy snapped, pulling his headset off and rounding on Crosby.

The scientist turned to run and crashed into the tall ladder that Rasputin had set wobbling. It swayed, tipped, balanced on one leg.

For a moment, everything was still.

Then it wasn't.

Giving in to the call of gravity, the ladder toppled over. It smashed into a tower of crates and boxes pushed against the wall, and the boxes on top began to slide. One crate smashed to the concrete floor and broke open, scattering wigs across the floor like a stampede of guinea pigs. Another tumbled through the air, PJ's *WATCH OUT BELOW* label rotating once, twice, three times through the spin.

It smashed into the side of the tank.

The glass cracked and fell apart, the frame warped, and a hundred thousand gallons of warm sour-milk water, blood syrup half-congealed in a goopy layer along the bottom, smashed through to freedom.

Lilah shinnied up the ladder to the cabin like her butt was on fire, reaching a hand down to haul Noa up with her.

The tidal wave rolled down, soaking Crosby and Troy, Tanner with Rasputin in his arms, and probably the snake as well, surging through the stage in a violent tsunami.

"Call Ed!"

"Call facilities management!"

"I'm calling my lawyer!"

When the water subsided, a drenched and dripping Crosby was fleeing out the door, Troy and Tanner—with his dog—close behind. Everything electrical flickered in a drumbeat faster and less regular even than Noa's pulse. A fire alarm sounded in the building, shrieking and bells ringing in a pulse of disaster. Noa jammed her hands over her ears, huddling against the wall like it would protect her from the noise.

Something popped, sparks flew, and then the alarm died. As did the lights.

The room was black, the air silent. Noa and Lilah were alone, in the dark, in the cabin six feet above the flooded sound stage floor. Noa took her hands down slowly and tried to focus her eyes on the faint red glow of the EXIT sign. All she heard was the sound of Lilah breathing and the gentle lapping of water as the rush settled.

Noa coughed once and cleared her throat.

"I don't suppose you know whether snakes can swim."

CHAPTER TWENTY-ONE

"YEAH," LILAH ANSWERED INTO THE darkness, the cabin wall against her back the only reference point she had before her eyes adjusted. "I'm pretty sure they can. At least water snakes can; we had them back home. And they can see in the dark."

A potentially venomous snake, a flood, a blackout, Wayne on the loose, and no one knew where they were. Unless—Lilah patted down her pockets but came up empty. "I lost my phone. We're stuck here," she realized with a start and a groan. Had she dropped it while running from the snake or chasing the dog, or was it down on the studio floor somewhere, under the floodwater? A strained giggle formed at the base of her ribs. She'd sound unhinged if she let it come out, but how stupid was this whole situation? "And there's definitely at least one snake in here. If we try and go down the ladder, we'll get bitten. Or electrocuted, if those sparks were a wire coming down. We're stuck here until someone wonders where we are.

"That's it, I'm done. I don't have enough cope left for this." First there had been the fight—no, first was the stalker, and the gossip column, then reading Noa's messages, then the fight, and *then* Wayne with his deranged proposal and his insistence on reliving one of her movies, and now she was stuck on set with Noa, and she had no idea how to begin to say even half the things that needed to be said between them.

A giggle bubbled up inside until it burst out in a fit of laughter that sounded as hysterical as she felt. She slid down the wall until her butt hit the floor and stayed there. It felt so good to laugh, to let everything come out, to sit there until tears collected in her eyes and her ribs ached.

Movement in the darkness was Noa getting up and fumbling her way toward Lilah. There was a thud followed by quiet cursing, then a scuffle and a faint rectangle of light brilliantly bright in the blackout. Lilah perked up. At least one of them had managed to keep her phone safe. Maybe they'd be rescued after all.

Noa picked her way across the floor, dropping down to sit next to Lilah. The shadows cast by the phone screen made everything look eerie and otherworldly, blue and black slipping and sliding around each other as the phone moved and the shadows danced.

"I've got a little bit left," Noa offered, and Lilah didn't get it. "Of 'cope,' I mean. I'll share," Noa offered, her own nervous laugh putting an end to Lilah's outburst.

Tears stung at the corners of Lilah's eyes. "What a mess," she said and groaned, because saying anything more specific felt dangerous. The phone gave her something more concrete to focus on, and she nodded at it. "Do you have signal?"

"I've got a couple of bars and a little bit of battery," Noa confirmed. "I'm texting Chrissy and telling her what's happened. She'll get us out of here. Somehow." She put the phone down on the wooden cabin floor and looked at Lilah, thrown into sharp relief by the rectangle of blue light. "What happened to you today?"

"Do you want the long version or the short one?" Lilah asked.

"However much you want to tell me."

Noa hadn't made a joke out of it or a demand, just sat there and waited for Lilah to choose. She could obey Mr. Gilbert's orders and continue to say nothing at all, or she could talk, spill out her fears and hopes to someone who'd broken her heart before. But who had also tried to attack a deadly snake with a mop because Lilah had been in danger.

Was it better to live a life closed off from trust or to take the risk? She knew what advice Zaidie would give.

Lilah started talking, giving Noa the basic outline of Wayne's threats, the way he'd come after her, and then the rest of the story spilled out: the messages, the nanny cam, the way he'd stalked her on location...

"You never said anything!" Noa cried out, the hurt in her voice so hard to hear. "That's why you were so upset? I could have helped, could have stayed with you, done something!"

"Mr. Gilbert ordered me not to tell anyone. He said he would take care of it, that he didn't want the bad publicity. I didn't think I could risk disobeying him." It sounded so weak saying it aloud, but it had been so important at the time. What did any of that matter now? "I didn't want to be the reason production shut down. Everyone would have lost their jobs." *You would have lost yours.*

"I wish I'd caught Wayne. I could punch that guy for everything he's put you through! Your life is a lot more important than a job, for the record." Noa bumped Lilah's shoulder with her own, side by side in the dark. "And if Dan Gilbert thought a stalker was bad publicity, wait until the media gets ahold of *this*."

Lilah laughed, the feeling of being able to let go of a held breath permeating every cell in her body. She'd missed this, regretted so much. But where did they go from here—could they somehow find their way back to being friends? Was she ridiculous to imagine that it was possible?

She grabbed Noa's hand and squeezed it tightly before letting her go again. "Thank you for the rescue." She fell silent after that, not sure what to say next—or if the responsibility was even hers right now.

"Anytime. So, um, I had a whole speech all planned out and practiced, but I already did the 'I messed up' part," Noa began, and Lilah's lips twitched up at the corners in a faint memory of a smile.

"Through a locked door. Did you want to take it from 'let me explain'?" Lilah replied. She wanted and didn't want to hear it, the conflict inside her heart making her mouth go dry. As hurt as she'd been at first, her pride most of all, she'd had time to cool down and reconsider her own role in the way everything had fallen to pieces. "Did you really practice a speech?"

"I'm really bad with words. I try and explain how I feel, and it all comes out wrong." Noa let out a long breath that shook a little at the end. "I try and say something like 'Lilah, you're an amazing person, and I love the way I feel when I'm around you,' and it comes out as 'wow, you're pretty.' So I tried to find something to say that was foot-in-mouth proof, and I don't think I did very well. I think we've firmly established that I'll never be a scriptwriter." Noa tried to laugh it off, waving her hand as though brushing away any commentary.

"Mmm." Lilah made a soft noise that neither confirmed nor denied the statement, still not quite sure where Noa was planning to end up.

"I wrote that stupid list because I was trying to convince myself not to fall for you," Noa confessed. "And that sounds incredibly dumb when I say it out loud, I know, I *know*." She held her head in her hands and groaned. "But I also know you have people hitting on you all the time. I really didn't want you to think I was scamming on you when you couldn't get away from me, so I tried to shake it off. Only the more time we spent together and the better I got to know you, the more amazing you turned out to be, and I just couldn't make any more excuses. I *was* falling for you, hard. And it scared me."

"So you texted Chrissy about everything you didn't like?" Lilah couldn't help relitigating it, beating the subject to death until she was sure that she understood. "Because you liked me too much to...like me?"

Noa made a noise like a strangled sob, a catch of breath that shuddered in her throat, and then silence fell for a moment. "Big feelings scare me," she said softly, so softly that Lilah had to strain a little to hear it even though they were sitting hip to hip in the darkened cabin. "It's easier to be flippant and make dumb jokes and pretend that none of it matters.

"Then you trusted me enough to come out to me, which was

so, so special, and by the time I realized just how *much* it mattered and that maybe there could be something good happening, I'd forgotten the list was even in there. And now I've blown it, maybe forever, and all I have left to say is that I miss you."

Lilah sat with the information for a minute and watched in the light of the little glowing phone screen. Noa was waiting for her to say something, but all she wanted to do was stare at Noa and appreciate her. Her curls, not pinned back today but free and full, spiraling down around her face. Her dark lashes and the way they swept across her high cheekbones, her strong shoulders and arms, her deft, talented artist's hands. Lilah cataloged them all as though for the last time. Noa was talented and driven; she had more passion for working on *Scareodactyl* than most of the cast and crew put together. She'd do amazing things if she had the chance.

Beautiful and talented and confusing—

And contrite. Contrite and ready to throw down for Lilah's honor and her life, wielding a mop against all comers. That image of Noa standing in her door like a Valkyrie riding to war, a bundle of floppy strings waving at the end of the mop handle as the snake was flung through the air, would stick with Lilah for a long time.

And now Noa was looking at her, waiting, and it was Lilah's turn. It would be easier to pour her heart out if she closed her eyes and imagined they were back in bed in the motel. But it would also be a cop-out. Noa was present in the moment, not hiding behind masks and playing pretend. Lilah owed her the same.

"I thought you might have been the person who submitted the blind item," she confessed. Noa's intake of breath hurt, and Lilah deserved that. "I didn't want to believe it, but it's happened before. Trusting the wrong person, I mean. And it said things that I thought only you and I knew. Now that I know about the camera in my dressing room, I understand, but at the time…" She curled her knees up to her chest and rested her chin on them. "So I looked at your phone to prove to myself that it wasn't you. That you weren't selling me out to the tabloids. That's when I found the list."

"And because you already thought that I might be lying to you," Noa prompted gently, more understanding than Lilah had the right to expect.

"I flew off the handle. I messed with your feelings and embarrassed you in front of your friends and never gave you the chance to explain. I'm sorry," Lilah breathed out, some of the terrible weight lifting from her heart.

Noa's hand found hers in the semidarkness and squeezed before she let go. She locked gazes with Lilah and didn't look away. "I was petty. I was mean, and I was jealous. I said some awful things. And I'm sorry."

"Jealous?" Lilah frowned, trying to make sense of that, and Noa's mouth quirked up in the corners. "Of what?"

"Of Claudia, mostly. The way you smiled at her, the way it seemed to be so easy for you two to flirt when I've been stumbling and tongue-tied since the day we met. I get close to you, and I can't think straight, no pun intended. Or maybe pun intended because that works too. So at the bar that night, when you were telling stories—"

"That was dumb of me," Lilah confessed, her face turning hot at the reminder of her own mistakes. "Can you—can you turn off the light? This is easier in the dark."

Noa did, and the security of the blackness curled around them again, broken only by the faint red glow of the emergency exit signs outside the cabin's safe three walls.

"I was so mad that night and so hurt. But not just because of the list. Some of what you said that night was right," Lilah confessed. "I wanted to be like you, right from the beginning. You seemed so sure of yourself, of who you are and who you love, and it's all so new for me to say out loud. Every day, people like Ed and Troy spend hours telling 'Lilah' what to say and how to say it. Sometimes I'm not sure who Lillian is anymore. Or if there's any way to find her again. But you had it all together."

Noa laughed at that, a long, loud, bitter laugh that made Lilah smile in tired recognition. "Oh my God, you are so wrong, it's almost amazing."

Lilah dragged in a ragged breath, fighting to get each word out past the lump in her throat. "And after I saw your texts...I wanted your friends to like me. I wanted you to see how well I could fit in with the group, that I wasn't just a shallow bimbo. That you were wrong, and I was worth something after all."

Groaning, Noa sagged next to her, their shoulders brushing against each other. She froze, but when Lilah didn't pull away, Noa leaned into her a little more solidly. "I am so, so sorry. You're a better person than I'll ever be."

Lilah made a face at the shadowed shape beside her. "Don't go putting me up on that pedestal again. If I hadn't snooped in your phone—"

"I shouldn't have written any of that down in the first place."

"Maybe it's better that you were honest. Maybe we wouldn't

work anyway." There. She'd said it—but she didn't believe it... not really. Lilah held her breath. Would Noa take the easy way out this time? Lilah's heart beat double tempo against her ribs when Noa's reply burst out of her.

"No! We absolutely would. We can. I think we can. The worst has already happened and...and now we're here, alone, where we have a chance to make everything right again." She fumbled in the dark, and Lilah felt a hand seize hers. She curled her fingers tight around Noa's so-familiar grip, let her hand be lifted, her knuckles pressed against Noa's lips.

The touch, so intimate, so tentative, sent shivers running through every inch of her. She remembered other stolen moments, and the thrill burned hot through her body and prickled fire under her skin. "Can we start over?" Lilah asked softly, clinging to that thread of hope. "A clean slate?"

"No," Noa replied, and agony ripped through Lilah only to vanish a second later in the soothing balm of Noa's next words. "But we can fix what we broke. And, um, if you're hungry, I brought the cheesecake."

"I figured you'd have eaten it by now," Lilah said, caught entirely off guard by the rapid topic change.

"What? No! You bought it for us to share," Noa replied, sounding a little offended. "I would never."

"So, what," Lilah laughed, the first time she'd felt light and free in what felt like a lifetime, "if we hadn't made up, you'd have left it in the fridge forever?"

"Nope. The freezer, like the world's saddest wedding cake layer. I'd be a modern-day Miss Havisham, drifting through life in

my backstage blacks, dreaming of cheesecake I would never eat."
Noa picked up her phone and turned the light on again, using it as
she fumbled in her bag and brought out a crumpled black shape
that might once have been a box. "It got a little squooshed, what
with all the running and the screaming."

"Is now really the right time to be making jokes?"

"I'm trying, but naked sincerity makes me uncomfortable,"
Noa confessed, and there was more honesty in that than Lilah was
willing to poke at. For now anyway. "If you're using the past tense,
does that mean we're back together?" Noa asked audaciously, and
Lilah grinned into the darkness.

"Depends on whether you remembered the Lactaid and a
fork."

"Both in the box. At least originally. They might be in the
bottom of my bag with a smashed eyeshadow palette at this point,
but that's all part of the adventure."

"Then you may have a deal." Noa's thigh pressed against
hers, their shoulders snug together, and it felt too right to ignore.
The first bite of cheesecake was more decadent than the first time;
maybe stress made her hungry. It was still cool from Noa's lunch
bag, the creamy caramel melting over her tongue.

"You're forgiven," Lilah declared magnanimously and stabbed
half blindly into the cake again. This time, she tried to aim the
fork at Noa's lips, not even the vague shadows cast by the phone
screen helpful now. She missed and almost stabbed Noa in the
chin before fumbling her hand into Noa's curls. Noa leaned her
cheek into Lilah's palm, a gesture of trust so complete that Lilah's
heart broke and mended itself a thousand times over in the span

of a breath. Her thumb found Noa's lips, and they parted under her touch, warm and inviting. Lilah slipped the bite of cheesecake between Noa's lips and felt the warm tip of her tongue take it, leaving the pad of her thumb damp.

They ate in relative silence, an intimate quiet broken only by murmurs of appreciation and laughter when their forks collided, unseen.

"So what happens next?" Noa asked, her voice breaking the silence once the cake was gone but for what Lilah suspected would be faint smears on the cardboard of the box.

"What do you mean?"

"Are we okay?"

Lilah hesitated, biting her lip to keep herself from being too forward. Only, this was *Noa*. And now that the air had been cleared, she didn't need to worry about Noa thinking she was too messy, too bossy, too pushy, too *anything* other than herself. She took a breath. "More than okay, I hope." Where she had recently had nothing but doubts, now she only had certainty. Lilah leaned in. She brushed her lips against where Noa's lips probably were and got a mouthful of chin instead. "Dammit."

"Hold still." Noa laughed, the sound a thrill that settled deep in Lilah's bones and filled her with light. Noa's hands slipped around Lilah's face, fingers sinking into Lilah's hair. Lilah held still, hardly daring to breathe for fear that this delicate bubble of a moment would burst. Noa's lips brushed hers, and Lilah sank into the kiss. Gentle exploration turned to a reclaiming, a reunion that sent stars bursting bright behind Lilah's closed eyes.

They parted, breathless, and Lilah emerged from the kiss into a world filled with everything new and bright. Her fingers and toes tingled, and a very different kind of hunger demanded her attention. There'd been no further texts from Chrissy, no sign that they'd be found soon. Did she dare? Giving in to impulse had worked well so far today.

She rose to her feet. Noa made a small sound of dismay, and Lilah reached for her hand. "Come on," she urged. "My butt's sore from sitting on the floor, and there's perfectly good furniture." *Like a bed.*

Noa caught on, and the light from her phone illuminated the cabin as they tumbled toward the bed. "Is it sturdy enough?" she asked, breathless and laughing.

"We dropped Mikal on it three times during rehearsal alone, so I think we'll be fine," Lilah retorted, the feeling of freedom making her bold. She dropped onto the bed on her knees and bounced once to prove her point. It wasn't the softest thing ever, but none of that mattered. She'd take a fold-down cot in a trailer if it meant getting to have this moment with Noa. "Now if you're going to worry, worry about my makeup. I'm hoping it's about to get completely wrecked."

Noa joined her on the bed, crawling on her hands and knees until she was kneeling in front of Lilah, her phone tossed onto the pillow where it cast a faint light over their small section of the room. Noa smiled, her full lips curving up into something more honest and open than Lilah had ever seen on her before. Other things burned in there as well, and Lilah's knees went weak. "I'm pretty sure we can find someone around here to fix it."

Arms around each other, their lips met again. And when the

phone screen turned off and cast the cabin into darkness, neither one cared enough to turn it on again.

———————

Drowsy and content, her head pillowed on Noa's shoulder, Lilah was faintly aware of a buzzing sound somewhere above them on the bed. She didn't feel like moving, not with Noa's arm tucked around her and everything in the world peaceful for once, but Noa shifted, patting around above their heads. Her phone flashed brightly, and Lilah closed her eyes against the unwelcome intrusion of the real world as Noa answered the incoming call. "Hello? Hey, Chrissy. What's happening out there?"

The tinny voice at the other end was on the edge of loud enough for Lilah to hear from where she lay curled against Noa's side, and she eavesdropped shamelessly.

"Animal control's here. They're gonna come in and corral the snakes, and the cops got Wayne. Mike snagged him while he was trying to get off the lot, and the LAPD finally bothered to drop by a minute ago. The power's been cut to the stage, so you guys won't get fried when they come to get you out, which should be any minute now. Unless you need more time alone?" Chrissy asked knowingly after she'd run out of news.

Lilah covered a giggle, and Noa snorted. "Nah, we're good. Come rescue us. I'm more than ready to go home. Unless you think they're going to try and keep filming tonight. Please tell me that's not happening. Denise is going to be ready to rip my head off for missing my call this afternoon, but she'll have chilled out by tomorrow." Lilah sat up and started feeling around for her clothes, dragging her jeans back on in the dark. Jeans, bra, T-shirt—

"Nah, not this time. And I wouldn't worry about Denise. Saving Lilah probably won you some brownie points with the production team."

"I didn't save her," Noa objected. In the light from her phone, Lilah saw her brilliant smile. "Not just me anyway. PJ helped. And then she saved me."

"Whatever. Just make sure you guys are ready for company because they're heading for you now."

Noa hung up and scrambled to get dressed. Lilah threw her a T-shirt and pulled on her shoes. Hair up? Hair down? Her hair had been down coming in, so no need to try and find an elastic in this mess. The bed was a disaster, but they could always claim to have taken a nap while they waited. That was if they were going to be keeping things private. Lilah chewed on her lip while Noa hopped on one foot, shoving the other into her running shoe. "I hate to break the mood, but what happens now?" she asked quietly.

Noa started to topple over, grabbing Lilah's shoulder to keep from falling. "Come over to my place tonight? Unless you want to go home instead, which I totally understand. But I'd like to...go out?" she said, hazarding a guess. "Sleep in? Do girlfriend things when we have time?"

"So we're going to be open and official now," Lilah clarified, laughing out of sheer relief. "And you wouldn't freak out if I, say, changed my relationship status on my socials? I think I'm ready. Though I should warn you, I have no idea what Wayne's done with the nanny-cam videos. You might be dating a social pariah and a gossip-blog punching bag."

Practically nose-to-nose, Noa stared at her, eyes wide, then recovered with a grin far more joyous than her usual sardonic twist of a smile. "Hell yeah. I'm a hundred times more embarrassing than you could ever be, so let's face social and professional ruin together. I'm in."

She was too cute, too sweet, and Lilah was not nearly strong enough to resist even if she wanted to. She kissed the end of Noa's nose, an impulsive gesture of affection that quickly changed to a thorough and penetrating kiss, Noa's hands slipping up under the hem of her tight T-shirt. Fireworks went off in Lilah's brain, an echo and a resonating fire kindling in her from every other kiss they'd shared so far. Only the sound of the doors opening made her jump away, sweeping her hair out of her face with both hands. Dim light from the hallway let her see a little more than before, illuminating the foot of water on the floor and the equipment lying in pieces.

"Anyone in here?" came the shout from the uniformed men at the door, their flashlights playing over the scene.

"Up here!" Lilah leaned out the cabin window, waving. The whole rescue only took a few minutes, the water draining out of the room as Lilah and Noa hopped over the knee-high barrier put up to stop the flood from escaping into the rest of the studio.

The hallways were eerily empty except for the couple of uniformed workers with nets and forked sticks who Lilah spotted moving through the sound stages as they passed the open doors. Two official-looking tanks sat near the door, one labeled *Gopher*

Snakes and filled with a half dozen writhing occupants, and the other *Rattlers*, with only one sad, sulking snake inside, much smaller and darker in color than the one that had been menacing her in her dressing room. Lilah gave a little shudder and picked up her pace.

The cast and crew were all outside, milling in groups in the parking lot, and a handful of people shouted greetings and waved when Noa, Lilah, and their rescuers emerged into the sunset. A police cruiser was indeed parked in the lot, Lilah noted with deep satisfaction, Wayne scowling in the back seat while one of the officers talked to Mike. Let him freak out. She'd won.

Sadie elbowed her way through to the two of them and made a gesture as though she were about to throw an arm around Lilah's neck, but she looked at them, did a double-take, and burst out laughing instead. "Uh-huh," she snort-giggled, and Lilah didn't get it.

At least not until she looked at Noa, really looked at her, and realized the pink designer T-shirt that had been snug on Lilah that morning was looser when Noa wore it. And *Lilah* was now in Noa's black shirt, one that had *Hello Mary Lou* emblazoned on it in a blood-dripping font. It was definitely not Lilah's usual sort of fashion, and her face turned hot at the obvious implication.

To hell with it. Wasn't she ready to come out publicly? Get over the fear of what everyone else thought of her? "It's exactly what you think," Lilah said, flashing her stunt double a grin that was more shaky than it should have been. Baby steps.

"You go, girlfriend," Sadie cheered, and the rush of her warm and obvious approval was a balm to Lilah's soul. "Pink suits you, by the way," she teased, winking broadly at Noa before jogging away.

"That's a pretty good first reaction." Noa breathed out a little sigh of relief. "So, um, can I have my shirt back?" Noa asked Lilah quietly, plucking at the fabric draping over her chest.

It would be the polite thing to do, but Noa's shirt smelled like her, all acetone and musk. If it was too late to get Noa signed on for the trip, Lilah was going to have months alone when she went to France. Cuddling the shirt at night would be a poor substitute, but it was a heck of a lot better than nothing. "No," she decided aloud and flashed Noa a guileless grin and a wink. "It's mine now."

"That's a limited edition! You can't get those anymore!" Noa protested, laughter in her eyes and her voice.

Lilah leaned in close, her hair brushing Noa's cheek. "Then come get it back."

She could practically see hearts beating in Noa's eyes when she pulled away, and the little rush of pleasure that came along with that was intoxicating. Lilah started moving toward the police car, the nanny cam in her bag evidence that she was eager to be free of, but Noa hissed under her breath.

"Shit!"

"Noa!" Denise was making a beeline for them, a frown on her face, and Lilah braced for the worst. Denise had been the thorn in their sides without even knowing it, and if she meant to punish Noa for missing her call today or for being with Lilah, Lilah had the chance right now to make things right.

"Denise!" Lilah grabbed Noa's hand and hung on, despite Noa's instantaneous panicked freeze. "I want to thank you, so much, for bringing Noa on board. She was amazing in there. You should have seen her! She realized I was locked in my dressing room and organized the whole rescue, and then when she chased away the snake? It was a real hero moment." Phrasing it like that brought memories of Wayne rushing back, and she stopped short.

Noa squeezed her hand tightly. "I was waving a mop at it. That's not exactly award material," she joked wryly, stepping in to fill the moment.

"You kept me safe," Lilah protested. "She saved the movie, really." She turned and said that directly to Denise, whose frown had vanished under the onslaught of praise.

She swooped on them instead of yelling, dolman sleeves flapping in the evening breeze, and gathered both of them up in an embrace that squeezed a surprised squeak of protest out of Noa. "I suppose I can't be mad at a hero for missing her call, can I? Thank goodness you're all right, both of you," Denise declared when she let them go. She looked them over, eyes narrowing a smidge at the T-shirts, which were obviously not on their original owners, but said nothing critical. "And, Lilah, what a day you've had! Ed's sending everyone home for now, but the new schedules will have to go out early tomorrow. We're going to have a lot of work to do to make up for this interruption, so get plenty of rest tonight."

She swanned off, making a beeline for the other department heads, and Noa looked helplessly at Lilah. "Does that mean she approves of us?"

Lilah shrugged helplessly. "Maybe if you play along, she'll forget that she told you not to date me?"

"I hate to bank on it, but that sure as hell sounds like her."

Noa pressed the heels of her hands into her eyes and breathed in, then out. "Okay. I'm okay, you're okay. Everything's good. I have no idea how I got from Thursday to now, but for the moment, everything is going really, really right."

"Don't overthink it," Lilah advised, only laughing at Noa a very little bit, and only because of her own almost delirious relief.

"Have you met me?" Noa asked dryly, and tangled her fingers with Lilah's as she passed. "I need to check in with Chrissy, okay?"

"I have to make a police report. Meet you back here when we're both done?" Lilah suggested. "And...one more request." Noa paused, fingertips trailing through Lilah's. "Be my date for the wrap party?"

"I'll go anywhere with you," Noa promised. And Lilah believed her.

EPILOGUE

"I SWEAR, THAT WAS BRAD Pitt over there," Lilah hissed at Noa under her breath as they gathered up their carry-on bags and Noa checked her pocket for the boarding passes for approximately the fiftieth time.

"I'm pretty sure he's got a private plane. Let me know if you see Kristen Stewart go by. Or Gina Gershon. She can still get it," Noa added with a wolfish grin. Chrissy's goodbye text flashed on her phone, and she paused long enough to text her back.

> **Noa:** Boarding soon. Have fun, no sex in my room, and tell Max they can have the yogurts I left in the fridge.
>
> **Chrissy:** Safe travels, mes petites choux!

Lilah laughed, slinging her bag over her shoulder. The utter chaos of LAX was always a trip, famous and not-so-famous faces all mingling in the crowds rushing from security to gate to concourse. It was a little piece of the city that she'd fallen for at first sight, and this time, she was hiking through it with the woman she'd fallen for at first sight. The smile spread wider on her face as she watched Noa rearrange her bag, tucking her reader in the outer pocket for easy access. "You were really absorbed in that book in the cab. Which one is it?" she asked, blinking innocently.

Noa gave her that *I know what you're doing* look but answered with a grin and a resigned sigh as she picked up her bag. "The one you sent me the link to last week, with the lesbian werewolf soul mates."

"And?" Lilah asked archly as they began to move toward the gathering line.

"And...it's really good."

"And?" Lilah prompted, grinning at the resigned and sheepish look on Noa's face.

"And you were right. You were right about many more things than I ever am, and you have excellent taste," Noa said, humoring her, eyes laughing. She tucked her hand into Lilah's back pocket for a moment, giving her a squeeze despite the dirty look shot their way from some bitter, little old lady waiting in the boarding line. There'd been a time when that kind of glare would have sent Lilah into a spiral of self-doubt, but no more. Not ever again. She had Noa now, and Noa's strength had made her a hundred—a thousand!—times stronger.

"I do, don't I?" Lilah replied and pressed a kiss to Noa's temple. "You should just listen to me about everything from now on."

Noa snorted softly but nodded and played along. "I'll consider it. Do you think crew housing will have Wi-Fi? I'm going to grab the sequels once we land."

"I would think so," Lilah began to answer. "France isn't exactly the back of beyond."

"Excuse me, Lilah? Are you Lilah Silver?"

Noa's hand slipped out of Lilah's pocket as they both turned, but the young fan who approached didn't seem threatening even if he looked like the frat-boy type. He seemed barely out of high school, for one, and the ball cap on his head was for Camp Kadimah. Spotting that made her feel a little bit more comfortable, that same way that seeing Noa's silver star had made all the difference three months ago. "Yes, that's me. Can I help you?"

His face lit up, and he started digging in his pocket. "No way, this is too cool. You're one of my bo—" He stumbled over his words, switching gears partway through, and Noa shot Lilah a knowing look. "My *friend*'s favorite actors. We just watched *Stairway to Terror* for, like, the fifth time last weekend." He pulled out his phone and gave her a beseeching look. "Can I take a selfie with you?"

Lilah nodded and tugged Noa's arm to get her into the shot. "Get Noa as well. She'll be more famous than me one day," she teased. Noa blew her a raspberry, but she glowed at the compliment anyway. "She's one of the best makeup effects artists I've ever worked with."

And because he'd played the pronoun game and because he reminded her a little bit of Noa, she took a chance: "That's how we started dating."

He paused halfway through getting his face in and taking the string of photos. "Seriously? You guys are…?"

"Girlfriends," Noa added sunnily, a little bit possessively, and

Lilah's heart still thrilled at the sound of the word. Fine, so she was a dork, but it sounded so good to hear Noa say it. She had the feeling that would never get old.

"I knew it! That's awesome. Adrian—that's my boyfriend—will be so stoked. That you're like us and we're in common and...yeah." He flushed red at the string of words he blurted out, so cute about it that Lilah had to resist the urge to give him a reassuring hug.

"Now boarding Delta Airlines flight 8553 to Paris. All passengers, please report to Gate 25. Delta Airlines flight 8553 to Paris, now boarding."

"Sorry, that's us. We have to go," Lilah said apologetically. Impulsively, she searched through her bag for a pen and paper, tearing a page from the back of her purple flowered day planner.

For Adrian. Always be proud. ♥ *Lilah Silver.*

"For your boyfriend," she told him, pressing the paper into his hand.

He took it with wide eyes and a smile that followed her as they headed for the gate, lingering for a minute before vanishing into the crowd.

"Here we see the movie star in her natural environment, making another fan for life," Noa teased her, and Lilah just smiled.

Economy seats weren't exactly luxurious, but one day, business class would be hers. At least she was going to be squished in next to Noa, and that wasn't exactly a hardship. Lilah stowed her bag and Noa's in the overhead bin and settled into her seat with a happy little sigh. "Ready for eleven hours of togetherness?"

Noa was poking through her carry-on, already pulling out earbuds and a splitter jack, her neck pillow propped up on her shoulders. "The start of three months of working together. It'll be twenty-four/seven togetherness," she laughed back, but that didn't scare Lilah in the slightest.

"It'll be like a honeymoon."

"A honeymoon where we'll be working eighteen-hour days."

"Shh. We'll find ways to relax," Lilah promised her, Noa's smile echoing her own. "Besides, most of that will be spent sitting around waiting for setups, and I'm determined to get good enough at *Mario Kart* to kick your butt by the end of principal photography."

Noa snorted. "You can try!" She stopped fussing as the plane taxied out, absorbed in her book again.

Lilah nestled in, resting her head on Noa's shoulder and watching the world recede away beneath them. Noa's warmth, the smell of Lilah's shampoo in her hair, the muscle of her shoulder and arm beneath and against Lilah, the faint vibration of her humming along with the music on their headsets—this was the way to travel.

"Do you really think I'm one of the best?" Noa asked, not exactly out of the blue.

Lilah popped out an earbud but didn't sit up. It was easier sometimes not to look, especially when what she wanted to say had been eating at her for ages, the tiniest of words feeling so big. Only right now, she was as safe as she could be, as happy as she'd ever been. "One hundred percent. I'm a little bit in love with you, you know."

There was silence for a moment, but that was okay. She'd

gotten a lot better at knowing when Noa's silences were bad and when they just meant she needed a second to process. This wasn't a bad one. "That's...that's awesome." Definitely a processing-error moment. Lilah hid her smile against Noa's shoulder.

"Tell you a secret," Noa murmured against Lilah's hair, and Lilah's heart thrilled to the sound and the feel of her voice, her breath, her everything. "I'm a little bit in love with you too."

The plane rose into the warm afternoon light, sun gleaming off the wing outside their window, casting a butterfly reflection on the chair in front of Lilah. Butterfly wings, so that together, they could soar.

DID YOU SPOT THE REFERENCES?

As a film fan and horror buff, I couldn't help but slide a few references into *I Kissed a Girl*—both to popular franchises and some more obscure classics. Did you catch them all?

DIRECT REFERENCES:

Hellraiser (1987)
One of Noa's many T-shirts.

Tenebre (1982)
Another piece from Noa's wardrobe. This is a deeply pretentious choice on her part, as only the original Italian release spelled it *Tenebre*. (The European release was *Tenebrae*, USA release was *Unsane*.)

Ginger Snaps (2000)
Noa's sleepwear at the motel.

Ringu (1998)

Lilah watches this when she's trying to learn to like horror movies.

The Exorcist (1973)

Lilah considers watching *The Exorcism of Audrey Rose.*

Audrey Rose (1977)

Lilah considers watching *The Exorcism of Audrey Rose.*

Jurassic Park (1992)

Mentioned in conversation between Lilah and Noa.

Bride of Chucky (1998)

Noa's travel mug, left in Lilah's trailer.

Twilight Zone (1983)

On producer Dan's list of cursed movies.

Poltergeist (1982)

On producer Dan's list of cursed movies.

Rodan (1956)

Noa jokes with PJ about the puppet's backstage nickname.

Hello Mary Lou: Prom Night II (1987)

Noa's T-shirt, which ends up on Lilah after the cabin rescue.

MORE OBLIQUE REFERENCES:

A card game called *Graverobbers from Outer Space*, based on horror b-movies.

Lilah thinks of Ishani's role as the "Bookish Girl with No Boyfriend," a card from the game. The card itself is a reference to Jamie Lee Curtis's role as Laurie Strode in *Halloween* (1978).

Blackula (1972)

One of the posters in Noa's room.

The Vampire Lovers (1970)

A second poster in Noa's room.

Creepshow (1982)

Nicknaming the monster puppet Fluffy, which was the on-set name for the monster puppet in *Creepshow*—Fluffy the Crate Beast.

Eegah (1962)

When arriving on location, Denise warns Noa to "watch out for snakes."

Six-Headed Shark Attack (2018)

During a makeup session conversation, Noa and Lilah discuss movies.

Pterodactyl (2005)

Scareodactyl itself is a riff on this fabulous low-budget schlock-fest.

Sharknado (2013)

Hamstergeddon is a riff on this and similarly titled animal and disaster movies.

Attack of the 50 Foot Woman (1958)

A movie reference dropped in backstage conversation.

Killer Klowns from Outer Space (1988)

Any time *Killer Carousel* or *Cannibal Carnival* are mentioned.

Friday the 13th movie franchise (1984–2009)

Tommy Jarvis is the name of a recurring protagonist/antagonist from four of the films.

Night of the Living Dead (1968)

The working title for this film was *Night of Anubis.*

Blood Moon Rising (2009)

Blood Moon Setting is a riff on this title.

The Cabin in the Woods (2011)

We literally have a cabin in the woods. Also, Ed's demand for "more blood" during Tanner's death scene is a reference to the outtakes from the epic Merman blowhole sequence in this movie.

The Shining (1980)

Dan references this when he's cussing out Ed.

The Old Guard (2020)

References to the director and one of the lead actors.

Snakes on a Plane (2006)

Snake on the Plain. I have no excuse.

NON-MOVIE REFERENCES:

Troma Studios

PJ's mug, as seen in the crew trailer on location. Troma is a movie studio and purveyor of ludicrous horror satire.

Actress Clea DuVall (*The Faculty, The Grudge, American Horror Story*)

Gay actress and director with some classic horror on her résumé. Lilah's character in *Scareodactyl* is named for her.

Reading Group Guide

1. Because she grew up in a small town and came out as bisexual later in life, Lilah felt disconnected from the LGBTQIA+ community. Do you think this is a common experience? Why or why not?

2. Why do you think it took so long for Lilah to feel comfortable coming out as bisexual?

3. Noa is very comfortable in her own identity but is quick to judge Lilah for her interests. Where do you think that's coming from? Do you feel Noa learns and grows thanks to her experience with Lilah?

4. When Lilah spots Noa's Star of David necklace, Noa braces for her reaction. What do you think Noa was expecting and why? What else was significant about their conversation?

5. As an actress, Lilah lives more and more in the public eye. How do you think you would handle the benefits and drawbacks of fame?

6. *I Kissed a Girl* highlights the real, authentic experience of working on a movie like *Scareodactyl*. How do you think you would like working on a set? Is there a department (makeup and special effects, costuming, props, stunts, etc.) that you'd particularly enjoy? Why?

7. The producers ask Lilah to keep quiet about the fact that she's been receiving threatening messages. What is their motivation here? Do you think that sort of thing is common?

8. Lilah feels pressure—thanks to her profession and the way she was raised—to always present a perfect front. How do you think that impacts both her self-image and how she interacts with others?

9. Do you think Noa was right to be angry with Lilah for pretending to be something she wasn't in front of Noa's friends?

10. Hollywood is often glamorized, but there's nothing glamorous about the hard work actors and actresses must do to get the perfect shot. Would you be willing to struggle for hours in a white water rapids set if it meant landing a film-worthy take?

11. Lilah has to face a fan who feels like she owes him her attention because of the way he feels when he watches her films. Fans have greater access to entertainment professionals than ever now, thanks to places like Twitter. What kind of boundaries

do you think are appropriate between fans and entertainers? How has the internet changed them?

12. Noa struggles to find a balance between her work and her personal life. Have you ever been in a situation where the "professional" thing to do conflicted with something you really wanted? What did you choose?

A Conversation
with the Author

How did Noa and Lilah develop as characters? Did you have them set from the beginning, or did they evolve as you wrote?

I knew from the start that their major conflict was going to be about false assumptions and different ideas about performing femininity, which meant they needed to be opposing forces in some fairly specific ways. Noa's rapid rushes to judgment evolved as a character trait; in the first few chapters of the first draft, she had much more of an anti-pink crusade going on. But as I drafted out some more scenes from the middle of the book, I realized that Noa's issues were different, and it would make for a much better balance. She's not about judging other women specifically; she rushes to pigeonhole everyone because being able to boil them down to an archetype makes her feel safer.

Lilah was always Lilah, I think; she appeared full-grown from my forehead like some kind of Athena. Her arc has always been about coming into her own, starting from a place of deep insecurity and discovering her own strength. She went through a couple of versions where she was snottier to Noa, holding on to her anger longer, but the core of the character has always been there.

Why did you pick a horror movie as the setting? What about the genre speaks to you?

Noa spells some of this out at one point, and that's a little bit of my love for the genre leaking through. On one level, a horror film gave me the chance to have some fun visual comedy with the props and effects, as well as an excuse to keep Noa and Lilah in close proximity during the appliance application process. On another, it gave me the chance to nerd out about some of my favorite subjects. Horror sits in this great place in fiction, because it's appalling and attractive at the same time; we can be scared and completely safe simultaneously, that roller-coaster kind of terror.

It also acts as a window to society's deeper fears and traumas. Individually, each horror movie isn't necessarily a message. But when we take a decade's worth of horror movies as a whole, we can see exactly what we were worried about as a culture. The 1950s, for instance, were all about the giant killer bugs, alien invasions, and mad science. The world had just been introduced to the atom bomb, and while Japan's kaiju genre is a direct commentary on the horrors of Hiroshima and Nagasaki, western film's obsession with science-gone-wrong was reacting to the same existential dread.

When we move to the '60s and the paranoia of the Cold War era, the mood shifts. We're asking the question "Is that person who they say they are?" which gives us brilliant films like *Invasion of the Body Snatchers* (where your neighbors are secretly evil aliens),

Night of the Living Dead (where your neighbors become flesh-eating creatures), and *Rosemary's Baby* (where your neighbors are baby-swapping Satanists). In the 1970s, it's panic about the decay of society and the violence lurking in every corner (*Alien, Texas Chainsaw Massacre, I Spit on Your Grave,* etc.) The Vietnam War and its aftereffects are responsible for a lot of this in both metaphorical and literal ways. The man who invented modern horror effects, Tom Savini, had been a photographer in Vietnam and used the anatomical knowledge he'd gained from photographing the dead to make his film creatures and corpses as horrifically realistic as possible.

Then once we're into the 1980s, we have the rise of suburban horror (*Poltergeist*) as well as the moral majority's influence on the slasher genre—anyone having too much fun out of wedlock is going to die horrifically. And so it goes.

The very short version of that long and somewhat winding answer is that horror is a very effective mirror of ourselves. And so Lilah's arc—the insecure woman surviving danger and heartache and finding her inner strength—is deliberately that of the classic Final Girl. Mirrors within mirrors.

Also, I got to fling fake blood and guts all over people, which is always fun.

Noa spends a lot of energy worrying about her professional reputation. Is that a big part of working in the entertainment industry?

If you're on a crew, reputation is everything. The majority of crew work is freelance rather than permanent contract, you're not the reason that people come to see a film, and there are a lot of people with the same skill sets who would love to step in and take your place. Being known as someone reliable, fast, and easy to work with is absolutely vital to getting hired again. Department heads will keep track of the people they enjoyed working with, and when a new project comes around, that list—and anyone people on that list can recommend—will be the first place they turn. There are open crew calls for productions, but in my experience, more often than not, you can end up working with variations of the same team on a dozen different contracts. Having someone higher up in the production hierarchy willing to vouch for you is the quickest and most common route to a crew job—and a career that lasts longer than one shoot. Noa got her job on *Scareodactyl* on Chrissy's recommendation, and ideally in the future Noa might be in a position to recommend PJ or Colin for something else. And so it goes.

If this were a DVD of the movie, would there be any deleted scenes or extras to share?

I had a whole sequence near the end where there's a mistaken-identity gag between Noa and Sadie. When Noa goes to the studio to apologize to Lilah, she comes across Sadie in the physio room instead and—thanks to the red wig and matching costume—assumes the girl on the bed is Lilah and stammers out her first try at the apology. I still think it was funny as heck but didn't end up working, unfortunately. It threw off the pace, was the wrong tone for that point in the book, and I was already working against my word limit. If someone ever made this into a movie, though, I'd angle to get that moment back in there! I adore Sadie and I'd like to have used her more.

What parts of writing were the easiest for you?

I had the easiest time with the day-in-the-life moments, particularly on set. Those silly and sometimes madcap moments, and the emotionally loud moments, are always the easiest. The fight came fairly early on in my drafts, and a lot of the big blowout fight remained exactly the same on page as it had in my first drafts. I have to push myself to slow down some sequences, to let the characters sit in their quiet moments and breathe. Thankfully my editor is very good at flagging those points where I've been in too much of a rush to get to the next bit!

Speaking of those on-set moments, were any of them things that could actually happen on a set?

While I have been on a location filled with harmless (yet bitey) garter snakes, I've never actually seen a box of reptiles released backstage. Many of the other scenes were drawn from things that have actually happened, though. The truck fire was a real moment from a history documentary I was working on. We had been using fire bars to get footage of flames so the post-production crew could do some composite shots of the village burning. The fire bars ended up being put away warm, and some of the props packed around them caught fire a few hours later. We had a sink at basecamp, thankfully, and had a bucket brigade going fairly quickly—it was out quickly, with minimal harm done!

Things like animals being smuggled into dressing rooms, actors smoking and eating in full costume, and poor Peter getting carted off to the ER with his disembowelment prosthetics attached are composites of similar sorts of events. Behind-the-scenes hookups and romances are fairly common as well, especially when you're on location for any length of time. When your coworkers are the only people you're seeing, for twelve- to eighteen-hour days, sometimes for months on end, all kinds of things can happen.

Acknowledgments

This book wouldn't exist without my better half, who introduced me to most of my favorite horror films and directors. He's also the one who drove cross-city at midnight to sit up with me after *I* made the mistake of watching *Ringu* cold in the early weeks of our relationship. *Scareodactyl* is also his fault. Whether or not that's a point of pride is left to the reader to decide.

Some of the other movie titles in Lilah's filmography came from our kids, who seem to have a knack for this sort of thing. That should probably concern me more than it does.

About the Author

Jennet Alexander has been a game designer, a teacher, a singer, a Riot Grrrl, a terrible guitar player, and an adequate crew tech and department head for both stage and screen. She grew up queer in the heart of a large Jewish community in Toronto, Canada, and now lives in a much smaller one with her partner, two kids, and two cats. Most of her wardrobe is still black.

You can follow Jennet on Twitter at @jennetalexander and find updates at her website, jennetalexander.com.